GRAVE MATTER

A DARK GOTHIC ROMANCE PSYCH THRILLER

KARINA HALLE

GRAVE MATTER

For Scott and Perry, the best sailing buddies a girl could have

"Lying to ourselves is more deeply ingrained than lying to others"

DOSTOYEVSKY

GRAVE MATTER

Darkly sensual, atmospheric, and inventive—New York Times bestseller Karina Halle blends horror romance and science fiction in a wildly unique standalone psychological thriller.

Grad Student Sydney Denik is getting a second chance. When a dream opportunity presents itself with a prestigious foundation doing promising Alzheimer's research, Sydney leaves the shambles of her old life to join a dozen other students at an isolated lodge hidden away in a remote, fog-shrouded inlet on Vancouver Island.

But the Madrona Foundation harbors more than brilliant minds. Everyone around her is hiding a terrible secret—including the resident psychologist she's falling in love with. A student disappears, and no one but Sydney seems to care. Ghosts walk the halls. Snow falls in the middle of summer. Dead animals move like the living. The more Sydney uncovers about the foundation, the more she begins to question her own sanity. And if Sydney isn't going mad, then the horrors in the surrounding forest are real, and the Madrona Foundation may be the biggest monster of all.

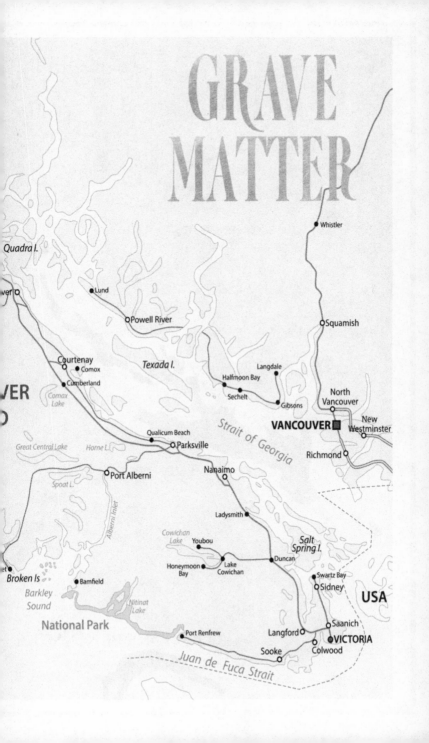

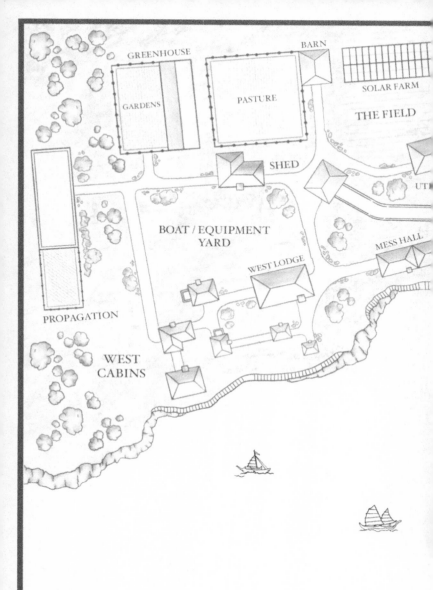

GREENHOUSE

BARN

GARDENS

PASTURE

SOLAR FARM

THE FIELD

SHED

UT

BOAT / EQUIPMENT
YARD

MESS HALL

WEST LODGE

PROPAGATION

WEST
CABINS

TO BROOKS PENINSULA

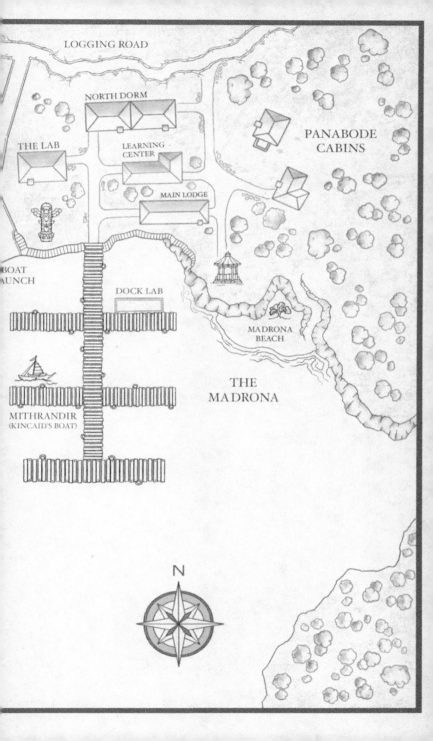

ALSO BY KARINA HALLE

Come Alive (EIT #7)

Ashes to Ashes (EIT #8)

Dust to Dust (EIT #9)

Ghosted (EIT #9.5)

Came Back Haunted (EIT #10)

The Devil's Metal (The Devil's Duology #1)

The Devil's Reprise (The Devil's Duology #2)

Veiled (Ada Palomino #1)

Song For the Dead (Ada Palomino #2)

CONTEMPORARY ROMANCE

Love, in English/Love, in Spanish

Where Sea Meets Sky

Racing the Sun

The Pact

The Offer

The Play

Winter Wishes

The Lie

The Debt

Smut

Heat Wave

Before I Ever Met You

After All

Rocked Up

Wild Card

Maverick

Hot Shot

Bad at Love

The Swedish Prince

The Wild Heir

A Nordic King

The Royal Rogue

Nothing Personal

My Life in Shambles

The Royal Rogue

The Forbidden Man

The One That Got Away

Lovewrecked

One Hot Italian Summer

All the Love in the World (Anthology)

The Royals Next Door

The Royals Upstairs

ROMANTIC SUSPENSE

Sins and Needles (The Artists Trilogy #1)

On Every Street (An Artists Trilogy Novella #0.5)

Shooting Scars (The Artists Trilogy #2)

Bold Tricks (The Artists Trilogy #3)

Dirty Angels (Dirty Angels #1)

Dirty Deeds (Dirty Angels #2)

Dirty Promises (Dirty Angels #3)

Black Hearts (Sins Duet #1)

Dirty Souls (Sins Duet #2)

Discretion (Dumonts #1)

Disarm (Dumonts #2)

Disavow (Dumonts #3)

PLAYLIST

The following songs (in no particular order) helped me write this book, though I also listened to various soundtracks, including *The Girl With the Dragon Tattoo* by Trent Reznor & Atticus Ross, *Westworld: Season 3* by Ramin Djawadi, and *Inception* by Hans Zimmer. The playlist can also be found on Spotify by scanning the code on the next page.

"The Beginning of the End" - +++ (Crosses)
"The Day the World Went Away" - Nine Inch Nails
"Change (In the House of Flies)" - Deftones
"Dissolved Girl" - Massive Attack
"Alibi" - BANKS
"Bury a Friend" - Billie Eilish
"Cinnamon Girl" - Lana Del Rey
"The Wake-Up" - How to Destroy Angels
"This is a Trick" - +++ (Crosses)
"Summertime Sadness" - Lana Del Rey
"We Come 1 (Radio Edit)" - Faithless
"Is That Your Life" - Tricky
"Butterfly Caught" - Massive Attack
"Sour Times" - Portishead
"Girls Float, Boys Cry" - +++ (Crosses)

"The Space in Between" - How to Destroy Angels
"The Night Does Not Belong to God" - Sleep Token
"Matador" - Faith No More
"Cadavre Exquis" - +++ (Crosses)
"How Long?" - How to Destroy Angels
"Body Electric" - Lana Del Rey
"Snow on the Beach" - Taylor Swift
"We're in This Together" - Nine Inch Nails
"Vivien" - +++ (Crosses)
"Ashes to Ashes" - Faith No More
"Head Like a Hole" - Nine Inch Nails
"Tomb of Liegia" - Team Sleep
"Runner" - +++ (Crosses)
"Into My Arms" - Nick Cave and the Bad Seeds

CONTENT WARNING

Grave Matter contains scenes of gore, body horror, animal/creature body horror, off-page animal death, mentions of suicide, visions of suicide, talk of Alzheimer's, loss of parents and parental figures, grief, difficulties with being neurodivergent, uneven power dynamics, and graphic language.

There are also some dark romance elements, such as morally grey main characters, abuse of power, and graphic sex scenes, which include degradation and praise kink, breath play, bondage with ropes and belts, and various other mild-BDSM elements. **If you aren't comfortable with a sexually-liberated FMC, or an unethical, obsessive MC that calls her a "dirty little slut" before making her get on her knees, then maybe think twice about reading this book.**

Your mental health is important to me, and this book contains all sorts of fuckery, so please proceed with caution.

Note: this book contains additional content at the end, including Book Club Discussion Questions for Grave Matter, as well as excerpts of other books with similar vibes.

CHAPTER 1

THE GIRL I was talking to the entire flight has disappeared.

I've stepped off the floatplane, the propellers still sputtering in rotation as I take the hand of a lanky man in a rain jacket who introduces himself as David Chen, manager of Madrona Lodge. But as I look behind me for the bright and bubbly Amani in her pale pink hijab, who I just spent an hour conversing with in the seat across from mine, she's no longer on the plane. The two other passengers are still on board—a bushy-browed man and a thin-lipped woman whom the co-pilot told me were new staff at the Madrona Foundation—sitting in the back row and watching me with idle curiosity.

But no Amani.

"Are you alright?" David says, giving my hand an unsettling squeeze, which brings my attention back to him. "I said I'm David Chen."

"Oh. Sydney Denik," I absently introduce myself, pulling my hand away from his as subtly as possible as I find my balance on the dock, meeting his inquisitive dark eyes for just a moment before I start scanning the plane again. "Sorry, I...I was just talking to someone on the plane, and now she's gone."

"Amani?" he asks, and I nod. "She went up ahead of you."

I look up the dock. There's a steep ramp, thanks to the low tide, and a long wharf leading to the land, but there's no sight of her. I frown. How is that possible?

"You likely didn't notice," he goes on. "Wouldn't be the first time a new student has become enraptured by the scenery here. We've even had a person fall off the dock because they were so distracted. It was quite the welcome, I'm sure," he adds with a chuckle.

But I was the first to step off the plane, I want to tell him. *I swear I was.* But I realize that arguing with the manager of the lodge wouldn't be the best start for me, especially when things are already so precarious. And perhaps he's right. Maybe I didn't notice Amani disembarking before me. Already, my brain feels a little fuzzy, probably from the relief of finally getting here without a hitch.

Amani talked the entire flight about how excited she was about being selected for the Madrona Foundation's student program, and I could hardly get a word in edgewise, which was fine by me. I try to stay silent when I first meet people, trying to figure out how to wear my mask, what kind of person I need to be for the conversation. So I listened and stared out the window at the scenery for the flight from Vancouver to this remote inlet on Vancouver Island's north-west coast, soaring over glittering straits dotted with white ferries, thick green forest, milky blue alpine lakes, and craggy, snowcapped peaks that have yet to thaw in the May sunshine.

But the further north we went, the more the landscape was blotted out by clouds and fog. In fact, our pilot had to circle for about twenty minutes before we landed, waiting for the mist to clear enough for a clear view of the water.

"Beautiful, isn't it?" David remarks. His hands go behind his back, and he rocks on the heels of his fancy dress shoes, which seem out of place on the dock. He sniffs the air in a perfunctory way, as if he's encouraging me to look at the scenery.

I expected the location to remind me of home—I grew up in Crescent City, California, so I'm no stranger to fog, ocean, and towering trees—but here, the elements are amplified, as if they have an edge to them. The fog is more corporeal yet delicate, reminding me of cobwebs that don't seem to move but *stretch* across the tips of the trees. The trees themselves—Douglas fir, western cedar, Sitka spruce—aren't as wide as the redwoods, but they're taller, their boughs are heavier, their trunks rich with moss and lichen. The undergrowth, too, is wildly overgrown, and my eyes have a hard time taking in all the different vegetation in riotous shades of green—salal bushes, Oregon grape, wild ginger, and massive sword ferns.

It's a biologist's fever dream.

And exactly why I'm here.

"I take it you didn't get a very good view of the Brooks Peninsula on the flight," David says, watching me as I look around. He gestures across the narrow inlet, the water dark emerald, glassy, and still, to the bank of clouds on the other side, obscuring what I assume is a forested slope. "Don't worry, you'll be up close and personal with the area soon enough. All the cures to humanity's woes, hidden just behind that mist."

I watch as the fog seems to creep across the water toward us.

You're finally here, I tell myself. *You made it. Relax.*

The weirdness of earlier has already faded. My ADHD brain is easily distracted, even when medicated, so it's entirely possible that Amani got off the plane before I did and I wasn't paying attention.

"Why don't I show you to your room and give you a tour of the lodge," David says, holding his arm out toward the dark, looming wood building at the end of the dock.

"What about my bags?" I glance behind me at the pilots as they start opening a hatch on the plane's pontoons and pulling out my luggage, a metallic black carry-on suitcase with a wonky wheel and a duffel bag I won at school that has The Cardinal emblazoned on the side, Stanford's basketball team.

"The stewards will take your luggage," he says. I hesitate, watching as they place them on the dock beside the plane. Something here is amiss, but I don't know what it is. "Come now, Ms. Denik," he adds with a touch of impatience.

He gestures again with his arm, and finally, I give him an apologetic smile. "Yes, sorry. Just getting my bearings."

"That's perfectly normal," he says, his voice jovial again. "And getting a tour will get you centered quickly."

Yet, as we walk down the dock, I have to look over my shoulder one last time. The two passengers are still sitting at the back of the plane, staring out the window and watching me. I wonder why they aren't getting off the plane, but I know I'll only annoy David if I ask another question. I have to put in more of an effort to get on his good side. He's not the one running the Madrona Foundation, but he is in charge of the lodge where I'll be spending the next sixteen weeks, and I don't need to give anyone here any excuse to check in with my school and find out the truth.

We start walking side by side down the dock. Aside from the floatplane tied up at the end, there's a handful of dinghies, Zodiacs, and fishing boats, crucial for getting around in a place as remote as this, plus a large, sleek sailboat called *Mithrandir* and several kayaks and paddleboards that are stacked on the dock. At the end of one slip is a small building that reads "Floating Lab."

Cool air rises off the water, washing over my cheeks, and I zip up the rest of my trusty Patagonia jacket I scored off a sales rack.

He notices. "Glad you dressed appropriately. You'd be

surprised how many people arrive here in the summer expecting hot, dry weather."

"I've been living in the Bay Area for the last few years. I'm used to it," I tell him, even though the area around Stanford can get really hot in the summer. You could be hiking the dry trails under the Stanford Dish, baking under the sun, while San Francisco is in a bank of cloud.

"I'll try to make the tour quick so as not to overwhelm you," David says, even though I'm so easily whelmed in general. "I take it you've done some research?"

"As much as I could," I admit, not wanting to tell him I've obsessively spent hours reading every single thing I could about the Madrona Foundation. "Whoever the copywriter is could be a novelist. They described the scenery so well."

And that's pretty much all they described. The Madrona Foundation is known for being a highly secretive organiza- tion, and their website only gives the media sound bites of their groundbreaking research finds. There was barely any write-up about the staff or the day-to-day operations—even the section about visiting research students and internships was given just a few lines. But the scenery and biodiversity was written with extraordinary care and detail by someone who clearly loves the area.

David chuckles. "Oh, that's Kincaid." Then he frowns, his face growing strangely grave as he glances at me. "Dr. Kincaid."

"The website also didn't give me any information on the staff here," I say, my way of letting him know I have no idea who Dr. Kincaid is, though I gather from his expression it's someone David doesn't like much.

"Well, you know how protective we are about our research," he says. "Which is why our first stop will be you handing in your phone."

I knew this was coming, but even so, the idea of being without the internet and my phone scares the hell out of me.

Each student that is accepted into this particular program is told that because of the foundation's nature, not only do we have to sign NDAs—which I did the other day—but we have to hand over our phones, and we weren't allowed to bring laptops, tablets, or any kind of electronic communication device until the program finishes at the end of August.

It will be good for you, I remind myself. *You need this break. From everything.*

David clears his throat. "Don't worry, you'll get used to being out of touch. You'll even welcome it. We've found it creates greater comradery between the students, as a bonus. And of course, you get to make calls every Friday, and your family will always be able to contact you."

He must know I have no family. I figure that's partly why I got accepted; they learned of my income and orphan status and decided to have pity on me. Then again, perhaps David doesn't know all the histories of each student. I bite my tongue and manage to refrain from saying anything, even though I have a hard time not correcting people when they're wrong.

"Since you've been on the website, you must know the history of this place?" he asks as we approach the lodge to our right. It's a dark and foreboding thing, even in the daylight, two stories high, worn wood recently stained a blackish brown. The length of it is perched on the rocks above the shoreline, reminding me of a predator about to pounce. A narrow boardwalk snakes along the front, peppered with the occasional wooden bench, and flower baskets hang on the railing, packed with delicate ferns, their tips wet with dew.

"Old cannery, wasn't it?" I say. The only sound is the occasional haunting call of a Bewick's wren and the water lapping at the rocks on the shore. I was expecting it to be bustling with the other students and researchers, but instead, the whole lodge seems to be holding its breath, like it's waiting for something.

Like it's waiting for you. The thought flits through my mind, causing the skin at the back of my neck to prickle. Even the row of four-paned windows along the front reminds me of a multi-eyed creature, ever watching.

"Correct." David's mild voice brings me out of my overactive imagination. "Was a functional cannery until the 1940s, crab and clamming at first, later salmon and halibut. It was then repurposed into a fishing lodge after that until we swept in fifteen years ago and transformed it into the foundation's lodge and headquarters."

"Am I the first to arrive?" I ask as I follow him to the black wood door, noticing a small video camera above it, pointed right at me. I self-consciously correct my posture.

"You're the last, actually," he says which takes me by surprise. "Everyone is already in the learning center getting oriented."

My stomach churns. I hate being the last one, even though it's common with my time blindness. It's why I set a million alarms and plan to be places far ahead of time (and yet still end up running late). But this was the plane they said for me to be on, so all of this is out of my control.

"So I'm late?" I whisper as he puts his hand on the doorknob.

"Not late. You're perfectly on time."

He opens the door and ushers me inside the building.

Immediately, I'm met with the smell of cedar and woodsmoke, the room looking exactly as a former fishing lodge should. There's a fireplace at the far end, small flames crackling, an elk head above the mantle. Shelves packed with books run along the worn wood walls, with small native carvings on display. In the center of the cavernous room are leather couches and upholstered chairs with plaid blankets draped over the backs and a couple of rough-hewn coffee tables carved from cedar. In the corner, a staircase leads to the second floor.

"This will be your common room," he says, gesturing to the cozy space.

To the left of me is a closed door with a reception sign on it. David leads me to it just as it opens and a woman steps out. She's about as short as I am, maybe five three, in her mid-forties, with a brown bob and thick-cut bangs with a cherubic face, wearing a blue flannel shirt and a load of silver bangles around her wrist.

"Sydney, this is Michelle," he says. "Michelle, Sydney Denik is here."

"Our last arrival," Michelle says, nodding profusely. Her smile is plastered on her face from ear to ear, a little too wide. She extends her hand, her bangles clinking together, and gives me a quick, albeit sweaty, shake. Her hand trembles slightly under my grasp.

"I was just telling Sydney she's not late. She's perfectly on time," he says as I fight the urge to wipe my palm against my jeans.

"Of course, of course!" Michelle exclaims loudly. "No, you're not late at all. Right on time, right on time. So nice to finally meet you."

"Did you already check Amani in?" I ask her.

Michelle frowns for a moment and exchanges a confused glance with David before she goes, "Oh, Amani. Yes. With the headscarf."

"Hijab," I correct her.

"Yes, hijab." She nods vigorously, smiling again. "Yes. Of course. Yup. She went straight to her room. Would you like to do the same? The stewards will bring your bags. Or David can take you right to the learning center and get you introduced to all the other students and the—"

"Before we do that," David interjects, "it's time that Sydney hands over her phone."

"Of course," Michelle says, her cheeks going pink. She

gives me an anxious look. "Sorry, dear, I know it's a painful process."

She holds out her hand expectantly.

I sigh and fish my phone out of my jacket. I tap the screen once just so I can see the wallpaper of my grandmother's smiling face one last time. But when I do so, something isn't right about the screen. Before it has time to register, Michelle has taken my phone from me.

"Wait, can I see that again?" I say, trying to take it back.

"Sorry," she says, letting out a nervous laugh as she quickly slips it into her back pocket. "I know it's hard, but you'll get used to it. Everyone says they appreciate talking on the phone and the landline so much more. You'll look forward to your Friday nights. And of course, there's—"

David clears his throat, cutting her off. "Now that the hard part is done, let me show you to your room," he says to me, putting his hand at my back briefly before giving Michelle a curt nod. "Thank you, Michelle."

"Yes. Of course," she says before she scurries back into her office.

Yet I can't stop thinking about my phone. About what should have been a picture of my grandmother, about a year before she died. It was one of the harder days, when Alzheimer's had taken over her nearly completely, but suddenly she remembered who I was. She looked at me and smiled. "Sydney," she had said, with so much love it broke me. It was so beautiful and pure and real. I'd taken a picture of that moment. That's been my wallpaper ever since.

But when I tapped on the screen, for that brief second, that's not the picture I saw. It was a different picture of my grandmother taken earlier that same day. In that picture, she was angry and confused, staring right at the camera, wanting me to leave.

A warning.

CHAPTER 2

"THIS IS where all your fellow students will be living," David says as we step onto the second floor landing. It's dark, despite it being daytime, with only a few sconces along the wood walls that emit a dim light along the hallway, six doors on either side with a couple at the very end. There's a creepy aspect here that I didn't expect, though it may have something to do with how unnerved I feel about my grandmother's photo.

You're imagining things, I tell myself. *You know it didn't change. And even if it did, you probably selected that other picture by accident.*

"And your room is right here," he says, pointing at the door right beside the stairs. A wooden plaque reads "Room One" in cursive above a carving of a madrona tree. "Showers are at the very end of the hall. There's also a shower in the floating lab for those who've been diving. Each room has its own sink and toilet though."

He takes out a pair of old-fashioned-looking keys, like the kind you see in a Gothic film, takes one off the ring, and hands it to me. "I know," he says, noting the wry look on my face, "but these rooms used to be for the cannery workers—why change the keys?"

I clear my throat, palming the key. "But you get to keep the other one?" I ask.

"We don't ever enter our students' rooms without their permission," he says with a slight smile. "But since keys are easy to lose, we like to hold on to one for safekeeping. Don't worry, when it comes to lab access, you'll have your own coded key card. We at least upped the tech in that department."

I should hope so, I think, taking the key and inserting it into the lock. It turns with a click that I find very satisfying.

I open the door and step inside. The room is small but cozy with a window overlooking a giant cedar, with glimpses of other buildings through the branches. On the walls, there's an oil painting of a starfish in a tidal pool on one side, a raven on a hemlock branch on the other. A large oak armoire sits across from a double bed with an embroidered red-and-black throw on top.

"Those are made by the Quatsino First Nations," David points out proudly. "The lodge borders onto their traditional territory, and we take great pride in our working relationship with them."

Uh-huh. He sounds like he's reading from a script. Generally, when corporations move on or next to native land, the local bands are the ones who end up getting screwed. I expect an institute like the Madrona Foundation, with all its money and research grants, isn't looking out for the indigenous people's best interests.

David's Apple Watch beeps, and he glances at it, frowning.

"If you'll excuse me, Sydney, I must go," he says, giving me a quick but flat smile. "Just make yourself at home. I'll go check on your bags and be back in a bit to continue the tour." He reaches into his jacket pocket and pulls out a folded piece of paper, thrusting it into my hands. "Here's a map to help get you oriented. On the back is a copy of your weekly schedule, though some things are subject to change. And in the drawer of your side table is a watch. You'll need it."

Then he turns and strides out of the room, closing the door behind him.

I hold the map and stare at the door for a moment, surprised by his sudden departure. Then I pull open the drawer, taking out a plastic watch with the Madrona Foundation's logo on it. It's so cheap and basic that it doesn't allow for any alarms, which is going to be the bane of my existence, though at least there's an alarm clock by my bed.

I tuck the watch in my pocket and decide to use the washroom, barely enough room for a small sink and toilet. Above the toilet is a vintage embroidery of what looks like my favorite fungus, *Omphalotus nidiformis*, its outline done in a bright green as if to show that it has bioluminescence. I stare at it for a moment, strangely entranced. These mushrooms are better known as ghost mushrooms, but they aren't usually the subject of embroidery or art, and they definitely aren't endemic to this area. I wonder if when I filled out my application, I had answered a "what's your favorite fungus?" question and they tried to make the room as personalized as possible. If so, that was awfully nice of them.

I sit down on the toilet and unravel the map, but before I can study it, there's a knock at my door.

"Coming!" I yell, finishing up and washing my hands before stepping out into my room. I open the door to find a stunning woman, tall with long pale blonde hair, wearing a bright red rain jacket, her legging-clad legs thin and miles long, Burberry plaid boots on her feet.

She has my luggage with her.

"Hello," she says to me in one of those raspy, sultry voices that belongs on a noir femme fatale. "I have your luggage here." Her bright green eyes flick over me with a sense of expectation. I feel like I've seen her somewhere before.

"Hi. Yes, thank you. I should probably, uh, tip you," I say, rummaging into my messenger bag, knowing I don't have any loose bills in there.

"No need," the woman says, bringing my suitcase and duffel bag inside, her Pantene Pro-V commercial hair carrying a hint of jasmine. "I'm not the steward. I just saw the bags on the dock and figured they could use a hand."

I stare at her, unsure if her beauty is blinding me or if it's something else. "Where do I know you from?" I ask, then realize I said it out loud.

She stares at me for a moment, her expression strangely blank. Then she smiles again. "You've probably seen me on campus. Stanford, right? I've given more than a few talks to the biology department, though that's been on the doctoral level." She pauses. "You're doing your coterminal master's in biology, focus on neurobiology, isn't that right?"

I stare right back. "You work for Madrona."

"We all work for Madrona here," she says. "For the next sixteen weeks, so will you." She pauses and extends her hand, and I shake it. "I'm Everly. Dr. Everly Johnstone."

My hand goes weak in her grasp.

Dr. Everly Johnstone is a certified genius and the head of the Madrona Foundation. No wonder she seemed familiar. It was her father, Brandon Johnstone, who started the foundation back in the day.

"Of course," I say, feeling stupid and taking my hand back. "I'm so sorry, I didn't realize who you were."

She breaks into a wide grin, her teeth so white and perfect they have to be veneers. "Oh, that's perfectly fine. I don't expect people to know who I am. I like to linger in the shadows of my work."

"Even so, you're Dr. Johnstone," I say by way of apology.

"I should have known." I've seen her on the occasional interview, even though she doesn't seem to do them as much these days. It's her father who gets more press time now since he started the offshoot company, Madrona Pharmaceuticals, leaving the foundation and its research to his daughter, or so I've read.

"Please," she says with an elegant wave of her hand. "Call me Everly. We're going to become a family here over the next while. I prefer a first-name basis."

"Sydney," I say, jerking an awkward thumb toward myself. "But you already knew that."

"I know everything about you, Ms. Denik," she says. "I'm the one who reviewed your application and approved you." Her gaze flicks over me for a moment, as if really seeing me for the first time, and her expression softens. "I'm really glad you're here, Sydney. You're quite a special girl."

I feel my cheeks go pink. I've never been one to handle any kind of sentimentality or compliments, and from the look on her face, it appears to be a mixture of both.

"I'm also glad to be here," I tell her. More than she knows. Especially when there's a chance this will all be taken from me at any moment.

I applied to the Madrona Foundation in January as part of my Senior Synthesis Capstone Project. The foundation regularly has internships for students during the summer months, so I decided to shoot my shot, even though I know that admittance is extremely competitive.

To my surprise, I was accepted. I knew my grades were good enough, I knew that the project I did last year with dark fungi had gotten a lot of attention in mycology circles, but honestly, anytime something goes well for me, I'm surprised, if not wary. Life has a way of conditioning you, and when you've gone to the school of hard knocks, you expect those knocks each time.

Once the shock wore off, I was more relieved than anything, especially since I would receive a stipend which would go a long way for me since room and board is included. In addition, I would help the researchers here in their quest to use fungi in neurological advancements. They'd already made promising strides in Alzheimer's treatment with a local, and previously unknown, fungus found on their grounds, and because Alzheimer's is so dear to my heart, I knew I could maybe make a difference here, if not produce something amazing for my capstone.

But then the knocks came, as they always do.

I fucked up.

I fucked up bigtime and made a huge mistake.

Self-sabotage has always been the name of my game.

And so, the day before yesterday, I received a phone call that I'd been dreading but knew was coming.

I'd lost my scholarship to Stanford.

Which meant I'm now unable to finish my senior year because I'm broke as fuck, and there's no way I can afford tuition.

But I sure as hell wasn't going to let this opportunity pass me by. I never got a chance to ask the administrator if that meant my internship at Madrona was called off, so I decided to chance it. And when I got my email from the airline yesterday, telling me to check in to my flight to Vancouver, I turned in my key to student housing, put the remainder of my belongings in my friend Chelsea's garage, and this morning picked up my bags and got on that flight.

Once I landed in Vancouver, I hurried to the seaplane terminal downtown, hoping and praying that I'd be allowed on board for the final journey to Madrona. The pilot asked if I was Sydney Denik, and then I got on that plane with the two staff members and Amani.

Somehow, by the skin of my teeth, I'm here.

I just don't know how long I have until someone figures it out. So far, neither David, Everly, nor the receptionist seem to think anything is off. Everyone has been treating me like I belong here. Maybe the department won't reach out to the foundation; maybe they'll be so glad to be rid of me that they'll purposely forget. Maybe because they already gave me my stipend in a lump sum, they can't recall it.

Or maybe the reason that David left the room so quickly is because he got a call from Stanford just now, and it's a matter of minutes before I have to face the humiliation of getting back on that seaplane.

The thought of it is like a fist over my lungs. True terror. Having a dream come true, getting just a taste of it, before having it all ripped away.

I've needed this win so badly.

Everly clears her throat, bringing my attention back to her, and nods at the map in my hands. "I know David has been called off somewhere, something to do with the solar farm. I'd be happy to take you on a tour. Did you want a chance to settle and put your things away first or—?"

"No," I say quickly, sliding the map into the front pocket of my jeans. "I can do that later." If I've got the head of the foundation offering to show me around, I'm not going to pass that up. David was fine, if not a little strange, but Dr. Everly Johnstone is an icon.

"Alright," she says with another easy smile. "Let's go."

She opens the door and glances at me over her shoulder, waiting for me to follow.

I let out a shaking breath. Part of me, the part that can't stand to lie, wants to confess everything right now, just so I won't have it weighing on me while I'm here, just so I don't spend my days wondering when the rug will be pulled out from underneath me.

The other part of me wants to lie for as long as I'm able to, with the hopes that maybe, just maybe, even if they find out what happened, I'll be able to convince them to let me stay.

So I manage to keep the fear inside.

I swallow the truth down.

I tuck it away.

And I follow her.

CHAPTER 3

ENCHANTING.

Lush.

Moody as hell.

Madrona Lodge, the name Everly uses to refer to the entire compound, is like stepping into a Grimm fairy tale. I think earlier I was too overwhelmed to get a good feel for the place, perhaps because David had been watching my reactions so closely, but now it feels like it's sinking in. The compound is immaculately kept, with neat stone paths that snake their way under the fragrant cedar boughs, dried needles lining the ground. The fog is still clinging to the tree-tops—ravens appear here and there like shadowed ghosts—but now, the mist is sliding down between the dark, rustic buildings, making the place seem like a dream.

Everly takes me to the left, past a giant totem pole that stands sentry at the boat launch, the mess hall, where the students and visiting researchers have their meals, then the west lodge, which is the lodge and dining room for the staff, and the slew of private cabins that the main researchers live in. Everly points out hers overlooking the inlet, number six. I would have thought that the head of the organization, who is probably worth near billions, would have something more extravagant, but it makes me like her more that she doesn't.

"Come visit me anytime," she says to me as I follow her down a path and away from her cabin. "I'm serious. Anytime, day, middle of the night, if you need someone to talk to, need someone to listen, I'm there. You're not alone."

I know she probably means it in a "hey, don't think of me as your superior, I'm super approachable" kind of way, but I'm starting to wonder why I'm going to need someone to talk to in the middle of the night.

She stops and points up the path where the trees thin out, and I can see a large expanse of grass with some boats and empty trailers on it. "You're going to get a soaker with those shoes if we continue."

"A soaker?" I ask.

She laughs. "Ah yes, I forgot that's a Canadian term. It means you're going to get your shoes wet. It's been raining cats and dogs over the last few days, so the fields are mostly puddles at the moment. But you won't have a need to be up there much anyway, aside from the propagation lab. Maybe the field below the solar farm for some bocce ball on a sunny day with a beer. The weather will clear at some point. Anyway, the rest is everything we need to keep this place running."

She leads me back toward the main lodge and tells me about how self-sustained they are, thanks to their solar farm, their own wastewater and potable water treatment plants, plus a new industrial-scale greenhouse they built to complement their garden, along with the chicken run and a barn and pasture where they raise a couple of pigs and goats.

"If you wake up to screaming, it's probably the goats," she says with a laugh. She glances over her shoulder at me, noting the puzzled expression on my face. "Because they're loud and ornery, not because we're slaughtering them."

Good to know.

"What's in the floating lab?" I ask as we pause near the wharf, gesturing to the shed on the dock below. The tide is even lower now, enough that the ramp is a near vertical climb, the briny scent of the ocean flooding my nose.

"It has pumped seawater, tanks, and tables to keep marine specimens for short periods," she explains. "A few of our researchers concentrate solely on marine and coastal biodiversity and nearshore habitats. Plankton, sea stars, kelp. Seeing the effects of climate change on bacteria and viruses in the water."

The sound of a twig snapping behind me turns my head.

A tall man steps out from the path underneath the trees and walks straight past us down the wharf. He doesn't even glance our way, and from the determined look in his eyes, I'm not sure if he even sees us standing off to the side here.

But I wish he would, just for a second, because he has to be one of the most intriguing men I've ever seen. Broad-shouldered in a black coat, his short hair a dark reddish brown, like the color of cedar bark at dusk, his face looking as if a famous artist sculpted it from marble, peppered with light stubble. Chiseled cheekbones, a strong jaw, and even with the faraway look in his eyes, his gaze is cold grey and intense as he scans the foggy inlet and makes his way down the steep ramp.

"That's Professor Kincaid," Everly says, her words quiet yet terse. "He'll be leading the studies in the learning center, along with Professor Tilden."

I watch as Professor Kincaid strides down the dock, his gait purposeful and graceful at the same time. He then gets on board the yacht I saw earlier.

"Is that his boat?"

She nods. "He lives on it."

"*Mithrandir*," I say, remembering the sailboat's name. How could I forget? He must be a Tolkien fan. "Wait, that's the same Kincaid that wrote the copy on the website? David referred to him as a doctor. I didn't know he would be teaching."

Everly doesn't say anything for a moment while my eyes are still glued to him, watching as he disappears below deck.

"Yes. He'll also be your psychologist," she says matter-of-factly.

I blink, not sure that I heard her right. I turn to face her. "My what?"

Her delicate taupe brows knit together as she searches my face. "Kincaid will be your psychologist. Didn't you read that part of the curriculum? Every student gets a weekly counseling session. Over the years, we've found it's crucial for those joining us. The isolation, not only in the sense of the location but being away from social media and the internet, can take a toll on students, especially as the weeks tick by. Add in the temperamental weather here, and you have the recipe for, well, mental duress, for lack of a better word. You wouldn't think it would be a big deal, but when things go south here, they go south really fast, and then…" She trails off, her expression darkening before she squares her shoulders and looks back at Professor Kincaid's boat. "Anyway, it's for everyone's safety and well-being. You'll come to like your sessions. Everyone does."

"So that man is my teacher *and* my psychologist?"

"Yes. He's a bit prickly at first, but you'll like him. Don't worry."

I am worried, actually. He might be easy on the eyes, but the only time I've willingly gone to a head doctor was to get diagnosed with ADHD.

"And if I don't comply?" I ask.

The corner of her mouth lifts. "It's mandatory, Sydney," she says with such finality that I know what the alternative is: I'll be sent on the first plane back.

Still, my first instinct—for better or worse—is always to

rebel. I grow tense, ready to protest. Forced counseling sessions with a shrink? No, thank you.

Everly seems to pick up on this. She turns to me and leans in a little closer, enough so that I get a whiff of that jasmine and feel myself drawn into the green depths of her eyes. *They match the moss on the trees*, I think absently.

"We have a saying here," she says softly. "Don't try to change the lodge. Let the lodge change you."

A memorable idiom for sure.

But still, I have to wonder…

Change me into what?

CHAPTER 4

WHEN I WAS eight years old, I decided my goal in life was to become a mad scientist. Not just any scientist but a *mad* one. My grandmother had a delightful collection of classic movies on VHS, and I remember playing the tapes of both the classic Boris Karloff *Frankenstein* and Mel Brooks *Young Frankenstein* over and over again until the tape ran thin. It didn't matter that one was horror and one was a comedy, both made me realize that becoming Dr. Frankenstein was a worthy goal for myself. I wanted to create life—I wanted to revel in it, in the magic of scientific creation that pushed the boundaries and bordered on insanity. I wanted to become so singularly obsessed with something that nothing else around me mattered. I wanted to leave my mark on the world, no matter what it took, even if it took my own mind.

My grandmother did what she could to encourage this obsession at a young age. Perhaps not my secret desires to succumb to madness, but at least the science part. We lived on a very modest budget comprised of her meager retirement savings and my father's job as a fisherman (okay, so we were *poor*). He was never home, so she was in charge of me most of the time. She'd often tell me that she wanted to be a botanist when she was younger but that her parents insisted her purpose was to be a housewife, so I became the girl who did what she never could.

She bought me cheap "scientific" kits from the dollar store, ones that were good for collecting and observing bugs or flowers. Sometimes she'd make them herself, and I'd sit around the beige linoleum table of our mobile home watching her hands, gnarled like the cedar roots outside the home, fasten a magnifying glass onto the end of pliers, telling me it was how scientists did their in-field extractions. Then I'd run out into the woods behind the trailer park in Crescent City and wouldn't come back until the sky was the color of bruised fruit and my bare legs were scratched pink by black-berry bushes and slicked with mud.

I'd like to say my findings were boring and benign, but they weren't. Oh, I wasn't pulling the legs off butterflies or frying ants under the microscope accompanied by a villainous laugh, just for the hell of it. My efforts were methodical and calculated. I sliced up the fungi that grew along rotted tree stumps, burning their edges with a match to see if they contracted or showed any signs of pain (they didn't, obviously, but I was curious). When my grandmother needed to defend her garden, I did the job of sprinkling salt on slugs, but really just to see how they would die. I didn't go into trying to torture things; everything was entirely in the name of curiosity and science.

And the pure fucking boredom of poverty.

But I also knew better than to tell my grandmother this when she asked me how my science experiments were going. As much as I coveted the term "mad scientist," I knew that telling her what I actually did would get me into trouble. Sure, a little boy can be excused for callous cruelty, but a girl doing the same thing, even in the name of research, would get me into deeper trouble.

See, boys are allowed to be mad scientists. But when

women do it? We're simply labeled crazy. And even at eight years old, I knew there was a difference.

Which is probably why the idea of mandatory psych sessions grates on me, because of how many times I've been told I need to "go see a shrink." Not because I'm a woman, per se (though I've noticed they never tell the men to get their head checked), but because I dealt with undiagnosed ADHD for so long. I hated how short my temper was, how the slightest criticism or rejection would feel like the world was ending, how some days, especially around my period, the smallest thing would set me off in a downward spiral. I'd been labeled "mad" and "crazy" and "fucking psycho" by more than a few ex-boyfriends (and one ex-girlfriend, who should have known better) just because I lacked emotional regulation.

When I was finally diagnosed, it was like a switch went off in my head. An explanation as to why I am the way I am. But even though more and more people are getting diagnosed as neurodiverse in some capacity, the stigma hasn't gone away. Many neurotypicals think most of us are faking it; they don't understand how we're not actually lazy but that there are brick walls that slide down, preventing us from doing things, even things we *want* to do. When they tell us not to worry about something or not to take something personally, they don't realize we often *can't*. And in the end, they shun us and side-eye us and make pithy comments about how "mentally unstable" we are, especially if we happen to present as feminine.

I don't want Everly to think I'm mentally unstable. I don't want Professor/Dr. Kincaid to think that either. And yet, if they find out the truth, that's exactly what they're going to think. If I'm below Stanford's moral standards, I sure as hell won't measure up here.

Thankfully, at no point has David appeared, demanding I be sent back on the next seaplane. Everly continued the tour, leading me to a short cliff overlooking the inlet with a cedar-shingled gazebo at the end, a place to hide from the rain and hunker down at the picnic table that had been scratched with hundreds of initials and doodles, and Madrona Beach, a strand of light sand so aptly named because of the lone madrona tree growing near the edge.

"We call them arbutus trees here," Everly said as she ran her hands over the papery and peeling red bark. "But my father thought the American name, madrona, had a better ring to it. The foundation was called the Johnstone Institute before he bought up the fishing lodge, and this tree sparked the change. Normally these trees aren't found this far north on Vancouver Island—they are concentrated more around Victoria and the Gulf Islands, where it's drier—but my father said there was something special about this tree, therefore something special about this place. And he was right."

One thing I've done on the tour is manage to keep a million questions to myself. I want to ask her about their fungus, the one that's only found here, the component that really makes this place special. The foundation is so secretive about it that I don't even know what the fungus looks like. I might have already walked past it and not known (I doubt it, though I did spot some rainbow chanterelle under a Sitka spruce).

After Everly takes me past the Panabode cabins, built for temporary researchers, and the north dorm, where the administrative offices are and miscellaneous visitors stay, we stop outside two buildings with a path connecting them.

"And here we are at the end of our tour and the two most important places," she says. She nods to the building on the left. "That's the lab. You'll find yourself in there once a week when Dr. Janet Wu is teaching. She's our genomics lab manager."

"Only once a week?" I ask. "I thought I would be spending day and night in there."

Everly studies me for a moment. "For most students, the introduction to the lab is gradual," she says carefully. "We have a lot of real work going on in there around the clock and our own way of doing things. I know you have plenty of lab experience, especially with eDNA and your project with *Archaeorhizomycetes*, which were fantastic findings, by the way. I can't wait to discuss that in detail with you. But even so, we do things differently at the lodge. I have no doubt by the end of summer, you'll be in there as often as I am."

Though she punctuates her speech with a bright smile, I can't help but feel a little disappointed. I needed this internship to lift me to the next level. The idea of working in the actual lab with this foundation, making a real difference, rubbing elbows with the technicians and doctors who were certified geniuses, would have meant I made it. It wasn't enough for me to just earn my degree; I wanted to become something more than just another grad student.

This place was supposed to make me into something *more*.

And now that it looks like I won't end up with a degree anytime soon, I need this more than ever.

"So then, what will I be doing here?" I ask, trying to hide the petulance from my voice. My Adderall is working overtime to keep my emotions in check.

"Plenty, don't you worry," she says, pointing at the other building. "That's the learning center. You'll have your morning class in there with Professor Kincaid or Professor Tilden. Your afternoons will be spent out on foraging expeditions."

"Foraging expeditions? To find more of your fungi?"

"Well, yes, that's part of it," she says reproachfully, and I realize I'm being too brash. "We have tried to grow the specimen in the propagation lab, but it doesn't seem to thrive. But you're not glorified mushroom foragers, if that's what you're worried about. You're searching for the next big thing, whatever that might be. The Brooks Peninsula is just at our doorstep, a piece of land as wild and untamed and unexplored as anything on this earth. The peaks there are untouched by the last ice age, with flora and fauna and fungi that don't exist anywhere else and have yet to be discovered."

"Is that how you discovered your fungus?"

"*Amanita excandesco*," she says.

It takes me a moment. "Is that the official name?"

She nods, and I do a quick Latin translation in my head. "*Excandesco*. So it glows? Is it luminescent?"

Her smile is coy now. "You will find out in time. How about we introduce you to the rest of the students." She puts a light hand on my shoulder and gestures to the door of the learning center.

I dig my heels in. The last thing I want is to be introduced to the rest of the students like it's the first fucking day of kindergarten. I was already a late arrival to begin with; surely they're done with class by now.

"It's alright, Sydney," Everly says. She presses a little harder in an effort to move me forward. "They're just your fellow grad students. They don't bite. Although there is one bad apple every season, isn't there?"

Just as long as it's not me, I think. I take in a deep breath. My social anxiety may be at an all-time high, my palms clammy, my heart thudding in my throat, but I can't let that hold me back in front of her. I just have to suck in the embarrassment.

She guides me to the door and opens it for me, ushering me inside.

The room is far more casual than I thought it would be. I was expecting to step into a lecture hall, but this has more of a meditation retreat vibe. There's a desk and a whiteboard, with a man dressed in a red flannel, holding a marker, standing in front of it, longish blond hair tucked behind his ears. I take it he's the professor, but he looks more like a thirty-something surfer. The ultimate guru.

In front of him are the students, some sitting at a couple of long tables, others sitting on giant pillows on the hardwood floor that's been piled high with various rugs. At the back, logs burn and crackle on the hearth, warmth filling the room. I quickly count ten students and notice Amani isn't among them. I guess I'm not the last after all.

"Ah, you must be Sydney," the teacher says to me in a gregarious voice, clapping his hands together. "Better late than never. I'm Professor Tilden, but you can call me Nick."

I raise my hand shyly, giving him an awkward smile.

Kill me now.

"Don't worry," he goes on, "I won't make you stand up here and tell the class three interesting things about yourself."

Thank fuck.

"I'll do it instead," he adds.

Cripes.

My face immediately heats up. "Everyone, this is Sydney Denik," he speaks slowly, saying my name like I'm hard of hearing. "Sydney is from Stanford University. She likes to play the tuba. And her favorite fungus is the ghost mushroom."

I snort, shaking my head.

"What?" he asks. "Not true?"

"I've never played the tuba in my life," I tell him, giving the class a bewildered look. I expect them to laugh, because of course they know he's joking, but they all stare at me with a strange look on their faces, as if they're concerned. They're probably just embarrassed for me.

"Oh, I see I got my wires crossed," Nick says. "Sydney here classified the phylum for a previously unknown dark fungus." He looks at me, brows raised. "Right?"

I nod, giving him a look that says *will you please shut the fuck up*?

"Alright, I'll stop torturing you," Nick says with a laugh.

Everly squeezes my arm. "I'm going to go, but it was lovely to show you around. I'll see you later, Syd."

Then she leaves, and suddenly, I feel completely unmoored. I wish Amani was here so there was at least another familiar face.

Luckily, a girl sitting near the end of the table pulls out the empty chair beside her, giving me a welcoming nod.

I scurry over there and sit down beside her.

"Thanks," I say, trying to keep my voice low as Nick starts talking about the generator output of the solar farm. Something about how the power to the lodges gets turned off from time to time to ensure electricity is always flowing to the labs, which is apparently why we have an arsenal of flashlights and candles in our rooms.

"I'm Lauren," the girl says. She's pretty and long-limbed with chin-length blonde hair a couple shades lighter than my own.

"Sydney," I say, even though she already knows that.

"Yes, the tuba player," she says seriously, then grins, her smile wide.

"Yeah," I say slowly. "That was hella embarrassing."

"Oh, don't worry. He made us all do that," she says. "One by one. Like the first day of camp. Which I suppose it is."

"That does make me feel a little better," I admit. Already, Lauren seems easy to be around. "What else did I miss?"

"Just a tour of the grounds," she says. "We then came back here, and he's just explaining how the lodge works in more detail."

"Oh, okay. Everly showed me around," I say.

She gives me an impressed look, and I realize I may have come off as bragging. But Lauren smiles. "Well, if there was a private tour, I would have opted for that one. But I guess you don't know three things about every person in this room now, do you? For instance." She points at a white guy with close-cropped brown hair at the front. "That's Albert. He's obsessed with sea urchins. And see that Japanese guy over there? That's Toshio, and he designed a video game with his friend that got bought out by Microsoft or something. That girl with the long dark hair sitting on the pillow? That's Natasha, and she has three pugs back at home, and she already misses them. And the guy at the end of this table? His name is Munawar, and he said he's only packed shirts with fungi puns on them."

"Hello, I'm Munawar Khatun from Bangladesh," the man says with a wave, leaning forward at the end of the table. "I'm wearing such a shirt today. It says 'I'm a real fungi.' Get it?"

He points to his shirt.

"Also, Munawar has really good hearing," Lauren whispers, leaning in close.

I can't help but laugh at that before I turn my attention back to the teacher. Nick goes on about how the system here runs, how our garbage is thrown into an incinerator every morning by their handyman, Keith, who must be addressed only as Handyman Keith, and that we'll have weekends to ourselves within designated areas.

"Does this mean we can party on the weekends?" Munawar asks. His voice is solemn, but his eyes are twinkling.

"It means you're free to do what you want within reason," Nick says. "You're all adults here, but this is still private property. We don't want you straying too far, not only because it's dangerous without an official chaperone but because the local tribe borders our land. It's unlawful to step onto their property, and we don't want to be disrespectful, now do we?"

Lauren puts up her hand. "Isn't this all of their property, technically?"

Another point for Lauren.

"We lease the land from the Quatsino Nation," Nick says.

"But yes, you're right, Lauren. We reside on their traditional territory."

"I want to know why it's dangerous without an official chaperone," a dude at the table in front of me says, his voice growing deeper as he talks, as if he's trying to be intimidating, while he leans back casually in his chair. "You just said we'll be spending a lot of time out in the bush, foraging and camping."

"Do you have experience with bears? Wolves? The Roosevelt elk that become so territorial they'll spear your guts out?" Nick asks, the first time I've ever seen him look remotely stern.

Lauren's been writing on a piece of paper and passes it to me: *That's Clayton. He's a dick. That's all you need to know.*

"Sure do," Clayton says, leaning back even further in his chair. "I'm from Montana. I probably killed a dozen bears before you were even born."

I exchange a dry look with Lauren. Dick is right.

Nick frowns. He's at least ten years older than Clayton. "That doesn't even make sense."

"What about drinking?" Clayton goes on. "I didn't see a bar in the mess hall."

Nick sighs. "Once a week, we go by boat to Port Alice for extra provisions. You give us the money, we'll pick up whatever you want. Cigarettes, alcohol, Archie Comics, you name it."

I exhale internally. At least alcohol won't be so easy to come by here.

And at that, class is dismissed. Nick tells us that dinner is at six every day, which is in an hour, and that there will be a few speeches at dinner, so we shouldn't miss out. I wouldn't anyway; my stomach is already growling. I'd only grabbed a bite to eat before my flight. Feels like a lifetime ago.

Everyone gets up and starts chatting with each other,

albeit a little awkwardly, which I guess is normal when you have a bunch of science students in forced cohabitation.

But that Clayton dick comes straight for me.

"So *you're* Sydney," he says. He reminds me of my jock boyfriend I had in high school, who also had curly brown hair and a permanently smug smile (and was also an asshole), though he wouldn't have been caught dead studying anything remotely scientific (or really anything at all...why did I go out with him again?).

"That I am," I say, conscious of how the rest of the students are watching us, as if they expect a fight to break out.

"You think you're special, huh?" he says.

"Clayton," a short Asian guy warns as he puts his hand on his shoulder. "Don't."

I shake my head, so confused. "I never said I was special."

Clayton squints at me. "Nah. You're right. I can see you're not."

Then he turns and walks away, the Asian guy following him as they exit the building.

"He is *not* a fungi," Munawar says, using air quotes around "fun-guy."

I glance at Lauren. "What was that about?"

She rolls her eyes. "Who cares? Don't pay him any attention."

Guess we found the bad apple, I think. I wonder if Everly knew about Clayton ahead of time. I'd hoped they only accepted students who aren't bad news.

Then again, I'm here.

Now that the altercation is over, the rest of us leave the building. The drama has made me feel like I've been sucked back into high school, which is annoying because we're all probably in our twenties. I guess that's bound to happen when you're stuck with your cohorts in forced proximity. I just hope it gets better over time, not worse.

Just as I was the last to arrive, I'm the last to leave the learning center. I follow behind Lauren as she exits, lagging a little to peer at a painting of a red-and-white Amanita on the wall, wondering if it's, in fact, their *Amanita excandesco.*

The door almost closes on me, but I push it open with my forearm before it does, stepping outside just as someone on the other side tries to pull the door open.

I run right into my future psychologist.

CHAPTER 5

"I'M SORRY," I cry out as I collide with Dr. Kincaid's chest. The man is built like a stone wall, but even so, he takes several steps backward, his striking eyes widening for a second.

"My apologies," he says, his voice sending a shiver up my spine. I've always been a voice gal. If a man has a low, gravelly voice, a little rough, a little rich, it makes me weak in the knees. If the man also happens to possess muscled forearms and strong hands, then that's Sydney's sex trifecta.

My gaze drops to his hands, which are clenching and unclenching into fists in a way that reminds me of the infamous Mr. Darcy shot from *Pride and Prejudice*. Those fit the bill, though I can't tell what his forearms look like under his black coat. It's thick and wool, more suited for winter than a mild evening. Two out of three ain't bad, though judging by the breadth of his shoulders, I'd wager his forearms would earn him the trifecta anyway.

Knock it off, I chide myself. *Lusting after your professor slash psychologist is the very last thing you need.*

Old habits, they die hard.

"If you'll excuse me," he says, still keeping his distance and gesturing to the door, which had closed. He seems to want to avoid me, and I figure it's because I'm probably staring at him with googly eyes.

But as he steps around me, I meet his gaze for a moment, and I swear the world goes still, like the fog wraps around us, blocking out the sporadic calls of the ravens, the haunting trill of the varied thrush, until there's only silence. His eyes are shadowed by his dark, low brows, his irises a ghostly shade of grey that matches the mist. His stare is intense, electrifying, burning straight into my soul, like he can see all of me.

And what he sees scares him.

Enough that he has to quickly look away.

"I'm Sydney Denik," I blurt out, not wanting him to walk away, not wanting my future shrink to already make some crash judgments about me. "I'm in your classes," I add, though I wince inwardly because of course I'm in his classes. We all are.

He freezes, his long fingers grasping the door handle. He nods, licks his lips, hesitating. Then he closes his eyes for a moment and turns to face me.

He meets my gaze again, and this time, the intensity is turned down. He still has a bewildering thousand-yard stare, but his brooding brows have softened. The corners of his eyes crinkle enough that I'd place his age in the late thirties.

He wipes his hand on his coat. "Sorry. Hands are clean, but they smell like diesel." He shakes mine, firm and hard, his palm warm, and it's as if a current of electricity runs from his skin to mine. Not enough to shock, but enough to make my nerves dance and send sparks down my spine. He holds on to my hand longer than is probably appropriate, and the longer he does, the more intense his stare becomes, until I can feel it start to unravel something in me, something I don't want unraveled.

He swallows hard, his full mouth forming a hard line, and then looks away, dropping my hand. Again, his fingers flex at his side.

"Wes Kincaid," he says, clearing his throat.

"Do I call you Professor Kincaid or Dr. Kincaid?" I manage to ask.

"Either one is fine," he says, his voice turning raspier. He clears his throat again. "Do you prefer Sydney or Syd?"

"Either one is fine," I echo. "I think I'll just call you Kincaid."

He gives me a soft, genuine smile, like I've amused him. His eyes light up, his face too handsome for his own good. "Then I will call you Sydney unless you tell me otherwise."

"My friends call me Syd," I tell him coyly. "I can't tell if we're going to be friends or not."

I know I'm sounding a little flirty, and I shouldn't, I *really* shouldn't, but he doesn't seem uncomfortable by it.

"I guess we'll see," he says. "Don't be late for your class tomorrow." His face grows stern, a look he does so well, but I can tell it's in jest.

"I won't," I say as he gives me a nod and then disappears into the building.

I stand there for a moment at the closed door, feeling strangely outside myself. The fog around me seems to be wisping away with the briny breeze, the light growing brighter. I sniff my hand. It does smell faintly of diesel, though I detect the scent of tobacco as well. He probably smokes.

Either way, it's not unpleasant at all. I keep my hand to my nose as I walk over to the main lodge, the scent reminding me of something I can't quite place but is comforting none-theless. Perhaps the smell of my childhood. My grandmother chain-smoked Marlboro Lights for the longest time, and my father always smelled of diesel from his fishing boats.

At the memory of them, my chest aches. Grief is funny like that. It lives alongside you, sometimes in silence, and then a random thought, or memory, or smell will punch through you like a fist, your bleeding heart in its grasp, and you have to relive it all over again. I often think of grief as a cycle from which there is no escape, an ouroboros, a snake of sorrow eating its tail.

My father died three years ago, and most days now, I can think of him without crying or getting sad. We were never that close since he was so rarely home, but we still had a good relationship. We were passing ships in the night, and with him, it was literal. Sometimes I think my struggle with object permanence—the ability to forget that certain things or people exist if they aren't present—is one reason why I'm not insane with grief all the time. It's one of the few concessions that my ADHD grants me. That and my ability to hyperfocus and grow obsessive over the things I care deeply about, which is why my grades are so good but only about the subjects I'm infatuated with (which is why that one calculus class I had to take was a bitch).

A raven's throaty warble draws my attention upward. It's perched on the top of the totem pole in front of me. I'd walked past the lodge without realizing it.

Instinctively, I reach inside my jacket for my phone to take a picture, since the totem at the top of the pole is a raven too, and with the fog as a background, it would make a stunning photo. But my fingers grasp nothing, and I remember my phone is gone, and I won't be able to look at it for a hella long time. The idea makes me feel twitchy, like I'm missing a limb, but I remind myself again that it's for the best.

I take my watch out of my pocket. Still have forty-five minutes to kill. I could go to my room and unpack, but it seems too daunting at the moment. I could wait in the mess hall, but I don't want to be that early, sitting all alone.

I decide to walk toward the gazebo, following the stone path as it undulates between salal bushes, the wet, rubbery leaves brushing against my legs, leaving damp spots on my jeans.

The mini peninsula that the gazebo is built on is treeless,

mostly rocky outcrops and moss, giving an unobstructed view of the inlet—on a clear day, that is. Right now, all I can see is the dock and the blanket of fog. Somewhere beyond it is the wild North Pacific Ocean, reefs and rocks and small islets breaking up their force until only gentle waves roll into the inlet. It's calm here, peaceful, and I sit on top of the picnic table, trying to do some deep breathing exercises. I hear the cry of a bald eagle, but the rest of it remains a ghost.

I tell myself it's okay to be sad sometimes. I tell myself that what's done is done. I tell myself that no matter what happens, even if they find out tomorrow morning that I lost my scholarship and I'm sent back home, I'll be alright.

And where is home? I think, panic simmering. I have no home anymore. I turned in my keys. I can't live on campus. I'll have to find a job when I get back, but until I do, I'll have nowhere to stay. It's not like I can afford to live in the Bay Area anymore, but where will I go?

I'm so very fucked.

I run my fingers over the old wood of the picnic table, over the carved initials and tag lines.

EJ+MP.

Nick smells like surfer bro.

Martin loves Amy.

Don't eat the walking ones, don't eat the talking ones.

Jessica is a…

Someone had written something, and then it's been crossed out.

Don't trust any of them.

They're all lying to you.

I pause over that one just as I hear a rustle in the bushes behind me.

I twist around to see a flash of a pastel pink hijab and a smiling, warm face.

My heart leaps.

Amani?

"Come on, Syd!" Amani yells at me, waving her hand. "You'll be late for dinner!" Then she turns and runs off into the bushes.

"Wait!" I yell, getting to my feet and bursting out of the gazebo. "Amani?"

I nearly slip on the moss, but I gain my balance and run down the path, trying to catch up, but she's damn fast.

By the time the main lodge comes into view, she's disappeared.

"Amani!" I yell, looking around, only to see Lauren, Munawar, and another guy step out of the building.

"Hey, tuba girl!" Munawar greets.

I run up to them. "Have you seen Amani?"

Lauren frowns. "Who?"

"Amani," I say, scouring the area. "She has a pink hijab. She wasn't in the class, but she was on my plane."

Lauren shakes her head. "No, I haven't seen anyone like that here. Ready for dinner?"

"I guess," I say reluctantly. Amani had said I would be late. Maybe she's already inside the mess hall.

"I'm Justin," the other guy says as we start walking. "Justin Wong." He's cute, tall, with thick black hair and a cocky smile. From the way his zip-up fleece fits him, it seems he works out too. "I did actually play the tuba in high school."

I laugh. "Maybe Nick got his wires crossed." I pause. "Hey, does it bother you guys that we aren't going to be working in the lab that much?"

"Lab work bores me," Lauren says cheerfully. "My major is forest biology. University of Victoria. I'm more happy to be out in the woods than in the lab."

"I'm doing marine science," Justin says. "I'll be in the floating lab when I'm not in the water."

I look over at Munawar and his fungi shirt. He smiles and nods at me. "I'm just happy to be here."

I feel I should be taking an example from him.

We enter the mess hall, which is a lot more elegant than the name implies. It resembles the common room of the main lodge, except there are long wooden tables done up with red checkered placemats and comfy-looking chairs. While the fireplace crackles and burns at one end, at the other is a bustling kitchen, the smell of roast chicken in the air.

I scan the room, but Amani isn't here.

One table is already full, so we take our seats at the other before the rest of the students file in. The sound of awkward conversation and scraping chairs fills the space as a staff member with braided grey hair comes out of the kitchen doors with two jugs of water and starts filling everyone's glasses. I keep looking around, expecting Amani to pop up at any moment. Perhaps she's in the washroom.

A door at the corner of the room beside the hearth opens, and David Chen enters, followed by Everly, Nick, and three people that seem familiar but I don't recognize: a white man in a tailored suit with shoe-polish black hair, very deep-set, beady eyes, and stiff posture; an Asian woman with glasses and long hair; a brown-skinned woman with layers of necklaces over a lab coat with a big grin, and a Latino man with a shaved head who waves at us. The door almost shuts before Kincaid squeezes his way through, joining the row of people who have gathered in front of the fireplace.

"Good evening, students," David says, clasping his hands together, "and welcome to your first day at the lodge. I know you're hungry, probably a little tired too, so we won't keep you long. I just wanted to introduce the team. Some of them you may know of, some you may not, but by the end of your sixteen weeks, the twelve of you will come to think of us as family."

Twelve. There were eleven of us at class. Amani hadn't been there.

I look around, six of us at one table, another six at the other.

Twelve.

There's a girl at the end with freckles and curly red hair. She wasn't in class earlier. She's resting her chin on her hand and watching David speak, enraptured.

I'm about to nudge Lauren and ask who that girl is when David's voice gets louder. I glance at him, surprised to find him looking right at me. I swear they're all looking right at me, waiting for me to pay attention.

"May I introduce to you to the CEO and the COO of the Madrona Foundation, Dr. Everly Johnstone and Dr. Michael Peterson," David says.

A few claps break out. Since I'm being watched, I clap too, even though the motion is causing my head to ache. That's nothing new when I haven't eaten for a while. I hope I get something in my stomach before I get really hangry.

Luckily, the appetizer, clam chowder in a sourdough bread bowl, comes out while Michael is talking.

"This is the seventh year for our grad student program," he says. He smiles every now and then, but it never reaches his eyes. There's something cold about his manner, and it's not just because his eyes are so deep-set, his brow so prominent that he looks perpetually angry. I automatically dislike him. "We started with a couple of students, then made our way up to six, and now a dozen. I'm telling the truth when I say the summer season is my favorite for this reason. You. You bring life to the lodge, to the land. If you can imagine for us researchers, we're in isolation for so long. We love our jobs, and you can't beat the nature here. It's like living in paradise, in the gaze of God's creation, while we ourselves create." He glances at the other doctors, who smile and nod, all except the Asian woman, who is staring at the floor, and Kincaid, who is gazing straight ahead at the back of the room, hands behind his back.

"But you all," Michael continues, looking at us again, "you all make our lives here a lot more interesting. You're not just students, you're not strangers, you are crucial to the work that we do here. You are one of us. So I think I'm not alone when I say, welcome to the family."

More clapping. If this were Everly's speech, I'd believe it, but for some reason, I don't trust a thing that comes out of that man's mouth.

I go back to my chowder. It's perfectly rich and salty, with chunks of wild salmon, and listen as the rest of the researchers introduce themselves. The Asian woman is Dr. Janet Wu, very soft-spoken and seemingly ill at ease being in the spotlight, the one who will be teaching us in the lab. Then, the woman with the necklaces, the bubbly Isabel Carvalho from Brazil, the genomics lab manager, and the man with the shaved head is Gabriel Hernandez from Mexico, who is the head of the marine sciences.

Then there's Kincaid. He keeps it very short. He just offers his name and doesn't say anything else. A man of few words seems to be the right impression of him.

When they're done, they walk off, and the roast chicken comes out. Even though I was hungry earlier, I could only eat half my chowder, and I'm not even sure I can eat the chicken.

I nudge Lauren again. "Who is the redhead?" I ask, trying to inconspicuously point to the girl.

She looks over and shakes her head as she spears her chicken with her fork. "No idea. She wasn't in class. Newcomer?"

But if she's new, what happened to Amani? There's a dozen of us here. Amani would make thirteen?

I don't voice this to Lauren though. I don't want to come across as obsessive and weird on my first day. Honestly, I don't know why I'm fixating on Amani so much.

Except that I kind of do. The more I think about this, the

more I'm not thinking about my actual problems. That proverbial shoe about to drop.

When dinner wraps up, I head to my room to unpack while Lauren, Munawar, and Justin lounge in the common room. I'd like to join them and attempt to be social, but I think the best thing for me is to hit the bottle of Nyquil I picked up at the Vancouver airport and go to sleep.

Except once I've unpacked, I can't find the Nyquil anywhere, or my Vancouver stickers and keychain. And some of my clothes are missing too. I swear I brought my white Stanford hoodie as well as my favorite nightgown (technically, an oversized Miss Piggy T-shirt that I've had for ten years and is hanging by a thread), and my black Nike sneakers. Now, all I have are my white ones, which probably won't last very long in this place considering how muddy it is.

I sit down on the edge of my bed and try to think about where I could have put my souvenirs and decide I must have left them on the seaplane. Luckily, I manage to find a bottle of melatonin and take one of those instead. Sometimes it works, sometimes it doesn't, but I'm afraid I won't be able to sleep, that my mind will be racing about all the what-ifs.

I do my best to make myself at home. I complete my nighttime routine of taking off my makeup, doing my skin care ritual, and face yoga for my TMJ, before turning off all the lights. I'm about to go to bed when I walk past the window.

I do a double take.

Standing beneath the cedar, lit only by the burning ember of a cigarette, is a shadowy figure. I can feel their eyes on me, even though I can't clearly see who it is.

They watch me, unashamed, unabashed.

Until they slowly turn and walk away.

And only then do I recognize him.

Kincaid.

CHAPTER 6

I'm dreaming.

I must be dreaming.

I'm on the bed, and the room is so dark. Cold air comes in through the open window, bringing in the scent of cedar and sea and tobacco.

I'm naked, staring at the ceiling, strong, warm hands gripping my hips as they pull me to the edge of the bed.

"Such a pretty pussy," a gravelly voice says from between my legs. "Such a tight little cunt for such a dirty fucking whore."

I blush, hot, his words making me as wet as his tongue as he glides it up between my thighs. I want him so badly I want to tear my skin right off.

"Tell me what you want, Syd," the man says, blowing on my clit until my legs clamp the side of his head. "Want me to lick your sweet cunt until you almost come and have to beg me for it? Get you so wet that you're squirting in my face? Or is that no longer enough to satisfy you? No. You want my cock shoved up that tight little hole, even though we both know it won't fit."

I groan, lifting my hips off the bed, the cool air washing

over my body and turning my nipples painfully hard, though it does nothing to quell the fire under my skin.

"I want…" I whisper, voice hoarse, unable to put into words all the things I do want. I want him to degrade me, I want the fear his words bring me, I want that release from all my beliefs. I want his cock and his hands and his tongue. "I want you to tell me to shut the fuck up and take it like a filthy slut."

An amused grunt. He raises his head, and I raise mine.

I meet his eyes, a dusky blue grey, a gaze that stares right into my soul.

"That can be arranged," Kincaid murmurs, giving me a deviant smile.

Adrenaline floods through my body at even the thought of it until everything goes fuzzy and eventually black.

Then there is nothing.

Nothing but need, and want, and—

A blaring alarm makes me jolt upright. Panicked, I look around for the source and smash my hand on the alarm clock beside my bed until it silences.

I let out a shaky exhale. Holy fuck. I press my fingers against my neck, my pulse racing. I can't tell if it was the dream that has my heart leaping or the hella loud alarm clock.

Probably a little of both.

It was a dream, wasn't it?

I lift up the covers, almost expecting to be naked, but of course I'm still in my fungi pajamas. Morning light is streaming in through my window, a window that is closed.

I remember now. Before I went to bed, I saw Kincaid standing beneath it, smoking a cigarette and staring up at me.

Had that been a dream too?

You should hope it was a dream, I tell myself as I get out of bed, walking over to the window and glancing at the cedar through the window, the light dim and grey. *The last thing you need is your professor creeping on you.*

And yet, the idea of it makes my pussy throb between my legs, though I'm going to have to blame that residual arousal on the dream.

I shake my head and glance at the clock. Six thirty a.m. We have class right after breakfast, which is at eight. What I need more than anything is a shower, preferably a cold one.

I grab my toiletry bag and a towel and poke my head out into the hall. I hear some rustling in the rooms, but one of the showers at the end is open, so I scurry down to claim it before someone else does.

The shower is nice and spacious, but I'm not in it for long until I hear a knock at the door.

"Five-minute limit," an unkind voice says. Immediately, I know it's Clayton.

I sigh and start getting the conditioner out of my hair without making a mess. It's purple, meant to counter the brassiness in my dark blonde hair. A travel size I stole from Target in a moment of poor desperation.

I get out of the shower and back into my pajamas just as he's knocking again, not about to risk going past Clayton in just a towel.

When I open the door, he's leering at me.

At my breasts, specifically. I keep a tight hold on my towel.

"I was hoping it was you," he says, barely meeting my eyes.

I scowl as I walk past him, giving him a wide berth, my hair dripping down my back.

"Hey, I think we got off on the wrong foot," he yells after me.

I ignore him. I don't want to make any trouble for myself, considering my position here, but if he continues this shit and gets even remotely close to sexual harassment, I'm reporting his ass.

I get back to my room, lock the door, and get ready. I shake the encounter with Clayton off, but my thoughts keep going back to Kincaid, to the dream. Had he really been standing underneath my window? I remember I was about to turn off the lights, and as I walked past the window, the burning ember of a cigarette caught my eye. The dream felt real in the moment but doesn't feel real now. It's faded away the way that dreams do. But him smoking beneath my window? That does feel real.

And so what? I think as I find a small blow dryer in the bathroom cupboard. He can't wander around on a smoke break? He probably wasn't even staring at me—it's not like I saw his eyes. It's not like I even know it was Kincaid. It could have been anyone.

But if anything, that thought makes it worse.

When my hair is dry, I spend a moment marveling at my reflection. That purple shampoo really did the trick because my hair looks a few shades lighter, a honey blonde now, making the blue in my eyes look saturated. I run my fingers over the sides of my face, focusing on my jaw, which has always been on the wider side, thanks to my incessant teeth grinding and clenching, but I guess that face yoga I did last night on my masseters did the trick because my face looks slimmer too. I feel like this is the first time I've really had a good, hard look at myself in the mirror. Some days I just sort of gloss over my reflection, like I'm too afraid to see myself, see who I really am.

But I force myself to look now. And I'm surprised to see a different version of myself looking back. Someone older, and hardened, and hopefully wiser.

Someone who definitely shouldn't want their new professor watching her through her window at night.

At breakfast, I eat with Lauren, Justin, and Munawar, who is so far keeping to his promise of wearing a different fungi shirt for each day because today he's wearing one with happy cartoon mushrooms that says *We Will Literally Feast On Your Corpse*. For some reason, I've lost my appetite, still full from the dinner last night, but I drink enough coffee to drown a horse.

The morning is warm, the sun bright somewhere behind the morning fog that sticks close to shore, sliding between the trees as we walk to the learning center. There's chatter amongst the students, a little more lively and comfortable than yesterday after everyone has gotten to know each other some. I stay close to Lauren since I can feel Clayton's gaze behind me and do my best to ignore it.

As we enter the building, Kincaid is leaning against the desk beside the whiteboard, his arms folded. He's dressed in slim-cut charcoal jeans and a black dress shirt that shows off the build of his muscular but lean upper body, not to mention he's rolled up his sleeves to his elbows. The trifecta is complete: his forearms are magnificent.

He meets my eyes for one electric moment, then moves his gaze on to the next person.

"Please take a tablet from the stack to your left," he says, his gruff voice tickling my spine. My dream had done such a fine job of mimicking him I'm already blushing.

I grab a tablet and follow Lauren to the table where we sat yesterday.

"The tablet is yours for the duration of your stay here," he informs us.

"Sweet, I can check my email," Munawar says.

"But of course, there will be no Wi-Fi for you to connect to," Kincaid continues, a slight curve to his mouth.

"Barbaric," Munawar mutters under his breath.

"At the end of your time here, you'll be able to transfer all your data to your computers back at home, so no work will be lost," Kincaid goes on. "I know we have a diverse group of students here from a variety of schools, working on different projects, so I hope the tablet will suffice. If you require something with more data, we can loan you a MacBook."

He unfolds his arms and picks up a textbook from his desk, taking out a pair of dark-framed glasses from his shirt pocket, slipping them on. The movement reveals a tattoo peeking beneath the edges of his sleeves, something like black feathers. My heart leaps.

"Glasses and tattoos," Lauren whispers as she nudges my arm, as if I'm not already blatantly staring at him. "No sign of a wedding ring either." She pauses and lowers her voice even more. "Not that I would ever condone sleeping with the professor."

I glance at her, and she gives me a playful wink. Jealousy unravels inside of me like a viper, sharp-fanged and completely unexpected. As if I have any claim to him just because I had that dream. Besides, I have been down this road before, and it only brought me shame and pain, and not the good kind.

Kincaid clears his throat, eyes down as he thumbs through the pages. "You're all here at the Madrona Foundation because you offer something of value—advancement in neurobiological research. While most of you are focused on mycology and lichenology, some of you are here from the marine sciences angle, but the outcome is the same. You are here to either discover new properties in species already classified, whether it be in the average oyster mushroom or strand of bull kelp, or to discover new species in a world that is nearly untapped."

He glances up at us. "How many of you applied for the program because of our advances in Alzheimer's research?"

I put up my hand, along with most of the students.

"That's what I thought," he says. "It's hard not to hear of the progress that we've been making here and not want to be a part of it. But the advancement was a happy accident, like most things are in science. We already knew that hyphae and mycelia showed decision-making capabilities. We knew that mycelia exhibited spatial recognition, learning, and short-term memory. And we knew that *Hericium erinaceus*, or lion's mane, had shown promise in neurological studies, enough so that it's been popping up in supplements that promise to make you smarter. Among its active compounds, only erinacine A had confirmed pharmacological actions in the central nervous system. Admit it, you've all tried that sludge they market as mushroom coffee. It works, but it's fucking awful. I'll stick to my espresso, thank you."

Kincaid gives us a wan smile and allows a few titters and murmurs in the room. "But despite the advances, we had yet to isolate the fungi's own intelligence from its compounds," he goes on. "Until one day, we did." He pauses, glancing down at his textbook and adjusting his glasses. His eyes close for a moment, frowning as if lost in thought. Then he opens them. "As you all know, to the detriment of your student loans, mycology is underfunded across the board. Most scientists are scrambling for breakthroughs, never able to raise enough funds for research. When Madrona discovered *Amanita excandesco*, the funds needed to properly study it became available. The Johnstones took a huge gamble in diverting their capital and interests away from an ecological observatory to one where mycology and other taxonomy could be used in pharmaceutical studies. It's more than paid off. The research being done in that building over there"—he nods in the direction of the lab—"is close to changing the world. Cures for Parkinson's disease, Alzheimer's disease, stroke, and even neurodevelopmental disorders such as ADHD and OCD, are at our fingertips. With what we've learned studying *Amanita excandesco*, we can now apply the research to many other organisms, and that's where you come in."

"But who says people with ADHD need a cure?" I blurt out.

His attention snaps to me, a strange look burning in his eyes. "I take it you have ADHD," he says calmly. He doesn't wait for me to confirm it. "Many take medication for it. Many would like to function as a neurotypical. This would be no different than taking prescribed stimulants, except, in theory, you would be able to take it once, and you'd be forever changed."

"Sounds good to me," a girl called Noor says. "I can barely remember to take my meds as it is."

But what if you lose the essence of who you are? I think, but I manage to keep it to myself because I'm sure the last thing Kincaid wants is for his speech to be derailed. I know it can be dangerous to think of ADHD as a superpower when so many people are clearly disabled by it, and the neurodivergent community is not a monolith, but even so, the idea of having it wiped away—for good—makes me pause.

"You said that Madrona discovered the fungus," Munawar says to him. "It was on your property here, was it not?"

He nods. "It was. Dr. Everly Johnstone discovered it while foraging."

"How did you know then that it possessed the same attributes as lion's mane?"

Kincaid shrugs. "A hunch, I suppose." Then he turns his focus back to his book. "Now, I'd like to list the types of fungi you'll likely find while you're here. I'm sure you've all seen *Chlorociboria aeruginascenes*, or blue stain fungus, painting the sides of the cedars out here," he begins and then launches into a very long list of all the fungi we'll encounter.

I write it all down on the tablet, doing my best to focus on my notes and not on Kincaid, though I have a hard time not trying to figure out what his tattoo is of, if he has any others hidden on his body, what he looks like naked. In my dream, I only had an impression of his form, and like most dreams, the details have completely washed away.

When class finally ends, I know I should leave the room along with Lauren and everyone else, but I linger behind. I feel pulled to Kincaid in ways I can't explain (okay, he's smart, and he's fucking hot, and maybe that's enough).

I stop by his desk, where he's gathering a few textbooks in his hands.

"Kincaid," I say.

He glances up at me and takes off his glasses, slipping them back into his pocket, his posture straightening. "Ms. Denik. I hope you didn't take offense to what I was saying." His voice is strained, and though he's staring into my eyes, he's unreadable.

I shake my head, feeling strangely off-balance around him. "I thought you were going to call me Syd," I say, but he continues to stare at me, his throat bobbing as he swallows. "Anyway, no. I didn't take offense. The idea just bothers me for some reason."

"Something I'd like to talk to you about during our sessions," he says, holding his books to his chest. I stare at his large hands splayed across the covers, the veins on his fore-arms. The fact that we'll have one-on-one sessions both thrills me and intimidates me. I want to be alone with him, but the idea that he'll be poking around in my brain disturbs me. I want to stay a secret to him, shadowed and mysterious.

Yeah right, I tell myself. *Like you've ever been shadowed and mysterious to anyone.*

He continues to stare at me, enough that his grey gaze

seems to unearth the ground beneath me. "Can I help you with something in particular?"

Oh, right. I didn't even have a reason for wanting to talk to him.

Or did I?

"Were you spying on me last night?" I ask, immediately wincing at how that came out. "I mean, I saw you last night outside my window. Seems you were staring up at me."

The corner of his mouth lifts. "I was."

"Oh?"

"Not the spying part, but I was outside the main lodge. I often have a walk before I turn in for the night. Checking for bears. Clearing my head. I suppose I happened to stop outside your window. I'll try to be more mindful next time."

"No," I say quickly. "No, it was fine, I just…"

"Thought I was spying on you," he fills in, giving me a quick smile. "Just what every professor needs."

"I wouldn't mind," I say.

God, what the fuck is wrong with me?

I expect him to laugh, but instead his expression darkens, enough that my blood runs cold. "I think you would mind very much," he says, his tone hard. Then he clears his throat, and his brow softens. "Is that all?"

Why am I stalling? I've already made things uncomfortable, but it seems I can't leave his side.

"Amani," I can't help but say. "There was a girl on my plane named Amani."

"Amani Farrokh?"

"I guess. I haven't seen her since I arrived."

He nods, his lips twisting in a somewhat apologetic smile. "Amani left early this morning on the first plane out. She wasn't feeling well."

I stare at him, blinking. "Wasn't feeling well? Is she okay?"

"I'm sure she'll be fine," he says. "Homesickness, I think. It can present itself in different ways."

"But she seemed fine last night."

The muscle in his jaw ticks, his gaze sharp. "You saw her last night? Where?"

"I was at the gazebo, and she came running out of the bushes. Told me to hurry up or I'd be late for dinner."

His pupils dilate, like a black hole in the fog. "Are you sure?"

I frown. "Well, yeah I'm sure. Are you trying to make me feel crazy or something?"

"No," he says quickly, shaking his head. "No, I would never disregard your thoughts. It's just surprising. Everly acts as the compound's nurse, and she had given her a sedative and put her to bed early. I suppose Amani could have gone for a walk after..." He trails off, mind going over something. "Anyway, this morning, she was ready to go back home. It was good to see she was making the right choice."

Something churns in my gut. Perhaps coffee on an empty stomach. "But she seemed so excited and happy to be here."

"This happens more than you know," he says sternly. "Every year, at least one student goes back. The isolation can be too much."

"Even with your weekly counseling?" I remark.

"I'm a psychologist, not a magician," he says. "Some minds are stronger than others. There is no shame in that."

"And my mind?" I can't help but ask. "Do you think it's strong enough?"

He studies me for a moment, something warm, close to affection, coming through his cold exterior. "I think that remains to be seen. But if I had to take a gander already, I would say yes. Shall we?"

Kincaid gestures to the door, and I follow him as he opens it for me. We step out into the late-morning fog.

"I'll see you later, Sydney Denik," he says to me with a faint smile before he disappears into the mist.

CHAPTER 7

AFTER LUNCH, a hearty vegetarian stew with beans and squash that I picked at, my appetite still not returning, the cohort split into two. Justin, Noor, sea-urchin-loving Albert, and the redhead Christina from Chicago went to the floating dock to do work with Dr. Hernandez while the rest of us were instructed to meet Nick by the totem pole.

The conversation with Kincaid is still on my mind as Nick starts distributing packs and foraging supplies to each of us. I really need to keep myself in check. Kincaid said he wasn't spying on me, and I believe him, but it's a worrying sign that I jumped to that conclusion. I don't know what it is about him, why he's already getting under my skin, but I'm going to blame it on a sex dream.

I've made mistakes before that have cost me dearly, and even though my sexual appetite can be extreme at times, my impulsivity can be restrained. Lusting after your professor is fine—as long as no line is ever crossed, and as long as it stays hidden away, siphoned into a harmless crush. Which means I need to stop being so...I don't know. I'm not flirting with him, not really, but I'm more comfortable with him than I ought to be. It needs to stop before I become too fixated and make bad decisions.

We head out along the logging road that runs behind the lodge. Nick tells us that it's rarely used these days since most areas around us were classified as protected land, though there is a logging camp about fifteen kilometers down the road.

"Camp number nine are our closest neighbors," he says as he walks ahead of us, a gnarled walking stick in hand. "If there's ever an emergency of some sort, which of course there won't be, just head up this road. It's tough going, but you'll eventually reach them. There's also the Checleset reservation to the south of us, bordering the entrance to the Brooks Peninsula, but it's boat access only, and you'd need permission first."

If it was an emergency, I'm sure they would be willing to help, permission or not, I think. I have to wonder what kind of emergencies happen at the lodge, but I don't want to bog down the atmosphere with that question.

The fog seems to lift as we walk along, the sun nearly breaking through the tops of the trees, and everyone is in good spirits, the bear bells attached to our packs filling the air with soft jingling. At Nick's prodding, I take out a compass from my pack and watch it move as we turn northeast, the land flatter to our right and a sharp mountain rising from our left where the Sitka spruce seem to reach into the sky. Ravens call out from the branches, occasionally swooping overhead, while the mournful call of the varied thrush comes from the bushes. I breathe in deeply, the scent of pine and fresh soil.

Clayton ends up walking right behind me, though he's thankfully in conversation with a black guy from London named Patrick.

"I'm just worried my brother will be drafted," Clayton says to Patrick. "War didn't seem a possibility when he joined the military."

I frown at that, wondering what war he could be talking about, when Patrick goes, "Shhhhhh."

Now I have to glance behind me. Patrick looks uneasy, quickly busying himself with the straps on his pack while Clayton glares at me.

"What are you looking at, princess?" he says. "Not used to walking places?"

"I was just curious what war your brother is being drafted into," I tell him.

He just stares at me for a moment, eyes boring into mine. "There's some skirmish in the Balkans," he eventually says. "Let me guess, you don't watch the news. Think you're too smart or woke for it or something."

"Clayton!" Nick barks at him from the front. "Enough."

Before I can turn back around, I trip over a rock, but Munawar's hand shoots out and grabs my arm, steadying me.

"Thanks," I tell him, giving him a flustered smile.

Munawar nods as he lets go. "I don't watch the news much either," he admits, his eyes kind. "Too much drama."

"Yeah, well, I used to," I tell him. "But I get so distracted it steals my focus, and I usually end up depressed."

"Luckily, we won't get any while we're here," Lauren notes. "I think we'll be happier for it. Though I wish I could keep up with the Kardashians."

"Do people still watch that show?"

She laughs. "You'd be surprised."

We walk for a little while longer, the logging road becoming overgrown with ferns and blooming pink fireweed in some places, before Nick leads us down a trail through the brush. Eventually, we come to a small clearing, the grass so rich and green it's almost neon, a few alder trees bordering a dark pond peppered with lily pads.

"This is where I'd like for us to forage," Nick says as he stops in the middle, lowering his pack to the grass.

"Everyone split up but remain in the glen where I can see you."

"Yes, Dad," Munawar says, which makes everyone laugh.

"Fine, you can go in twos if you want to explore deeper. Just make sure you're talking the entire time," Nick concedes with a sigh. "Keeps away the animals, even though your bear bells should do the trick. And have those compasses handy. I don't want you getting lost. The forest here can play tricks on you."

Lauren looks at me expectantly. "Well? Shall we explore?"

I nod eagerly. Under Nick's watchful eye, we head east to where a faint deer trail zags through Oregon grape and stinging nettle, the latter we are careful to avoid. The alders turn into cedar and fir, the forest becoming darker as we go. I know we're heading toward the water, so it should be opening up, not becoming more overgrown, dense, and tangled, the branches overhead touching each other and blotting out the sky.

"It's kind of creepy," Lauren says, but she's smiling.

"Yeah," I agree, looking around. Nothing but dark trees and the wild underbrush. "Makes you feel like something is watching you," I add, trying to creep her out a little more.

"Something probably is," she says playfully, tucking her hair behind her ear. "Trees have eyes, don't you know?"

We eventually come to a stop by a grove of cedars, Lauren taking out her water bottle with the Madrona Foundation logo on it and downing it. In front of us is a beast of a western cedar, meters wide, bigger than all the rest, and I instinctively place my palm on the rough, red strips of bark. My eyes fall closed, thinking about what Lauren said. Trees might not have eyes, but they communicate to each other through the mycelia that travels under the earth. The mycorrhizal network allows trees to shoot more nutrients to saplings, such as those in the shade, giving them a better chance at survival. They see without eyes.

"This is a mother tree," I whisper, the oldest and most established, with the deepest fungal connections, the one to recognize distress signals in other trees and send them more water. I feel like if I concentrate hard enough, I can almost feel the tree trying to talk to me.

As if it thinks I'm in distress.

You're right, I can't help but think. *I am in distress. I feel like my whole world is about to collapse any day now.*

Suddenly, an image flashes through my mind.

A dark-haired girl in a nightgown, hanging from a tree, her neck broken.

Dead.

I gasp and step away from the tree, my eyes flying open.

"Looks like blue stain fungus," Lauren says. She's kneeling beside me, fingers trailing over the blue streaks on the bark, not noticing my reaction.

Chill out, I remind myself, and the image of the girl starts to fade from my mind until I can't remember what I saw, but I know that I saw something.

"Worth sampling?" she asks, finally looking up at me. She frowns. "You okay? You look a little pale."

"I'm fine," I tell her quickly. "Let's keep going."

"Sure," she says, wiping her palms on her jeans as we continue along the path. I trail behind her. My head feels swimmy, my gait off-balance. I think the lack of food is finally catching up with me, and yet I'm still not hungry.

I'm lost in my thoughts, blindly following Lauren, when she suddenly stops, and I slam into her back.

"Oh my god," she gasps.

"What?" I peer over her shoulder.

In front of us, in a small clearing of dirt and pine needles, is a mound of soil with a cross made of sticks at one end.

A grave.

A grave that is covered in fungi, the fruiting bodies of the mushrooms sprouting across it. There must be hundreds of them, various sizes of the same variety, so white they're nearly translucent, their gills a bright orange.

Suddenly the air fills with a whiny droning noise, like mosquitos.

"Should we sample them?" Lauren asks me uneasily.

I shake my head. "No. We need to turn back and tell Nick."

She nods, biting her lip until it's white. "Yeah. I'm sure it's...I'm sure they know. But the mushrooms, I don't recognize them. They're like..." She takes a step forward to get closer. I reach for her to hold her back but miss. "They're like Amanita, but I've never seen one with orange gills like this. Reminds me of jack-o'-lantern mushrooms but not completely orange. We should do a spore print."

"Since we don't know what species this is, it could be poisonous," I tell her, watching as she kneels down beside the grave. She makes a show of taking out a rubber glove from her pack and putting it on before she pulls out an aluminum flower, a dropper of water, and a small knife. "It's probably poisonous."

"I'll be careful," she says, reaching with her knife for the nearest mushroom, about the size of her thumb.

"But what if this is *it*?" I ask her, crouching down and grabbing her arm. The droning sound is louder here, and I feel a wave of nausea, but I hang on. "What if this is *Amanita excandesco*? If this is their fungi, maybe we shouldn't be tampering with it in any way, at least without their permission."

She seems to think that over and reluctantly puts the knife away.

"Don't you think Nick would have warned us?" she asks.

"Maybe he didn't think we'd find any. I think we should go back now. Anyway, it feels wrong to harvest mushrooms from a grave." I can't help but think of Munawar's shirt and shiver. They literally *are* feasting on something's corpse.

"I never pegged you for the sentimental type," she says as she straightens up. "Alright, let's go back. This shit is too creepy, even for me."

We walk back on the path, our pace quicker, and it's about ten minutes before we see the grave again.

"How the fuck?" Lauren says, looking around wildly. "How did we walk in a circle?"

The air is growing colder now, the light dimmer. I reach down for my compass and realize the hairs on my arms are standing up.

"Okay, let's try again," I say, holding it out.

Lauren comes behind me, and we turn back on the path again. At one point, it veers off through a grove of hemlock, the branches bare and spindly, the bark covered with lichen and spiderwebs hanging off the ends, but the compass is telling us it's the wrong direction.

We go back a few feet and then see the trail we were supposed to take, barely visible from this angle because of the density of the ferns. Then we pass the mother cedar, which I avoid looking at in case I hallucinate about a dead girl again, until we hear chatter in the distance, and the trees start to open up into the glen.

"There you are!" Nick says, putting his hands on his hips. Most of the students are gathered around him, looking bored. "We were about to come looking for you two."

"We went further than we thought," Lauren says. "Sorry."

"We found a grave," I tell him bluntly.

Everyone snaps to attention. Nick's brows go up. "A...grave?"

I nod, out of breath. "Yeah. A mound of dirt with a cross on the end. Covered in mushrooms we couldn't identify."

"I wanted to take a spore print, but we weren't sure if it was, you know, Madrona's famous fungus," Lauren says.

Nick seems to think that over for a moment. "A grave. Well, it's possible if you went far enough toward the inlet that you came across Everly and Michael's old dog, Grover. Was it a cross made from sticks?"

I nod.

"Then that's probably Grover," he says. "He was the most beloved member of the team. What did the fruiting bodies look like?" We describe them for him, and he smiles. "Your instincts were correct. That is *Amanita excandesco*. I'm glad you didn't sample them as the spores can be a nuisance if disturbed. I'll make a note to tell Everly to check on the grave."

"So, to be clear," Lauren says, crossing her arms. "You want us foraging and making new discoveries, but you don't actually want us foraging for your fungi."

He gives her a stiff smile. "I appreciate all discoveries. I just didn't know the fungi were ever found in this zone. If any of you come across them, please don't pick them, but let us know instead."

"It would help if we knew what they looked like," Patrick says. "Why don't you take us to the grave so we know?"

Nick looks at his watch. "You know, it's getting late," he says. "We need to head back. The clouds look like rain."

I look up just in time to see a bald eagle soaring past, the clouds behind it looking dark and ominous.

We start walking back to the logging road, Lauren, Munawar, and I lagging behind.

Munawar leans in and whispers, "I bet the reason he doesn't want us to know what they look like is because he doesn't want us collecting them for ourselves. Maybe they are dangerous, or maybe they don't want their property stolen and sold to someone else."

"But it's not really their property," Lauren points out. "I've looked up their patent application for the fungus. It was denied. You can't patent something that you didn't create. Unless they find a way to cultivate and crossbreed it with something else and then get that patented, but it sounds like they have trouble propagating."

"Doesn't mean we're allowed to take them," I point out. "Pretty sure it's in the NDA we signed. Not a single organism can go back with us."

"Hmmm," Munawar says.

I glance at him over my shoulder and see the contemplative look on his face. "Don't even think about smuggling them up your butt."

"I would never," he says, but from his smile, I know that's exactly what he was thinking.

By the time we get back to the lodge and dinner rolls around, I'm absolutely beat. I'm a fairly healthy person, not a thin one by any means, my size fluctuating between ten and twelve, but I've always been active with hiking, sometimes jogging if I'm training for a fun run, and my muscles are usually pretty strong and defined. So it's strange that I feel like I could sleep forever as soon as the evening hits. It's like my muscles have atrophied.

After dinner, I join the others in the common room, where mugs of hot chocolate with marshmallows and plates of crumbly butter cookies are handed out. I force myself to nibble on a cookie, but the sugar does nothing to perk me up.

"I think I'm going to go to bed," I tell Lauren in the armchair beside me. Munawar, Justin, and Noor are on the couch, deep in a conversation about some TV series I've never heard of. But when they see me looking at them, they abruptly stop talking.

"Already? It's eight p.m.," Lauren says, glancing at her plastic watch.

I yawn to prove a point. "I know, but I've just been so exhausted all day. Ever since I got here, really."

"It's the fresh air," she says. "But I've been watching you pick at your food. You're like a bird. You're not eating enough."

I give her a tired smile. "It's not a bad change, believe me. Usually, I wolf down everything in sight and in five seconds flat." I pat my stomach. "My IBS is grateful."

"Alright," she says warily. "I'll see you in the morning."

I say my goodbyes to the group and head toward the stairs. I feel a prickle at the back of my neck and turn around to see Lauren whispering with the others. Once they see me looking at them, they break apart.

I feel my cheeks go hot, and I quickly go up the stairs. It's probably nothing. I'm sure they weren't talking about me, and if they were, it probably wasn't anything bad. I'm sure they asked why I was going to bed so early, and Lauren explained.

But still, after years of feeling like an outsider, of having a hard time picking up on social cues, I always doubt myself when it comes to making friends. A few bad apples when I was young, and I'm suspicious of everyone.

I push it out of my mind and get ready for bed. No need for melatonin this night; I'm practically falling asleep on my feet. No need to do my TMJ face yoga either. It's like my jaw muscles have reduced, my face slimmer. I'm probably a lot less bloated, thanks to the reduction in food. You'd think I would be elated at the weight loss, but I'm not. It's actually kind of concerning since I never wanted to lose weight in the first place.

After I wash my face and put on my pajamas, I get into bed and turn off my lamp. The room is barely dark, twilight thick in the sky and moonlight spilling in through the window.

I get out of bed to close the curtains. It's been raining ever since our foraging excursion, but the skies are clearing now. The moon is visible, just beyond the cedar tops, almost full, with fast-moving clouds passing over it like gauze. I stare at it for a moment, feeling a strange sense of wonder, of feeling plugged in and drawn to it, when movement below catches my eye.

I glance down to see someone underneath my window. He's shaped like Kincaid, but with the moon behind him, I can't see his face.

Yet I know he's looking at me.

His cigarette glows once, and then he turns and disappears into the trees, the puddles rippling in his wake.

"Just out on your nightly walk," I say softly.

CHAPTER 8

I'M NERVOUS.

It's my first counseling session with Kincaid, and I have no idea what to expect. I'm standing outside the north dorm, under the slight overhang of the roof, trying to stay out of the drizzle, but I can't quite make myself open the door and walk inside the building.

It doesn't help that I saw him again outside my window last night, but I should be grateful it didn't result in another sex dream. In fact, I slept pretty well and didn't wake up until my alarm went off. I still feel tired though. All the coffee at breakfast didn't help; neither did the toast and peanut butter I pecked at like a bird, much to Lauren's amusement.

I take in a deep breath and step inside the building. It's warm in here, smelling of woodsmoke. There's a long hallway with a handful of doors, and at the end, it looks like it opens up to a small common room, similar to the one in the main lodge.

I slowly walk down the hall until I find a door that says Dr. Wes Kincaid.

You don't have to tell him anything, I remind myself. *Showing up is mandatory. Showing yourself isn't.*

I rap on his door.

"Come in," comes his now familiar voice.

I turn the handle and step inside. His office is dark, venetian blinds over the windows that are half-shuttered. Bookshelves crammed with books line all the walls, along with several diplomas, and artifacts that seem to be collected from a bunch of cultures: a lacquered vase, a broken pot, a small Peruvian statue. It smells good, like santal, and I spot an incense holder on one shelf, as well as various candles.

He's standing at his desk, staring at something white and square in his hands that he quickly slips into his pocket before he takes his seat and finally meets my eyes.

"Please, come in. Sit down," he says, gesturing to the empty chair on the other side of the desk.

I walk across the room, my shoes squeaking on the hardwood, feeling self-conscious. The worn leather creaks as I sit down in the chair.

He folds his hands over the desk, and I take note of his attire today, a grey button-up under a dark vest. He looks every bit the psychologist today, including his eyes, which are flicking over my body and face as if searching for something.

Unfortunately, his professional attire doesn't make him any less sexy.

He clears his throat. "How are you?"

I shrug. "Can't complain."

His dark brow arches up. "Well, that is good to know. Before we start, I should tell you that I'm videotaping this session." He points at a small web camera on the windowsill behind him.

"Don't you need my permission for that?" I ask, my body stiffening, hating the idea of being on film.

His smile is stiff. "Not here, I don't. You conceded to that in your NDA."

"Do you have a copy of the NDA so I can double-check?" I

ask grumpily. "Doesn't seem fair that I have no computer access to check what I signed."

"How about we get to that later. I only have an hour with you a week, and I want to make it worth my while."

I sit back in my chair, my hackles up. It doesn't matter how handsome he is, I'm going to be as stubborn as humanely possible for the next hour. Which, of course, isn't easy when I have a tendency to blab about everything, especially when the subject is *me*.

"Tell me, Ms. Denik," Kincaid says in his smooth voice. "Have you been sleeping well?"

"You would know," I answer. "You're the one who keeps standing outside my room at night."

He splays his hands in innocence. "Merely my evening walk."

"Right. Bear patrol."

The corner of his mouth lifts. "Yes. Someone has to keep you safe."

"How long have you been working here?" I ask, looking around the room. "This place seems very lived-in. I like it."

"Five years," he says. "But we aren't here to talk about me."

"That's a shame. You're far more interesting than I am."

A flash of something in his eyes, intense and unreadable. "That's not true. You know it too. You know you're special, Sydney."

I roll my eyes. "Everyone wants to believe that."

"But it's true. That's why you're here. Do you know how many applicants we get each year? Thousands. Aspiring neuroscientists, biologists, geneticists—everyone wants in, but only those who are special enough, like you, are accepted. You have proven your worth. Tell me about how you discovered the dark fungus."

"I had heard about dark fungi and saw Dr. Nilsson's most wanted list on a website. I was already interested in DNA sequencing and molecular data and decided to apply it to the list. The idea that there are millions of unclassified fungi out there that we can't really see, in the land, the sea, the air, all this DNA that we can isolate but can't attribute to any known organism...it's fascinating."

Normally, when I'm talking about dark fungi, I get really passionate and animated, so I'm surprised I'm playing it so cool.

"So you followed your curiosity."

"Yes."

He leans in slightly, watching me closely. "It had nothing to do with the fact that whatever you discovered would be linked to you, that you would become known for it. That you would be recognized and deserving of the accolades."

I swallow thickly. "I mean, I guess."

Okay, that had a lot to do with it. My ego loved the idea of discovering something before someone else, loved how people would know the name Sydney Denik, even if just within a small circle of mycology nerds.

"Would you consider yourself to be an ambitious person?" he asks, bringing out a pen and pad of paper and writing something down.

"Yes."

"Have you always been ambitious?"

"Ever since I was young," I tell him. I launch into how I wanted to be a mad scientist growing up and how my grand-mother was my enabler.

He at least seems amused by my confession. "I see," he says, smiling slightly, his grey eyes seeming warmer. Then he grows serious again. "Has your ambition ever taken on a dark side?"

I stare at him for a moment, my heart lurching.

He can't know, can he?

Oh, but wait. He has access to the internet. Of course he can.

"No," I lie. He doesn't need to know, and if he does know already, I don't need to repeat it. Besides, it's a leap to say it was because of ambition. I thought Professor Edwards actually liked me. It was him who used me, not the other way around. It was him that lied and said he wasn't married. It was him that made me lose my scholarship to Stanford.

"Do you feel ambitious here at Madrona?" he asks. "I imagine your capstone project is at the forefront of your mind."

I blink a couple of times. "Actually, no," I admit. "I haven't really thought about it since I got here."

Because there is no capstone for me anymore, I want to admit to him, just to get the truth out there.

Kincaid scribbles something down, and my thoughts about Edwards remind me to stay professional, no matter how good his hands look as he writes.

"How have you been sleeping?" he asks again, glancing up at me. "You never answered the first time. You deflected."

I make a face at his candor. "I think I'm sleeping okay. But I don't feel like I have. I've been pretty tired since I got here."

"How is your appetite?"

"Nonexistent. The food is really good, I'm just not... hungry. I don't know. Feels like I lost weight since I got here."

"Are you on any medication?"

"Yes. I have an IUD. And I take Adderall."

"How much do you take?"

"Only ten milligrams. Just twice a day. But I plan on cutting back. I could only get the pharmacist to give me two months' worth. You know, they automatically think you're dealing drugs if you get three, heaven forbid. So I'll cut back to one a day while I'm here."

He leans back in his chair, tapping his elegant fingers along the edge of the armrests. "Do you care to do a little experiment with me?"

My brows go up. "What kind of experiment?"

"Well, two experiments, actually. One is that I want you to keep a diary. Write in it every night before you go to bed. Just a sentence or two about your day or at least how you're feeling. Mentally, physically."

He reaches into his desk drawer and slides a faux-leather notebook toward me.

I take it, turning it over. I love a good notebook. "You won't be reading it, will you?"

"No. It's not for me to analyze. It's for you to analyze."

"Okay. What else?"

"I'd like you to stop taking your medication for a couple of weeks."

I stare blankly at him. "Why?"

"I think you'll sleep better."

"I need it to function," I tell him, feeling a little panicky.

"Stimulants can be very helpful, but from the symptoms you describe, feeling tired despite sleeping, not having an appetite, I think we can manage your ADHD through behavioral therapy. You're only on ten milligrams. That's something we can try to manage without drugs. And that diary should help."

I shake my head. "No. I need to be able to think while I'm here. I need my brain at its best. I need to concentrate on my capstone." I lie about the last one.

"You'll be fine. I promise. Just a couple of weeks, and if you don't see a difference, go right back on them. You have to conserve them anyway." He pauses, licking his lips, his gaze sharpening on mine. "Don't you trust me?"

I feel my breath hitch in my chest. "I don't know you," I whisper.

"Haven't you ever trusted someone you don't know before?"

"Yes. And it never ended well."

He nods slowly. "I understand. Well, then I'm asking you

to trust me, Sydney Denik. I only have your best interests at heart." He swallows. "Please."

I find myself agreeing. "Okay."

He gives me a genuine smile, one that makes his eyes crinkle, lines along his cheeks lighting up his face for one brief, beautiful moment.

Wow. I can't help but smile back.

"I won't let you down," he says. Then he coughs lightly and turns his attention back to the pad of paper, the spell between us broken. "How are you getting along with the rest of the students?"

I shrug. "Uh, I mean, I've made some friends, I think."

"Does that come easy to you? Making friends?"

"Define friends," I say wryly. "I seem to get along with most people. On a surface level, anyway. I think I'm easygoing and fun. People seem to want to be around me…"

"And below a surface level?" he asks, leaning forward on his elbows and steepling his fingers together.

I fall silent at that, digging deep. "I think I have a hard time keeping people engaged. Because even though I feel like I'm honest, I'm also holding the real me back."

"You're masking."

"Yes. Not consciously. I have to know someone and trust them to let them see the real me, and when I do, that's when I often lose them."

"I bet the real you isn't that different from the one that people see," he offers quietly. "Sometimes others pick up on the fact that you're masking, and so they think perhaps they aren't worthy of being shown the true you. It's not always about people not accepting who you are. Sometimes it's about them feeling like they aren't good enough for you or worth your time. Sometimes people just want to feel worthy of being let in."

I rub my lips together as I think that over. I'd never thought of it that way. "Maybe," I concede.

He studies me for a moment, his gaze so inquisitive that I have to stare down at my nails. Normally, I've picked them raw, one of my stims, but lately, they've been looking good. I'd paint them if my polish didn't chip after a day.

"And how are you dealing with the lack of communication and internet?" he finally asks.

"It's only been three days," I inform him. "I'm fine."

"You let your friends back home know where you are, of course."

"Yep. My friend Chelsea has all my stuff. She knows I'm out of contact."

"All your stuff?"

Oh fuck. He doesn't know I was kicked out of housing.

"There was no point being in student housing over the summer if I was going to be here," I say smoothly.

"Of course." He stares at me, and from the barely perceptible wince, I can tell what he's about to say next. "You wrote down a lot on your application...I know you lost your father a couple of years ago. And your grandmother a year before that. Are there any other relatives that you have a relationship with, that you stay in touch with?"

I shake my head. "I have an aunt, but we don't really talk."

He writes something else down, then looks up, his forehead wrinkling.

"You lost your mother at a young age too," he says softly.

"Postpartum depression," I tell him. I don't have to tell him the rest.

"You've experienced a lot of loss during your life. How old are you?"

"Twenty-six."

"Oh. You seemed older," he says. "No offense."

"I'm not offended. It's just rare to hear." Everyone usually thinks I'm younger than I am, probably because I have a baby face. Oh, and I'm incredibly immature.

"And how has your relationship with death changed? Do you think about it often? Do you fear it?"

The questions are starting to make me uncomfortable now. I shift in my chair, the leather groaning loudly. "I don't think about it. I used to fear losing my family, but after my grand-mother and my father…there's no one left for me to lose. I guess that's the silver lining, isn't it?"

I give him an awkward smile, and he scribbles something down.

"I fear my own death though," I go on. "I fear dying before accomplishing all the things I want to accomplish, before I get to experience things and leave my mark on the world. But everyone fears that. Don't you?"

His eyes soften. "I do. It's a very human reaction. It comes down to purpose. We want to find our purpose before our death." A beat. The rain starts to pick up outside, spattering on the window. "Have you found your purpose yet?"

I let out a caustic laugh. "Are you kidding? No."

Kincaid leans in slightly, a conspiratorial look in his dusky eyes. "I think you'll find your purpose while you're here, Syd. I really do."

I hate how sincere he looks and sounds when I know he's just playing to my ego and saying things he knows I want to hear.

And yet, I believe him.

"You called me Syd," I tell him. "Does that mean we're friends now?"

"If you're trusting me, then I suppose that's fair to say." He glances at the clock on the wall. "Well, I think that's it for today."

"It's only been thirty minutes," I tell him.

"I like to break you in slowly," he says, his voice becoming rough for a moment, a smolder in his gaze, and, fuck, I can't help but think of sex.

"Okay," I practically squeak.

"Better to quit when things are going well, don't you think?" he says, looking cool and professional again. "I'll see you tomorrow in class."

And just like that, I'm dismissed.

"Are you going to get anything tomorrow when they go to town?" Lauren asks me. "I was thinking of getting a box of wine if you want to split it. I know it's not very classy, but it should last a long time. Might be nice to have some at dinner."

We're sitting at the picnic table at the gazebo with Munawar, Justin, and Natasha. The skies cleared during dinner, so we decided to forgo the common room and watch the sunset. I'm sleepy, as usual, but force myself to stay up.

It's a beautiful evening, too, a low bank of fog sitting over the entrance to the inlet and the ocean beyond. The water is still, and everything is bathed in soft gold, a raft of sea otters in the distance. Even the breeze is warmer than it has been, coasting over my skin, making everything seem magical. It's a view that deserves a glass of wine, but…

"Count me out," I tell her. "I'm cutting back on drinking."

Last time I drank was when I showed up shitfaced to Professor Edwards' house, and everything went swiftly downhill from there.

"That's fine. I'll get it anyway," she says. "More for me."

"How was your session with Dr. Kincaid?" Natasha asks. She's normally quiet, barely says more than a few words to anyone except Justin, whom she's been flirting with all night. "I really hope he doesn't make me talk about anything personal."

"It was fine," I tell her. "And only half an hour to start. He doesn't seem to be too invasive so far."

"Did you find out if he's married?" Lauren says with a wink, the setting sun shining on her hair.

"*No*," I tell her. "That's none of my business." I want to tell her that married men lie too, but that would be opening a can of worms.

"You have the hots for teacher?" Munawar asks as he buttons up his jacket, looking visibly cold.

"No," Lauren and I answer in unison, which just makes the rest of them laugh.

"Sydney!"

A voice calls out from behind me, and I twist around to look, half expecting to see Amani again, even though I know she went home.

"Who's there?" I ask, though all I see are the bushes.

"What?" asks Lauren.

"I thought I heard my name," I tell her, motioning for everyone to be quiet.

"Sydney!" the person yells again, further away this time. The voice sounds so damn familiar, but I can't place it.

"There!" I exclaim, looking back at everyone. "Didn't you hear that?"

Justin snorts. "That sounds like an elk bugle. I don't think the elk here know your name."

"No, it said Sydney," I tell them, getting to my feet.

"Where are you going?" Lauren asks.

"I'm going to go see who it is." I walk out of the gazebo, my ears straining as I try to hear if they call for me again, and head into the bushes.

"Sydney!" Lauren cries out as I hear her run after me. "That's right, I'm calling you too! Don't you know about folklore? Don't answer things that yell for you in the woods!"

I had heard about that but figured it was some Appalachian stuff. At the very least, I knew not to whistle at night. But the person was indeed a person and very clearly yelling my name.

It really did sound like Amani, I think, *but that's impossible.*

I come to a stop where the path forks, the right heading to the beach and the Panabode cabins, the other toward the main lodge. Suddenly, there's a rustling sound, and I swear I see someone running into the trees beyond, pink cloth trailing behind them.

"Amani," I say under my breath and start running that way.

"The girl who went home?" Lauren asks, following close behind.

"I don't know, maybe," I tell her, slowing down as the path gets rocky and starts going downhill to the beach. "Maybe she didn't really leave."

"Why would they lie? And why would none of us have seen her? Why hide her?" Lauren asks. "I swear, your imagination needs to be scaled back."

She's right though. When we get to the beach, there's no sign of Amani or anyone, just the calm waves lapping on the white-sand shore, the peeling orange bark of the lone Madrona looking extra fiery in the sunset.

"Maybe you should consider taking up drinking again," Lauren says, looking me over. "You're kinda stressed, whether you know it or not."

"I'm fine," I tell her, scanning the forest illuminated by the sun's glow. "I could have sworn I heard my name."

"Probably an elk, like Justin said. There's an estuary not far from here and their calls are made to carry. Come on, let's head back. We left Munawar alone with Justin and Natasha, and I'm afraid he's about to turn into a third wheel."

By the time we get back to the gazebo, however, all the activity has left me exhausted. I know the sun won't set for a bit, but I'd rather be asleep by then.

I excuse myself and head to the main lodge. The common

room is quieter than normal, with only Noor sitting in an armchair by the fire, reading a book. Everyone else must be out enjoying the nice evening.

I head up the stairs, pausing at the landing when I hear a door above me shut, and a key turning, the sounds close enough to be coming from my room. I round the corner, and suddenly, Kincaid is running down the stairs.

"Kincaid?" I call out to him as he brushes past me, the scent of sweet tobacco and cedar whipping past, but he doesn't stop.

I watch as he disappears out the front door, and then I hurry up the stairs to my room. I quickly unlock the door and step inside, locking it again behind me.

Was Kincaid just in my room?

I turn on all the lights and look around, inspecting every-thing. Nothing seems to be taken; everything is exactly as I left it or as much as I remember.

Then I notice something that I can't believe I didn't notice before.

Poking halfway under the bed are the black Nike sneakers I thought I forgot to pack.

CHAPTER 9

I'M DREAMING AGAIN.

Kincaid's office. Moonlight spills in through the blinds, leaving slashes of cold light amidst the darkness. I'm on my knees, the thick rug cushioning me as I reach up and unzip Kincaid's pants in a teasing manner.

I glance up at him, and he's staring down at me with quiet intensity, made all the more feral by the moonlight in his eyes, turning the grey to the color of a grave.

"That's it," he murmurs, his voice feeling like fingers down my spine. "Let me use you."

Heat flares between my legs. I want him to keep talking like that.

I want to *feel*.

I slowly take his dick out of his pants, large, thick, and perfectly sculpted. It's hot to touch in my palm. I give it a squeeze, which makes his nostrils flare.

"Look at you, my little pet," he says through a hiss. "Holding my cock like you've held countless others. But you don't know how to please me, do you? You're not quite good enough. Not yet."

That's what you think.

"Prove your worth to me," he goes on, voice growing hoarse. "Prove you're something more than a useless little slut, a vessel for my pleasure."

"Yes, Doctor," I say, knowing he loves it when I call him that.

I wrap my lips around the head of his cock, the salt of his precum making my taste buds dance. I love taking him like this, feeling every inch of him in such a vulnerable, raw way. Like I'm a heathen, worshipping the devil. I love how he looms above me, all power and control, that I'm subjected to his whims, used solely for his gratification.

"So cum hungry, so desperate," he purrs. "I can smell how wet you are from here."

I moan, pressing my tongue along the ridge as he grabs my hair, making a tight fist as he starts pumping his hips, thrusting into my wet mouth.

"Keep going. Taking my cock like the good little bitch you are."

The praise thrills me, shoots straight to my pussy, and I start writhing in desperation, knowing how it will make him degrade me again.

I need to hear it. To hear both.

I slip my hand between my thighs.

"Disobedient," he growls, yanking my hair in a deliciously painful way. "You know that sweet cunt belongs to me, pet. You know you don't have permission to touch what's mine."

Maybe I want to be punished, I think, sliding my fingers deeper until I feel how wet I am.

I'm coming in seconds.

"Oh god," I yell out into the pillow, my cry muffled. My heart pounds in my ears, my body jerking as the orgasm slams through me.

And then I lift up my head and realize where I am.

Lying on my stomach in bed, the covers kicked to the side.

I remove my hand, my arm sore from having been trapped under my body.

Holy shit. What a fucking dream. First time I've actually woken myself up masturbating.

I turn over, breathing hard. I'm covered in a thin sheen of sweat.

That was wild.

I slowly sit up, trying to will my heart to return to a normal pace. I forgot to write in my diary before bed, but perhaps jotting down my dreams is a good start.

I'm about to turn on the bedside light when suddenly, I hear the floorboards creak outside my room.

I squint, looking at the crack under the door. There's faint light from the hallway, but a shadow is moving, as if someone is passing by.

I get up and walk quietly across the room, my limbs feeling like jelly. I pause with my hand outstretched, too afraid to open it and find someone like Clayton leering outside. God, is it possible that I was moaning really loud, enough to wake someone up? Was I calling out Kincaid's name? Fuck, I hope not.

I place my ear against the door instead, and listen.

Someone is *whispering*.

I jolt, pulling my head away.

What the fuck was that?!

Fear washes over me like an ice bath. I suck in my breath, feeling frozen on the spot.

Slowly, I find the courage to put my ear against the door again.

There's a low hiss, like someone letting air out of tires, but the hiss sounds a lot like someone—or something—speaking.

Pleeeeeeeease, it says.

Then, all is silent.

Suffice to say I didn't go back to sleep after that, which wasn't awesome because it was three in the morning. I stayed up with all the lights on, busying myself with a mycology book I had taken from the common room. It was only when first light brightened the darkness at five a.m. that I finally calmed down enough to let myself think about what happened. The problem was, the sex dream and the voice saying *please* outside the door started to blend together, until I couldn't be sure if the latter had been a dream as well.

It was safer to think it was.

The morning class with Kincaid was weird, but only because I was making it weird—I kept thinking about my dream and his strange behavior last night. Had he gone into my room or not? If he did, why? Did he bring me my shoes, or had they always been there and I overlooked them? The more I try to think about it, the more I can't remember, like everything is becoming a blur.

So I did my best not to stare at him and stayed focused on his lecture about the role of fungi in aquatic web systems and biogeochemistry, all of which were fascinating to me, especially how they relate to dark fungi. My ego wants to think he created that lecture just for me after our conversation, the way it tickled my brain and got all my neurons firing.

Lunch was another hearty meal of turkey and white bean chili, which happens to be one of my favorite dishes. My appetite increased a little, and I was actually able to finish a whole bowl, even though I ate slower than I ever have in my life. Lauren seemed proud of me.

Now, we're all standing on the dock, waiting for Kincaid and Nick. The mycology cohort is supposed to go on a boat expedition to an area that isn't accessible by road and is too far to walk.

"This is exciting," Lauren says to me, a damp breeze messing up her hair. "I hope we see whales."

"I want to see the megalodon," Munawar says. "Jason Statham has nothing on me." In keeping with his promise, he's wearing a shirt that says *Me, Mycelium, and I*, which he promptly zips up under a puffer jacket. It's chilly out, the fog thick as soup in places, but at least it's not raining.

Kincaid and Nick appear at the top of the ramp and stroll down single file, Kincaid towering over the surfer dude, both of them dressed in heavy-duty rain jackets, Kincaid's olive green while Nick's is bright yellow.

"Looks like you're all dressed for the weather," Kincaid says to us, meeting my eyes for one intense moment, harkening back to my dream. My cheeks burn, and I look away. "If you need hats, gloves, or a poncho, they're in bins on the Zodiacs. You never know when the weather will turn. We'll be splitting up. Munawar, Natasha, Lauren, and Toshio with Nick. Sydney, Patrick, Clayton, Rav, you'll be with me." He gestures to the sleek black boat to our left.

I look at Lauren in surprise that we're being split up, and she grabs my arm in an overly dramatic gesture.

"Noooo, Sydney," she cries. "I'll never let go."

I know she's joking, but I really don't want to be separated from her, especially as I'll be in a group with both Clayton and Kincaid, two people I have very opposing feelings about.

"Life jackets are on your seats," Kincaid adds. "Put them on."

I get into the boat, which looks like it might take tourists whale watching with the two-by-two seating configuration down the middle. There are even straps on the seats to hold us in. I take the first seat and give Rav a grateful smile when he sits down next to me. I like him, and from the way he and

Lauren give each other the eye, I know that yet another romance is budding on the compound.

I slip on the life jacket, which barely fits over my boobs, then pull down the harness, clipping me into the seat.

"We'll take it slow out of the inlet," Kincaid says, getting behind the wheel at the back of the boat and yanking the cord on the motor until it roars to life. "There's a raft of otters we don't like to disturb, as well as the herons who like to nest along the shore. They can get quite ornery. Once we get out of the protected waters and past the barrier rocks though, that's when things might get a little bumpy. Remember, that's the North Pacific out there. No other landmass between us and Japan. The wind is picking up a little, so there's going to be some chop, but the swells should be tolerable today. Anyway, we'll let Nick's group go first and be the guinea pigs. They'll radio back if it gets too bad, and we'll stick to the inlets instead."

Rav and I wave to Lauren in unison as Nick's Zodiac pulls away from the dock and heads down the inlet, their wake leaving glassy ripples that spread out toward the shores.

"What are the chances of us seeing whales?" Rav asks Kincaid. "Orcas?"

"There's always a chance, though lately, we're more likely to see humpbacks and greys at the moment," Kincaid replies. "Everyone ready? Hold on."

The boat pulls away from the dock, and soon, we're zipping along at a comfortable speed. The wind is cold, and I regret not grabbing a hat, but it's also exhilarating to be out on the water. We slow as we go past the otter raft, which is basically a bunch of adorable sea otters with chubby, fluffy faces lying on their backs beside each other as they snooze and eat. Possibly the cutest thing I've seen.

We then zoom around an island that lies sentry at the start of the inlet before we approach the fog bank. Being in the front, everything rushes toward me like a roller-coaster ride until my nose is cold and I know my cheeks are stained pink, my hair a mess that keeps escaping the satin scrunchie I've tied it back with.

Soon, rocks appear through the fog, waves crashing over them, giving us our first glance at the wild ocean. The waves build, swells sweeping toward us, and we meet them with a smack, water crashing over the bow. I yelp as I get sprayed, along with Rav, then start laughing.

"Well, that woke me the fuck up." Rav chuckles, wiping the water off his forehead.

We hold on tight, the waves getting smoother and further apart as the boat leaves the inlet, careening up the coast. You can't see much with the wind and sea spray whipping in your face, but to one side, the ocean seems to go on forever, no horizon, only grey. For a moment, I have the disorienting feeling that I'm close to falling off the edge of the Earth.

But then I notice quite a few small fishing boats in the distance, bobbing between the waves, and it feels good to know we're not quite as isolated as it feels. Being at the lodge really makes you feel cut off from the world.

To the other side is the Brooks Peninsula, a long, giant mass of land made of steep, forested slopes, the top covered in clouds. Nick's boat turns inland and heads to a beach close to us, but Kincaid keeps going.

"I know a better beach!" Kincaid yells, his voice barely audible over the wind and engine.

We go further up and around a point until I see a long, wide stretch of cream-colored sand dotted with giant driftwood, the dark green forest behind it. There are a few rocks that Kincaid maneuvers the boat around, but once we get close to shore, we don't drop speed as much as we should.

"Hang on!" he yells.

We crash through the surf, spray flying everywhere, until the Zodiac slides up on the sand, coming to a halt that nearly gives me whiplash.

"I didn't think mycology could be so exciting," Rav jokes.

"If there's no dock, this is the only way to get you off and keep your feet dry," Kincaid says. I glance back to see him lock the engine up out of the water, then stride along the boat and leap over the nose and onto the hard sand, the surf breaking behind us.

Kincaid holds his hand out for me, and I quickly unbuckle myself, slipping my hand into his. His hand is as cold as mine, and yet I still feel a warmth spreading, skin to skin. I swear he even gives it a squeeze, but that could be just him trying to steady me so I don't eat shit when I land in the sand.

Everyone else follows, and we take off our life jackets, tossing them into the boat.

Kincaid turns to face us, handing out pads of paper with golf pencils attached. "This is a very special spot. There's a cliff wall about a hundred feet into the forest, running parallel to the beach. It's perpetually wet with rain runoff, and the forest is mainly hemlock, which makes it a favorite of all types of fungi. Stay between here and the cliff, make lots of noise with your bear bells, and you should be fine. Spread out at least several yards between each other to ensure we're getting a proper survey."

"There's no rules about foraging for the Madrona fungi?" Rav asks. "Because Nick certainly frowned upon that."

Kincaid nods, his gaze going to mine. "I have been briefed about what Lauren and Sydney discovered yesterday." I wince. The way he says it sounds like it wasn't a good briefing. "We won't be foraging at any rate; this is purely surveying. If you do find something, I brought my Polaroid camera, otherwise just make a note on your notepad. Don't touch anything."

Everyone starts walking off while Kincaid takes the rope from the Zodiac and fastens it around a giant piece of driftwood halfway up the beach.

"Will that hold?" I ask, wanting to stay and talk to him instead of surveying with the group.

"Should do," he says with a grunt, pulling the Zodiac a couple of feet. He's hella strong. "We'll only be here about an hour. The tide is slack right now, best time for a beach landing. By the time it starts going out, we'll be ready to go."

He finishes and walks back to me, dusting his hands off.

"Black runners," he comments, eyeing my shoes. "Smart. White ones get dirty very fast out here."

I can't help but stare at him, remembering last night. "This is going to sound odd, but…" I pause, waiting until everyone else walks out of earshot. "Were you in my room last night?"

He doesn't even blink. "And why would you think that?" he asks, his voice flat.

"You ran past me down the stairs, didn't even look at me. Before that, I heard a door close and someone locking it. It sounded like it was my door."

"I had to go into Christina's room to retrieve something for her. It was a pressing matter." He frowns, folding his arms with a hint of a smile on his lips. "I suppose I should be flattered. First, you think I'm stalking you outside your window, now you think I'm breaking into your room. Tell me, did I take anything from you?"

"No," I say, feeling flustered and wishing I hadn't brought it up. "Just these shoes appeared when I couldn't find them before." I hold out my foot.

"So, you think I went into your room and gave you your shoes? Which I assume means you think I have some sort of foot fetish and stole them to begin with?"

"Well, I do now," I joke, cheeks burning.

He holds my gaze for a few seconds.

"Did you take your pills this morning?"

I shake my head. "No, actually, I'm following your rules. Are you going to blame this conversation on that?"

He laughs. It's a lively, genuine sound that makes my

stomach flip, such a contrast to his composed exterior. "Perhaps. Did you write in your diary?"

"I forgot. But I will. I promise."

"What about your appetite? Your sleep?"

I don't bother filling him in about not getting back to sleep because I was too scared.

"Still tired, but my appetite has returned."

"Good," he says. He sucks in his lower lip and watches me for a moment, like he's about to say something else. Then he nods at the forest. "You better hurry."

I take that as a sign to leave him alone.

I nod and then scurry along the white sand until I'm entering the forest. I have a feeling that if it was a sunny day, this beach would look tropical. The air is filled with birdsong and the jingle of bear bells, mine attached to the bottom of my jacket. I try to stay away from the others. I don't want to go too far, but I like the idea of exploring by myself. It's always more fun for me to discover and survey on my own, going at my own pace and having conversations in my head that I don't have to share with anyone.

I head to the right, where the slope isn't as sharp and where a creek empties out into the ocean. I walk through the hemlocks until I'm at the base of the cliff, but I must be at the tail end of it because it's not very high.

A twig snaps behind me.

I whirl around.

There's nothing but the trees.

Trunks, branches, and shadows.

But one of the shadows is shaped like a man.

And I realize someone is *there*.

Standing completely still.

Staring at me.

CHAPTER 10

I FREEZE.

It's Clayton.

"What are you doing?" I ask, really hoping he doesn't try anything, or I'm going to have to scream. "He told us to stay far apart."

"I just wanted to talk to you," he says, slowly coming closer. "Figure out what's really going on."

He steps forward, but I put my hand out. "Stay right there."

Thankfully, he listens.

"Do I make you uncomfortable?" he asks, scratching at a spot below his ear.

"Yes." Shit, my heart is racing. I hate confrontation like this.

"Why?"

"Because you're an asshole," I tell him bluntly. "At least you are to me."

He lets out a bitter laugh, shaking his head. "We're more alike than you think."

"What does that mean? No, we're not. You don't know me."

"I know more about you than you think."

I glare at him, calling his bluff.

He gives me a sinister smile. "Neither of us should be here."

I swallow at that. My stomach twists uneasily.

He doesn't know about my lost scholarship, does he?

"You know it," he goes on. "I think it's cruel that you're here at all. That any of us are."

"Cruel?"

"Don't you wonder why they have us doing surveys and foraging? It's all bullshit. It's all busywork. They'll never let us actually see what they're working on. It's all a ruse, all a way to make the foundation look accessible and honest when it's not. We were chosen for a reason. Do you really think you're some sort of genius because they accepted you here? I shouldn't have gotten in at all. My grades were never good enough."

I blink slowly, trying to understand what he's saying. "Well, my grades were good enough," I assure him, raising my chin slightly.

"Right. They must have been. Since you're so special."

"Stop saying that. I put in the work. I deserve to be here."

"They think you're special," he says. "That's not a good thing, Sydney."

I look at him a little closer. His eyes are bloodshot, his fingers twitching slightly. "Clayton, look, I don't know what you're going on about. I really don't. If you want to call me special, fine. But if I am, then we're all special. And whether this is busywork, I don't know. We all have different reasons for being here. They can't exactly cater the curriculum to everyone."

Suddenly, he comes closer, stopping a couple of feet away. Too close. I back up, but my back hits the slimy rock wall. "Don't you see, Sydney?" he says, his eyes wild, his voice raw. "They're lying to you. They're lying to all of us. And we all go along with it because we want to be someone so badly. That's how they get us. Our need. Our want. To be seen and heard. But they don't care. They don't see us like that. They see us as something to be used and disregarded until there's nothing left of us."

"Okay, you're freaking me the fuck out now," I say, putting my hands out. "Please go and leave me alone, or I will scream. I swear it."

He exhales, visibly trying to control himself, but his face crumples, tears in his eyes. "I went to a fortune teller a month ago. She said I'd never leave this place."

Okay, that's it.

I start walking fast, away from Clayton, looking over my shoulder while trying not to bump into the trees. He stands there watching me until he eventually turns around and goes back the way he came.

Meanwhile, I've ended up in a little pocket of bushes and rocky outcrops covered in moss and tiny maidenhair ferns, the trees clearing a space. I stop, not wanting to go any further, and let out a long breath. I still feel a little shaky from that interaction, even more so because he wasn't making much sense. Is he on drugs? He must be on drugs. His eyes were red, and he was acting erratic and twitchy, much different than the insolent douchebag from the first day. Perhaps this place is getting to him. The isolation must be taking its toll.

Kincaid had said one student always goes home. Maybe Amani won't be the only one this year.

I decide to wait a few moments before I head back, making sure there's no chance of running into Clayton again.

Until something catches my eye.

Up ahead on the rocky ground is what I first think is a fallen branch, lying across the moss.

But…

It's not.

It's a leg.

An animal's leg.

Oh god, I think, my fingers clenching at my chest.

It looks like a...paw.

A dog?

Against my better judgment, I creep forward. I don't want to see what it is, but at the same time, what if it's alive and hurt and I can help?

I peer around a salal bush and gasp.

It's a fucking *wolf*.

Not just any wolf, but a dead wolf, half of its body rotted away. Sinew stretches over the bones like pink gum, fluffs of fur sticking out in places. Underneath a couple of exposed ribs, I can see the heart, bright white and...fuzzy.

Nausea rolls through me. My hand covers my mouth, trying to keep from vomiting. The more I look at the wolf's lifeless, decomposing body, the more disturbed I become. Thin white strands loop around the exposed skin and muscle, looking like tendons at first, but then I realize that's not what they are at all.

It looks like...mycelia. Like fungi have sprouted up from inside the wolf, which isn't strange at this stage of decomposition, and yet...

The fuzzy white heart twitches inside the rib cage.

No.

I freeze. Blood fills my ears until it sounds like a hammer.

I stare at the unmoving heart, wondering if some unseen maggots are writhing underneath, making it move. It seems too large for its body, and as I keep staring, I realize the white fuzz is hyphae, each tiny white hair moving together, like seagrass in a current.

The heart pulses again.

Once.

Twice.

It's *beating*.

The wolf's legs twitch, causing fur to shed.

I stare in horror. Lead in my veins. I can't move, can't breathe, can't think.

The wolf opens its mouth, a long exhale that makes its chest expand, its ribs *cracking*. A black tongue slips out between its teeth, growing longer and longer and—

It raises its head and looks at me with one milky eye and one empty socket.

Release me, the wolf hisses.

Then it lunges at me.

I scream.

I scream so loud that my whole body shakes and my vision blurs and I stumble backward, the wolf's rotting jaw snapping at me, a tooth catching the edge of my raised arm as I try in vain to protect myself.

I fall backward onto the moss, still screaming, my head banging against a rock.

But the wolf stops.

I struggle to sit up, expecting to see it face-to-face, to stare into that one milky eye, for its teeth to gnaw my nose off.

Instead, it's slinking off into the bushes in retreat, and then it's gone.

"What the fuck, what the fuck," I cry out. I look down at my arm. There's a long red mark, but it didn't break skin.

"Sydney!" I hear Kincaid's voice from behind me, echoing through the trees. "Sydney!"

"I'm here," I say, trying to shout, but my voice cracks.

What the fuck just happened?

I hear rustling in the brush, and I twist around, expecting to see the wolf coming at me from behind, but instead, it's Kincaid, bursting through the underbrush.

"Are you alright? What happened?" he asks, his voice strained with panic. He runs right over to me and crouches down. Then he reaches out and cups my face in his hands, so strong, so warm, brushing the hair off my forehead in a gesture that is so intimate and tender that it disarms me even further.

"I don't know," I whisper, conscious of how close our faces are, of how his winter eyes are vivid with concern. "There was a wolf."

His pupils dilate. "A wolf?"

He looks behind him, and I raise my arm to show him the red mark, which has already faded to pink. "It tried to bite me, but it didn't break the skin."

He runs his finger over the mark, a soft touch. "A wolf," he repeats. "Are you hurt anywhere else?"

"I hit my head on the rock."

He gently runs his hand over the back of my head, and I wince. "There's a bump, but you should be alright," he says. "Still, we need to get you back, have Everly look you over. Then we need to find this wolf. The sea wolves here have never attacked anyone. They're shy creatures. It could be rabid."

"It wasn't rabid. It was dead," I say.

He stares at me as if he didn't hear what I said.

"What happened?!" Rav yells.

I turn to see him and Patrick at the edge of the clearing.

"She had a fall," Kincaid says. "Nothing to worry about. The moss can be slippery."

He grabs my elbows, ready to pull me up, and I give him an incredulous look. Why isn't he telling them the truth?

His eyes narrow slightly as he tugs me to my feet.

A warning to keep my mouth shut.

"We should head back now, make sure she's alright," Kincaid says to the others, putting a hand at my lower back and guiding me forward.

"Shit. Sydney, you sounded like you were being murdered," Rav says as I pass him.

I give him a faint smile. I want nothing more than to tell him I saw an undead wolf, but I'm realizing that might make me seem crazy. Even a normal wolf might be enough to worry and panic the others.

Still, I don't feel good about keeping it inside, and I know I'll have to talk to Kincaid about it later.

We're halfway through the forest when I realize something.

The only person who didn't come running was Clayton.

"It's bruising, but it didn't break the skin," Everly says calmly as she handles my arm, cleaning it with solution. "Still, I think I'll have to give you a tetanus and rabies shot just in case. Then a series of shots over the next couple of weeks."

"Do you have to?" I ask.

I'm sitting in the nurse's room, which is beside reception in the main lodge. The room is only accessed through reception, which meant a lot of Michelle fussing over me as they led me in here.

Kincaid is here with Everly, leaning back against the door with his arms crossed, as if he's barricading it. His expression is serious, his brows lowered, creating shadows over his eyes, his mouth firm.

"Better to be safe than sorry," Everly says, giving me a sympathetic smile. "It sounds like the wolf was rabid, and we can't take that chance. Rabies is fatal once the signs show, and the last thing we need here is…well, *that*."

The wolf wasn't just rabid, it was dead! I'm screaming inside to tell her the truth. But I don't want Everly to think I'm losing my mind, even though I know what I saw. Kincaid is already looking at me like I need to be in a psych ward.

She walks over to the cupboard and starts pulling out a few syringes. I can't look, turning my attention to the posters on the wall, one of which reads *Do You Know the Signs of Mushroom Poisoning?*

"Can you roll up your sleeve?" she asks.

The arms of my sweater are fairly tight. "No."

"Please remove it, then."

"I'm not wearing anything underneath."

"That's fine," Everly says patiently.

I look over at Kincaid as if to say, *but he's standing right there.*

But he doesn't look away, doesn't protest and say it's inappropriate like I thought he would.

I meet Everly's eyes again, and she smiles faintly. "We're all adults here, Syd. It's nothing we haven't seen before."

I gulp. I suppose she's right. At least I'm wearing a bra, albeit a cheap black one from Target.

I pull my sweater off over my head, feeling utterly self-conscious. I can feel Kincaid's gaze burning my skin, visceral and real, and I don't have to look at him to know that he's staring at my breasts.

I swallow hard, feeling both on display and vulnerable yet desired at the same time, and I force myself to close my eyes as Everly wipes my upper arm with a sanitizing pad.

"This shouldn't hurt much," she says.

I wince as the needle breaks the skin, grinding my teeth together. I hate that I have such a low pain tolerance.

"One down," she says. "One more to go. Just breathe."

I get through the second shot, and when I open my eyes, Kincaid is still staring at me. His nostrils are flaring slightly, but his forehead is lined with concern.

"All done," Everly says, sticking two circular Band-Aids on. "That wasn't so bad, was it?"

It was awful, I think, in ways I can't really explain.

I give her a stiff smile. "No."

"And how is your head? Still no dizziness?"

"No more than normal."

Her thin brows come together, a deep line forming. She definitely doesn't have Botox. "You're normally dizzy?" She glances over at Kincaid with a sharp look, as if this is somehow his fault.

"Yeah," I tell her. "But it's probably because I don't eat enough."

"Right," she says slowly. "Hopefully, your appetite will return. All this exercise and fresh air, plus the food here is so good. Did you know our cook, Andrew, used to work at a Michelin-star restaurant? Only the best for the Madrona Foundation." She gives me a prideful smile. "The best minds need the best nutrients."

She straightens up. "I think we're done here. You can put your sweater back on. And please let me know if you experience any memory loss, confusion, strange headaches, things of that nature."

I quickly put my sweater back on and stand up, adjusting it.

"Thank you," I say to her, but I stare down Kincaid as I leave the room, trying to send him a message with my eyes.

I need to talk to you.

I leave the room, dashing through reception so Michelle doesn't bog me down with her blathering (the woman always seems on the verge of hysterics), and then step out into the common room.

Lauren, Munawar, and Rav are sitting on the couch, getting to their feet when they see me.

"Are you okay?" Lauren cries out as she hurries over to me. "Rav told me what happened."

He didn't tell you everything, I think. *Because none of you know everything.*

After the wolf encounter, Kincaid sped us back to the lodge as quickly as he could. He didn't even slow down around the otters, though they didn't seem to care. We got back before Nick's team did, and he quickly ushered me in to see Everly.

"I'm fine," I assure them, lying through my teeth. How the fuck can I be fine after all that?

I hear the door close behind me and see Kincaid step out of reception.

"Dr. Kincaid," I say, trying to sound as professional as possible. "Is it possible I could talk to you. In your office?"

He swallows. "Of course," he says, striding over to the lodge door and holding it open. "After you, Ms. Denik."

I give the others another reassuring look before I step outside.

It's a wall of grey, so misty now that the air is wet with it, almost drizzling. I follow Kincaid toward the north dorm, neither of us speaking. In the distance, I can hear the goats bleating on the farm section and the sound of an ATV. A raven close by makes a hoarse clicking sound before it swoops down in front of us, nearly touching the top of Kincaid's head before it lands in a cedar on the other side of the path.

"That's Poe," Kincaid says. "He's one of our resident corvids."

"Original name," I remark. "Don't tell me he's tame."

"He can be when he wants to," he says, glancing at me over his shoulder. "But he doesn't belong to anyone but the forest. He's good luck to have around."

"I always heard that ravens were omens."

"They are," he says, opening the door to the north dorm. "But it's up to the beholder to decide what kind of omen it is."

The image of the dead wolf, its furry white beating heart, slams into my brain, along with Clayton's words.

I saw a fortune teller. She told me I was going to die here.

No, wait. That's not what he said. He said, *She told me I would never leave this place.*

Already, I can't seem to trust my memory.

We go down the dark hall, and he leads me into his office. I notice he keeps it unlocked.

"Take a seat," he says, going over to the window and pulling at the blinds enough that it dims the room. I'm reminded of my dream and have to force my brain to push the images away. I concentrate on him turning on his camera and then lighting a candle on his desk with a silver Zippo engraved with something. He slips it into his pocket before I can get a better look, the air filling with the scent of santal and musk.

"Do you have to film this?" I ask, sitting down in the leather chair. "This isn't another counseling session."

"I don't know what this will be," he says, taking his seat across from me and folding his hands on the desk. "And yes, I do have to film it."

"What do you even do with the videos? Watch them?"

"Yes," he says simply.

I shift in my seat, hit with a strange sense of desire. "Why?"

"Because you fascinate me, Syd," he says. "And I'm your doctor. I'm trying to…make you better."

I hope I'm not blushing. "Why do I fascinate you?"

"Many reasons. One of which is why I suppose you wanted to talk to me. You think a dead wolf attacked you."

"I don't think, I know! It was dead," I tell him adamantly. "*Was* being the operative word."

"Tell me what happened, from the beginning," he says, taking out a pad of paper and a pen.

"Well, first, I had to deal with Clayton, who followed me through the woods."

His gaze snaps to mine. "He did what?" His tone is incredibly sharp.

"He followed me…" I say uneasily. The change in Kincaid is palpable, like he's turned into a predator.

"Did he touch you?" he grinds out.

"No! No, nothing like that. He was just trying to make me uncomfortable. Telling me weird shit."

His expression hardens. "Like what?"

"It's hard to explain. He wasn't making much sense. He kept saying that I was special, but he, like, had no basis for it, and yet the idea angered him. And that neither of us deserved to be here. That this place was...cruel."

He inhales sharply through his nose. "Cruel? In what way?"

"I guess because we're all just doing busywork, and we'll never be shown what work you actually do in the lab. Like Madrona is just leading us on and making us think we're important when we're not."

Kincaid runs his tongue over his teeth while he sits back in his chair. "That simply isn't true. You have lab with Janet, I mean Dr. Wu, first thing in the morning."

"I'm not agreeing with him."

His lips twitch with amusement. "But you do, Syd. I can see that clear as day. Don't worry. You'll be integrated soon enough into the workflow. I'm sure the lab can use a mind as brilliant as yours."

I scoff. "Certainly doesn't feel brilliant. I feel dumber by the day."

"That will pass," he says. "Once you're in the lab, I'm sure you'll come alive. You'll see what we're doing firsthand. The advancements we've made even over the last week will astound you. It won't be long until..."

"Until what?"

He blinks, a somber look. "Until the next phase." He swallows hard. "Well, I'll be sure to give Clayton a talk."

"No," I say quickly, leaning forward in my chair. "No, please. It's fine. I'm an adult. I can handle him."

"He's distracting you. But you're right. I'm sorry. I can get...protective at times."

I recall the way he held my face when I'd fallen, something like madness in his eyes.

"Anyway, I hope this talk has been helpful," he says, moving in his chair like he's about to get up.

"What? No. What about the wolf?"

He hesitates, then settles back down. "Ah. Yes. The wolf. Tell me about the wolf."

I can't help but glare at him. He's being so dismissive, like it's all in my head. So I tell him what happened, all the details, making sure I sound as measured and rational as I can.

"I know it's not possible, but that's what I saw." I end my story, my tone firm.

"I see," he says carefully, scribbling in his book again. "And what did the fruiting bodies look like?"

"I didn't see any. It looked like it was just mycelia."

"Looked like, but you can't be sure?"

I let out a caustic laugh. "Sorry, I was too busy trying not to die to get a closer look."

He stares at me patiently. I would kill to know what he's thinking, what he's written down in his notepad. I bet I wouldn't like any of it.

"The forest can play tricks on us," he finally says, and I grit my teeth in response because of course he's going to say that. "You were obviously emotionally upset from your interaction with Clayton. You haven't been eating right or sleeping right, and you haven't taken your medication that keeps your emotions in check. I have no doubt you came across an injured and dying wolf. You probably surprised it, hence why it both attacked you and quickly ran away. We'll send a drone out later to the area and see what we can find. If I had to guess, I'd say the wolf won't be bothering anyone anymore."

I can't help but glare at him. "Fine," I grumble, getting out of my chair.

He swiftly gets out of his and steps around the desk,

reaching out and grabbing my arm before I have a chance to leave.

"Don't make me worry about you," he says, his voice gruff, his grip hard.

I glance at his hand, and he slowly removes it.

"Don't make me worry either," I tell him.

I leave.

CHAPTER 11

"SHIRT OF THE DAY," Munawar says as I approach the horde of students standing outside the lab building.

I glance at it. It says *Morely Grey* with a picture of a morel mushroom.

"Get it?" he asks. "Like morally grey characters."

"Oh, I get it," I tell him. "In fact, I might just steal it from you."

"You can have it if you want," he says, grabbing the hem and starting to lift it up, his round belly poking out.

"No, no," I cry out, laughing.

"Munawar," Lauren says with a grin. "Look at you, willing to give your shirt off your back."

He shrugs, cheeks dimpled.

"Sorry I'm late," a breathless voice says. Dr. Janet Wu appears from behind us with her key card in hand, her white lab coat flapping around her. "Had a minor emergency in the propagation lab."

She's petite, young, and pretty, with delicate bones and square glasses perched on the end of her nose, her long black hair glossy in the faint morning sunlight. She gives everyone an apologetic smile as she passes, though she visibly stiffens when she sees me.

I don't blame her—I am a hot mess this morning.

I'm exhausted, as usual, despite eating my entire bowl of oatmeal at breakfast, my muscles feeling limp and sore, probably from the hike into the woods, not to mention a bruised ass and head from when I fell. Plus, the arm that got the shots won't stop aching. I couldn't sleep on the side I normally do.

I also wouldn't be surprised if she heard on the grapevine about my encounter with the wolf. I'm pretty sure there's no such thing as doctor-patient confidentiality here. My rejection sensitivity dysphoria usually kicks into high gear because I have this ability to assume that everyone hates me deep down, but lately, I think I'm giving people reasons to look at me askew.

Once the door is open, we all pile inside. The lab is a lot smaller than I thought, with a door at the other end that doesn't seem like it leads outside, considering the size of the building. It reminds me of the labs at Stanford, purposed for learning more than doing anything.

Dr. Wu flicks on the lights and tells us all to grab a seat. Chairs are stationed along the counters that line half the room, microscopes, test tubes, scanners, and IVD instruments interspersed.

I sit down next to Lauren, one of the few seats that have a window. It's only now that I realize the windows are one-way since I could never see inside the building.

Dr. Wu stands at the front of the room in front of a whiteboard that bears the ghostly scribbles of markers from the past.

"This is MiSeq, the DNA sequencer," she says, patting the machine beside her. "I know this machine better than I know my own husband. Just kidding. I don't have a husband."

Some of us laugh at her cute yet awkward humor, yet as I look around, I realize this isn't actually *the* lab. It's just a learning lab. It's just for us. The real work of the Madrona Foundation must be done elsewhere.

To say I'm disappointed is an understatement.

It's while I'm looking around the room that I catch Clayton's eyes. He looks worse for wear, and he gives me a look that says *I told you so.*

I quickly look away, trying to focus on Dr. Wu instead.

"I'm really excited to be teaching the lab this year," she says, pressing her palms together. She's so soft-spoken and genuine that I really like her, and I have a pressing need for her to like me. I guess I'll have to be an exemplary student.

She starts talking about her role at the foundation, how long she's been working here, and the current advancements they've made with *Amanita excandesco* and neurology.

"As you all know," she continues, focusing on a space on the wall behind us, "a variety of N-methyl-D-aspartate receptor antagonists have been able to halt stroke and traumatic brain injuries. When we discovered *Amanita excandesco*, we found it had similar properties to *Hericium erinaceus*. With the proper sequencing, we were able to isolate cyathin diterpenoids that showed biological activities as stimulators of NGF synthesis. In rats, at first, but eventually pigs and goats."

She then goes on to tell us about how they found *excandesco* can cross the blood-brain barrier, going where lion's mane can't, and that the research they've done has built upon this, trying to figure out if simple supplements of their fungi can actually start either reversing inflammation in the brain or preventing it.

Suddenly, Dr. Wu trails off. She looks down at the floor, and her lower lip starts to tremble. "Then we…" she begins, her voice cracking. "Then Madrona Pharmaceuticals brought the funds and the equipment to…"

She covers her face with her hands.

Everyone in the class exchanges a *what the fuck* glance, not sure what to do.

Dr. Wu lifts up her head, tears streaming beneath her glasses. "I'm sorry, I can't do this."

She turns and hurries out of the classroom, slamming the door behind her.

The fuck?

"What the hell was that?" Lauren asks. "Oh no. Do you think maybe she *did* have a husband, and now her husband is dead?"

But I'm barely listening to her.

I'm looking at Clayton.

He's smiling at me.

My stomach clenches.

"Let's go," I say to Lauren, immediately getting to my feet and leaving the room. "Class dismissed."

"What if she comes back?" she asks, though she's right behind me. The rest of the class decides to do the same, branching out as we step outside.

"Then they'll know where to find us," I tell her. "It's not like we can go far."

"Want to go skip rocks on the beach?" Munawar asks.

"What are we, twelve?" Rav laughs.

"Sounds good to me," I say. Anything to be out of that lab, to be away from Dr. Wu's breakdown and Clayton's fucking weird-ass vibes.

We take the path to the left and follow it through the bushes and down the rough dirt slope until we're at the beach. I sit on a log beside Lauren, watching Rav and Munawar try to skip stones, both of them failing. The rocks sink with a *plunk*.

"How's your head?" Lauren asks.

"It's fine," I tell her. "Just sore to touch."

She leans in closer, a sly look in her eyes. "Rav said the two of you looked very close. You and Professor Kincaid. You know, when you fell."

I roll my eyes. "He was just worried about me."

"Uh-huh," she says. "I don't think you see what I see."

"Apparently not," I say. I bite my lip to keep from asking what it is. But it doesn't work. "What do you see?"

She plays with the zipper on her UVIC hoodie. "Oh, just that he's always looking at you. Staring at you. Even when you're not looking. *Especially* when you're not looking."

My heart skips a beat, and I hate it for that. "Really? I haven't noticed. He's always got that intense look, you know?"

"Yes. You're the reason for that look. He sure as hell doesn't look like that when I'm talking to him."

I look down at my nails. "He said I'm fascinating," I confess, feeling a little embarrassed. "Though I'm not sure I should repeat what he says during our sessions."

"Baby, you tell Lauren everything," she says, giving my sore shoulder a squeeze.

"Ow!" I cry out, enough that Rav and Munawar stop skipping stones.

"What? I'm sorry. I didn't mean to hurt you," she says. "Are you okay?"

I nod, the truth on the tip of my tongue. The need to confide is overwhelming.

"They gave me a tetanus and rabies shot yesterday," I whisper. "On that arm. It's still really sore."

Rav and Munawar have stopped in front of us, flat stones in their palms.

"For hitting your head?" Rav asks, a brow raised quizzically.

"No." I take in a deep breath. "I'm going to tell you something, and you're going to think I'm crazy, just as Kincaid and Everly did, but you're my friends, I think."

"I'll still give you this shirt off my back," Munawar says, lifting up the hem with his free hand.

"We're your friends," Lauren says imploringly as she

tucks a strand of hair behind her ears, her green eyes serious. "You can tell us."

I glance at Rav and Munawar, and they nod. I know Kincaid didn't want me to say anything, but what's the harm if he doesn't believe me anyway?

"Please don't, you know, stop talking to me if you think I'm full of shit," I say to them. "I don't think I could handle that, not in a place like this."

"We promise," Munawar says.

So I take the leap, and I tell them what happened yesterday, starting with Clayton and ending with the undead wolf slinking away into the forest.

"Why did Professor Kincaid lie to us, then?" Rav asks. "He just said you hit your head. I knew you didn't though. You sounded as if you were being attacked."

"I don't know. I guess he didn't want you to panic if there was a rabid wolf around, especially since we were a small group isolated from the rest."

"It really does sound like it was rabid to me," Lauren says. "It's possible that it was so rabid that the disease was basically keeping it alive."

"Also," Rav says slowly. "Well, aren't you thinking what we're all thinking?"

"I have no idea," I tell him. "What are you thinking?"

"Just me? Okay, well, *Amanita excandesco*. The mushrooms. Is it possible that the famous fungus has been ingested by the wildlife here? We all know by now that *Ophiocordyceps unilateralis* affects certain ants. What if it's in the wolves? What if this strain of fungi can create zombie wolves instead of zombie ants."

"That's not what I was thinking," says Lauren, curling her lip in disgust.

"Yeah, me neither," I say. Fungi can't survive in high temperatures found in warm-blooded mammals, like wolves or ourselves. There are theories that humans actually evolved to have our specific high body temperature on purpose. Plus, that's not how that particular fungus spreads.

"I think you've seen too many episodes of *The Last of Us*," Munawar tells him.

"The video game?" I ask. "They made a TV show of it?"

"You haven't seen it?" Munawar asks in disbelief. "Every single mycology student is hooked on the show. Pedro Pascal? Hello?"

"Munawar," Lauren snaps while Rav kicks him in the leg. "Stay on task, okay?"

His face falls, chagrined. "Sorry."

"It's just an idea," Rav says quickly. "We have to have theories, don't we?"

I sigh, putting my head in my hands. Even though it's morning, I could easily crawl back into bed. "I don't know. Maybe I was stressed out and hallucinating. Wouldn't be the first time."

Everyone goes silent. I glance at them, their eyes filled with pity.

"Do you hallucinate often?" Lauren asks quietly.

"No," I say, unsure if I'm lying or not. "Only yesterday, when I thought I heard someone calling my name."

"You're not sleeping well, I can tell," she says, giving my knee a pat. "At least you're eating more. Maybe you need a day off to relax. Tell them you need a mental health break. They'll understand."

"It's barely been a week," I scoff. "I have fifteen more weeks to go."

"Then it's a great time to get yourself right. We have a long summer ahead of us here."

For the first time since I arrived, I feel the weight of our tenure here.

It's starting to feel suffocating.

CHAPTER 12

WAKE UP, Sydney.

My eyes snap open to a dark room.

Who just said that? Was that in my dream?

My heart is already racing, the blood thumping in my ears, and I take in a shaky breath as I hold the covers to my chest, trying to bring my brain back online.

The room is freezing. I can see my breath when I exhale. The nights have been comfortable so far, but tonight, I have to wonder if the heat is even on. Perhaps they shut down the heat pump at night sometimes to conserve power, and this is the first time I've noticed. That said, the day had been warm and sunny, finally feeling like summer is on the way.

After Dr. Wu's breakdown, we stayed on the beach, all of us eventually having a stone-skipping competition and enjoying the weather until lunch rolled around, and then it was time for yet another "foraging" expedition with Nick. We took the logging road to the west, taking lichen samples from a stand of maples. Nick told us that Dr. Wu was going through something very personal at the moment, the loss of a friend, and that next week, Everly would take her place in teaching.

At dinner, my appetite stayed steady, and I was able to enjoy the grilled spring salmon and roast veggies before I went to bed, early as usual, though I made a point of writing down in my diary.

I sigh, hoping I can get back to sleep, and settle further into my pillow, careful not to lie on my aching arm. I feel the weightlessness of drifting back to sleep when I hear something that pulls me out of it.

A loud *groan* outside my door.

The floorboards.

"Fuck," I whisper to myself, my body going still. Not this again.

I tilt my head to look at the door.

The light under the frame is dim, a strange white glow.

There's a shadow of two feet standing in the hallway.

I breathe in sharply. The cold air solidifies in my chest, fear settling in my bones as if trying to make a home in the marrow.

What the fuck?

Please let that be a student, I can't help but think. *Even Clayton would be fine.*

I don't know why my mind is jumping to the supernatural, but it's kind of a given with a creaky old lodge like this one and zombie wolves in the forest.

The person moves, shifting their weight from one foot to the other, and something about that both makes me think they're anxious and also makes me think it's not a ghost.

Then they move, the floorboards creaking as they walk down the hall.

Stay put, I tell myself.

Let them go.

Don't get up.

And yet I get up, as if my blood is thick with metal and someone outside is wielding a giant magnet. I step into my slippers, grab my robe and cinch it against the cold, then go to the door.

I don't want to listen; I don't want to hear that awful inhuman voice hissing *please*. I already heard a wolf talking—that was enough.

Release me, it had said.

That was the one part I left out when talking to Kincaid, Everly, and the others about what had happened. They didn't need to know *that* part.

Instead, I unlock the door, put my hand on the knob, and yank it open.

The hallway is darker than normal. Instead of the sconces glowing at intervals along the wall, there's only one light midway down the hall, casting everything else in shadow.

At the end of the hall is a blur of a person, a girl in a white nightgown, a flash of long dark hair as she disappears into the shower room.

I stare at her for a moment, trying to get my eyes to adjust to the darkness. It could be Natasha—her hair is similar—but there was something unnerving about the way she walked, the way she held herself like she was...

Broken.

I stand there, waiting for her to close the door of the shower room.

But she doesn't. It remains partially open, enough that I can see inside. Or I would be able to if there was enough light. It's blacker than black, not just shadows, but like a void.

And the lodge is so silent it's like it's holding its breath along with me. I can't hear anyone else, no one snoring or turning in their sleep, and no sound of the shower or someone undressing in the room.

What is going on?

I find myself padding down the hallway in my slippers, trying to avoid creaky floorboards. As I pass by the light I realize it's a nightlight, one that would turn on if the power went out.

As I get closer to the end of the hall, I finally hear a sound.

Coming from the shower.

A rustling sound like...

Raspy breathing.

I stop just outside the door, afraid to pull it open, afraid to ask if they're okay, if they need any help. My chest feels constricted, like it's squeezing my heart and making it smaller and smaller, the beat irregular as it tries to escape.

I reach out with my hand.

It's shaking.

Cold air breathes down my spine, my skin sharp with goosebumps.

I grab the knob.

Pull it back.

I'm staring into the abyss, into a black void where there is nothing but death and infinity. There is no one in the shower, and I fear there is no one left alive anywhere. It's just me and this never-ending darkness, swallowing me whole. It's the lodge eating me alive.

Creak.

Behind me.

I whirl around to see my door at the end of the hall closing.

What the fuck?

I take off down the hall, running to my door, grabbing the handle.

It won't turn. I can't open it. I jiggle it repeatedly, but it won't budge.

I kept the key in the lock on the other side, and now someone is in there, not letting me in.

Hell, I don't even want to go in now.

Look through the keyhole, I think.

But I can imagine doing so. I imagine leaning down and looking through the keyhole and seeing that wolf's white eye staring back at me.

I back away. I could ask Lauren or Rav for help, but what would they do? I need to find David Chen and get the other key.

I decide to talk to Everly. She did say to come by her place to talk, even in the middle of the night.

I quickly run down the stairs and then out into the night.

The fog is thick, obscuring the moon, and I hurry along the boardwalk, careful to not slip on the damp planks, my slippers having no tread. I pull my robe closer, the cold, damp air biting at my skin. Everything is dark, save for a few lights here and there, the water as smooth and dark as obsidian glass.

I reach Everly's cabin and stop outside her door. I don't want to wake her up, especially not since she already had to deal with me yesterday, but I don't have a choice.

I rap on it quickly, my fingers hurting from the cold. God, it's May. It's supposed to be mild here. Why is it so cold?

Through the windows, I see a flashlight's beam moving erratically, and then the door opens, Everly on the other side with it in her hand, wearing silk pajamas, a sleep mask pushed up on her forehead.

"Sydney. What happened? Are you okay?"

She steps out and reaches for my head, patting it over, as if I hit it again.

"Someone's in my room," I tell her. "I heard someone outside my door. I went to investigate down the hall, but I guess it was a trick or something because they went in my room and locked my door. I can't get in, and the key is in there."

She frowns. "Someone is playing a prank on you?"

I fucking hope it's a prank, I think.

"One of the bad apples you talked about." I look down at the flashlight. "Is the power out everywhere?"

"Generator is down," she says. "Just for a couple of hours."

"Why?"

"Routine," she says, grabbing my hand. "Here, you must be freezing. Come inside, I'll light some candles."

She pulls me inside and shuts the door, then leads me across a dark room to a couch, putting a blanket on my legs. "Get warm and wait here. I'm going to go wake up David and get the spare key, and then we can all go over together."

She goes over to a candle on the coffee table, grabs a pack of matches, and lights it. Then she slips on her coat and shearling boots. "I'll be right back."

She leaves, the flashlight shining in the trees outside the window before it disappears.

I look around Everly's living room. It's at least a lot warmer here than it was in the lodge. In the flickering candlelight, scented like oranges and cloves, a Christmas smell, I make out modern furnishings and fancy art on the walls. It may be a small cabin like the others, but I have no doubt everything in here costs thousands of dollars.

"Hello."

I jump in my seat, letting out a yelp.

A man steps into the room, gathering his flannel robe around him.

Not just any man, but Michael Peterson, Everly's husband. It takes me a moment to recognize him. I haven't seen him around since that first day.

"I'm so sorry, I didn't know we had a guest," he says, his voice monotone. "Where is Everly?"

"I was locked out of my room. She went to get David." I offer my hand. "I'm Sydney."

"Sydney," he says slowly, like he's savoring the word, even though his eyes are cold as always, his prominent brow creating the deepest shadows. He comes over to me and stands right in front of me, towering. "Yes, I recall Everly talking about you."

He doesn't shake my hand.

I awkwardly take it back, my cheeks hot. "Good things, I hope."

"Yes, yes, very good things." He takes a seat in the leather armchair across from me. "Tell me, Sydney, how are you?"

"Other than having to bug Dr. Johnstone in the middle of the night, and her husband, because I was locked out of my room? I'm fine."

"Oh, don't worry about me," he says. "I rarely sleep. The mind, you know." He taps the side of it. "It doesn't stop."

"I hear you on that."

He gives me a small smile, but it only makes me uneasy. He leans forward on his elbows and stares at me. Doesn't say anything else, just stares.

And me, well, I've never met a silence I can't bluster my way through.

"Really lovely home you have here," I say, looking around, though I'm not really seeing anything. He's still staring at me, and it's starting to make me nervous. When is Everly coming back?

"How long have you lived here for?" I ask for the sake of asking. "Do you have like a normal house somewhere else? I imagine you do."

He leans back in his chair, brow raised. "I'm not here as often as my wife. I am here when there is important work going on. Otherwise, you'll find me in Carmel. Carmel-by-the-sea. Have you ever been?"

"No," I tell him.

"But you're a Northern California girl. That surprises me."

How did he know where I was from? I guess Everly told him.

"Carmel is a rich area. I grew up poor," I say bluntly, just to see him squirm a bit.

He does no such thing. "Is that so? What a tragedy that is."

I shrug awkwardly. "It wasn't so bad. I had a nice grandmother."

"And your father, who died at sea," he says with a sigh.

My muscles tense. I give him a sharp look. "How did you know that?"

"I know everything about every student." He gives me a tight smile. "So much information in my brain, sometimes I get confused between who is who over the years. But yes, Sydney Denik, I know all about Sydney Denik. So much terrible loss. You must wonder why death is so fixated on you."

Okay, I *really* need Everly to come back now.

"I just chalk it up to bad fucking luck," I say, an edge to my voice warning him to stop talking.

He chuckles. It's an empty sound. "I see. Yes. Bad luck. That I can agree with. You are a woman of bad luck. And yet, you're also a miracle. You're here. You're one of the few who get to experience the foundation at its most raw state. You're getting a glimpse behind the curtain, passage beyond the velvet rope. You're going to set an example for the years to come."

"An example of what?" I ask.

But he only grins at me, his teeth very white, his eyes terribly unkind.

I don't want to be alone with this man.

Suddenly, the door bursts open, and Everly steps inside with David Chen in tow.

"Sydney," David says as I jump to my feet, so happy to leave. "Everly told me what happened. We went ahead and checked it out for you. There was no one in your room."

I shake my head vehemently. "No. There was. I know there was. I couldn't get in!"

"We believe you," Everly says, placing the key in my hand. "I think someone was playing a prank. But they knew they would be found out. They left before they could get in trouble." She lowers her voice, peering at me. "Do you know who it could have been?"

I want to tell her it's Clayton, and after my session with Kincaid, I feel like that's what she expects me to say. But I don't know if it was him or not. He's already so erratic I don't want to involve him if it wasn't.

"I have no idea," I tell her. I can tell she doesn't believe me.

"Well, it sounded like a harmless prank," Michael says. "Glad that all got sorted. I'm going to bed now. Nice meeting you, Syd."

He saunters off, and I look back at David and Everly. "So there really wasn't anyone there?"

No ghost standing in the corner, facing the wall Blair Witch style?

"No," David says. "And the key was back in the lock, on the inside, but it wasn't turned. Students do pranks sometimes, but I can understand why it would have been upsetting."

"Come on, I'll take you back," Everly says, guiding me to the door.

We step out into the fog, David leaving us to go check on the generators. Everly doesn't say much as we walk, pine needles crunching beneath our feet as she takes me along the tree-lined path behind the lodge instead of the boardwalk.

"I'm sorry for waking you up," I tell her.

She shoots me a soft smile, barely visible in the darkness. "I told you to. Day or night. I'm glad you did, otherwise you'd be sleeping in the hall. Or worse, having a fight with a fellow student. That's the last thing you need while you're here."

I swallow thickly and nod. "Yeah."

"I was meaning to talk to you anyway," she says.

"Oh, what about?"

"I got a phone call from Stanford."

I stop dead in my tracks.

I can only stare at her while she stops and faces me.

A cunning smile. "You sneaky little bitch."

CHAPTER 13

I GULP.

Everly laughs. "I mean bitch as a compliment, though you're definitely sneaky. I can't believe you lost your scholarship and still decided to fly all the way to Canada to see if anyone would notice. You have some nerve."

Fuck. Fuck, fuck, *fuck*.

I feel like the forest has turned into a black hole, and I'm sinking, no way to climb out.

"My goodness, Syd," she says to me. "You look absolutely terrified. Come on. I'm allowed to make fun. You definitely proved how devoted you are to working at Madrona."

"I'm sorry," I whisper. It's all I can say.

"Don't be sorry," she says. "Well, I shouldn't say that. Your apology is necessary and appreciated. But it's done now. Come on, let's get you inside."

She grabs my hand and pulls me along around the lodge, past the cedar where I always see Kincaid standing. I glance up at my window, wondering what he sees when I'm there. The light in my room is on, which means he can see me clearly.

Strange thing to think about, considering you're about to be sent home.

I follow Everly into the lodge, but instead of going upstairs, she takes me to the couch nearest to the hearth, the flames low. "Here, sit. I'll get the fire going."

She goes and grabs a couple of logs from the basket and throws them in. They crackle and pop, embers and sparks. Then she walks to the hot water dispenser and grabs a mug, plopping a tea bag inside, and fills it.

I stare back at the fire, watching as the flames rise, feeling sick to my stomach. I want to keel over right here, crawl into a ball, and simply disappear.

Everly comes over with the tea and hands me the mug. "Chamomile. Should help you sleep after all this commotion and warm you up."

I wrap my cold fingers around it. "Thank you," I say quietly.

"You know, I think it's ridiculous that they took your scholarship away. You didn't do anything wrong. He's the one who did."

I wince, closing my eyes. "Great. You know everything."

"Sydney. It happens," she says, sitting beside me and putting her hand on my knee. "So you had an affair with your professor. You wouldn't be the first."

I give her a pained look. "I didn't know he was married. He never wore a ring, never mentioned a wife or anyone. He lied by omission."

"Men lie," she says simply. "Especially men with power. They gaslight you."

He certainly did. It was Professor Edwards' daughter who found out about the two of us. She sent me a threatening message on my Instagram, telling me the truth about her mother and father, which then made me spiral. I drank too much and then found out his real address and made my way over there to confront him. He answered the door, and I called him every name in the book, except I was so drunk I wasn't making much sense. His daughter stood behind him, recording the whole thing on her phone. The way she framed it, it looked like I had turned into some drunken and obsessed stalker.

The only saving grace was that school was officially done for the year, so I didn't have to return to campus to face him in my chemistry class or see the looks of my fellow students because I know that video went viral. I thought maybe if I just stayed offline, I would escape from all of this unscathed.

And then the school called.

And that was that.

"I'm really sorry," I say again, my shame as hot as the fire. "I shouldn't have come here. I should have let you know. You flew me all the way out here for no reason. I'm sorry I pretended. I just…I was scared. It's no excuse, but I had nowhere else to go. I lost everything, and—"

"Syd," she says sharply, though her eyes are kind. "It's alright. I understand. As I said before, you have nerve, and that's a really admirable trait. That shows guts. That shows risk. That shows you are willing to do things that other people are not willing to do. You are willing to lie and cheat to get ahead. Your ambition is that strong, and ambition is what creates geniuses."

I look down at my tea, waiting for the other shoe to drop, the part where she says *but you have to go home*.

"Does everyone know?" I ask meekly. "Does Kincaid?"

"Yes," she says. "All the staff know of this." She pauses, and I don't dare look at her. "You really care what Wes thinks, don't you?"

I'm not about to answer that. I make my face as blank as possible, the mask held tight. The absolute last thing I need is for her to think that I'm interested in Kincaid, much like I was interested in Professor Edwards. Of course, I have a type. An older man, intelligent, successful in his field, dominant in bed with a penchant for ropes and whips and some good old-fashioned degradation and praise kink. But Kincaid is only the latter in my dreams.

"I don't want anyone thinking ill of me," I finally say, my voice steady.

"They don't," she says. "They all feel the way that I do."

I exhale heavily and take a sip of tea. It's too hot. "So, do I have time to say my goodbyes, or are you shipping me off next morning on the first plane, like Amani?"

She tenses beside me, and when I look at her, she's frowning. "No." Then she shakes her head. "No. We're not sending you back, Syd. You're here to stay."

My eyes widen, a flicker of hope in my chest. "Are you serious?" She nods. "But why?"

"Because of everything I just told you. Your ambition. You're still ambitious, aren't you? You're still ready to prove yourself, to give yourself to the foundation, to leave your mark on the world?"

"Yes?"

"I don't believe you. Once more with feeling."

"Yes!" I say, louder now.

"Good girl," she says, activating my need for praise. "Now, finish your tea and get warm. The power will come back soon. I'm going to head back home and get some sleep. I suggest you do too."

"Okay," I say. Though I think I'd rather fall asleep on the couch in the common room than go back to my bed. "Thank you."

She gets up and stares down at me, then reaches out and brushes a strand of hair off my face. "Such lovely hair," she says. "Blonde really suits you."

I try not to blush nor reject the compliment. "Thank you."

"Remember, you're family now," she says, straightening up. "You're part of Madrona. If you ever feel at odds with this place, you just have to tell yourself: don't try to change the lodge, let the lodge change you."

Then she gives me a sweet smile and walks off, closing the door behind her and leaving me alone with the crackling fire.

Relief immediately floods through my body, and I practically melt into the couch.

I did it.

The truth finally came out.

I don't have to hide or worry anymore.

You're safe, I tell myself. *The worst is over, and you survived.*

But why does it feel like I'm lying?

"Heavens, Sydney, are you alright?"

A hand vigorously shakes my shoulder, making me wince.

I open my eyes and glare up at Michelle, who is staring down at me, her eyes wild with fright, her lips a shocking pink. The room is bright, and I blink.

"I'm fine," I say with a groan, sitting up. I look down and see a fleece blanket draped over my body, a star symbol stitched in the corner, but I don't remember Everly putting one on me.

"Do I need to get David? Or Everly? Is it your head?" Michelle is flapping her hands like a bird.

"I'm fine," I repeat. "Please. I was with Everly last night. I decided to sleep here. It was…warmer." She definitely doesn't need to know what happened last night.

"Oh," she says, hand on her chest. "What a relief."

Then she bustles off toward reception.

I exhale and look up at the wood beams, hearing footsteps and doors closing from above. The sun gets up so early here, and it's already streaming in through the windows, making the dust motes dance. The idea of going to my room seemed impossible last night, but in the light of day, with students beginning to wake, I don't feel as scared anymore.

I get up and fold up the blanket, taking it upstairs with me in case the power goes out again and I need the warmth. I stop outside my door, hesitating. Up here, there are no windows, and the hall is dim, though hearing someone's alarm clock go off comforts me.

I insert the key and quickly open the door.

It looks the same as always, the covers pushed to the side. Whoever was in my room didn't touch anything. Still, I slowly walk around to make sure. If my missing Miss Piggy shirt reappears like my shoes did, it really means I've lost my marbles.

But I don't see it. I walk into the bathroom, to the mirror, and stare at myself. My face doesn't seem as gaunt as it did a week ago, which is a good thing. I'm starting to look more like myself, more like the person I was before I came to Madrona.

I don't want the lodge to change me, no matter what their motto is. I want to stay Sydney Denik, even though she's a fucked up hot mess.

Who apparently has a ghost problem.

That had to be what it was, right? A ghost?

I know I saw that woman in the hallway.

But what if you didn't? I think. *What if you thought you did? What if it was Natasha, and she went into her room instead, and you got confused? What if it was Clayton who went into your room and locked you out? What if no one locked you out and you were just pulling on the door wrong, or perhaps because you left the key in the door, it somehow relocked itself?*

And what if it was Kincaid?

I don't know what to think, but the most logical reasoning is that there was no ghost, it was Natasha, and I was the one who locked myself out. It at least makes the most sense. After all, I did hit my head. Maybe it's a delayed concussion fucking up my brain a bit.

I get dressed into a pair of ripped stretchy jeans and a long plaid shirt, tie back my hair, and decide to go for a walk before breakfast since it's early enough. I bring my puffer jacket since the night had been so cold and head outside.

The morning is still bright, blue-skied, and filled with birdsong, the sunlight making me wish I brought sunglasses. I've barely had a need for them here.

I decide to head up to the logging road, wanting to feel the openness it affords and the sun on my face. I glance at my watch. If I go for twenty minutes, then turn around and come back, I'll be just in time to catch breakfast.

I'm about five minutes into the walk, sweating enough to unzip my jacket, when suddenly, it goes dark.

As in, the sun just *disappears*.

I glance up to see storm clouds, fluffy and charcoal-covered, making the world turn a shade of dark grey. There hadn't been a cloud in the sky earlier, and yet, like a switch has turned off, it's overcast.

The air becomes chilled, and I shiver, zipping my jacket back up, but it does nothing to keep me warmer.

Something isn't right.

All of this is terribly wrong.

I look around, trying to figure out what it is.

The light is different. It's not just grey and dim, but…it's weak.

I make a fist, my fingers already feeling numb. I hold my hands to my mouth and breathe on them, my exhale turning into clouds.

Then I hear laughter. From somewhere up ahead, around the bend.

"Hello!" I yell.

The laughter gets louder. A woman. Everly?

A man starts laughing too. Could be Michael, though I can't imagine him laughing.

I start walking faster, and then I'm jogging, running around the bend until I come to a halt.

There's no one there.

The laughter has stopped.

The road is an empty straightaway for a bit before it curves down around another corner.

At that corner, a lone maple resides amongst a copse of cedars and hemlock.

The maple tree is dead.

Nearly all the branches are bare, with big brown and rust-colored leaves spread out along the road.

What the hell?

I'm staring at the tree, wondering what happened to it, when I hear twigs snapping in the woods.

I gasp, twisting around.

Fear chokes my throat, and I listen, wide-eyed, straining to see, to hear.

Snap.

There's someone moving amongst the trees.

A dark shape in the forest, walking parallel to me.

"Who is that?" I cry out. "What do you want?"

Suddenly, the sun comes out again, my vision going white, my hands above my eyes as I wince through it.

Kincaid emerges from the trees, dressed in his black coat.

There you are, as always. The thought flits across my mind.

"I'm sorry," he says, looking mildly flustered. "I didn't mean to scare you. I was worried. I—" He frowns, his gaze sharpening. "Jesus, are you alright?" He gestures to his nose. "You're bleeding."

"What?" I bring my fingers under my nostrils and touch my skin. It's wet. I take it away to see fresh blood.

My stomach churns. I hate nosebleeds.

"Oh, shit," I say as he strides over to me, fishing in his

coat pockets. He takes out a navy handkerchief. Of course he would have a handkerchief.

I take it from him and hold it under my nose, feeling like an idiot. The cloth smells like him, that warm tobacco and wood that makes me feel like I'm draped in a warm blanket.

"Do you get nosebleeds often?" he asks, standing close, too close. Normally I wouldn't mind, but not when I have blood pouring from my nose.

"I used to get them all the time as a child, but not since then," I say, my voice nasal. I give him an awkward look. "This is mortifying."

He studies me with those cool grey eyes, the color reminding me of the weather's quick change. The temperature is creeping back up by the second.

I frown at him, realizing he must have been following me. "Were you on bear patrol again?"

His head shakes faintly, and he swallows. He has a gorgeous neck, something I don't think I've ever admired in a man before. Then my gaze goes to his lips, full and firm, lips I never kissed in my dream.

His mouth looks like he's holding back secrets.

"I was worried about you."

"So you said."

He gives me a sympathetic tilt of the head. "I know about what happened last night. I also know that you shouldn't be walking off into the woods alone when you have a head injury."

"So you're my guardian angel?"

"I'm no one's angel," he says darkly. He puts his hand at the small of my back. "But I like to think I can protect you. Come. Let's walk back. You don't want to miss breakfast."

"Protect me from what?" I ask as we walk side by side. His hand lingers on me for a few seconds more before it falls away.

"From yourself," he says.

"You don't know anything about me," I tell him, feeling annoyed.

"You keep saying that, and yet, every day, I know more and more," he says softly, hands clasped behind his back. "One day, I'll know everything."

My stomach flips at his assuredness. "You won't like what you find."

"I like what I've found so far," he says, gazing steadily at me. "I like it very much." He clears his throat and looks away. "This place can mess with your mind, Syd. I'm sure you're discovering that by now. The isolation…"

"Is it just the isolation?" I ask.

His dark brows come together. "What do you mean?"

I shrug. "I don't know. Just seems like there's something about this place. Something I can't explain."

"Like rabid wolves in the forest?"

"Something like that." I rub my lips together, unsure if I should continue.

Don't tell him everything, I think.

He exhales loudly. "I know we keep talking about the isolation here and the lack of contact with the outside world, for students at least, but it really does play tricks on the mind. Enough so that students have become a danger to themselves." He pauses. "There's always the threat of suicide."

He says that last part so quietly that it takes a moment to register.

I stop walking. "You mean someone killed themselves? Here?"

He turns to look at me. "Yes. The first death was the hardest."

"The first death? How many people have died here?"

He stares at me for a moment, his jaw tight.

"Four."

CHAPTER 14

"Four? There have been four suicides here?" I repeat, a sickly churn in my stomach. "Oh my god. Were they all students?"

"Three students," Kincaid says. His eyes are glassy as he glances away into the forest. "One researcher."

"Fuck," I swear. "Why the hell wasn't that in your brochure highlighting the dangers? Warning: in addition to not having internet access, students might stumble into a bear, a rabid wolf, or become unsubscribed to life."

"It's not funny, Syd," he says, his tone cold.

My eyes widen. "I don't think it's funny. I think it's horrific. Don't you have to disclose that or something? Shouldn't this be in the news?"

"What happens here never makes the news unless Madrona approves it," he says, a bitter tinge to his voice. "After the third death, we put fail-safes up."

"*Your* counseling is a fail-safe?" I ask incredulously. "No offense."

It could explain why he has to record everything. Maybe he goes back over the footage and looks for the signs.

I hope to hell he doesn't find any in me.

"It has been."

"But you just said after the third death, you started counseling. When did the fourth death happen?"

"It was the researcher, a couple of years ago," he says quietly. "It was…unexpected."

I shake my head. "Damn. So you were called here just to try to keep the students and researchers from dying? No pressure or anything."

He chuckles, his grave expression loosening. "No, actually. I'm not here because I'm a psychologist. I'm here because I'm a neurosurgeon. They needed someone when they started doing clinical trials. Of course, I happen to have a license in psychology. The two go hand in hand."

"You're a neurosurgeon?" Somehow, he got even sexier.

"Yes, well, I've heard all the brain surgery jokes, believe me," he says, smiling slightly as he starts walking again. "To be honest, I much prefer psychology. People fascinate me. The brain is interesting in of itself, but it's the people who possess the brain that, well, to be sentimental, I guess they give me my purpose."

I follow as he veers off down a narrow deer trail. "Where are we going?"

"Back to the lodge," he says, glancing at me over his shoulder. "You have breakfast waiting."

"Honestly, I'm not very hungry anymore," I say. "I would rather talk to you."

I want to know more about the suicides.

I want to know more about you.

He doesn't say anything for a moment. Fallen branches snap under our feet as we walk, robins calling to each other from a nearby alder. "Very well," he says. "We can talk on my boat. If you don't mind, of course."

Joy fizzes up inside me. He's inviting me on his boat?

"I'd like that," I say, feeling so terribly shy all of a sudden. I dab the handkerchief at my nose again, and luckily, the blood has stopped. "Gives me a chance to wash up before the students wonder what happened to my nose."

"You must promise to eat something though," he says. "I'll whip you up some breakfast."

"Oh, no, seriously, I don't—"

"It's no bother, Syd. I like to cook. And you need to eat. It's a requirement this morning."

A few seconds pass before I dare to say, "Did anyone ever tell you that you're bossy?"

We step out onto the stone path leading to the docks, where I walk beside him.

"Some people like that I'm bossy," he says with a smirk.

I bet.

I follow him down the ramp, the tide high so that it's almost level, then to his boat.

"*Lord of the Rings* fan, huh?" I say, gesturing to the name of the boat. *Mithrandir.* Gandalf's name given to him by the elves.

"Only those worthy pick up on it," he says, climbing on board with ease. "I assume you know it means *Grey Wanderer* in Sindarin. Until I found myself at Madrona, I was a wanderer myself."

"Nerd," I say under my breath.

He laughs and reaches down, grabbing my hand, holding tight, my skin dancing at his contact. "Just put your foot on the fender step there. That's it. Put all your weight on it and push up."

I push off the horizontal bumper hanging from the open gate, and he pulls me up the rest of the way until I'm on his teak deck. He leads me to the cockpit before he lets go.

"Welcome aboard my humble abode," he says, appraising me. "You seem fairly comfortable on it already."

"Not my first time," I tell him. "I mean, I don't frequent fancy sailboats like this, but my father was a fisherman."

He gives me a polite smile. "Ah, that explains it."

Though he must know what my father did. He'd mentioned his death before, and Michael was the one who brought up the details last night.

You must wonder why death is so fixated on you.

At that thought, I shiver.

"You alright?" Kincaid asks.

"Morning chill," I say. From where we are in the harbor, the sun hasn't quite reached over the tops of the forest yet.

"I'll fix that," he says, reaching into a rubber sleeve that contains a winch and pulling out a key. He inserts it into the wood salon-style doors. "Coffee?"

"Yes, please," I tell him as he opens the doors and slides back a glass hatch, stepping down into the boat.

I go after him, five steps down until we're inside. It's nice and warm down here, with gleaming teak accents, a seat and chart table to the left, a small kitchen to the right. Down a step is the living area, couches and two chairs around a dining table, with another couch across the aisle. Beyond that, a closed door, probably the captain's quarters.

"If you need to wash up, this is the head," he says, gesturing to one of the three doors behind us. "It's a motorized toilet, so you don't have to worry about anything challenging, though if you're used to fishing boats, then I have no doubt you can handle anything. I'll make you coffee."

I thank him and go inside. The space is small but manageable and clean. I use the tiny toilet, terribly self-conscious about the fact that he can hear me pee, though the whir of a Keurig machine quickly covers it up.

After I'm done, I wash my hands, admiring the soap. It's some fancy shit with a black-and-white label, the kind you see on a lifestyle influencer's feed. I sniff my skin. Smells like being a rich neurosurgeon.

I dry my hands on the fluffy monogrammed towel, something about it snagging my memory for a moment before it disappears. I know I shouldn't, but I pull back the knob on the mirror to reveal a medicine cabinet underneath.

I reach in carefully and pull out a thing of oil face wash by some Korean skincare company that costs an arm and a leg at Sephora. There's also a tub of La Mer skin cream that costs even more.

Expensive taste, I think. *But we like a man who takes care of his skin.*

Curious, I dip my hand over the slight ledge, and my fingers grasp something else. I bring it out and hold it in front of me.

A tube of MAC lipstick.

Oh.

Oh.

A sour taste fills my throat as I pull off the cap.

The color is bright pink, similar to the color Michelle was wearing this morning. No. That's just a coincidence. They can't possibly be an item. That's *not* possible. I hold it up to the light coming in through the half-drawn curtains above my head and peer at it closer. The shade is a little darker, more subtle and sophisticated than Michelle's.

But regardless of whose it is, there's a lipstick in his medicine cabinet, and so now I'm assuming the facewash and La Mer aren't for him in the end.

Shit. Does he have a girlfriend?

Is he married?

You haven't even done anything, I remind myself. *Just a harmless crush and sex dreams that are out of your control. But you better fucking figure it out soon.*

I sigh and then use some of that oil cleanser to wash the blood off my face.

When I use the towel again, that's when my brain figures something out.

The monogram on the towel is one of a star and rope intertwined.

The symbol matches the one on the blanket I found on me this morning.

I burst out of the washroom to find him placing two coffees on the table.

"Everything alright?" he asks.

"Did you put that blanket on me last night?" I blurt out.

"I did," he confirms without skipping a beat. He sits down in a chair and gestures to the couch beside him. "Have a seat."

I do as he says, and he slides the mug of coffee toward me. Black, just the way I like it, though I notice he drinks his with cream.

"Everly told me what happened," he says, having a sip of his. I'm only now noticing that he's taken his coat off, so he's wearing just a navy blue Henley that shows off the muscles of his biceps, the width and firmness of his chest and shoulders. I have to pry my eyes away from his body and focus on his face, which of course isn't a hardship.

"But it happened so late," I say. "She said she was going to bed."

"We have a WhatsApp group chat here," he says dryly. "Some nights, I can't get an honest sleep without someone alerting me about something."

Alerting you about what? I want to ask, but I need to stay on track.

"So Everly told me what happened, more or less, and I figured I would go check on you," he says, swallowing down his coffee. "I found you in the common room, sprawled out on the couch and snoring away."

Oh god. How sexy of me.

"I went back to the boat, grabbed a blanket, and put it on you," he says, his palm cradling his mug. "Figured you must have been cold, and I couldn't figure out if I should wake you or not."

"So you were watching me sleep?" That should sound creepy, but somehow, it doesn't.

He lets out a huff of amusement through his nose, his eyes mischievous. "I prefer the term observing. A doctor observing his patient, making sure she's sleeping soundly."

I take a sip of my coffee, and he gestures to it with his chin.

"Sorry it isn't espresso," he says. "The machine is broken, and I haven't had time yet to take it to a repair shop. They aren't easy to come by around here."

"No, the coffee is fine. I like it black."

"Right," he says, scratching at his jaw. "I should have asked you if you wanted cream and sugar with yours. I'm sorry."

"It's perfect," I assure him. "Anyway, well, I guess thank you for looking out for me. My guardian not-angel."

The corners of his eyes crinkle, and he gives me a closed-mouth smile as he stares at me, unabashed. Sometimes he reminds me of a hero from a Victorian novel, the classic features of his face, the timeless quality of that jaw and those high cheekbones, combined with the reservation of a man who's seen a lot but rarely talks about it.

"What?" I ask, feeling myself get pulled into those grey eyes. It's like being lost in the fog.

Careful. Don't keep making the same mistakes. Don't let history repeat.

"Nothing," he says softly.

Man, his psychologist mind must work overtime with me.

"Are you married?" I ask. Like a gun, point-blank, like I should have asked Professor Edwards instead of assuming.

He blinks but doesn't seem taken aback. "No."

"Girlfriend?"

He gives his head a small shake. "No."

"Boyfriend?"

A smile. "No."

Relief floods my veins, though it still doesn't explain the lipstick.

Doesn't mean he doesn't have one-night stands. You're probably not the first student who wanted to jump him. There was probably a girl just like you.

I push that voice away.

"I did have a fiancé many years ago," he says, his voice a little gruff now. "Keiko Lynn. But when I started here, she couldn't handle it. She thought she could, but this wasn't the life for her. Living on a boat in one of the most remote locations on the coast. The isolation, the fog, the rain. My work. She broke it off and moved back to Japan."

"Oh, I'm sorry," I say, feeling dumb now.

He shrugs lightly. "Nothing to be sorry about. Everything happens for a reason. Why do you ask?"

"I'm just curious," I tell him. "You're a neurosurgeon. That's quite the catch. You're also someone who says he used to wander but now...doesn't. I just wondered if you had a family somewhere. Michael had mentioned he has a house in—"

"When did you speak to Michael?" Kincaid says abruptly, his eyes blazing.

"Uh, last night. When I went to see Everly."

His jaw clenches, his fingers start picking at some tape at the corner of the table where a crack in the wood has formed.

"Something wrong?" I ask. The change in his demeanor is razor-sharp.

He doesn't say anything. "No. I'm just not fond of him."

I exhale noisily. "Whew. Well, that makes two of us. He gives me the fucking creeps."

That brings out a slight smile, though his gaze is still hard. "Good. Stay away from him."

A thrill runs through me. He really is protective.

"But why? He's the COO."

"Just trust me," he says. "He doesn't have your best interests at heart. He doesn't have anyone's best interests at heart. If it were up to him, I wouldn't be counseling anyone or teaching. I would be back in the lab. I would be doing something I don't want to do. That I would have to refuse to do. He doesn't care about the students, no matter what his speech said. He only cares about profit."

"And Everly?" I've been wondering how she can be married to him when they seem so different.

His expression goes neutral. "Everly cares about more than profit." He looks away, licking his lips. "It was her idea for the counseling."

"So who was the first person that died?"

"You're a morbid one, aren't you?"

I shrug.

"Farida," he says quietly, staring down into his coffee. "Farida Shetty. We chalked it up to a troubled mind. She was from India, she'd been missing her home already even before she got here. The isolation made it worse."

"How did she kill herself?"

His gaze flicks up to mine, reproachful. "She hung herself."

"My god."

Then, the image of what I saw when I leaned against the mother cedar flashes across my eyes.

A dark-haired girl in a nightgown, hanging from a tree, her neck broken.

"What was she wearing?" I ask, my voice cracking with fear.

He frowns. "Why?"

"I just want to know," I say quietly. "When did it happen? In the night?"

The line between his brows deepens. "Yes, in the night. Looped the noose off the branch of a strong cedar." Each word is a knife to my gut, twisting my reality. "Ms. Shetty was found in her nightgown by Handyman Keith. He was in hysterics, poor guy. Not sure he's ever really recovered. He's someone who should have counseling, but he's as stubborn as a mule."

I let the information sink in, falling through my skin like melting snow. I stare into my coffee, a black hole.

Nightgown.

Broken.

The girl in the hallway.

"She had dark hair, didn't she?" I whisper.

He doesn't say anything, and when I look up at him, he's staring at me with an expression of quiet horror. That's a look you never want to see on a psychologist.

"Why do you ask?" he asks, his voice strained.

I finish the dregs of my coffee, though it will only make my racing heart worse. "Just wondering," I eventually say, putting the empty mug down.

He studies me for a moment, then plucks the empty mug from the table and gets up, stepping up around to the kitchen behind me. "You're lying to me," he says calmly as he puts the mug under the Keurig. "As punishment, I'm making you breakfast, and you have to eat it."

I don't protest about either one. I really don't want to lie. He already thinks I'm a special case anyway.

Still, I don't explain further. I start nervously picking at the tape at the corner of the table and stare at a painting on the wall, a famous painting of a bald eagle by Robert Bateman. I've seen it so many times before, and yet it still captures my attention. The eagle, posed in a haunting cry as it perches at the top of a dead tree, wings partially spread, the mist and forest a grey cloak behind it.

The Keurig whirs on, breaking the silence, while Kincaid starts taking stuff out of his fridge, placing it on the counter. I hear the click of a propane stove.

When the coffee is done, he puts the full mug in front of

me and sits back down. His sleeves are rolled up now to his forearms, showing the end of his tattoo. Up close, I can clearly see the feathers.

"Thank you," I say, holding up the mug. I nod at his tattoo. "A raven?"

"Are you trying to get my shirt off?" he muses.

Don't say yes. Don't say yes.

"Maybe."

Damnit, Sydney.

He smirks. "I'll take my shirt off if you tell me why you asked about Farida's hair."

"That's extortion."

"Take it or leave it."

I watch him for a moment, trying to read him at a deeper level, but as usual, his eyes hold so much back. Is he serious about any of this? Are we flirting? Is he aware that this whole exchange would be considered highly inappropriate, especially since he knows why I lost my scholarship?

He might not be a good man, the thought comes to me, bringing awareness into my bones. *He might be a bad man.*

And yet, who am I to talk, anyway?

I'm not a good person either.

I look at the painting on the wall. "The reason I left my room last night was because I saw a woman matching that description, in the hall. A woman who then disappeared."

"I see…"

"And before that, I saw an image of her when I was touching a cedar. It felt like…I don't know, this will sound silly—"

"As silly as ghosts?" he says, as if he's making fun of me, but when I look at him, his expression is grave.

"Worse," I admit. "It felt like the tree gave me that image. Perhaps it was the tree she hung herself from? Either way, I saw a girl in a nightgown, with long dark hair, hanging from a tree. I didn't see her face—it was just a flash, but it was there in my mind, clear as day."

"When was this?"

"On a foraging expedition. The one with Nick where Lauren and I discovered the grave."

He looks off, deep in thought, his face more handsome in profile. "I see." His gaze returns to mine, a fervent look in his eyes, making them look more blue. "And what do you make of that?"

"Ghosts?"

"Do you believe in ghosts?"

"I've always *wanted* to believe in ghosts. I've never seen any though. Until now. How else would you explain it?"

We both fall silent as we mull that over. Bacon starts to sizzle on the stove.

"Could be a coincidence," he says, getting up, his massive frame towering over me. "Things can always be a coincidence."

I twist around to watch him cook. My sex trifecta has just turned into a quadfecta: large hands, nice forearms, gravelly voice, and the ability to make me breakfast.

"Are you going to take your shirt off now?"

He manages a laugh. "While I'm cooking bacon of all things? I like inflicting punishment, not taking it."

I try not to let my mouth drop open. Did he really just say that?

Damn.

"After the bacon," I tell him.

He shoots me a wry look. "I said I would do it. I didn't say when. Perhaps when I take the group to the lake. We can go swimming."

That's not what I had in mind, but I know better than to push it.

Besides, now that the threat of his shirt coming off is gone, I'm thinking back to what he said about it being a coincidence. That may be fine and dandy about me seeing a woman who looks like Farida who also happened to die in the same way, but it doesn't explain the fact that I saw her to begin with, both in my mind and in the hall.

But then there's a phrase that I've heard at least three times since I've been here.

This place can play tricks on you.

CHAPTER 15

"GOOD AFTERNOON, EVERYONE," Everly says cheerfully from the front of the lab classroom. "Dr. Wu is still on a break, so I will be taking over her class today."

It's been a week since our last lab session, where Dr. Wu ran out crying, and it's gone by in a flash. After that breakfast with Kincaid on his boat, I've felt a lot closer to him, but he's been elusive outside of the classroom. I don't feel brave enough to go to his boat and say hello, but I'd be lying if I said I haven't been roaming the grounds, hoping we'd bump into each other, or looking out my window at night, hoping to catch him on bear patrol. Staring at him during class just hasn't been enough, though when he does meet my gaze on occasion and holds it, the electricity is enough to fuel me for the rest of the day.

It's a little like lovesickness. I'm not in love with Kincaid, but there is a flickering there, buried deep inside, that wants to spark. It wants to become a fire to ravage me whole. I am prone to falling fast and hard and then either falling out of love when I've grown bored or tossed to the side because they've finally come to terms with the fact that I am *too much*, and that's something I can't hide forever. I know that given half the chance, I could fall hard for Kincaid too, but one would think I'd learn from my mistakes, especially so soon after I've made them.

So while I've wanted to see him, talk to him privately, it's for the best that I haven't.

It's dangerous when you get what you want.

The weather has also helped the time blur. It's been so foggy that some days, you can't see more than a few feet in front of you. Because of that, all the days just sort of roll into one when you don't see the sun.

Today is no exception. All the lights inside the lab are blazing because the fog envelops the building, the tinted windows making it look like twilight.

I turn my attention back to Everly. She looks gorgeous, as usual, even in her lab coat. Though I now realize she's wearing it for appearances since this isn't the real lab.

She flicks her long blonde hair off her shoulder with graceful fingers and starts talking about how hyphae and fungi can possess a form of consciousness and how Madrona has sharpened their study on finding out if this use of consciousness can be helpful in tailoring specific medications using *Amanita excandesco*.

"The bigger question we are looking at right now," she says, pacing back and forth, "is *if* individual hyphae are conscious, what happens when an interconnected colony of thousands of these individual cells comes together? Does it become a hive mind, for lack of a better word? Or do they retain their independence? If we can separate the hyphae, can we ask them to do individual things, targeting different neurons?"

Munawar taps me on the shoulder, and I turn in my seat to face him. "This is way more interesting than any of the lectures Nick gives us," he whispers. He's wearing his shirt of the day. This one says *M.I.L.F.*, with the subtitle underneath *Man, I Love Fungi*.

"I feel like I've learned more in the last ten minutes than I have the last few weeks." His eyes dance. "Of course, Professor Kincaid is compelling too, am I right?"

I turn back around and roll my eyes. I don't like that smug look on his face and what he's insinuating.

Everly talks for a little longer and then passes out some slides with some organic matter for us to use in our microscopes. I can't help but think about what Clayton said, that this is busywork. Still, the organic matter turns out to be hyphae from *excandesco* itself, so it's nice to get a closer look at the infamous fungus.

Eventually, the hour is over, and Everly dismisses us. I'm walking toward the door with Lauren, Rav, and Munawar when Everly says, "Sydney, can I have a word with you?"

"Ooooh," Munawar teases. "Someone is in trouble."

"She's not," Everly says with a smile. "But you will be if you don't scoot along." She makes a shooing motion with her elegant fingers.

The look on his face is priceless before he practically runs out of the room, Lauren laughing after him.

I stare at her expectantly. She said I'm not in trouble, and yet my palms feel clammy. I want Everly to like me, but at the same time, even though she's been nothing but understanding and kind, she makes me nervous.

"What can I do you for?" I joke in a bumpkin accent.

"Just wanted to see how you're feeling," she says. "How are your arms? Any vaccine side effects?"

I've had to get two more rabies shots since the initial one, rotating arms as we go. "Both are sore now."

She nods. "We're almost done." Her eyes coast over my body and face, appraising me. "And how are you mentally? I feel I need to check in."

"You don't trust Kincaid to do that?"

Her smile is tight in response. "Wes is not here as a friend. But I am. I worry about you, Syd, my star pupil."

She reaches out and ruffles the top of my head like I'm a dog.

I laugh awkwardly, moving my head out of the way. I smooth down my hair, trying not to show my annoyance. "Yeah, right, star pupil. We haven't even had any testing done yet."

"You know we don't test you here. If you made it this far, you've passed. All this time is for you to concentrate on your capstone project." At the mention of my capstone, my stomach turns. She gives me a sympathetic look. "But of course, you don't have to do one anymore, do you? So tell me, Syd, what are your plans, then, while you're here? I'm letting you stay, but you still need a focus, a purpose. You need to contribute *something* to Madrona."

"My existence isn't enough?" I joke.

"You would think," she says dryly. "No, you're too brilliant to hold anything back from us."

I really wish she would stop saying that because I know I'm not. I fold my arms across my chest. "Can I be honest with you?"

"Are you ever not honest?" she says with a wink.

"If I'm so brilliant, if everyone here is brilliant, then why are we doing basic busywork in the lab? Why not integrate us into the real lab and see how Madrona really works? You made us sign NDAs. If you're worried we might see something we're not supposed to—"

"Like what?" she interrupts.

"I don't know. I have no idea. You keep talking about the research and the testing you've done in trials and all the amazing things that your fungus can do, but we haven't seen it."

"These things take time," she says calmly. "I like to lay groundwork first."

"So I'm right, then. This isn't the real lab."

She looks around. "Oh, we do work here," she says before

her gaze returns to me, a sly look in her green eyes. "But you are right. This isn't the main lab. They're downstairs."

"There's a downstairs?" I ask, surprised. "There's more than one?"

"Would you like to see?"

"Well, yeah."

"Come, then," she says as she walks to the other end of the room toward that other door. "But promise me you won't tell anyone. I don't want the other students to think you're getting preferential treatment."

"I swear," I say, making the sign of the cross over my heart. I know my Catholic grandmother will be watching me closely to make sure I don't break it.

She takes out her key card from her lanyard and passes it over the door. It unlocks with a click, and she pulls it open to reveal a dark staircase. She steps inside, and motion detector lights flick on.

I follow her down the narrow stairs, my pulse quickening with excitement. Finally, I'm going to see where the real magic happens.

At the bottom of the stairs are two doors across from each other. I'm trying to map it out in my head with the shape and size of the building above, and it seems both rooms must continue underground beyond the learning lab's foundation. I have to wonder if there's a tunnel system of sorts.

She swipes her card at the door on the right and steps in, flicking on the lights beside her. This lab is twice the size as the one upstairs, filled with the hum of machines, many of which I've never seen before.

"I thought the lab was running all the time," I tell her, surprised that it's empty.

"It is," she says. "The technicians are in the testing lab at the moment, across the hall. I would take you in there, but they aren't to be disturbed."

"Technicians," I say slowly. "Like Dr. Carvalho?"

"Yes."

"Who are the other technicians?" I ask because I have yet to see anyone on the compound that I haven't recognized. "Dr. Wu?"

"Part-time workers," she says. "They spend most of their time in the lab and live in the west lodge. That's probably why you haven't seen them," she adds, as if reading my mind.

"Ah," I say, glancing around the lab again.

"Can you imagine yourself working here?" she asks idly.

Weeks ago, I would have said yes with no hesitation. Now, I have to think about it. "I guess it depends what I would be doing."

"Whatever it is you want," she says. "If you play your cards right, there might be a job for you in the end. Imagine how that would solve all your problems. You'd live here, be paid very well, and you'd be ushering in groundbreaking research. You would leave your mark on the world for generations to come."

Yes. All this research we still don't know much about, and by design.

"How close *are* you to finding a cure for Alzheimer's?" I ask her.

Her brows rise. "Very close. We have practically found the cure. It just needs perfecting before we can open up the trials."

"But I thought you were already doing clinical trials."

"Closed clinical trials," she says. "We have been testing on animals."

I make a face. "But Kincaid said…"

Her posture stiffens. "Wes said what?" she asks in a clipped voice.

"That he was originally your neurosurgeon."

Her eyes narrow for a second before her expression relaxes. "He was. He still is, though Michael has taken over his role. Wes cares very much about saving people, whichever way he can do it."

Ah, so Michael happens to be a neurosurgeon as well. I would not let that man anywhere near my brain.

"So the studies have only been done on animals?"

"Not quite," she says.

Her secrecy is starting to grate on me.

"You know, the reason I wanted to study here was because of what your interviews and press releases had promised. Alzheimer's is dear to my heart—that's the whole reason I'm here. My grandmother died from it."

"I know." She nods, her eyes soft. "Sometimes I forget you…"

She trails off.

"Forget I what?"

"Forget that you've been through so much." She sighs, shaking her head in sympathy. "Too much. It's too much for one person, Syd."

Her attention is making me uneasy. "I turned out fine," I joke.

She doesn't laugh though. Her eyes narrow as she stares at me. "I wouldn't say that."

I bristle, feeling the sting.

"I turned out okay," I clarify.

Her lips purse as she considers that, her demeanor changing. "Yeah. You turned out okay. Considering, you know. Everything. You could be better though." She reaches out with her fawn-colored gel nails and brushes a strand of hair off my face. "Maybe you just need more time. Need to grow older. Need to learn. I forget that you're still just a grad student."

Just a grad student?

"Technically, not anymore," I mutter.

"Of course. I tell you what," she says after a moment. "You continue to do well and prove yourself, and then I'll let you in on the ground floor. Find your purpose at Madrona. Find something that excites you. Figure out how to be useful. Use that hyperfocus of yours and narrow in on something worthwhile. Surprise me."

Hyperfocus. That reminds me I haven't taken my Adderall for at least ten days now.

"If I prove myself, then will you actually let me in, actually let me see what you're doing here?"

"I promise," she says, then reaches over and flicks off the lights, plunging us into darkness except for the green and blue glowing lights of the various machines.

This time, I'm on my stomach.

Completely naked, my breasts pressed against the table in Kincaid's boat.

My hands are fastened together behind my back. I can tell it's rope; the fibers are cutting into my skin, tied painfully tight, just the way I like it.

I look up, expecting to see the painting of the eagle on the wall.

Instead, it's a painting of a grave, mushrooms growing on top of it.

Something under the soil is moving, unearthing.

Something in the painting is real and being born.

"Don't look at it." Kincaid's voice is rough and commanding in my ear. "Don't do anything unless I tell you to." He runs a hand down my spine, from my shoulders to my ass, and it takes me a minute to realize he's wearing a glove. He brings his hand back up and then presses my head against the table.

"Stay completely still," he says gruffly. "Don't fucking

move an inch, don't fucking make a sound, or you're going to bed with your hands tied, your swollen cunt begging for it." He leans in, licking up the rim of my ear, making me shiver. "Then again, I do love it when you beg. I think your cunt does too."

He pulls back, and I keep my eyes closed, my face pressed against the table. Cold air caresses the back of my thighs, and I hear the smooth sound of leather being whipped out of his belt buckle. I have no time to brace before—

CRACK.

The belt comes down across my ass, a sharp, sweet pain.

I yelp, unable to help myself. I feel electric, alive.

"What did I just say?" Kincaid growls. He reaches forward and makes a fist in my hair, holding my head back, mouth at my ear. "You disobedient little slut."

I squeeze my thighs together, trying to relieve the ache.

He immediately reaches between my legs and parts them.

"I'm going to take my fill of you now." He reaches back, and I feel the head of his cock press against where I'm open and wet. I can't help but move my hips, wanting him, needing him in deep.

"Please," I beg him.

But nothing happens.

Suddenly, he's no longer behind me.

I'm no longer on a table.

I'm on the goddamn floor in my room, practically writhing on the rug.

What the actual fuck?

I roll over and stare up at the ceiling, catching my breath.

Another goddamn dream.

But how did I end up here on the floor?

I sit up. The way my body still pulses tells me I came in my sleep again.

I can't tell if these dreams are intensifying my attraction to Kincaid or helping in some way. Maybe I can keep my distance if I keep getting what I want in my dreams. But getting off on the floor of my room is next-level weird shit.

I get to my feet, unsteady, feeling a little embarrassed, even though no one saw me.

Though I kind of wish Kincaid did.

With him in mind, I go to my window. The alarm clock says three a.m., never the best hour to be awake, but maybe he happens to be on bear patrol.

But when I look out the window, I don't see anyone at all. Just the moon filtering through the trees, making the ground look like it's covered in shards of light.

There's a knock at my door.

Quick and light.

I freeze, ice trickling down my spine.

Fuck. Not again.

Not again.

This time, I'm *not* leaving.

Another knock.

Then…

"Sydney," a girl's voice whispers excitedly. "Hurry up. It's happening! It's actually happening! Meet me at the field."

She sounds familiar.

She sounds just like…

Amani?

But it can't be.

The floorboards creak, followed by the sound of someone running down the stairs.

I quickly slide on my slippers and put on my housecoat, unlocking the door and pulling the key out of the lock. The hallway is empty and still poorly lit, but at least the power is on this time.

With my heart in my throat, I make a point of locking the door and then slipping the key into my pocket. Then I run down the stairs to the common room just in time to see the front door closing.

I hurry along, the fire down to embers, the room dark, and then burst out into the night. I catch sight of Amani running around the corner, and I follow along the path, running after her until we go past the lab and hit the gravel road that leads from the boat launch to the maintenance yard, the ground crunching beneath our feet and echoing in the trees.

She keeps going into the grassy field where empty boat trailers sit and then stops and starts twirling around with her arms raised to the sky.

"Isn't this amazing?" she cries out.

I stare at her, trying to figure out what's happening, *how* it's happening, when I realize why Amani is spinning around and grinning like a fool.

White flakes are falling from the air.

It's snowing.

It's fucking *snowing*.

The cold hits me at once. My shins, my nose, my cheeks, the exposed section of my chest as flakes hit my skin and melt. I hold my robe closer, wishing I could make sense of this, wishing my brain could just keep up.

"They said it doesn't snow here, not even in winter, and yet look at this!" she cries out, her breath freezing in the air. "This is a dream come true."

I can only stand where I am and stare, blinking away the flakes that gather on my lashes. "You're not real," I whisper.

"Aren't we lucky?" She continues to twirl, then points at me. "You're so lucky that Everly didn't care about your scholarship. Teacher's pet that you are."

I slowly walk toward her, terror starting to seep into my bones like the cold because Amani was sent home on the plane. Amani isn't here. Someone else took her place.

But what if Amani didn't go home at all?

"Amani. Are you okay?" I ask her, my voice shaking. "What happened to you? Where have you been staying? How do you know about Everly and my scholarship?"

"Sydney Denik, the golden child," Amani says, laughing now. Round and round she goes. "Who would have thought? Well, that Professor Edwards dick will rue the day you become more successful than he is."

I stop. No. None of this is right.

I look up at the sky. It's still snowing, the flakes illuminated by the lights from the barn. It's so quiet outside, so still, and the snow is getting thicker.

It's getting colder.

This is real, I tell myself, feeling the flakes on my skin and in my hair, the biting ice. Snow in early June, strange but possible. *But is she real?*

Suddenly, she picks up a snowball and throws it at me.

It hits me right in the face, caking it.

I gasp, quickly brushing the snow out of my eyes, my nose and hair. When I look down at my hand, it's smeared with red. Either the snow cut my face, or my nose is bleeding again.

I look up, blinking through frosted white. Amani is gone.

I spin around, looking for her.

"Amani!" I call out.

There are only the trees, their branches now layered with white, like icing sugar. They stand there, stoic observers, giving no insight.

She may have run to the logging road, to the barn, or to the woods, or just back to wherever she came from. But I don't want to follow her anymore.

I don't trust her.

I don't trust my mind.

I don't trust this place.

CHAPTER 16

I HURRY down the path through the rain, the ferns reaching out and brushing against my jeans, my jacket held above my head in lieu of an umbrella. I'm early for Kincaid's session, but I didn't want to waste any time in talking to him, and I'm eager to get out of the rain.

I first took a quick detour to the maintenance yard. After the snow last night, I had to go and check to see if there was any left on the ground. Of course, with the rain, there's no trace of it.

I'm running across the gravel path when I hear rustling behind me.

I stop, thinking perhaps I'll see Amani again.

But there's no one there. Rain drips from the cedars, splashing on the leaves. And yet, I have that uneasy twinge in the base of my skull, the feeling of being watched.

It's not the first time since I've been here that I've felt eyes on me, eyes that seem to only be found in the trees.

I start hurrying along again, hating that prickle at the back of my neck, and reach the north dorm. Once under the shelter of the overhang, I shake the water off my jacket, then open the door and step inside, still dripping all over the floor.

Wincing at the puddle I'm leaving, I walk slowly down the hall, careful not to slip, when I notice Kincaid's door is open a crack.

I'm about to knock when I hear Everly from inside.

"She's different," Everly says with a heavy sigh.

I gulp, hoping they're not talking about me.

I lean in closer to the door, trying to hear.

"She's better now," Kincaid says.

"You would say that" is Everly's snippy remark.

"She's better," Kincaid repeats, his voice hard. "Her appetite has returned."

Fuck. They are talking about me.

"I bet it has," she comments.

"What is *that* supposed to mean?"

"It means that you're very obvious about your obsession with her."

Obsession with me?

Hell no, he hasn't been obvious.

But then I think of him standing outside my window.

I think of when I've caught him staring so openly at me.

I think about him following me on my walk.

I know that the two of us share some kind of connection, but I've honestly thought it's all been in my head. So to hear this is…something.

Kincaid is silent for a moment. "It can't be helped," he concedes miserably.

That would sound romantic, but the way he says it makes it sound like some incurable disease, like he's dying.

"Obsession leaves when you stop feeding it," Everly says. "You need to stop feeding it. You need to focus on your own mind for once and rein it in. Focus on your work. Focus on me! I know you, Wes. I know what you're like, your need to fixate and control…the spiral you're about to go down, the writing on the wall…"

"What if she feels something for me?" He says this so

quietly I have to strain to pick it up above the hammering of my heart.

"She doesn't," she says matter-of-factly. "She just thinks you're hot. She just wants to sleep with you. Poor thing."

"And if it's more than that?"

"Then you act like a professional," she says sternly. "You're her doctor, for god's sake. You can keep it in your pants, can't you? You need to be there for her as a doctor. Not as a friend, not as anything else. You need that distance, or things will get really fucking messy. It's already fucking messy." She pauses, sighs. "She's just not smart enough."

The fuck?

Her words stab me right in the chest. Suddenly, I have a flashback to grade school where I overheard class hottie Ryan Corrigan telling Vicki Bessey that he hated being next to me in math class because I looked so stupid while I tried to figure out the equations. I struggled through my calculus in college because what he said stayed with me, made me think I was an idiot.

So to hear that from Everly, of all people, after she just called me brilliant, her star fucking pupil, is a real trip.

She's been lying to me.

"She *is* smart," Kincaid snaps at her. "She's just adjusting. These things take time. She'll prove herself, just not now."

"Well, you're not working hard enough, Dr. Kincaid," she says.

"Neither are you," he says quietly. "The other students—"

"You leave them to me. They might be useful in time." I hear her walking toward the door. "Patience is key."

I can't be caught here. I quickly turn around and scamper down the hall and into the common room. I stand there, heart in my throat, back against the wall, praying she doesn't follow the trail of water to find me.

Then I hear the door close to the outside.

I exhale heavily, clutching my chest. Jesus.

I take a moment to compose myself. The last thing I want is for Kincaid to think I heard anything. I lightly tap my fingers on my face and neck, trying to calm myself down and stay steady.

When I'm finally ready, I walk back down the hall and knock on Kincaid's door. This time, it's closed.

"Come in," I hear his voice.

I open the door and pop my head inside. Smoke wafts toward me, smelling like sweet tobacco. Kincaid is sitting at his desk and staring at that small white square piece of paper again before he slips it into a drawer. It takes me a moment to realize that it's one of those mini Polaroid photos, like the one he brought for documenting when we went to the beach. A hand-rolled cigarette smokes from an ashtray on the windowsill, where it's been put out.

"Take a seat," he says, and when he meets my eyes, I can see the frustration in them. I would give anything to know exactly what they were talking about. Am I being tested somehow to prove how smart I am, prove I'm good enough to work at the Madrona Foundation? Is this actually more of an internship than anything else? Is that why we're all here?

Fuck that, I think, hating the idea of being tested unknowingly. *I'll never work here.*

But then there's that part of me that doesn't want to rebel, the part that wants to work here, that craves that recognition and the significance in my life. I'm not sure which one is stronger.

Kincaid and I stare at each other for a moment.

His obsession with me…

Why me?

"You look tired," he finally says.

I bristle at the comment and nod at the dark circles under his own eyes. "So do you, doctor."

He nods, running his hand over his jaw. "Yes. I haven't been sleeping well either. Perhaps it's contagious."

I sit up straighter. "What's contagious?" I frown.

"You're not sleeping well," he says. "I assume you haven't been."

"Well, I haven't had a chance to talk to you," I tell him. "Not since breakfast on the boat."

He inhales sharply. "I'm glad you brought that up." His eyes flick to the wall. "I think that was a mistake."

"Breakfast?" My stomach drops.

"There are boundaries between a doctor and a patient, and I think that I crossed one by inviting you into my private quarters. I'm sorry."

Fuck. He really is putting in the distance now after what Everly said.

"I just thought it was really nice," I tell him quietly. "I felt a little less…alone."

That softens something in his face for a moment before it hardens again.

Please be obsessed with me, I think. *Please want me like I want you.*

His gaze is unreadable. "Tell me how you've been," he says.

I exhale and sit back in my chair. "You want the truth?"

"I only ever want the truth."

Do you tell me the truth?

"I've been having dreams."

He grabs his pen and his book and starts writing. "What kind of dreams? When did they start?"

"They started pretty much my second night here," I tell him. "They're sex dreams."

He pauses, eyes glued to the paper as he swallows hard. "Oh. Well, that's not cause for alarm."

"They're about you."

He drops the pencil, his jaw tense. "I see." His gaze burns as he meets my eyes. "It would be inappropriate for us to discuss this more."

It sure would be.

"Don't you want to know what we were doing in the dreams?"

He leans back in his chair and covers his face with his hands before dragging them down. He stares up at the ceiling. Then nods, just once.

My heart skips several beats, knowing he's relenting, knowing he wants to hear this, and I take a deep breath. "The first one, you were going down on me in my bed at the lodge. The second one, I was giving you a blowjob here in the office. The third one, you had me on my stomach on the table in your boat, tied up, edging me, punishing me with your belt…"

His eyes fall closed, and he's breathing heavily. I wonder if he's hard. I wonder if he's picturing doing all of that right now.

"Do you want the details of exactly how it felt?"

A muscle in his jaw feathers, and he gives his head a shake.

"I'm not sure what to say," he says after a moment, his voice hoarse. He clears it and sits forward, meeting my eyes. His gaze is unreadable, blank and grey. "But it's nothing to be ashamed of."

"Who said I was ashamed? Those dreams are the best part of going to sleep."

He swallows audibly. "Please don't say things like that."

"Why not? You wanted the truth. That's the truth." I lick my lips, buoyed by a strange courage, by a deep desire. "I want to get on my knees right here and crawl under that desk and—"

"Stop!" he suddenly yells, getting to his feet, as if I was actually about to do that. His expression is one of both fear and fury. "Don't say another fucking word about this. I am here to help you, Sydney. That is it. That is all I am to you!"

I flinch at his words, my face flaming, immediately feeling

stupid. I thought maybe if I pushed him enough, I could see that obsession. I thought maybe I could make him give in. I thought maybe I could see some inkling of feelings for me.

But all I see is a boundary being thrown into place.

It's probably for the best, but I can't sit here and talk to him, not after this.

"I better go," I say, quickly getting out of my chair and running to the door.

"Sydney," he growls, calling after me. "Wait, come back."

I don't come back. I run down the hall, cheeks flaming, careful not to slip on the wet puddles I originally left behind, then run out into the rain.

"Sydney!"

I stop and turn around, surprised to see him running after me, getting soaked.

"Please," he says, reaching out and grabbing my hand, holding it. "I didn't mean to yell. I shouldn't have yelled. I'm sorry."

I try to take my hand from his, but his grip is strong.

His grip is always so strong, perfect for keeping me in place.

"I crossed a line, I get it," I say, feeling helpless, like I'm caught between wanting to go and stay. "I pushed that line on purpose. But I know my place. And I know yours. *Doctor.*"

He shakes his head, rain streaming over his beautiful face. Fuck me for actually having feelings for my goddamn psychologist.

"I…I…" he begins. Then he raises his head, looks over my shoulder, and abruptly lets go of me. Without another word, he turns around and strides back to the building.

I turn around to see what's caught his eye.

Michael is standing still by the totem pole, an umbrella over his head, staring our way.

He meets my eyes.

So, so cold.

Then he walks off.

I stand there in the rain until I'm drenched from head to toe, then make my way to the main lodge, wondering where I went wrong while knowing exactly why it went wrong.

History is struggling to repeat itself.

CHAPTER 17

"ALMOST THE LAST ONE," Everly says sweetly before she jabs the shot in my arm.

I grit my teeth together. "Almost? I thought this was the last? It's been two weeks."

"We'll do another one next week," she says, removing the needle. "Just to be safe." She places the circular adhesive on my arm and tells me to apply pressure, which I do.

"But the wolf still didn't break the skin."

"Just to be safe," she repeats, putting the needle away and snapping off her gloves. She folds her arms and stares at me, head tilted, long blonde hair hanging like a curtain of wheat. "How are you?"

Just peachy. Ever since I learned you think I'm a moron.

Though it was a couple days ago that I overheard her talking to Kincaid, her words still sting.

"Fine," I say.

She smiles thinly. "Good. Good to hear. I hope you've been thinking about what I told you. About wanting to prove yourself. Have you given it any more thought?"

"Not yet," I admit. "I'm looking for inspiration."

"Inspiration is all around us, Syd," she says. "The forest

here…there are cedars that are five hundred years old, Sitka spruce that are close to a thousand. All those years, all that history, all those ghosts."

I look at her sharply. "Ghosts?"

"You think this place doesn't have ghosts? It's built on ghosts. On the indigenous who have lived here for thousands of years. On the trees that have fallen. On the animals whose bones sink into the soil. All these ghosts connected and living underneath our feet through networks of mycelia." Her eyes spark. "History stays alive here. I know you feel it. We all do."

"Maybe I'll make my study on ghosts, then," I manage to say, the hair at the back of my neck prickling.

She grins, her smile too wide. "I hope you do."

The rest of my day was thankfully uneventful. The rain hadn't stopped since yesterday and continued through dinner, leaving everyone in a soggy mood. My arm was super sore from the shot, and I cursed Everly for making me have another one next week, but perhaps they know something about rabies that I don't.

I didn't have class with Kincaid, and I hadn't seen him anywhere, which probably means he's avoiding me yet again. First, he kept his distance after the boat breakfast; now, he's doing the same after our argument in his office.

Which I still feel stupid about. Every time I think about what I said, I feel a rush of shame in my chest. What was I thinking, being so bold and brazen?

But you saw that look on his face, I remind myself. *He wanted you to tell him the details of your dreams.*

Still, the rejection has made its way into my bloodstream, clouding everything I do. It's hard to shake, hard to forget.

I'm standing in my bathroom, about to take off my makeup, when suddenly, there's a loud knock at my door.

My breath hitches in my throat.

It's ten at night.

Cautiously, I poke my head out of the bathroom to see a shadow on the other side of the door, the knob turning, rattling.

Fuck no.

"Sydney!" a voice yells. "Get up! The ocean is sparkling!"

"We also have wine!" adds Munawar.

I exhale with relief and head over to the door, opening to see Lauren, Munawar, and Rav with boxes of wine in hand.

"Get your shoes and your coat," Lauren says quickly. "The phosphorescence is going off tonight!"

"And Nick just got back from the Port Alice run, so we have provisions," Munawar says, lifting up the box of wine and attempting to pour it into his mouth. It explains the ruby stains on his *Amateur Mycologist with Questionable Morels* sweatshirt.

"Save some for the rest of us," Rav says, smacking him on the back, which only makes him spill more wine on his shirt.

"Okay, just wait for me, please," I tell them. I'm remembering Amani knocking on my door and taking off, and I'm afraid that if they go without me, I'm going to end up in a snowy field again.

They hang out in the doorway while I slip on my sneakers and hoodie.

We then leave my room, and I lock the door behind me before we clamor down the steps. In the common room, a group is cracking open beer cans by the fire, and Munawar yells at them to come join the show.

With that group now joining ours, we head out into the night. Twilight still stretches across the horizon, but the darkness is coming quickly, the stars appearing in the clearing sky as the rain clouds move to the north. The group is laughing, yelping, drinking, and for the first time since I've been here, I feel like I'm part of the gang.

"Have any wine to spare?" I ask Lauren as we pile down the ramp, our footsteps on the metal grid echoing across the inlet, shaking the dock at the bottom.

"I thought you would never ask," she says, pulling out one of the disposable paper cups from the common room's water cooler. Once we're level on the dock, we stop, and she makes me hold the cup while she pours red wine from the box, and then we continue on our way to the end, where there are no boats tied.

On the way, we pass by Kincaid's boat. From the looks of it, he's not home. Unless he's sleeping. All the lights are off.

"Is this wise to be partying beside the professor?" Munawar asks.

"We're in our fucking twenties, Munawar," Justin says, his words slurring slightly. "Nick is the one who got us the booze. We're allowed to do what we want."

Then Justin grabs Natasha's arm and pulls her close to him, and they start wildly making out.

Lauren snorts. "Geez. We get it, you like each other."

We all walk around the couple until we reach the end of the dock. Lauren drops to her knees and then leans over the side. The water is black, reflecting the sky, though if you look close enough, it does seem to be sparkling here and there. Could be the stars though.

Then Lauren dips her hand in, and the water comes to life, glowing a sparkling green and blue.

"Whoa!" a few people say in unison, and suddenly, we're all sitting by the edge of the dock. I get down on my side and reach down, my fingertips trailing over the water. It's freezing cold, but that doesn't matter when you're able to make light streaks by moving your fingers around.

"Magic," I say to myself, marveling at it. We have bioluminescence at home, but not that frequently, and it's just never that dark out. But here, there are no other lights aside from the dim ones on the dock and at the lodge, zero light pollution in the night sky when the nearest town is a hundred miles away.

Munawar and Rav decide to go to the beach to get some stones to skip, so I get comfortable sitting on the dock next to Lauren. Justin and Natasha have climbed into a fishing boat, and one can only imagine what's happening there. Everyone else is drinking and splashing the water around until it sparkles.

I take a sip of my wine. It's cheap, but it tastes good after not having any for a month.

"You going to let your hair down tonight?" Lauren asks, pouring herself another cup. "Relax a little?"

"Maybe," I say.

She touches her cup against mine. "Alright, well, here is to that maybe. Don't you dare go to sleep before the night is over."

"No promises," I say, downing the contents and handing it to Lauren.

"Off to a good start," she says, filling it back up.

"I hope so," I say as I take it from her. I'm already feeling a little fuzzy-headed, but it also feels like a weight has lifted off my shoulders. I need to keep myself in check though. I don't need to be drunk and hollering gibberish while pounding on Kincaid's boat.

"How have you been?" I squint at her. "I mean, really."

"Fine," she says, though her voice sounds clipped. She looks around, and I have a feeling she's looking for Rav. "It's been good."

I watch her closely. She seems a little thinner than she was, hollows under her cheekbones, and in the darkness, the shadows under her eyes deepen. I feel bad that this is the first time I'm noticing. As usual, I've been too wrapped up in my own brain, in my own worries. "Are you sure?"

She drinks her wine and nods. "Yeah. I mean, you know. I don't think it's a secret that I have a thing for Rav."

"And he has a thing for you. I've at least noticed that," I say. "So? How is that going?"

"Well, nowhere because neither of us has made a move. God, I feel like I'm in high school again." She sighs and looks off into the dark inlet.

"That's not a bad thing," I say. "You have all summer to explore that. You don't want to jump into anything right away." I look over at the fishing boat that's rocking slightly, the ripples making the water glow. "What happens if Natasha and Justin break up tomorrow and they have to deal with seeing each other for the rest of the summer? No, thanks."

"That's true," she says. She leans over and dangles her hand in the water again and sighs. "But actually, I'm not sure how I can survive the next couple months. I wonder if I can request to go home early."

My eyes widen as I'm struck with fear.

"Why? No. You can't. You can't leave me."

She gives me a soft smile. "You can leave too."

But I can't. I have no money and nowhere to go.

I shake my head. "Why do you want to leave?"

"You mean, aside from the fact that I would fucking die to just check my email and Instagram for a minute?" She brings her hand out of the water and peers at it, flicking tiny pieces of seaweed off her pruny skin. "I just don't feel tested here, you know? My senior synthesis was supposed to be on fungi that survived the ice age, and yet, we haven't gone anywhere near the peninsula yet. The classes are all over the place. Professor Kincaid's are thought-provoking, but they're still holding so much back from us. Lab work with Everly is just lip service. I just feel like I might be wasting my time."

She's right about all that.

"How are your sessions with Kincaid?" I ask.

She shrugs. "Fine. He's not very thorough. We just mainly talk about this and that. What TV shows I'm missing, how it feels like the world is passing me by while I'm stuck here." She pauses and shoots me a furtive glance. "Though I don't tell him everything."

I frown. "What aren't you telling him?"

"Sometimes this place vibes me out." She finishes her drink and then leans in close. "I'm not going crazy, don't worry. But sometimes it feels like I'm being watched. When I walk to class. When we're foraging. When we're in the common room. It just feels like…eyes on me. Studying me."

I swallow hard.

"And sometimes," she goes on, her voice lower. "I see things…in the forest."

"What things?" I whisper back, feeling my stomach churn from the wine.

She closes her eyes and shakes her head. "I don't even know. Just…things. Like…shapes. Shadows. Sometimes I think I see glowing eyes."

"Well, there are a lot of wild animals here. Could be anything."

"I think the forest plays tricks on us," she says.

I want to fight against that, but I know she's right. "Yeah, well, the other night, I thought I saw Amani again. She was knocking on my door. I followed her outside to the boat yard, and it started snowing."

"Snowing?"

"Yep. I can't figure out if Amani was real or not, but the snow was. It was cold. I felt it. I watched it melt. It was real. And gone with the rain in the morning. The forest really is playing tricks on us."

"Well, snow in early June this far north isn't totally impossible. And it has been cold lately. Maybe a freak weather system passed over us?"

"Still doesn't explain Amani," I say quietly, staring down at my empty cup.

We both go quiet, thinking.

"Do you think I'm crazy?" I ask.

"No. Do you think I'm crazy?"

"No." We both laugh. It feels fucking good to laugh, to put it all out there.

"We come with rocks!" Munawar yells, and we twist around to see him approaching with Rav, both of them with handfuls. They start trying to skip them into the ocean, creating dazzling sprays of water and light.

I keep drinking, I keep laughing. I tuck my worries away and force myself to pay attention to my friends, to live in this very moment. This much, I know, is real. This is what counts. But if Lauren ever tries to leave early, I'm leaving on that plane with her.

And Kincaid?

If things in a few months are the same as they are now with us—full of tension that has nowhere to go—then I'm going to have to cut my losses with him. Hell, I should probably do that sooner than later. It's only making things complicated.

"Okay, I'm going to bed," I tell them after a while. Rav comes over and helps me to my feet. The dock sways, or maybe I'm swaying because of all the wine. That's the problem with drinking a box of wine in tiny cups—you have no idea how much you've had.

"I'll come with you," Lauren says, trying to get up but falling back on her ass and giggling.

"No, you stay," I tell her, stepping away from Rav. "I'm going straight to my room."

"Promise you won't go for a walk in the forest!" she yells, trying to grab me and sprawling out along the dock. "The forest has eyes!"

"Take care of her," I say to Rav and Munawar. "I mean it."

Munawar gives me the salute, which I know means he's on the case.

I stagger down the dock past *Mithrandir*, but the yacht is still completely dark. Perhaps he's working late in his office.

But I'm still mindful enough to know that visiting him would be a very bad idea, so as soon as I stagger up the ramp, steeper now thanks to the lowering tide, I head straight into the lodge and through the common room. Noor and Toshio are playing a game of backgammon by the fireplace, and I wave to them before I head up the stairs.

I hesitate a little before I unlock my door, wanting to give any ghosties time to hide, and then I open it and step in.

I flip on the light, though I could have sworn I left it on for this very reason, then take a look around the room. Everything looks normal. I go over to the bedside lamp and flick it on for extra light.

Then, I slowly start getting undressed. I take off my hoodie, long-sleeved T-shirt and bra, then step out of my yoga pants, throwing them onto my bed. Then I cross the room to my dresser and take out my pajama top, pulling it on over my head. I spilled coffee on the bottoms this morning, so they're in a pile in the corner of the room, waiting for laundry day.

I turn around and go to the bathroom sink, grabbing a tub of cleansing balm and rubbing it on my face, staring at myself in the mirror. My eyes are a little glassy, and I look exhausted. I just hope I don't have a hangover tomorrow.

I rinse my face, mentally making a note to drink more water. I'm patting my skin dry with a towel when I hear a *thump* from behind me.

I go dead still.

My heart sticks to my chest.

Slowly, very slowly, I turn around to look.

My room is empty.

I step out of the bathroom and look around, wondering

what it could have been that made the noise when I notice all my clothes are in the middle of the floor.

I stare at them blankly. I could have sworn I placed them all on the bed in a pile.

And my hoodie is almost totally under the bed, only the arms sticking out.

I take a deep breath, trying to calm my hummingbird heart, and then walk across the room and stop.

What if there's something underneath the bed?

I know it's a silly thought—why should there be anything under there?

But I can't help it. Goosebumps cover my arms, my spine like ice.

Just get on your knees and look under the bed.

I stare at the hoodie.

I can't do it.

I crouch down and quickly reach for the arms.

Just as a large, fat spider comes crawling out from under the bed, toward my hand.

I shriek and stumble backward, banging into the wall hard enough for the painting of the raven to fall down. The spider, seemingly scared, scurries back under the bed.

"Jesus," I swear, leaning against the wall, my hand on my chest. I glance at the painting, hoping I didn't break it.

But…there's something not right about it.

There's something stuck behind it.

A round, black metal object.

I reach down and pick the painting up, peering at the back closely.

Then, I flip the frame over and examine it.

Up close, I notice one of the raven's black eyes is extra shiny.

Dread creeps up my throat.

Oh my god. Please don't tell me.

I flip it over again, and I try to pull the black object off. I have to yank and twist, and finally, it comes out, destroying part of the painting in the process, but I have to know.

I let the painting fall to the floor and turn the object over in my hand, noting the USB slot in the side, peering into the lens.

Someone's put a fucking camera in my room.

I clutch my stomach, feeling sick. I put the camera in my pajama top's pocket, then go to the other painting on the opposite wall above my head. The center of the starfish is a glossy lens as well. I take that off the wall and rip the camera out.

I look around wildly, wondering where else they could be.

The ghost mushrooms.

I run over to the bathroom and lift the embroidered picture off the wall.

There is no camera on the back of the frame, but there is a small round microphone.

Someone has been watching me.

Listening to me.

Spying on me.

Stalking me.

And in the depths of my heart, I know who it is.

Kincaid.

CHAPTER 18

I DON'T WASTE any time.

I put on my slippers and robe and I'm running out of my room, not bothering to lock it. What's the point when people like Kincaid can enter any damn time they want?

I hurry down the stairs, past Noor and Toshio, still playing backgammon, who watch me curiously as I run outside with no pants on. Drunken singing emanates from the dock below but I head for the north dorm, hoping to find Kincaid in his office. If he's in his boat despite the party on the docks, well, I might have to wait. The last thing I want is to make a scene in front of everyone.

The north dorm is unlocked, and I step inside, closing the door behind me. I hurry down the hall and frantically knock on Kincaid's office door.

I'm breathing hard, still drunk, still livid, and I know I need to control myself, I need to calm down and handle this rationally, but I can't. I feel like everything I've been going through these past weeks has come to a boiling point.

Before I have time to take a deep breath and count to ten backward, a last ditch attempt to thwart my rage, the door swings open with Kincaid on the other side.

I hate how fucking good he looks, even working late at night. Black dress shirt unbuttoned, sleeves rolled up, his dark hair spiked up as if he's been running his hands through it. His expression is slightly unhinged, a wild sort of concern that belies any professionalism between us.

"Sydney?"

"I need to talk to you," I manage to say, anger bubbling over as I storm past him into the room.

He closes the door behind me, and I slam my hand down on his desk, displaying the two cameras and microphone.

"What is this?!" I shriek, whirling around to face him. "Tell me what this is! And don't you dare fucking lie to me."

He strides over to me but as soon as he spots them, his pace slows. He stops in front of me, a sharp inhale.

I watch his face closely. I'll know a lie when I see it.

He meets my gaze and swallows. In the dim light of his office, lit only by a couple of candles that emit the scent of santal, and a lamp in the corner, his eyes are the color of a thunderstorm, mirroring how I feel inside.

"I can explain," he finally says, licking his lips.

"Then explain it," I snipe, leaning back against his desk and crossing my arms. "Explain why there are fucking cameras in my room. Was it you? Was it Everly? Michael?"

"It was me," he says. He says it so simply without an ounce of remorse.

I grind my teeth together, huffing through my nose. "Do they know?"

He stares at me for a moment then shakes his head. "They don't know. If you want to report me to them, I completely understand. My studying of you is…unauthorized."

"Studying?" I repeat. "You call that studying?"

"Observing, then."

I blink at him, my mouth open. "You violated my privacy! What have you been doing, just sitting in your office, watching me get undressed? Watching me sleep?" The horror hits me. "Oh god, you knew I was having sex dreams! You saw it! You heard it!"

He doesn't say anything. His face remains so impassive that I can't help what I do next. My anger rolls through me like an earthquake, my palm shooting up and across to SLAP him in the face.

The sound reverberates across the room, and my palm stings, sharp spikes of pain.

His nostrils flare but he takes it.

He doesn't repent nor does his expression change.

He just stands there and takes it.

"Say something!" I scream at him.

"What do you want me to say?" he says, gruff but still calm.

"Tell me why!"

"You don't want to know why," he says quietly.

"Fuck you!" I shout, and I attempt to slap him again.

This time his hand catches my wrist and holds my palm inches away from his face.

"You've been drinking," he says. "You need to calm down, for your own good."

"Don't you dare tell me to calm down," I sneer. I feel violent, out of control, like I'm finally unraveling, every thread that had threatened to come loose is finally being pulled. "As if I don't have a right to be upset! To be horrified!"

His grip on my wrist tightens. "I won't let go until you do. Come on, Syd. Let's get your heart rate down, take in a deep breath."

"Fuck you," I say, trying to pull out of his grasp, but he reaches out and grabs me by the back of the neck. I automatically freeze.

"Calm down," he repeats sternly. His grip on my neck is as strong as the one on my wrist and for a moment I feel true fear. It penetrates my alcohol-induced bravado, a sharp shard of clarity, and I realize I've been a fool. I came here alone to confront my teacher, someone I barely know, someone who has all the power and all the secrets, and I stoked him into these flames, a fire that could consume me whole.

He could hurt me. It would be my word against his. Who would believe me after all the stuff I've been saying? I'm sure his computer is full of files about me and my behavior.

About how crazy I am.

"There," he says softly, still staring deep into my eyes. "Breathe. That was fight. Next is flight. But right here I see fear. It's good to be afraid of me, Syd. It's good to be afraid of everyone. Promise me you won't lose that."

What the fuck is he talking about?

"Why?" I whisper, noticing the grip on my neck has loosened. He starts to move his thumb back and forth over my skin, rubbing it. It's bringing my heart rate down but it's doing something else to me. Making my knees weak. "I hate you," I whisper.

"I know you do," he says with a sigh. "You deserve to hate me. I hate me too."

And yet somehow that angers me, like it's the easy way out.

"Tell me why you were spying on me," I say through a clenched jaw. "Are you...obsessed with me?"

It sounds absolutely stupid when I say it though there is no other word.

A small, sad smile on his lips. "We're all obsessed with something, aren't we? We all have our little fixations. You know that better than anyone."

I swallow hard. "This is more than a little fixation, *doctor*. Cameras, standing outside my window, following me on walks, those are all more than a little fixation."

"I know," he says, gaze dropping to the floor. He lowers my hand but he's still holding on. "It can't be helped. The moment I first saw you I knew I was done for."

My cheeks burn. I remember that moment like it was yesterday, bumping into him outside the learning center. "You looked like you were scared of me," I mutter.

"I was. Because I knew." He pauses, glancing back at me to meet my eyes, his brow crumpled. "And I know my role. I know my position. I know that this power imbalance is why I can't ever act on anything. I was doomed."

His words are starting to sink in, to have an effect.

I can't let them drown me because I'll just put my hands up willingly.

"And so you decided to put cameras in my room? Because the one during our sessions wasn't enough?"

He lets go of my neck and wrist and walks across the room, running his hands over his face. My skin aches where he held me. Some sick part of me hopes it leaves a mark. "No," he eventually says. "It wasn't enough."

He stops by an ornate mirror on the wall and stares at himself.

"I just don't understand," I say.

"Come here and maybe you will."

I hesitate and then walk over to him. He moves out of the way, gesturing for me to take his place.

I step in front of the mirror and stare.

I look like a fucking mess. Streaks of mascara under my eyes that the cleanser didn't get. My hair wild, my robe hastily fastened.

Though for a moment, just for a second, I think I see a flash of something else.

But no, it's just a trick of the light.

Kincaid stands to the side of me and says, "Do you see that girl?"

I see her, I think. *Sydney Denik, hot mess express.*

"That's what I'm up against," he says, his voice so low and rough that it sends fingers up my spine. "That's who makes it so damn hard to come to work every day because I have to pretend. Pretend I don't want her. Pretend I don't need her. Pretend I *don't crave* her."

Fuck, I'm turning into a puddle on my feet. The way he said he *craves me* is combining into a messy brew, along with every other feeling I've had tonight, until I'm not sure if I want to slap him again or fuck him senseless.

"The only thing I'm allowed to do is try and save her," he adds. "And so I watch you. I don't need to watch you undress or fuck yourself in your sleep. I need to make sure you're alright."

I blink at his words and stare at his reflection in the mirror.

"I should report you," I tell him, though it doesn't sound like I mean it and I hate that. Hate how weak he makes me feel.

"You should," he agrees solemnly. "It would be the right thing to do."

"Would you be sent away?"

He shrugs.

I have a feeling he wouldn't be. They need him here.

"And no one else watches me?"

"Not like I do," he says, a sharpness in his gaze. "They don't have your best interests at heart."

That's apparent now. I feel bamboozled by Everly after hearing what she said.

I turn to face him. "Why do you need to save me? Are you saving me from them? What is really going on here?"

"I told you. I need to save you from yourself. I know your background. I know what happened to you. I know the things you won't let yourself see, the things you won't let yourself face. This place…" He shakes his head. "This place will lead you into the forest one day and never let you out. I can't let that happen to you."

"Please tell me that's metaphorical."

"It's the forest of your mind, Syd. The Lodge, it messes

with those who are most vulnerable. I've seen it happen time and time again. I don't want any harm coming to you, not if I can stop it."

My chest suddenly feels cold, constricted, like my ribs are made of ice. "You're the one who made me go off Adderall. I haven't been able to think clearly ever since."

"Yes, you have," he says. "Tell me, have you noticed your symptoms? Has it felt like you've been missing your meds?"

I rub my lips together, trying to think. "I don't know. It's hard to tell. There's just so much happening."

"You have to keep trusting me."

"Oh, so you can keep spying on me?"

"The cameras are recent, Sydney," he says. "I put them up a few days ago."

And just like that, I'm angry again.

"Do you know how it feels to have your trust violated by the one person who asked you to trust them?"

"I do. And I hate that you feel that way," he says. "I apologize, deeply and sincerely. But I still need you to trust me."

I stare at him. I can tell he really is sorry for making me feel this way, but I don't think he's actually sorry about doing it.

How deep does his obsession with me go?

How can I find out?

Or should I cut my losses and run?

"I want to go home," I say quietly. The admission surprises me, but the moment I say it, I know it's true.

Kincaid looks like I slapped him yet again. His face falls, his brow crinkling in something like sympathy, something like pity. "Where is home, Syd?"

And of course he's got me there. I have no home. No school, no job, no money, no prospects, no home.

You have nothing, a voice whispers in my ear. *You are nothing. Nothing but alone.*

That's when it strikes me, a poisoned lance that spears

deep in my heart, one I've tried so hard to shield myself against.

I am so alone in this world.

So completely unmoored, untethered, and alone.

I cover my face with my hands and burst into tears.

There's a pause, perhaps another look of shock from Kincaid, but then he's up and beside me, wrapping his arms around me and holding me against him. I press my palms against his chest, a feeble attempt to push him away, but his arms are strong and they keep me in place. He holds me, tight, so tight, until I relent and place my cheek against him. The tears stream down and he puts his palm at the back of my head.

"You're going to be okay," he murmurs. "Trust me, you're going to be okay."

How? I think. *How?*

"I have no one," I sob against him. "I truly have nobody. Not a single soul in this world loves me. Do you know how awful that feels?"

"I do," he says, kissing the top of my head. That makes me melt into him further, undoes another thread that was so tightly wrapped around me, that was holding me together. "I wish I didn't."

"I just thought I could still get through life without it mattering," I say, my chin trembling so hard that my words are staccato. "I thought I was okay with being alone, just me, stuck in my head with only myself for company. I've always been so different, but I took pride in it, and when others complained of loneliness, I thought that was something that happened to other people and not to me. But I was wrong. I was so fucking wrong."

He doesn't say anything to that, just continues to hold me, his palm cradling the back of my head.

And yet I can't stop the words from flowing any more than I can stop the tears. "I had my grandmother, she loved me more than anything. She loved me enough to make up for the loss of my mother. She loved me enough to fill that void when my father was gone, at sea for days and weeks at a time. And then I lost her. I lost her to that horrible disease, one that ripped me from her memory until I was nothing to her, a nobody."

I take in a shaking breath. "And then I thought that maybe I should become closer to my father, that this was a sign to try to get to know him better, even though he worked all the time. So I made the effort, and so did he. Our time was so brief. It was too brief. I finally felt like I saw the man in the shadows of my life, and then he was taken from me. We didn't have enough time together. We never have enough time!"

"I know," he says. "We don't."

"Now what? Now the only people who loved me uncon-ditionally are gone and I have no one else. There's just me. I only have myself, and I don't even feel like I know myself anymore. I don't even *like* her."

Silence fills the room. I can hear his heart beating against my ear, quick but steady. I inhale his scent, that sweet tobacco and cedar mixed with the warm santal from the candles.

"You'll find someone, one day," he eventually says.

"You don't know that," I snap, the anger at it all.

"But I do. Because I know you are someone worth loving. That you are worthy of being loved. And there is someone out there who will one day lay down their life for yours."

If he wasn't holding on to me, I think I'd be on the floor.

Can it be you? I think, settling deeper into his arms. *Can your obsession turn to love without either of us going up in flames?*

"You just need faith," he goes on, voice soft. "You just need patience. You just need to keep surviving for now. It won't always be this way, I promise."

"But I don't see the way out," I whisper. "I don't see how I'll ever stop being too much for someone. Too impulsive, too brash, too reckless, too self-centered, too cold, too sensitive, *too much*. Too me."

He exhales loudly and kisses the top of my head again, and my god, I want him, want him to be what's on the other side of being patient. Or being *a* patient.

"There is always a way out," he says. "Oh, Syd, sweetheart. If only you knew how much your words break me."

Sweetheart?

I pull back enough to glance up at him. He stares down at me, his eyes glassy with emotion.

"You're a good person," he says, swallowing hard. My eyes are glued to his lips, a compulsion running through me, something heavy in my veins that feels pulled to him, iron to a magnet.

I can't help myself.

I stand on my tiptoes.

And with the taste of my own tears, I kiss him.

CHAPTER 19

Kincaid kisses me back.

No hesitation.

Not even a little.

My lips press against his, my mouth parted slightly, and suddenly my whole world has been overturned. I melt into him, his lips soft yet hard, yielding to me for a moment before he lets out a whimper that resonates in my chest. It's a sound of yearning finally fulfilled, of emotion that's been trying to escape.

But that whimper swiftly turns into a throaty growl and he's kissing me like he's suddenly realized how ravenous he is, rough and commanding, taking what's his. I give myself to him, knees weak, wanting to be eaten up like dessert on a platter, wanting to be used by him in whatever way he chooses, so long as I'm devoured whole.

I'm yours, I'm yours, I'm yours.

He grunts into my mouth, his tongue licking inside mine, as he holds me by the back of the neck again, so possessive and strong.

Take, take, take.

Please, please, please.

Pleasure curls inside me like smoke, my skin erupting in goosebumps as his scent fills my nose, and the taste of whisky on his silken tongue clouds my head. My thighs squeeze together, trying to soothe the ache that has always been there for him, that ache that infiltrates my dreams.

And yet this still feels like a dream, a heady hallucination. Everything about him is so hard and soft at the same time, the wet, silky quality of his tongue as it fucks my mouth, the hard press of his lips, the tight grip of his hand on my neck, the other hand now gripping my jaw as if he thinks I might escape.

I could never escape this. He is the undertow, his kiss pulling me down to my fate. Or maybe it's my doom. It's too hard to tell.

Suddenly he pulls back. It's like an elastic band. I stare up at him, my body pressed against his, breathing hard. He's gazing wildly at me, his pupils dilated, his eyes dark under the shadow of his brow. In them I see bewilderment, shame, and something that ripples with so much intensity that I can't even recognize it.

"I can't do this," he says through a ragged inhale. "I can't do this."

"You're doing it," I tell him, my hand going to the small of his back and pressing him against me. His erection pushes into my thigh and I let out a gasp. Everything I dreamed is proving to be right.

"Fuck," he grunts, and I grind against him, wanting more of those delicious sounds.

"Yes, fuck me," I whisper, my hands going to his pants and trying to unbuckle the belt.

"Sydney," he rasps, his head going back, leaving his neck exposed. I stand on my toes and lick his Adam's apple, tasting of soap.

Another powerful grunt vibrates in his chest and I'm dropping to my knees, the rug soft on my bare skin.

"No, Syd," he says roughly, his eyes blazing with desire as he stares at me. "Please, I don't have the willpower."

"That's the idea," I say sweetly as I gaze up at him, unbuttoning his dark jeans and sliding the zipper down slowly. The sound is like thunder in the quiet of the room.

"I'm not allowed," he says, breathless, but then he's making a fist in my hair, pulling tight on my strands until I feel a spike of pain, the ache in my pussy intensifying.

"I won't tell anyone." I grin at him. "Just use me. Come inside my mouth and I'll be your little pet."

He swallows audibly, his throat shiny where I licked him. "Fuck, Sydney. Don't tempt me."

It's as if he doesn't know that I love to rebel against authority.

I reach into his pants and pull out his cock. It's so hot under my fingers, and I struggle to grasp the size of him, long, thick, and hard. The candlelight reflects on his swollen crown, a drop of precum glinting.

I lean forward and lick it up, sliding my tongue through the slit, pushing in slightly until he lets out a gasp. He yanks my hair, swearing, "Fuck, fuck, fuck."

God, I've never felt more powerful than I have here on my knees. I'm undoing this calculating and controlled—*obsessed* —doctor, and I can bring him pleasure that he's trying so hard to deny.

Obsess over me, I think. *Please. I need your obsession.*

I want his possession.

I open my mouth wide to take him, but now he's in control, forcing himself past my lips, holding my head down as he hits the back of my throat. I immediately force myself to relax, avoiding the gag reflex as he pushes in past the point of no return.

He's swearing again, quiet, rough remarks about how well he fits, how good I take him.

"I want you to choke on it," he says through a groan. "Dirty little slut."

Fuck.

The pulse between my legs is sharp now, a painful knot of pressure that screams for release. He knows exactly what to say.

Somehow I bring him in deeper, and his pace begins to quicken and quicken until suddenly he gasps and pulls back, his dick sliding out of my mouth.

"I can't," he says, though it's apparent he's struggling for breath, struggling to stay in control.

He tucks his cock back into his pants and zips himself up.

I can only stare at him, mouth open, shocked by his willpower coming through at the last possible minute.

He gazes down at me, that cock straining against his fly, begging to be free, and I watch the fight in those shadowy eyes, a battle between desire and the need to fuck, and duty and the need to stay professional.

"Crawl over to the desk," he commands.

I blink at him. "What?"

His jaw is tense as he repeats himself. "I said, crawl over to the desk, my little pet." He pauses. "That is what you wish to be called, isn't it?"

Oh *fuck* yes.

"Yes, doctor," I say, pouting slightly, as if he's inconveniencing me. Inside I'm fucking thrilled that he's actually asking me to do this. I don't think I've ever been so giddy and turned on in my life. It's making my head spin.

I crawl over, hands and knees on the hardwood and the rugs, and he walks backward in front of me, as if I'm trying to catch up with him but can't.

He stops in front of his desk and holds out his palm, commanding me to do the same.

I pause mid-crawl, dropping my upper body so that I'm on my elbows, so that he has a good view of my tits under the neckline of my top. I'm not sure if it helps that I've dreamt about being with him before, but there's something so natural about all of this. He runs his palm over his dick, giving it a squeeze through the fabric of his pants, his smoky eyes glued to my cleavage. He inhales sharply, the muscle in his jaw ticking, his neck corded as if he's bracing for something.

"Get on the desk," he orders.

I straighten up, about to ask him in which way, but he grumbles, reaches down and grabs me by the arms, hauling me roughly to my feet. Before I can do anything but gasp he puts his hands around my waist and picks me up, placing me on the desk.

He doesn't say anything else, just places his palm on my chest and pushes until my back is on his desk, my head hanging off one side, my legs hanging off the other.

Then he parts my legs with a bruising grip and reaches up to my hips, fingers curling over the waistband of my underwear. He starts bringing them down over my thighs, his movements urgent, like he's afraid he's going to change his mind.

"I'm going to hell," he murmurs.

But he doesn't stop.

If he's going, I'm going too.

He pulls my underwear to my knees then suddenly straightens up.

Leans over me. Reaches for something on the desk.

I raise my head up just in time for him to shove a pencil in my mouth.

"Bite down on that when you feel like screaming."

I smile, tasting the wood. Guess he already figured I'm a loud one.

Then he moves back into place between my legs, grabs my hips, and lowers his head.

My whole body tenses in anticipation, my fingertips digging into the desk.

But he doesn't do anything, not at first.

I can feel his breath tickling me, making my hips squirm, and I'm so close to just bucking up into his face so I can get some pressure, some sort of release.

"So fucking pretty," he says, his voice gruff, and it's apparent he's staring at my pussy, just open and on display for him. "So fucking *beautiful*."

He touches my clit with his fingertip and I grind my teeth against the pencil, moaning, wanting more. He rubs it slowly then drags his finger down, the pressure now like a feather, until it reaches where I'm terribly wet.

"So sweet," he groans, teasing around my entrance. "So desperate."

I gasp, agreeing with him, unable to keep from holding back. I try to thrust my hips toward him.

It only makes him withdraw his finger, leaving me to whimper.

"Such a greedy little cunt for such a good student," he surmises, his stark words making me feel dizzy with desire. "I can smell your desperation. I can see it."

I make a noise of want, muffled by the pencil.

He lowers his head and blows on me.

I shriek, the pencil nearly falling from my mouth.

Suddenly he's on me, devouring me with lips and tongue, a feverish attack, a messy one. He's licking me up and down, sucking my clit into his mouth, biting lightly, while his fingers start to fuck me by ones, by twos, by threes. He works them in and out of me while he devours and I am moaning, bucking, nearly falling off the desk.

Several times he has to grab my hips and pull me back down or pull me back up and then he's right back at eating me, like his appetite will never be vanquished.

This feels right. It feels like a million different things but it feels right.

Like I'm his to be tasted, like I'm his for whatever he wants.

In the back of my head, I know he's going to try and pull back after this, I know he's letting himself give in because he wants me that badly. But I'll worry about tomorrow, tomorrow. For now, my pussy is being ravaged by my psychologist, right on his office desk, and that's all I need. One good orgasm might undo weeks of strife.

"Oh fuck," he gasps against me, and his breath hitches, his body stiffening. Then a long moan that vibrates against my clit.

Did he just come?

In his pants?

The thought of it is enough to push me over the edge, to let go.

"God!" I cry out through the pencil as the orgasm slams through me, shaking my limbs, making my body feel like it's rising off the desk. An exorcism. I keep writhing, my eyes pinched shut but seeing stars, my nails clawing wildly at the wood, the air squeezed from my lungs. If he wasn't gripping my hips so hard, if his mouth didn't continue to eat with abandon, I think I might shatter into a million fragments.

At least the pencil does.

It snaps in half and I have to spit it out, the taste of wood and lead mixing with the highest point of ecstasy.

Finally he pulls back, breathing hard and I'm delirious with glee. My body twitches, effervescent.

He swallows audibly, a ragged exhale, and I raise my head to look at him, my abs burning.

His eyes are unfocused, the glassy grey of the inlet, as he grabs me by the elbows and pulls me forward so I'm sitting up right, then cups his hand over the back of my head. His forehead touches mine and we both try to get our breaths back.

No words are spoken.

None need to be said.

Not now.

Finally he lets go and straightens up.

My gaze drops to his crotch, seeing the wet spot.

I look up at him with a brow arched. He did come, didn't he?

He gives me a chagrined look that says *yes* and clears his throat. His mouth is shiny with my desire. "Some things can't be helped," he says, by way of explanation.

He's said this before and I have to agree.

Him, me, us, *this*…it can't be helped.

CHAPTER 20

"Today, we're in luck," Nick announces from the front of the Learning Centre. We've only just found our seats, tablets at the ready. "And it's a nice change of pace. We're going on a field trip."

"More foraging?" Rav says with a heavy sigh, leaning back in his chair as if he's being crushed by the thought.

"*No*," Nick says pointedly. "We'll leave the foraging for when we go on the camping trip to the peninsula next week. This morning I'm taking you to the—drumroll please." He does an exaggerated imaginary one that makes my eyes roll. "The propagation lab."

Oh? I sit up a little straighter. So does everyone else.

That *is* a nice change.

"Finally," Lauren says tiredly. "I thought we'd never make it over there."

I glance at her. Dark circles ring under her eyes, her face ashy. I look over at Munawar and Rav. They don't look much better. Even Munawar's shirt isn't a fungi-pun. Instead it's the Madrona Foundation's logo, which still features mushrooms, but somehow that's worse. Like he's becoming one of *them*.

Is this place getting to us all?

If this is what three weeks of fog will do to you, what will three months?

Or is it more than just the weather?

I swallow the pit of uneasiness in my stomach. It's something I'll have to talk to Kincaid about after lunch. I have a session with him, and it will be the first time seeing him since our tryst in his office.

I'm still not sure how I feel about what happened, though I've literally done nothing but think about it.

On one hand, *fuck*.

It was exactly what I wanted, what I needed. I thought nothing could top my dreams but Doctor Kincaid knew exactly how to fix me. At least in the moment. When I close my eyes I can still feel his tongue inside me, the rough way he held my hips, the fist in my hair. The dirty, thrilling way he obliged my kink, called me his little pet, like I was one of his possessions. I want all of that to happen again, and soon.

But on the other hand...it was hard to ignore the shame in his eyes.

That he crossed a line he didn't want to cross.

That he made a mistake.

Oh, his desire for me was more than apparent.

The way he ate me out with abandon.

The way he was so turned on that he came in his pants, like he was a horny teenager unable to control his hormones, not a neurosurgeon in his late thirties. I have to admit, that was the hottest fucking thing I've seen in a long time.

But he is my doctor.

I am his patient.

He is my teacher.

I am his student.

He says he's the one keeping me safe.

But every moment I'm with him, I feel I'm one step closer to danger.

I'm starting to hate this place and yet I've never felt so...*alive*.

And yet, as we get up and file out the door, following Nick as he leads us under the cedar boughs, ravens calling from the sky, I feel like death is around the corner. Perhaps not waiting for me, but waiting for someone. I feel it on my skin, like the clammy kiss of the damp air.

It's hard to ignore death when so many people have died here.

I push those thoughts out of my head. Perhaps I'm too morbid for my own good.

The propagation lab is past the maintenance yard and barn, the furthest building west on the property. The walk is fairly wet and muddy since it's been either raining or we've been blanketed by fog for the last few days. Our shoes squelch as we unsuccessfully try to avoid puddles. At least the clouds are moving fast today, a warm breeze coming from the ocean that brings the scent of seaweed at high tide.

Nick swipes his keycard and the door beeps. He pushes it open and flicks on the lights.

"Everyone spread out along the aisles and don't you dare touch anything," he says.

The excitement is palpable as we walk inside. It looks like a greenhouse except all the windows have been blacked out. Thin shafts of light pierce the places where the coverings don't quite reach, illuminating the dust and spores floating in the air. I get the feeling that they are retractable, able to usher in daylight when needed.

Instead of rows of plants, however, there are rows of fungi, some growing from mossy surfaces, others from soil. So many different kinds—bleeding tooth, ghost fungus, stinkhorns, amethyst deceivers. The air is musty with their scents, some sweet, some sour, and the metallic loam of the soil.

Nick is speaking but none of us are listening. It's impossible to corral us, we're like cats and the mushrooms are the catnip. We're spreading out down the aisles, marveling at all the different varieties, some of which are hard to grow outside of mother nature, touching while Nick continues to berate us for doing so.

"Look," Lauren coos, stopping to peer at some parrot waxcaps, elegant green fungi, their surface as shiny as lip gloss. "These are my favorite. I thought I'd have to go all the way to Australia to see them."

But while I see several of my favorites, many of which I still wonder at what magic—or science—Madrona has in order to grow them in such a setting, I don't see their famous *Excandesco*. I know they've said a few times now that they have struggled to replicate it in the lab, but I was still hoping it would be here. Or at least their attempts at it, though I'm sure they keep that under wraps too.

After a while though, I grow bored. The lab is starting to feel claustrophobic and stuffy. The fact that I can see all the spores floating around, probably remnants of the earth stars that shoot theirs out into the air, makes me a little wary about breathing them in. I know breathing in spores can't hurt you but...I don't know. This place is called a lab, after all. I don't want to take my chances.

"I need to get some fresh air," I tell Nick. "I'll just be outside."

"You okay?" he asks. "Smell can be gnarly, can't it?"

I just give him a close-lipped smile and head over to the door, pushing it open and stepping out into the fresh air. I have to blink at the light for a moment. The greyness feels like the sun after being in such a dark tomb.

I take in a few deep breaths, then my restlessness gets the best of me. I decide to walk to the barn. Though I've heard the goats at all hours and the roosters in the morning, I haven't actually gone to the barn yet, just walked past it.

There's a fenced paddock on one side of it where the goats

are grazing, and the chicken run on the other. I lean against the fence and decide to watch the goats for a bit. They're one of my favorite animals, and despite them being all creepy-eyed, I find them super cute and entertaining to watch.

But the moment I lean against the fence the goats all raise their heads to look at me. They bleat and cry and start running in the opposite direction, toward the far corner of the fence.

"What the fuck?" I mutter out loud. Since when do goats hate me? Most animals love me. Maybe they just don't get enough interaction here.

They're experimented on, I remind myself. *Remember what Everly said about the testing? They might not be here for goat milk.*

I shudder. I have always hated animal testing, even though I know it's necessary in some regards for medical science. Still, it's the worst aspect of getting into any neurobiology field. I know the testing on rats is what helps us develop the drugs that treat things like Alzheimer's, or hell, even Adderall would have been tested on them at first. But it doesn't mean I have to like it.

I decide to head over to the chicken yard instead, feeling the sting of the goat's rejection. The chickens at least run up to me, clucking about.

"I wish I had some food for you," I tell them.

They cock their heads in unison, demanding treats.

Suddenly a god-awful noise fills the air, like nails down my spine. The chickens all cluck at once in alarm.

It sounded like a baby goat but also…not a baby goat.

The wind blows around my hair, this time carrying a chill with it, and I look toward the entrance of the barn from which the sound came. It's dark. Darker than it seemed a couple minutes ago. I can barely see what's inside—some bales of hay, a few stalls.

The bleating shriek sounds again.

I jump.

It's louder now.

It sounds like something is in trouble, and as much as I'm already freaked out, that's something I can't ignore. Even though, as I step into the barn, I feel the darkness close around me. It's physical, like the damp air, a blanket to weigh me down.

A noose.

Go get Nick, I think. *Go and tell Nick.*

But like all those times before, my body moves without me telling it to. I feel wildly out of control, I'm just one foot in front of the other, going toward the terrible, terrible sound.

My heart is in my throat, my lungs shallow as low tide.

"Are you okay?" I manage to call out as I carefully creep forward into the darkness. Eventually my eyes adjust to the grey light coming in through the windows at the side, but it only deepens the shadows.

And then I see it.

Against the far wall, by the floor, something is writhing.

It's pink.

Shiny and pink and attached to the wall.

At first I think it's like a piglet that's stuck in some kind of web, or like the liquid stuff they use as insulation. Maybe it was stuck behind the wall and it's trying to burst through. My brain is going for the most rational explanations first, trying to make sense of what I'm seeing.

But as I step close and it opens its mouth and lets out another ear-piercing scream, one that cuts to the bone, I realize how horribly wrong I was.

A baby pig stuck in the wall makes sense in this world.

What I'm looking at doesn't make sense.

In any world.

It's a baby goat. Devoid of all skin. Just the pink, red, and deep burgundy layers of muscle, creamy lines of fat. It doesn't have any eyes; instead it has long snaking lines emerging from the sockets, blending into the wall, spreading up it like mold.

The goat thing screams again.

Revulsions slams through me and I vomit. I can't help it.

I throw up right on the concrete floor of the barn, unable to keep it in, unable to understand what I'm looking at, except to know that it's wrong. It's so wrong. My grandmother would be making the sign of the cross right now, swearing that this thing did not come from God, did not come from nature.

The goat doesn't notice. It struggles, the sound wet, sluicing, its bare muscles rippling as it tries to escape its fate. The white filaments coming out of its eyes are coming out of its mouth too, poking out beneath the muscles like snakes.

Mycelia, I think. *They're not filaments, they're mycelia.*

It's being devoured whole by the fungi.

I'm about to vomit again when suddenly I hear footsteps behind me.

I turn around, hand at my mouth, to see Nick walking toward me. With his face in silhouette, I can't see his expression, but even he is putting me on alert. It's the way he walks. Purposeful. Powerful.

"What is this?" I manage to say, trying to keep from throwing up again. "Nick. This poor baby goat. What's happening to it?"

He stops beside me, and I can finally focus on his face. Gone is the hippie surfer dude who catches the wave breaks not far from here. He's someone else now. Maybe the person he was always underneath.

"Something that you aren't to repeat to anyone else," he says. His brown eyes are hard, his words harder. "You didn't see any of this."

"But what is it?" I exclaim. "What happened to it?!"

He just stares at me. "You need to go back to your cohort and forget you ever saw this."

I shake my head. "I can't. I need to…"

The goat thing screams again.

"Please, just put it out of its misery!" I yell.

"I'll deal with it," he says. "Go back."

But I feel like standing my ground.

"Or what?" I ask.

His eyes narrow. So damn cold. So damn serious. "I'll get Everly and Michael to recite to you the NDA that you signed."

"It never said anything about not talking about the things while we're here!"

"Did you even read it?" he asks with a derisive snort. "I mean it, Sydney. Talk about this and you'll have a lawsuit on your hands. How the fuck are you going to pay for that? You don't have a job, you don't even have a scholarship. You have nothing."

My jaw clenches. Fuck him. He is just a bro in disguise, a corporate asshole underneath.

He jerks his head toward the light, and I go.

I'm both happy to be out of there and yet so fucking disturbed that when I leave the barn, I don't even bother catching up with the other students who have already walked ahead, dispersing for lunch.

I go right to Kincaid's office and bang on the door with my fist until he opens it.

His expression is both guarded and relieved. Happy to see me and yet…not.

"You're early," he says with a raise of his brow.

"Close the door," I say quickly, rushing in and sitting down in the chair, my head in my hands, rocking back and forth like a mental patient.

I hear him close it, then lock it, and he comes over to me, crouching beside the chair, hand on my knee. "Syd," he says softly. "What happened?"

I can tell from the way he says my name that he thinks I

had another episode. That I'm going to talk about Farida's ghost, or perhaps another student, or Amani.

I straighten up, moving my hands away. "I saw something just now. In the barn. Nick made me promise not to talk to anyone about it. Said the NDA is enforceable, even here."

"What was it?" he asks, gazing up at me, brow furrowed.

"Was that a lie, what he said about the NDAs?"

"You don't have to worry about that right now," he says calmly, giving my knee a squeeze. "You're allowed to tell me. Tell me what happened. What did you see?"

I take in a deep breath and fill him in, feeling queasy all over again. I can't get the image of the pink creature out of my head.

"What...*was* that?" I ask.

His face has remained impassive this whole time. Nothing of what I've said has surprised him.

"It sounds like something that belonged to the lab," he says.

"Something that you may have worked on?"

A dark brow arches up. "I have also signed NDAs, Syd."

I give him a dirty look. "Oh. I see. A little hard to trust you when you're not even allowed to be honest with me."

"That's what trust is," he says simply. "It's faith."

"Well, pardon me if I'm not feeling faithful at the moment. Everywhere I look here there's one steaming pile of lies after another."

"Lies in order to protect the foundation," Kincaid says, straightening up. He walks around his desk and sits down, folding his hands in front of him. Back to being my shrink again. "The work here is..." His eyes roam the room as he searches for the words. "Important."

"And mysterious."

The corner of his mouth lifts. "Very much so. We are doing good things here. I may not agree with Everly, Michael, or even Nick half the time, but I wouldn't be here if

I didn't think we were making a difference in the world. We have the ability to change disease. To change life. Prevent death."

I cross my arms and lean back in my chair. "You sound like you're reading from the company brochure," I grumble. "Oh, but wait, you're the one who wrote it."

He lets out a dry laugh. "I did."

But I don't find it funny.

"Should I be worried?" I ask.

"About what?"

I shrug, sighing as I drum my nails along the edge of the armrest. "The other day you said I should fear you. Then you ask me to trust you. You ate me out on this very desk, then you do your hardest to avoid me. I can't figure you out. I don't know if you're on my side. I don't know what sides there are."

"I'll never not admire how bold your choice of words are," he says, smiling slightly.

I look at him askew. "That's it? That's all you've got to what I just said?"

He stares at me for a long moment, frowning slightly. "I have much I would like to say, Syd. But much that I can't."

"Ugh, fuck this," I mutter, getting out of my chair. "Fuck you, Mr. Can't Tell Me Shit."

He's quick. He's around the desk and pushing me back against it, his hand at my throat. "Every single thing I do is in your best interest," he says, his voice tense, rough with warning. His eyes blaze like a thunderstorm. "You either trust me or you don't."

I swallow against his palm. "Hard to trust you when you're choking me, doctor."

His nostrils flare and his hand drops away. He clenches his teeth and looks away, though I'm still bracketed against the desk, the edge digging into my ass. My heart beats wildly against my ribs, wanting to provoke him more, push him over the edge so he can choke me, pull my hair, have his way with me again.

"Are you ashamed of what we did?" I whisper.

"No," he says quickly, his gaze snapping to mine. "Not even a little."

I smile slyly, satisfied with that answer. "You know, next time you can come inside me. You don't have to mess up your pants again."

I swear I see his cheeks go pink above his days old stubble. He lets out a small, embarrassed laugh. "You'll never let me hear the end of that, will you? My body acting like I'm in fucking high school again."

"I took it as a compliment," I tell him. "Still, the offer stands."

The levity in his eyes fades like a cloud darkening. "There won't be a next time, Syd."

I nod. For once I don't feel the crush of rejection because I know he's lying.

We are inexorable.

Locked-in.

He steps back from me, and I straighten up.

"Was that our session or am I free to go?" I ask.

He puts his hand at my back and guides me toward the door. "Let's take a rain check. I think you know now that you can talk to me at any time. For now, though, I need to talk to Nick."

My eyes widen with fear as we leave his office. "Are you going to tell him I told you?"

"You'll be fine. You're allowed to tell your doctor anything."

We step outside into the mist. I go one way toward the main lodge, and he goes toward the lab.

Suddenly Clayton steps out from behind a tree.

"You saw it, didn't you?" he says.

He looks fucking awful, and it makes me realize I didn't

see him in the lab today, nor have I seen him much over the last few days. His absence has been refreshing, but still I'm a little concerned.

Especially at the wild look in his eyes.

He looks absolutely feral, and not in a good way.

"See what?" I ask uneasily. I look around for a way out and see it in the form of Kincaid who has spotted Clayton and is striding purposefully toward us.

"The experiment," Clayton says. "Sometimes they escape. But you knew that already, didn't you? You've seen them."

Is he talking about the wolf?

Wait. Amani?

"Clayton," Kincaid barks as he gets closer. "I need a word with you."

"Am I in trouble, professor?" Clayton sneers, stepping back.

"You know you're supposed to leave Sydney alone," he says, glancing at me briefly. My heart twists at how possessive and protective he is, yet there's an uneasiness deeper down. I have to wonder if Kincaid already gave him the lecture about following me.

Clayton just laughs. Loud and unhinged.

I can't help but move back.

Something isn't right with him.

I give Kincaid a look like he needs counseling asap but Kincaid only nods at me in return.

"You better go, Sydney," he says grimly.

I stand there, looking between the two of them, before I nod and walk off.

When I reach the lodge, I look over my shoulder, but they've both disappeared.

CHAPTER 21

"OH MY GOD, SUNSHINE," Lauren exclaims as we step out of the lodge. "And holy fuck I think we can actually see the peninsula."

We walk over to the totem pole for a closer look, and sure enough, beyond the sparkling inlet and the forest of fir and hemlock on the other side, the mountainous mass of the Brooks Peninsula rises up into the blinding blue sky.

"I was starting to think it didn't exist," I say, taking a sip of my coffee from the paper cup, though now I don't think I need the caffeine. The change in weather alone is enough to perk me up.

It does the same to the rest of the students, everyone a little louder, with a little more spring in their step as we walk over to the learning center. The air is cool and soft, smelling of cedar and fresh-cut grass, birds call out from the trees, and everyone looks a bit healthier in the bright light.

Which is good timing because the camping trip is tomorrow and it would suck if the weather was awful. I once went camping with my father when I was eight years old, in Redwood National Park, and it poured the whole time.

Looking back, it's one of my fondest memories of my childhood because I actually had my father's undivided attention, and I felt like the luckiest girl in the world despite the water seeping into our tent, but my poor father complained endlessly, feeling bad. Obviously he really wanted to have the perfect trip with his little girl.

Tears well in my eyes at the memory, grief as slippery as an eel.

We head inside the classroom and take our seats. Kincaid is at his usual spot, leaning against the desk, his arms crossed over his chest. He's wearing a dusky blue button-up that matches his eyes, the sleeves rolled up. I can't believe he's had my vagina in his mouth and yet I haven't seen the full extent of his tattoo.

"Morning," he says gruffly to the class. "Today we're going to spend our time discussing the camping trip to the Brooks Peninsula tomorrow. We'll be leaving bright and early, six a.m., so it's best that we go through it all now. This is a trip for all students, including those in marine sciences, and it's something we all need to be fully prepared for."

He pauses and clears his throat. "Before we get into that, however, I must inform you that a student had to be sent home. Clayton Wade."

I stiffen, my stomach twisting in knots.

Murmurs fill the room as we all look around, noticing he's not here.

What the hell?

"Unfortunately," Kincaid goes on, avoiding my eyes as I stare blatantly at him, "Clayton wasn't adjusting to life at Madrona the way that we had hoped. He was put on the first seaplane out this morning. Let this be a warning to all of you —if any of you are struggling in any way, please come talk to me. Schedule an extra counseling session if you can. This is a wild, tough land to inhabit, even with all the comforts of the lodge, and the isolation can get to even the hardiest of minds."

Kincaid then starts discussing the trip, but I'm no longer listening. Clayton was acting strange yesterday. Hell, he's been strange this whole time. I have to wonder what he discussed with Kincaid the other day. What was it that made him want to leave? He was a creep that seemed to mistrust the foundation, but I never heard him say he wanted to go, just that his fortune teller told him he wouldn't.

Wait, Kincaid said that Clayton was put on a plane, making it seem like it wasn't Clayton's idea. Was he forcefully removed from the premises?

Was it because of me?

Lauren nudges me. "Should be nicer without him around," she whispers. "Did you get Clayton in trouble?"

I shake my head. "Not on purpose," I whisper back.

Kincaid's focus is on me now so I press my lips together and force myself to pay attention.

When class is over, however, I head right to his desk, wanting to ask him what really happened with Clayton, because I'm not sure it's as simple as all that. But as soon as I approach, Everly enters the learning center.

"Good morning, Syd," Everly says to me cheerfully, though her smile is strained. Even in the morning she looks chic with a matching black yoga set that shows off her long skinny legs. "Sorry to cut you off at the pass, but I need to speak to Wes. Alone."

I look at Kincaid and he just gives me a subtle nod.

"Okay, no worries," I tell them, playing it cool. Of course, I only say no worries when I am absolutely full of worries.

I open the door, looking over my shoulder to see Everly's sharp eyes on me, waiting for me to leave.

Where am I?

Where the *fuck* am I?

Is this another crazy dream?

I sit up.

It's pitch black and I'm outside.

Not in my bed, not in my room, but *outside*.

Oh my god, oh my god.

I start feeling around with my hands, brushing over moss and ferns and twigs.

I can hardly breathe. Blood pounds in my head.

I know I'm not asleep. Everything is too real. Too cold. I can feel moisture seeping in through my pajama bottoms, the ground damp, the air thick and clammy. I breathe in sharply, my lungs weak and shallow, my nose catching the scent of the sea and pines and petrichor.

It's so dark, too dark.

How did I end up here?

Did I sleepwalk?

Was I...taken?

There's a helplessness embedded in my bones and I fear that most of all. Because this shouldn't be possible and my mind is no longer my friend.

My mind is turning on me.

And I am terrified.

So I sit, frozen in fear, unable to move. My eyes are starting to adjust, picking out the outlines of the trees above me, their branches moving in the breeze. Far in the distance I see the glow of a light, which hopefully means I'm not far from the lodge.

I need to get up, I need to work my way through the woods, toward the light.

And yet I wonder if I can just stay where I am. Stay still. Stay hidden. If I lie back down and fall asleep, will I wake up in my bed again? The last thing I remember was after dinner packing for the camping trip in one of the backpacks they loaned us, then getting into bed when the sky wasn't even dark yet, a bruised twilight.

You're losing it, I tell myself. *You're truly losing your mind. You've been losing it all this time.*

I have to find Kincaid. I have to talk to him.

I dig my fingers into the moss, cool, soft and damp, trying to feel what's real, trying to hold on to reality.

But the more I dig my fingers in, the deeper they go, until my fist is buried and I have a terrible feeling that something is going to reach out from underneath, grab my hand and pull me down.

I suddenly yank my hand out, the thought enough to get me up on my feet. I stumble, off-balance on the uneven ground, and I'm about to fall sideways when my hands catch the rough bark of a Sitka spruce.

It's a wide, rough trunk, an old tree, and I lean against it, trying to catch my breath, trying to push away all the scary images I have about what lurks beneath the moss, what hides between the trees. It feels like something is watching me, perhaps many somethings.

Stop that! I chide myself. *Stop thinking like that. Find your way to the light!*

But the tree feels comforting. The more I lean my head against it, the more I swear it whispers: *rest, rest, rest.*

It's just the wind, though, moving the branches above me.

It's just the wind that says, *stay, stay, stay.*

That whispers, *Sydney.*

Sydney, you're home.

I straighten up, my heart pounding. The wind is playing tricks on me. Everything here plays tricks on me, even the people.

Especially the people.

I take in a deep shaking breath, my body trembling.

I start walking, grateful for my slippers, one uneven step in front of the other, my ankle nearly giving out on a few occasions. My eyes have adjusted enough to see that I'm in a small, open area in the middle of the forest and as long as I don't look directly at the far-off light, I can see where I'm going.

That is until my toe catches on something, and with a cry, I go flying to the ground, landing in a pile of soft earth.

Soft, overturned earth.

I gasp, pushing myself upright but my hands sink in until the dirt is at my elbows. I'm about to panic when I realize that what I thought were stars behind my eyes are actually stars in front of my eyes.

The ground is covered in them.

Teal glowing stars with orange underneath.

Excandesco.

Excandesco, which means to flare and burn in Latin.

I'm staring at the Madrona mushrooms, glowing in their bioluminescence, and they're all around me, lighting up the earth like fallen stars.

I marvel at them, feeling like I'm floating in the phosphorescent sea, but there's a warning digging at the back of my skull. Something telling me to get up and keep moving. Something that says I need to get out of there, now.

I try to move, my knees sinking into the dirt now. For a second, I have a stupid worry about having to launder my damn pajama pants again, but that thought is quickly wiped away when I realize what this mound of soil I'm sinking into actually is.

It's a grave.

It's the dog's grave that Lauren and I stumbled upon.

It's been unearthed.

And I'm crawling in it.

Nope, nope, nope, I think as revulsion rolls through me, about to pull my hand out when something in the soil starts to wrap around my wrist.

I scream.

I rip my hand out in a panic, frantically crawling through the grave, crushing the mushrooms, dirt flying everywhere, until I finally reach hard ground. I stagger to my feet, running straight into a tree that nearly knocks me backwards again, and I look wildly for the light.

I push off the trunk, lungs squeezing, heart galloping as I try to run through the dark forest, branches scratching at my body, pulling at my hair like they mean to hold me captive. I can't help but feel like something is still around my wrist and I keep touching it to make sure there's nothing there, brushing all the dirt off me as I go, zigzagging through the trees.

I'm close to the light when suddenly the air changes, and I feel something heavy at my back.

A dark presence, suffocating and ominous.

Dread personified, looming behind me.

Coming after me with the snap of branches and a low, hungry *growl*.

I yelp and push myself to run harder and faster than I ever have, until I burst through the trees and find myself behind the Panabode cabins. I've never been so happy to see Madrona Lodge before.

I keep running though, down the winding paths, straight to the ramp. I clamor down as it shakes wildly, then speed along the dock, nearly slipping twice before I reach Kincaid's boat.

I scramble onboard, half crawling, my slippers nearly coming off as I fall onto the deck.

"Kincaid," I cry out, my voice hoarse.

The sound of the salon doors swinging open.

"Sydney," he cries out, and then he's wrapping his arms around me, pulling me to my feet.

I collapse into his arms. "Oh god. It was awful."

"You're shaking like a leaf," he says, running his hands down my arms. "Your skin is ice cold. What happened?" He pulls a few leaves from my hair and stares at them in amazement.

"Didn't you hear me scream?" I ask.

He shakes his head. "Come, let's go inside, I'll make you a tea."

I nod as he leads me over to the doors and helps me down the steps. He grabs a blanket and puts it over my shoulders, then sits me down on the couch.

"What happened?" he asks again, going to the sink and filling the kettle with water. The boat's cozy low lighting and the warmth from the heater is already making my heart slow, the fear seeming further away. I have to look down at my nails, at the dirt embedded in them, to remember what happened was real.

It *was* real, wasn't it?

I take in a deep breath, slowly exhaling before I start. "I woke up in the forest. I have no idea how I got there. I went to bed early after I packed for the camping trip and the next thing I knew, I was lying on the forest floor."

He pauses. "I see." He puts the kettle on the stove. "And then what happened? You said you screamed."

"I got up and saw the light from the lodge, tried to find my way out when I..." I decide not to tell him about the wind and the trees whispering my name.

Telling me I was home.

"Yes?" he prods, lighting the stove and coming back to sit across from me, hand on my knee. "What?"

"I fell into a grave. That dog's grave that Lauren and I discovered. Grover. It was covered in the glowing mushrooms. It was empty, like someone had dug it up or...whatever was buried had crawled out."

If it was even dog, I think. I know I heard a growl of something behind me, but that could have been anything.

Anyone.

Oh god.

I look at Kincaid fearfully. "I know you must think I'm crazy."

"I don't," he says but he's frowning, breathing in deeply through his nose. "I'm just trying to tackle this one step at a time. The first and most important thing is figuring out how you woke up in the forest."

I nod. "Yes. Exactly. So how did that happen?"

"If only I still had cameras in your room, we could see for ourselves," he says quietly. God, he's right. Maybe he should put them back. "But we can only speculate. Do you have a history of sleepwalking?"

"When I was younger."

"Just like your nosebleeds." I nod. "Have you had any more?"

I think about when Amani had hit me in the face with a snowball. Had the snow cut me or was my nose bleeding?

"I'm not sure."

His brows knit together. "You're not sure?"

"Maybe. I was hit in the face with a snowball. It's hard to say if the ice cut me or not."

He blinks slowly, then sits up straight. "A...what? A snowball?"

"I woke up in the middle of the night and Amani led me outside to the field, where it started snowing. She threw a snowball at me."

"When did this happen?" he asks carefully.

"I don't know. Time is a blur. A week ago?"

His gaze sharpens, the grey becoming flint. "And you

never told me. You know you're not supposed to keep secrets from me."

I laugh. "Oh, how the tables have turned. Sorry I didn't tell you, guess I was distracted by a million other fucking things happening that I have no explanation for."

He stares at me for a moment, the wheels turning behind his eyes. "It's interesting."

"Oh yeah, snow in June and having ghosts wallop snowballs at you is real *interesting*."

"Amani isn't a ghost," he says. "As far as I know, she's not dead. She was here and then she went home."

"So then what? I'm hallucinating her?"

"Yes. That is the most logical explanation. Same as when you saw her before."

"Then the snowball was a hallucination too?"

"It can be."

"And snow in June?"

"We're too close to the ocean for that to happen. On the surrounding mountains? Sure, if a strange cold front moved in from the north. But not down here."

Well, fuck.

So I really did just imagine the whole thing.

Wait.

Or did I?

"What happened with Clayton?" I ask suddenly.

His gaze thins. "What do you mean?"

"You know what I mean," I tell him. "One minute he's harassing me, the next he's being sent home on a seaplane."

"I thought that would have made you happy," he says stiffly.

"Happy?" I exclaim. "You did that for me?"

"Of course."

I can't help but stare at him. "You put Clayton on the seaplane and sent him home? For me?"

"I did."

I can't decide if this is terribly romantic or something else.

"What…" I begin. "And he went willingly?"

He nods.

But I don't believe him.

I remember Everly coming in to talk to him this morning. "Did Everly know?"

"She knew he was being a nuisance to you. She wanted him gone. So I got rid of him."

Got rid of him.

Just like they got rid of Amani…

CHAPTER 22

"IT'S BETTER NOW that Clayton is gone," Kincaid says, getting up and going to the kitchen. "He was trouble. Shouldn't have been accepted to begin with, but sometimes Michael and Everly take pity on those less fortunate, students that don't have a lot of family or money."

"People like me," I say as he pours tea into the mugs.

"No," he says sharply. "You're smart. Your grades prove it. You have potential. You're not here out of pity."

"That's hard to believe when my grandmother and father's death keeps being brought up, as well as my lack of funds." I think about what Nick said, that I don't have a job, or scholarship. That I had nothing. "There was that space on the application form that asked us to list any hardships we had gone through. I regret filling that out now."

And my mind is running away on me, my mind that I can no longer trust.

What do I actually think happened? That Kincaid murdered him?

No.

But if I start hallucinating him, like I hallucinated Amani, then something else is going on and it's not the fault of my brain.

He brings me the mug of chamomile tea and sits down. Sighing, he runs his hand over his face, and I glance at the brass clock on the wall, realizing it's two in the morning. No wonder he's exhausted, I woke him up mid-sleep.

Then again, he's wearing his clothes, so I guess he was already awake.

"I know this is scary, Syd. But everything you've told me isn't surprising."

"What about the unearthed grave? I hope that was surprising."

"It was," he says slowly. "But it was dark. You don't know what you fell on."

I'm about to protest, to tell him I know it was the grave. But maybe he's right. It was pitch black. I could have been anywhere. It could have been any lump of dirt.

"But the mushrooms, the *Excandesco*," I tell him. "I saw them glow."

"They do glow at night, faintly, but especially when disturbed. But they aren't that rare. I'm sure we will find some on our trip—" He eyes the clock. "In four hours."

I know this is the right time to say hey thanks for the tea and company and head back to my room to try and get some sleep, but I'm not leaving. I feel undone and unfulfilled.

"Then how did I end up in the forest?"

"My honest opinion is that you were sleepwalking. Just like with your nosebleeds, you're reverting back to when you were younger. Regression is common under high stress situations. It can also show up as hallucinations. We talked about this at the beginning, how even feeling an affinity to Amani in such an isolated, lonely place can make our brains latch on. And you've said yourself that you weren't in a healthy place mentally before you came here."

"Unhealthy enough to hallucinate?"

"You told me you have nothing, Syd. No home, no family, nothing. You lost your scholarship, your lifeline to your degree. Yes. I think that's enough. That's enough to push anyone's mind over the edge." He takes a long sip of his tea. "Sometimes our brains have a hard time letting go. Letting go of events, letting go of places, letting go of people…"

"Is that why you have lipstick in your bathroom?" I spring on him, deciding to turn the tables.

Shame rains down on his face. He looks down at his mug, the steam rising, and doesn't answer.

"Is that your ex's lipstick?" I ask.

He nods.

My heart pinches in response.

"How long ago was it when she was last here?"

"A few years," he says.

I try to act casual and blasé, as if it doesn't bother me that he still keeps her stuff after all this time. "Well, you should probably throw it all out because it's past its expiration date. No one wants to put on moldy La Mer."

"Moldy La Mer," he repeats, smiling softly. "Perhaps we could study it in the lab. Might be even better than the original."

I'm too tired to find it funny. "Since it's so rare for you to talk about yourself, don't mind me while I psychoanalyze the torch you carry for her."

"It's just lipstick, Syd," he says. "It doesn't mean anything."

"So why did you really break up?"

"I told you."

"But…isn't love about sacrifice? I know that if I truly loved someone I would have put up with whatever inconvenient location I had to live in."

"Perhaps our relationship wasn't as strong as I thought," he says bitterly, his gaze unkind. "Sometimes when people fall in love, they stay in love, because they were lucky. Other people have a wrench thrown into their relationship. Sometimes other people enter the picture and fuck things up. You don't know what you'll survive until something like that happens."

"So shit got fucked up and then Keiko Lynn took that opportunity to go back to Japan."

"Are you done?" he asks testily.

I shrug. "I just don't get how you can be hung up on the past and yet…"

"And yet what?"

I shake my head. "Nevermind." I take a long sip of tea.

"And yet what?" he repeats, putting his hand on my arm, the grip firm.

"And yet find yourself fixated on me."

Part of me wants to look away, because what I've said is just so raw, for both of us, but I force myself to meet his eyes. They blaze as they hold me in place, the intensity enough for me to cause the hair on my arms to rise.

"Because you are my future, Syd," he says, his voice low and gruff. "Because that's all there is. The past doesn't exist anymore. Only now and tomorrow is what does. And I want you—now and tomorrow."

Before I can say anything, he leans forward and grabs my face, pulling me into a hard, deep kiss that makes my toes curl. I melt into him, surrendering all control as he claims me with his mouth. He tastes like flowers from the tea, like mint toothpaste, smells like home: the trees, the wild ocean.

That whimper rises up from him again, rattling his chest, sinking into my bones—a plea, a promise, desperation for me, for more. Our kiss deepens suddenly, like a ravenous beast has been unleashed, his tongue strong as it fucks my mouth, everything becoming wet and messy and raw.

Oh god, I think as the pleasure spikes through me. *This might be the best kiss I've ever had.*

I never want him to stop.

And yet, greedily, I want more.

I want to feel this way across my entire body. Not just my mouth claimed, but every inch of skin.

The grip on my jaw tightens as another hand goes to my neck, choking me slightly, pressing on the windpipe enough to cause me to suck in air, the threat of suffocation.

He pulls away, breathing hard, his mouth wet as he stares at me with heavy-lidded, burning eyes. His grip on my neck remains, possessive, on the border of being too much, while his other hand lets go of my chin and starts unbuttoning the front of my pajama top.

"I am a fool," he murmurs as he swiftly undoes my shirt. "I am but a weak fool when it comes to you, sweetheart."

He slides his hand inside my open top and gently cups my breast, his thumb slowly rolling over my nipple. I gasp, the nerves shooting straight to my core, heat pooling between my legs.

"God, you're perfect," he says, his other thumb now massaging my throat as he continues to hold me in place. His head dips down and he licks at my breast, tongue strong and flat, sucking in my nipple until my head rolls back and I'm writhing against him. The pressure on my neck increases, and I'm feeling lightheaded, and I never want him to stop.

But then suddenly he does stop, releasing my neck just as I let out a moan.

"Sorry," he says, giving me a sheepish look that contradicts the storm in his eyes. "Choking you is the last thing I should do."

I swallow, my neck already tender. "Then what's the first thing you should do?"

A wicked grin flashes across his face, a dimple appearing in his stubble.

He reaches down and grabs me by the waist, hauling me up and flipping my stomach down onto the table, knocking over the tea, the contents spilling everywhere.

I let out a yelp of surprise and he grunts, pushing me down with one hand, the other yanking down my pants and underwear until I'm totally bare.

He lets out a hiss, pausing for a moment, then grabs my arms and holds my wrists at the small of my back.

"I have this need to restrain you," he murmurs, his voice thick with lust. "To pin you down like a butterfly. To marvel at your beauty but to know that you are caught, that you are mine." He exhales a shaky breath. "Does that scare you?" he adds quietly. "There's not many women who understand the things I desire, at least in the bedroom."

"It scares me in the best way," I tell him, my voice muffled as my cheek rests against the table. "And I understand completely. It's what I need."

"You will want a safe word. Something that lets me know I'm taking things too far. I don't wish to harm you in any way."

"Ocean," I say, the word just coming to me.

He lets out a happy sigh. "Ocean. That's perfect. You're perfect for me, Syd."

Because you have found a kindred spirit in me, a depraved soul who knows your depraved soul, I think, but I don't voice this to him. It's too cheesy and sentimental, too much for what's actually going to happen, which is pure, raw sex. I can be this way when something finally feels good and right; I fall fast but I never keep it to myself. I have to tell the world, or at least the person I have feelings for, which only makes them run.

Which is why I tell him, "Restrain me. Please, doctor."

At least one of us won't be able to run.

He swallows thickly, lust clouding his eyes.

"Don't fucking move," he says, harkening back to my dream.

Is it possible that my dreams are of the future?

While he disappears somewhere in the boat, I look up at

the painting on the wall. In the dream it was one of the grave, but now it's the eagle again, thank god. I shut the memory of the night out of my mind, refusing to think about what transpired right before I got here.

Kincaid comes back into the cabin. "Good girl," he says, the praise making me blush. "How well you follow my instructions. Perhaps I'll be more lenient on you."

"Don't," I tell him, pressing my cheek against the wood. "I don't deserve it."

He chuckles and I hear the smooth sound of something being unraveled.

Rope.

"You're right about that, my pet," he growls. "But I'm the one who gets to judge, not you. Now shut the fuck up and don't speak until you're spoken to."

Holy fuck. Yes, doctor.

He grabs my wrists again, wrapping rope around them. Unlike the one in my dream, this rope is soft and smooth, the same kind used for the sails on deck. When he finishes with my wrists, he brings the rope underneath my body, wrapping it up to my shoulders and back down over the bottom of my ass and over my thighs, keeping them together until I'm restrained all over.

The fact that he's using Shibari rope bondage on me makes me want to melt into the table.

You're a dream come true, I can't help but think. Literally.

"Perfect," he murmurs roughly, gliding his hand over me, following where the ropes criss-cross my body. "Almost a masterpiece."

Then I hear him undo his belt, the slick slide of leather. It makes my heart pound against my chest, and my body feels like it's on fire. I brace myself, waiting for him to whip me with it.

But to my surprise he wraps the belt around my throat, tightening it like a collar. Not enough to choke me but enough to keep me under control, which he demonstrates by giving it a tug.

"There," he says. "Now it's a masterpiece. Now you're truly mine."

I hear him take off his Henley and his pants. I try to turn around and look at him but he tugs on the belt sharply as a warning. "Stay," he commands.

I swallow against the leather and nod, though I find it criminal that he's staring at me all tied up and naked and I can't even get a look at his body, or his tattoo. At least I already know what his cock looks like.

He positions himself behind me, long fingers curling over the rope around my waist, while his other hand pushes down at it where it hugs the bottom of my ass, making room for his cock. The head of his dick presses between my legs, teasing where I'm wet.

"Soaked," he says gruffly. "All this for me." I can hear him smile. "You're going to need it."

He pushes inside me with one hard, stretching thrust.

I cry out, stars behind my eyes as his cock sinks in deeper, all the way to the hilt. He groans loudly, his breath ragged as he inhales.

"Fuck, your cunt is tight," he grinds out, both hands now curling around the rope, holding on.

I am fucking tight. My eyes are watering from the intrusion, his dick shoved in so deep that I can't even breathe. I'm stretched so far that the pain showers down on me like sparks.

"Breathe," Kincaid says as he slowly pulls out, his length dragging over every nerve. "Breathe, my pet. Breathe through it. You can take it, I know you can."

I suck in a breath, holding it in before exhaling, and the pain starts to turn to pleasure, the agony melting until my cunt is throbbing and pulsing with need.

"Fuck, yes," he rasps, "that's it. That's it, sweetheart. Keep taking it."

He pushes in again and this time I'm ready, expanding around him, the tight, slick glide of him hitting my g-spot, making my core feel like it might explode.

"You'll let me use you," he says breathlessly as he starts to pound away at me, his hips pistoning against my ass. "Tell me you're mine to use."

"I'm yours to use," I say through a gasp.

"Tell me to fill you up until it's coming out your mouth," he grunts.

Oh, Jesus have mercy.

"Fill me up until it's coming out of my mouth," I say, adding, "Doctor, please."

"Shit," he swears. "You know exactly what to say. Such a little slut, aren't you? Just willing to be used like this, used solely for my fucking."

"Yes," I cry out. My body shakes on the table, the whole boat now starting to list back and forth from his relentless movement. "Use me, please. Take what you want, I beg you."

A low, rumbling sound emits from his chest as he picks up the pace. There's subtle cruelty in his fucking, his movements rough as he plunges into me, his hands yanking at the ropes until they dig deep into my skin. Every now and then he grabs the belt and yanks at it like a leash, pulling my head off the table, and he's muttering things like, "you take me so well, good girl, greedy little slut, yes just like that."

Meanwhile my clit is so swollen, so needy for release that I start squirming on the table, trying to adjust my hips so that the hard ridge of his cock rubs against it, but he only pushes me back down.

"Beg me for it," he growls.

"Please," I try to say, but my words are weak, trembling, my body trying to break against the ropes that hold me in place. I've never felt so desperate before, like it's a creature trying to crawl out of me. "Please let me come."

He grunts again and then reaches down, stroking my clit.

I'm so wet, so wild, that it only takes one hard pass of his finger before my orgasm crashes over me. I erupt with a cry that fills the boat, that must soar up into the sky and down into the ocean below. If it weren't for the ropes restraining me, I am certain there would be pieces of me spread across the waves. I'm sure it would be impossible to put me back together. Where my body can't go, my mind does, floating and freewheeling as it gathers up a million different emotions like a tumbleweed.

He pumps hard, a couple of short, deep thrusts before he stills and releases with a loud, breathless groan.

"Sweetheart," he rasps. "You're too good."

He pushes in one last time, grunting as he goes, and then he leans forward, one hand bracing himself on either side of me. Breathing hard, he places shaky kisses down my spine before he undoes the belt around my neck.

"You're perfect," he tells me again, his voice gravelly. "So obedient and willing for me."

I feel like I'm dissolving into the table. To my surprise, I have tears in my eyes, every feeling inside my chest stirred up like sediment.

He reaches around and starts undoing the rope next, sliding it out from under my body until I feel released. "Stay here, please," he whispers, and honestly I couldn't move even if I tried.

I hear the tap running and then he comes back and presses a warm wet cloth between my legs, cleaning me up with so much tenderness that my heart flutters.

I exhale and close my eyes, relishing the feeling of being cared for, doted on. I may not have anyone in my life to love me, but at this moment, somehow I feel loved.

Then he whispers for me to sit up. He helps me to my

knees then bends over the table and literally picks me up. I'm a heavy girl but he does it with ease and carries me, pressed against his bare chest, through a narrow door to the captain's quarters.

He lays me down on a V-shaped bed. I stare at him. Though he's lit from behind, I can still make out the tattoo on his arm. A raven, with a faint moon behind it, its feathers trailing down to his forearm.

"What does your tattoo mean?" I whisper.

"It means I like ravens," he says, but there's levity in his voice. "To many local tribes here, a raven is known as the keeper of secrets."

Very apt indeed.

"To me," he continues, "they are omens, but where one can decide whether it's good or bad. It reminds me of perspective. And to be frank, it reminds me of here. I got this tattoo done during a supply run to Campbell River, back when I was new to Madrona and in love with this nature. I still am."

"Ravens are also psychopomps," I tell him, remembering my lit classes, and also because I like the word psychopomp. "Connecting the living world with the world of the spirits. A mediator between life and death."

"I like that," he says, giving me a soft smile before he climbs into bed with me, pulling up the covers. "But I don't want you thinking about death right now. I want you to sleep. We have to be up in a couple of hours."

He pulls me to him so that he's spooning my back. I twist around slightly, looking up through the glass hatches to see a million stars in the sky. They make me feel so small and inconsequential that I have to look away. I snuggle back into Kincaid as he drapes his arm around me and holds me tight.

"I can fix you, Syd," he whispers in my ear.

"How?"

"Trust me."

CHAPTER 23

WE START off the trip into the peninsula, not by hiking, but by ATV. When we all met by the totem pole just as the sun was coming over the ridge, we were led by Nick over to the ATVs parked in the maintenance yard. Kincaid showed up a minute later, then Dr. Hernandez with a cart full of supplies, plus tents, one to each person.

It was hard not to look at Kincaid, to pretend that we hadn't been in each other's arms until his alarm went off at 5 a.m. and I had to run to my room to shower and get ready. It helps that I'm so exhausted I can barely see straight.

But the ATV is waking me up. I'm sitting beside Lauren and Munawar. Rav and Patrick are in the front beside Dr. Hernandez who is driving us to our drop-off point. The other two vehicles are driven by Nick and Kincaid, taking the rest of the students and supplies. I purposely picked the one with Hernandez, which prompted an odd look from Lauren. Truth is, I need some space away from Kincaid to clear my head— I'm so afraid that everything we did last night is visible, like he scrawled his lust on my body. Which I suppose he did, but those rope marks are hidden.

And I wasn't about to sit with Nick, not after the baby

goat incident. Now that I've seen that dark side of him, now that I've seen his surfer persona is an act, I don't want anything to do with the guy. He officially gives me the heebie jeebies. Between him and Michael, I wonder who will give me the creeps at Madrona next.

The trip on the ATV is supposed to take about 90 minutes, following a logging road as it heads toward the peninsula. The weather isn't as beautiful as it was yesterday. There's morning fog in patches and some clouds in the sky, but it's still dry and warm, and when the sun does burst through it illuminates the scenery in a million shades of green.

I remember being awed by all that green the first day I got here, even though it had been cloudy at the time. Feels like a million years ago. Time has ceased to exist here at Madrona, and if it weren't for the weather getting incrementally warmer as the days go by, along with the flowering of the Nootka roses and blackberry bushes, I wouldn't even notice spring blending into summer.

"Oh look!" Lauren says, nudging me to look at a black bear and her cubs off in the distance. One of the moments again where I wish I had my camera. I make a note to ask Kincaid if he brought his Polaroid. I'm sure we'll see lots of wildlife on our actual hike.

Suddenly, I picture the baby goat stuck on the wall of the barn and I feel sick to my stomach. That image will forever be burned into my brain. That knowledge that Madrona is doing something they shouldn't be doing.

"What's wrong?" Lauren asks, leaning in to be heard over the roar of the ATV and the crunch of the rocks beneath the tires.

I shake my head, Nick's threat ringing in my head. "Just a little motion sickness," I say loudly and we bump around. "How are you feeling? You still thinking of going home?"

"I don't know," she says. "Now that we're out here in the wild?" She leans back, closing her eyes and breathing in deep.

"No, not really. I've been looking forward to this damn trip ever since they announced it. I don't even know if there's a point to it, I mean why are the marine sciences people like Justin and Dr. Hernandez here since we'll be in the mountains? More busy work, I'm guessing. But if it gets us out of the lodge, then I don't care. I was starting to go insane."

"You and me both," I tell her, which prompts an ironic smile.

She's right. This camping trip is coinciding with some nicer weather, that's for sure, but it's also happening at a time where most students are starting to buckle under the fog and isolation. It's probably well timed to give us a little freedom every now and then so that we don't rebel.

Then again, maybe the lodge wants us out of its hair. Only Everly, Michael, and the researchers are left behind, the students all gone.

A trickle of unease rolls down my spine.

Did they get rid of us on purpose?

Is there something going on back at Madrona?

Or is there something going on here? a voice whispers.

I ignore it. That's all I can do, though I know it's burying itself under my skin. I'm going to be on high alert. Not for bears and wolves but for…

I don't even know what the threat is.

I just know it would be a mistake to let my guard down, no matter where I am, no matter who I'm with.

I glance over my shoulder at Kincaid driving the ATV a little ways behind us. In his olive raincoat and aviator glasses, he looks equally at ease driving this beast of a machine up a steep mountain road as he does when standing at the front of the classroom, textbook in hand.

I'm lucky I have him in my corner, I think.

Even though I still don't trust him completely.

I trust him sexually. I trust him to look after me.

But that's where it ends.

I'm still not sure if Kincaid is actually a good person or not.

I don't think you can work for Madrona otherwise.

And I don't really know Kincaid at all.

"Making sure he doesn't drive off?" Lauren asks wryly as she leans in.

I face forward, feeling the cool air as we climb higher, making sure my cheeks don't burn. "Just admiring the view."

"I bet you are," she says.

Eventually the ATV comes to a stop in front of an industrial-looking building with a green tin roof, in the middle of a big empty lot, an odd sight surrounded by so much beauty. We're told by Hernandez that this used to be used by the loggers but the logging in the area stopped a long time ago, just at the end of the park.

We climb out of the ATVs, eager to stretch our legs. Dr. Hernandez passes out protein bars as a snack to hold us over until lunch, and our water bottles get filled from the trailer at the back of Nick's vehicle.

Then Kincaid hands us all our tents—his finger touching mine for too long when he hands me mine—and tells us to drink up the expensive stuff while we can. From now on we'll be drinking water from streams and lakes, our water cleaned with purifying tablets.

Then Nick waves goodbye and gets on his ATV before driving off.

"Why is he leaving?" Munawar asks.

"What am I, chopped liver?" Dr. Hernandez jokes. "Nick has some stuff to attend to back at the lab."

Please not baby goats...

"And I never get to go on this expedition," Hernandez continues. "Neither do the marine sciences students, normally. So it's a nice change of pace. Although now that I'm here, I'm a little intimidated. Are you sure it's three days in and three days out?"

Kincaid grins at him, wrinkles appearing at the corner of his aviators, causing my stomach to flutter. "Don't be a wimp."

I adjust my tent on my back, and we all get into single file, Kincaid at the lead and carrying a rifle for protection, Hernandez bringing up the rear, our bear bells jingling from our packs. I'm glad Hernandez is here since I wouldn't have felt very comfortable with Nick, but even so I wonder what lab work Nick is staying behind to do.

I try not to think about it. I'll only get myself into a tizzy.

Instead, I concentrate on my senses to put me firmly in the present. The sound of whisky jacks calling from the trees, no longer cedar but mountain hemlock and balsam fir, and the crunch of the ground beneath our feet. The smell of the crushed needles, the sharp mountain air, and flowing streams. The feel of the sun as it penetrates the canopy above, warming my skin despite the temperature getting cooler. The taste of the water on my tongue, and the sight of all of us students in a line, walking toward something, even if we don't know what it is.

I feel a pang of camaraderie for my cohort. I really have gotten to know and like all of them.

Except for Clayton. Though at the end there, I wasn't really afraid of him anymore. I felt like he was trying to tell me something, as if he was looking out for me. He was just so strange and abrasive about it, it was hard to decipher.

I really hope that Kincaid told me the truth. That Clayton was put on a plane and sent back home. I hope he was trying to prevent something disastrous from happening, that he wasn't just looking out for me in an overly protective manner. As sweet and romantic as the gesture was, it puts a lot of pressure on me. I can handle myself and I could have handled Clayton. Girls become experts at dealing with creeps after a while, even if it exhausts us to do so, even though we shouldn't *have to* do so.

We hike for a couple of hours until we have our first break. I'm tired and lightheaded, not used to this much exercise, nor this little sleep. Kincaid keeps staring at me, and I can tell he's mentally checking in on how I'm doing. I give him a tepid smile from time to time. It isn't until lunch is over, simple ham and cheese sandwiches that Hernandez passes out, that I perk up a little and we continue walking.

The trail is rough and hard to follow in places, even as we enter the provincial park. I can tell that no one ever comes here except those at Madrona. Every now and then as the trail switchbacks through open rock and scree, we see a foreboding forested mountain in the distance, and the jagged shape reminds me of a jawbone.

"That's Mount Doom," Kincaid says.

Of course it is.

"Technically Doom Mountain," he goes on, "but, you know, doesn't have the same ring to it."

We keep going, down again and into the thick forest.

Kincaid keeps talking, doing an impressive job at throwing his voice back at the twelve of us, Hernandez included, but I don't catch much except that the peninsula was only first explored by botanists in 1975. Before then, no one knew what a treasure trove of fungi, moss, lichen, and plants were here.

We finally stop at our place to camp for the night—a grassy clearing scattered with tiny white and pink flowers, surrounded by lodgepole pine and hemlock. My feet are burning and I'm so tired I want to crawl right into my tent and go to sleep, but I have to put together my tent first.

I stare at it dumbly, not moving, until Kincaid comes over and helps me out.

After he's done setting it up like a pro and in record time, another incredibly sexy thing about him, he leans in close. "Want to take a walk?"

My stomach flips. "Right now?" I whisper. I look around.

Everyone is busy struggling with their tents, but no one is paying us any attention.

He nods and then walks off toward the edge of the field.

I try to play it cool. I skirt the edges of the clearing and then duck into the forest. Kincaid is quite far up ahead so I move as fast as I can so that I don't lose him, and suddenly we're in the dark woods. The air is cool and damp here, soft as a kiss on my skin, and the sounds of a babbling brook comes through the bowed trees.

Kincaid stands under the branches, lifting off his shirt.

"There's a stream we can clean off in," he says, nodding further down into the forest. "Cold as hell but it will make us feel like new again after that hike."

But I'm barely paying attention to him because all I can do is stare blatantly at his body. Yes, I saw it last night, more than this, but now it's the early evening and the light is bright and he looks like a forest god with his taut muscles, his smooth, slightly tan skin, the raven tattoo on his arm.

I feel like if there was a male Dryad in ancient Greece, that Wes Kincaid would be one of them.

I waste no time in stepping out of my clothes, stripping for him until it's all scattered around me. Standing in a forest totally naked makes me feel like a fairy nymph too.

And I know I'm not built like a fairy, either. I have cellulite on my thick thighs, I have a belly despite the weight I'd lost early on. But standing in front of Kincaid like this, watching as his cock hardens against his jeans, the lust building in his gaze as he lets it roam over my body, my skin shivering as if being licked by flames, I feel like a mythical creature.

"The stream can wait," Kincaid says before he strides toward me, grabbing me by the small of my waist. He pulls me in for a kiss, hungry and fast. Like a feral animal he starts kissing down my neck, nipping at my collarbone, then to my breasts, licking and sucking until I'm crying out.

Just when I think my knees will buckle, he puts his arms

around me and lowers me down until I'm nestled in the soft moss and the cushiony foliage of pink alpine azalea. His hands are rough, moving fast as they part my thighs, leaving myself open for him as the dappled sunshine slides in through the branches above.

I watch, enraptured, as he lowers his head between my legs, his arms wrapped around my thighs, securing me in place while holding me open. He admires my pussy for a moment, then glances up at me through his lashes, his smile crooked and devious.

Then he plunges his head down, attacking me like a starving man, his lips, mouth, and tongue wet, strong and forceful.

A gasp is caught in my throat and I throw my head back. The trees seem to crowd over me as if protecting us, and I'm starting to feel both delicious and light-headed. Dizzy in the best way, like the air is shimmering and melting.

My head rolls to the side and I notice the mushrooms surrounding us.

Some tiny, some large. All a near translucent white with orange gills.

"*Excandesco*," I breathe just as Kincaid's tongue plunges inside me, making me choke on the word. My eyes pinch shut, riding out the wave of pleasure, and when I open them again, the mushrooms seem closer somehow.

What is happening? I think, but at the same time, I don't care. My head is too heavy to keep up and I sink further back into the moss, letting the sensations swirl around me.

Kincaid continues to lap at me, ravishing me until I sink so deep, it's as if I'm starting to become one with the moss. My mind is shooting through the stars, and I feel like my soul is starting to disintegrate.

"Don't stop," I whisper. I open my eyes to see the tree branches reaching for me, wanting me, craving me. The air is filled with orange dust that sparkles in the sunlight and I breathe it in, deep as I can, feeling it fill my lungs, infuse the blood in my veins.

I am one, I think. *We are one.*

I raise my head and glance at Kincaid, the orange dust collecting on his hair, his shoulders as he continues to eat me out, each stroke of his tongue making my body writhe. But when I try to move, I can't.

I glance down and see thin strands of mycelia coming out of the moss, wrapping delicately around my wrists and ankles. It holds my legs apart for Kincaid as he devours me, and the pink flowers of the alpine azalea press against my bare skin, as if they're kissing me. When I look around, the mushrooms are even closer now.

They move when I'm not looking.

Slowly coming for me.

This isn't real, the faint thought pushes through the murkiness of my mind. *This isn't happening. You're hallucinating.*

But if I feel any fear, it vanishes as Kincaid brings me to a climax. I come hard, the mycelia tightening like the very ropes Kincaid used last night, strapping me down in place.

I am the forest's captive, it's possession, I think as my body keeps convulsing and bucking up against his mouth. The mycelia dig into my skin, tighter, tighter, while inside I feel as if I'm being split into atoms. I am one with the earth, souls joined to souls, a network ever reaching. My vision is of pulses of light traveling through space and time and—

"Sydney!?"

I open my eyes.

Lift up my head.

See Kincaid staring at me between my legs, looking concerned.

I blink and then look down at my wrists and ankles.

No mycelia.

I look around the forest.

The trees are back in their place, and there are no mush-rooms at all.

Like they never existed.

"Are you alright?" he asks, sounding slightly panicked. There's no sight of orange dust anywhere.

I give him a lopsided smile, feeling so strange. "I just…"

But I don't know how to finish the sentence.

Am I alright?

"You seemed like you were in another world," he says, slowly straightening up and sitting back on his knees. "I kept calling your name but you wouldn't respond. Scared the shit out of me."

"I guess the orgasm was just that good," I manage to say, pushing myself up so that I'm on my elbows. I'm not about to tell him that I hallucinated the forest pinning me down so he could have his way with me. I mean there's weird—like seeing Amani and snow in June—and then there's *weird*. As much as Kincaid rolls with my mental health punches, I think that would stretch his compassion, even for him.

He helps me to my feet, giving me a quick kiss, then takes me by hand to the stream to wash off.

He takes off his pants, his cock half-hard, and I drop to my knees to finish him off. It's only fair, and I make quick work of him, swallowing his release down my throat.

Then we go into the water. It's cold as hell and I can only wander in to my thighs, crouching down in the water to clean myself. At least it's waking me up, snapping some sense into me. I feel like I'm being pulled out of a dream.

Both of us stagger out of the stream, the sky opening up just in time for the sun to heat up our skin. Though the altitude is higher here, that means the rays are stronger and we are quick to dry off.

I grab my clothes and excuse myself to go pee.

"Don't go far," he warns, slipping on his boxer briefs.

"Wouldn't dream of it," I tell him, stepping behind a couple of trees.

Not when the forest seems to do things when you're not looking.

I finish peeing and then pull on my underwear and leggings. I'm just dragging my shirt over my bra when I hear a rustle in the bushes.

I quickly yank the shirt down in time to see a blue ballcap and dark head appear above the yellow flowers of Oregon grape on the slope beneath me.

Suddenly a man looks up and freezes when he spots me standing there.

He's native, dressed in a short-sleeved black shirt and jeans, a backpack on one shoulder.

"It's *you*," he says, his voice stern, dripping with disdain. "Haven't seen you in a while. You planning on fucking me over again? Didn't get enough out of us, huh?"

I can only blink at him. I've never met this man before.

"Excuse me?" I say, my voice uneasy.

He lifts up the brim of his ballcap and frowns at me. Then fear comes into his eyes.

"No," he says, shaking his head. "No. Sorry, so sorry. It's not you. You're not her."

Then he turns around.

"Hey!" I yell at him, but he doesn't stop, quickly disappearing into the bushes as if he's running away from me.

What the fuck?

"Sydney?" Kincaid says, appearing beside me. "Who were you talking to?"

I point into the bushes but there's no trace of the man.

"There was a man," I tell him, which makes him frown. "No!" I quickly say, frustration running through me. "No, this was not a hallucination. You can go catch up with him, he's just down there. There was a man. A native. He thought I was someone else."

"Who did he think you were?" he asks, scanning the brush and forest below us.

"I don't know. He said that he hadn't seen me in a while and wondered if I was fucking him over again."

Realization dawns over his face and he nods. "I see. He thought you were Everly." He glances at me. "Everly has had issues with the natives here. They're afraid of her, of everyone at Madrona."

"Issues as in she's fucking them over?"

"Yeah."

"Good lord, what now? Is there anything ethical about Madrona?"

"We're doing good work," Kincaid says with a sigh. "But it comes at a cost. Madrona leases the land, but because the fungi is found on their land, Madrona has taken all the profit. Me and a few others had set it up so that the natives were supposed to get a percentage of sales from the pharmaceutical company, but unbeknownst to me, a new contract was drafted up that essentially cut them out. The Johnstones had their sneaky fucking lawyers word it so, burying it in language and made it iron-clad. When the attorneys tried to fight it, the natives were left out."

I curl my lip in disgust. "That's fucking ridiculous. It's their land, all of this is. They're owed everything."

"I know," he says sadly, but he's grinning at me.

"Why are you smiling?"

"Because," he says with a sigh of relief. "I wanted to know where you stood on this whole thing. It's a relief to know that you feel the same as I do."

"Well, of course I do. I have *some* morals."

"Then you keep those morals," he says, his eyes flashing with intensity. "Because I've seen what ambition does to a person. I've seen what it's done to Everly. Everything gets thrown aside in pursuit of significance or the almighty dollar."

"You really sound like you hate it here," I tell him. "Why don't you sail away and quit?"

"One day," he says, looking off. "One day I'll do just that. But I can't quit now. As long as you're here, I'm here."

"Oh no," I tell him, even though my chest feels light. "Don't say you're staying for me."

"I'm staying for you, sweetheart," he says, grabbing my hand and holding it up to his mouth, pressing his lips against my skin. "I'm burning up for you. You're my fever, Syd. No cure."

CHAPTER 24

THAT EVENING, after everyone has gone to sleep, I creep through the darkness over to Kincaid's tent. Luckily he pitched his close to mine so I don't have far to go.

He unzips it for me, and I crawl inside, not wanting to be alone. The memories of the mycelia wrapping around me, the flowers licking me—I keep thinking that if I close my eyes I'll be devoured by the earth without Kincaid there to pull me out.

But we don't sleep. We have sex instead, quiet and controlled movements that keep the tent shaking to a minimum. Kincaid takes his time, slow and teasing as he pushes in and out, pausing to lick up my body. Sometimes he goes down on me again, a thirsty boy who can't seem to get his fill, and then he's rolling me over on my back and taking me from behind.

At some point in the haze of sex, footsteps crunch outside the tent and a light appears, showing a silhouette.

I freeze but Kincaid keeps fucking.

"Wes," Hernandez whispers. "Are you awake? Where did you put the extra stakes?"

Kincaid places his hand over my mouth and clears his

throat. "They're underneath the bag with the extra blankets," he says evenly, as if he's not currently thrusting his dick into me.

I stare up at Kincaid, wide-eyed, and he grins down at me, clearly enjoying the fact that we're fucking in front of his co-worker, who currently has no idea but could catch us at any second.

"Thanks. Sorry to wake you," Hernandez says as he shuffles away.

"Wasn't asleep," Kincaid says after him, and quickly brings me to climax, never taking his hand away.

After that I sleep soundly, no bad dreams or anything until Kincaid rouses me awake at first light. "Better get back to your tent. The moment that sun is up, everyone will be awake."

I thought I got back to my tent in the grey dawn without anyone seeing me, but later Lauren pulls me aside and says, "I saw you sneaking out of his tent."

My stomach churns uneasily and I give her a sheepish look. "Well, you did say he was always staring at me. Just wanted to see if it was true."

I expect her to laugh because she has always been teasing me about Kincaid, but she doesn't. Her expression is grave, tone serious. "I want you to be careful," she says. "He's taking advantage of you."

I frown. "No, he isn't. What do you mean?"

She puts her hand on my shoulder and gives it a squeeze. "Just be careful with him, please."

After that, everyone has a breakfast of oatmeal and nuts and we're tasked with taking down our tents. But I can't help thinking about what Lauren said. I know Kincaid isn't taking advantage of me, because I'm the one initiating everything. I want her to know that, but I have a hard time getting her alone without Rav or Munawar around.

Just as we had all tucked our tents into their respective

packs, Kincaid, who had been conversing with Hernandez over something that looked serious, listening to a small radio in his hand, turns to us.

"Can I have your attention?" Kincaid booms, giving us an uneasy smile. "I'm afraid I have some bad news. The weather center is calling for a massive pacific storm to hit us in forty-eight hours, with the first bands coming in at twenty-four hours. The peninsula is exposed to the elements on all three corners and the weather is usually foul as it is. We can't risk it and will have to head back to the lodge immediately."

Everyone breaks out into a disappointed groan, myself included.

"I know, I know," Kincaid says. "I'm just as upset about it as you, especially as the weather right now is brilliant for once. But things change here, and when they do, they change fast. We can reschedule the trip for next week, as soon as the storm clears, I promise. At least then you'll know what to expect."

"Can we have better food than sandwiches?" Munawar asks.

Kincaid chuckles. "Yes. I promise."

So with that, we all get our packs on, knowing we're going to be heading back down instead of up.

It's funny, being away from Madrona has helped my head clear for the first time. Not counting my bizarre sexual plant hallucinations in the forest, since I still don't know what the fuck that was about. I decide to wrap up that moment with a little bow and shove it back in my head, where it can collect dust along with other memories I don't want to look at ever again.

At least the hike back down goes faster than the one going up. I try to focus on the positives about returning to the lodge early, and the only one I can come up with is the fact that it's much easier for me to sneak into Kincaid's boat in the middle of the night instead of a tent. And that's enough of a perk for me. Having sex with Kincaid is the only thing that feels normal these days, like he's the only thing keeping me remotely sane.

But when we finally reach the ATVs, the weather has started to change. It's much cooler, with a wet ocean breeze, and the clouds are stiflingly low, threatening us with rain.

Of course since we're back early, there isn't an extra ATV for us.

"There's not enough room for everyone," Kincaid says, rubbing his jaw in thought.

"I can ride in the trailer!" Munawar offers.

"Still not enough room," Hernandez says. "We have two ATVs and three groups, so one group will have to stay behind while the other drops people off and comes back for you."

"I have the rifle," Kincaid says. "And I'm the only one licensed to have one. I'll stay behind."

And I'm not going back to the lodge alone. "I'll stay, too," I speak up, and I don't give a fuck if that seems weird. I purposely avoid Lauren's stare, but then she says, "I'll stay too."

"Me too," say Munawar and Rav.

Patrick, who was with us on the way up, shrugs and says he'll also stay.

"Now, to find out which one of you can drive an ATV," Hernandez says, clapping his hands together.

Surprisingly Natasha raises her hand. "My parents have a dairy farm outside Chicago. I can do it."

So Natasha gets behind the wheel, looking very comfortable, and Hernandez gets behind the other as the rest of the students pile in. They wave and drive off, leaving us in their dust.

I swallow hard. "Now what?" I say, looking at Kincaid for guidance.

"We can sit here and twiddle our thumbs, or we can get moving," he says. "I say we get moving. I'm sure we'll be halfway down by the time they return for us. Beats waiting."

We start walking down the logging road. The rain seems to hold off and the wind dies down to nothing. But in its place rises the mist, condensing on everything, leaving the atmosphere cold, dank, and spooky. The forest rises up from other side of the road, but you can only see a few yards through the trees and the tops become covered in fog.

None of us say much at first, the air filling with a thick, eerie silence punctuated only by the crunching of our shoes on the dirt, and the soft clang of the bear bells. The fog seems to bring the mosquitoes, and I try to wave them away as they whine in my ears.

But as I'm doing so, something in the misty woods catches my eye.

There's something there, something dark lurking, sliding between the trunks.

"Hey guys," I say, raising my voice. "I might be seeing things, but is there something to our right? Look between the trees."

Kincaid instinctively reaches back to touch his rifle as everyone looks where I'm staring.

"I don't know, it's hard to tell when we're moving too," Rav says. "Maybe we should st—?"

"No," Kincaid cuts him off, taking the rifle off his shoulder. "No, we keep walking. We keep talking. Loudly."

"Okay great!" Munawar says. "Because I think there's something to our left."

Our heads swivel to the other side of the road. I squint to see what looks like moving bushes until something rises up out of it, a black shape.

"What is that?" Lauren whispers. "Is that a bear?"

"Maybe it's a wolf," I say, looking back to the other side now. Whatever it is closest to me on the right, it's staying just out of view, a murky dark shape amongst all the blackberry bushes that rustle as it brushes past. If the fog would clear a little, we would get a better look, but none of us want to venture closer.

"No, I think it's a bear," Kincaid says. "Two adult bears on either side of us."

"Grizzlies?" Patrick asks in a shaky voice.

"Black bears," Kincaid says. "Which normally stay away, as you know. They don't want to bother us, we don't want to bother them. They could be curious, escorting us out of their territory. That's why they're not coming closer."

But at the mention of bears, I don't picture the mother and cubs we saw yesterday. I picture something else. I picture the baby goat, I picture the wolf. I see a bear with its fur sliding off its skull, exposing the white bone of its long jaw, the sharp teeth, the empty eye socket filled with writhing mycelia. I imagine a beating heart covered with mold, lungs filled with orange spores.

And the more I stare at the shapes in the trees, the more I think that's what I see. The bear moves strangely too, limping, dragging its feet, and sometimes when the mist clears in places, I think I see wild fur standing straight up, like a hyena.

Please let this be a normal bear, please let this be a normal bear.

I catch Kincaid's eyes as he looks back at me, and from the grim expression on his face, and the way he's holding the gun, I can tell that he's thinking the exact same.

"Seriously, fuck this place," I grumble under my breath.

But when I glance at the others, expecting to see admonishment, they nod in agreement.

Fuck this place indeed.

We keep walking. We ring the bells louder. Munawar starts singing the Bangladesh national anthem at the top of his lungs and then rattles off the players on his favorite cricket team. I think we all feel like we're going absolutely insane listening to him, but all the while, the bears in the brush keep following us. Even when Kincaid suggests we walk faster, the bears keep pace with us, their movements becoming even more erratic.

"How long can we keep this up?" I say to Kincaid.

"As long as it takes," he says, brandishing the weapon. "Don't worry, I have enough bullets."

Normally I would protest, hating the idea of shooting a bear, even in self-defense. I think I'd rather get a little mauled first than cause death. But I know these aren't normal bears. I feel it my soul, in my blood, in my bones. I mean I actually feel it, like my veins are vibrating.

Then the fog starts getting thicker, nearly blotting out the trees, but we can still see the bears, which means they're getting closer.

Much closer.

"I want to run," Rav says, his breath shallow. "When do we run?"

"Never," Kincaid says sharply. "We never run from a bear. We keep doing what we're doing, and eventually—"

He stops talking as the roar of an engine is heard.

"Oh, thank fuck!" Lauren yelps. "They're here!"

Headlights flash through the fog and the ATV nearly takes us out, unable to see us until the last minute.

"That was close," Hernandez says, skidding to a stop. He looks at our faces, then the gun. "What is it?"

"Bears!" Kincaid yells, ushering us all to climb in. With no spare seat, he climbs in the trailer at the back and thuds his fist against the metal. "Go, go, go!"

We barely strap ourselves in before Hernandez takes the ATV at a wide angle and I'm dangerously close to the edge of the road, the blackberry and salmonberry bushes brushing against my thighs.

And that's when I stare right into the mist, right into those trees, and see the shape of a creature charging at me. Just a flash of an empty eye socket, white skull and matted hair, mouth open in a guttural roar.

The ATV peels away just in time, rocks and dirt kicked back, and Kincaid bounces in the trailer behind us, rifle out and aimed as we speed down the road.

"Did you see that?" I whisper to no one in particular.

"I saw it," Lauren says firmly.

The relief is palpable.

She saw the half-dead creature.

I'm not fucking crazy.

"Look!" Rav yells.

We watch in the distance as the creatures come to the middle of the road, still half-buried by the fog so only their outlines can be seen. They don't run after us but the bears are joined by others. It looks like a dozen of them have gathered, watching us leave, before the mist swallows them entirely.

Lauren reaches over and grabs my hand, giving it a squeeze. I squeeze her hand back. "Rabid bears, maybe?" she asks.

"Maybe," I say. But I know now that's not it.

It's not even close.

By the time we get back to the lodge, the mist has cleared a little, and we march right into the dining hall for dinner. The atmosphere is still tense, especially for those of us who saw the bears, and we mostly eat in silence. Even the other groups seem to be on edge as we dig into our chicken pot pies. Though the fire roars from the hearth, I can't seem to shake a chill.

After dinner some of us hang out in the common room, snacking on cookies with mugs of hot chocolate. I hang out with the usual crew, though Patrick has joined us now, all of us sitting in the chairs in the corner, talking about what we saw, trying to make sense of it. Lauren and I seemed to be the only ones to see the bears melting faces but the others don't dismiss us. Instead they believe it. Everything about that encounter seemed to be against the laws of nature.

"Strange vibes," Lauren says, nibbling on a cookie and dusting the crumbs off her thighs. "Not just from the journey, but like here." She motions around her. "This place. The lodge."

I have to agree. I feel with us coming back early we interrupted something. I know the lodge is just a bunch of buildings, but some days, particularly at night, I feel it has a personality of its own—and it's not a nice personality. Moody, perhaps. And tonight, I feel like it wants us gone, like we're not supposed to be here.

"Okay, I'm actually going to have an early one tonight," Lauren says, getting to her feet.

"Yeah me too," Rav says, stifling a yawn. He and Lauren lock eyes and a knowing look passes between them before they wave goodbye to us and head up the stairs together.

"Oh, they are so doing it," Munawar says.

I elbow him, almost causing his hot chocolate to spill on his shirt that says *All Mushrooms are Edible—Some Only Once.*

"Nah, they are," says Patrick. "Good thing I don't share a wall with either of them."

And at that the rest of us decide to turn in.

I say goodbye to the guys, unlock my door, and step inside my room. I head straight to the sink, washing all the camping off my face and hands until I feel clean and refreshed, even if my mind is still in the murk.

Suddenly an impossibly loud, clanging alarm sounds, and the room starts flashing red, like I'm in a submarine and a missile is coming. I yelp and cover my ears with my hands, unable to block out the noise as a shuddering sound starts to shake the building.

"Warning," a robotic voice announces over loudspeakers I didn't even know existed. "Dangerous animal reported in area. Please seek shelter immediately. Warning. Dangerous animal reported in area. Please seek shelter immediately."

"Oh my god," I cry out, running to my door and opening it to see everyone filing out of their rooms, some excited, some in a panic.

"Do you think it's the bears?" Munawar says, grabbing my arm, and I can't tell if he's excited or not.

"What bears?" Natasha asks, holding Justin's hand.

Further down the hall I spot Lauren and Rav stumbling out of her room, their clothes askew, their hair messy. If I wasn't starting to panic myself, I'd think it comical that the lodge is cock-blocking her.

"We're locked in!" someone yells from downstairs.

We all clamor down the steps to the common room where Toshio is struggling to open the door. It only moves an inch before it hits metal siding.

"No way, they have automatic shutters," Justin says. "This is like living in the middle of a bank robbery!"

The door to reception opens and Michelle steps out, red-faced and looking flustered as hell, her palms raised.

"Don't panic everyone!" she shouts. "Remain calm. This happens sometimes, it's probably just a cougar."

"Yeah but cougars avoid people if they can help it," Noor points out. "They're not velociraptors trying to find their way in."

"I did not need that visual!" Munawar shrieks.

Chaos. It's utter chaos.

"And why are the windows not covered?" Lauren says, peering out of one.

That gives me an idea. I decide to run up the stairs and back to my room.

I hurry over to the window to get a visual. I can see people running beneath the trees, and though I can't make out who they are, some of them are carrying rifles.

Jesus. I guess this really is a big deal.

I keep watching, waiting for someone else, something else, but it seems like they've all run off some place I can't see. I'm about to head downstairs and join the rest when movement catches my eye.

It's crawling all crouched, like an animal, and pale, but then it straightens up once it's under the cedar tree across from me, looking decidedly human as it climbs up. The cedar branches begin to shake, and every now and then I can see glimpses of hands, of feet, of a face, until finally it moves out onto a branch at eye level with me.

A scream dies in my throat.

It's Clayton.

It's hard to tell at first because his face is covered in shadow, but the shadows are slick and when I realize it's covered in blood, my mouth waters with nausea.

He's staring right at me, naked. He's been cut open down his chest, staples holding him back together. His fingers curl around the branch and he's trying to speak, to tell me something.

I'm about to open the window when suddenly he twists to look behind him and a bunch of people run under the tree. A gun goes off, shaking the window, and Clayton is hit, falling out of the tree and to the ground in a lifeless heap.

I scream.

I scream and I scream and then someone down below looks up at me, his face in shadow.

Michael.

Then he disappears and Clayton is dragged out of sight, just as Lauren and Rav run into my room, followed by the others.

"What is it, what happened?" she cries out. "I heard a gun!"

I point at the tree, shaking my hand violently. "Clayton! It's not a cougar, it's Clayton! He was in the tree and they shot him. Oh my god, they fucking shot him, they killed him!"

"Clayton?" Lauren repeats.

"Clayton went home on the seaplane," says Patrick.

"I know but he didn't! Kincaid lied, he lied." Oh my god, he lied to me. "He lied to us all. They're all lying to us! That was Clayton. I know it was. Go outside and check, there will be blood! They shot him out of the tree!"

"Okay, calm down," Michelle says from the door as she pushes her way into my room and through the crowd, grabbing me roughly by the shoulders. "You're the one who is lying, Sydney. Clayton went home. You saw a cougar."

"No I didn't," I snarl, trying to get away from her. "Let go of me! Get your fucking hands off me!"

Michelle's nails dig in harder, her awful pink lips in a sneer, and then Lauren is there, yanking at her sleeve.

"She said to not touch her, now fuck off!" Lauren yells, and then Natasha steps forward, grabbing Michelle by the other arm. If I wasn't freaking the fuck out I'd be utterly touched by their support.

I stumble backward until I hit the wall. "I am not lying! I saw Clayton. They lied about him, they're keeping him here, he looked operated on and—"

"Alright, alright, what's going on here," says Michael.

I freeze when I see him walk in the door, followed by Everly and David. "Everyone clear out, including you, Michelle."

"No!" I yell, trying to hold on to Lauren. "No, I'm not going to be alone with you people. You're murderers!"

"You're overreacting, Sydney," Everly says in her calm voice. "It's okay, everyone here knows that you're prone to such things."

I shake my head in confusion. "What do you mean everyone here knows?" I stare at Lauren. "What did they tell you?"

She just stares at me, blinking.

"They know you've been through a lot," Everly says, coming closer. She looks at Lauren and gestures with her head for her to go. Lauren looks torn. "It's okay, Lauren. You're a good friend. But clearly she didn't see Clayton in the tree. None of that makes any logical sense. If you don't believe us, we have logs of the seaplane. We have his flight information from Vancouver back to Montana. We would be happy to show you, but first we have to deal with poor Sydney." She pouts at me.

"Fuck you!" I yelp and try to run at her, but Michael jumps in front of me and with a quick maneuver wrenches my arms behind my back.

"Everyone out!" Michael bellows. "David, escort them all to their rooms."

David tries, but it's like herding cats, none of the students want to go anywhere.

"Don't leave me alone with them," I plead.

"That's enough Sydney," Everly snaps. She looks at everyone. "As you can see, she's in need of treatment and TLC. Please, go back to your rooms. We're just going to check her over in the nurse's office. We'll release her when we're done."

"Now!" Michael barks, and that's enough for everyone to jump and then start slowly shuffling out of the room.

"You need to calm down," Everly says, turning her back to everyone as she brings out a needle from her coat and jabs it in my arm. "There. Now we can take you to get your rabies shot. You're due for your last one."

I feel the shot almost immediately. The room starts to swim and my knees buckle. It's only then that I notice Michael's dark shirt has been splattered with blood.

"You're going to be okay," Everly says as the world starts to get fuzzy. "You're having an episode. But don't worry, Nurse Everly is going to make it all better."

CHAPTER 25

My mind keeps slipping in and out of reality. One minute, I'm floating in darkness, an eternal void, and the next, I'm being dragged down the stairs, Everly on one side of me, Michael on the other. I can hear the students asking if I'm going to be okay. I can hear them asking each other if I really am crazy. One of them mentions that I tried to attack Everly and I'll probably be reprimanded, maybe sent home.

But I'm not taken to the nurse's office. Suddenly, the door is opening, the shutters gone, and I'm brought outside into the cool night air. The mist is damp against my skin, and I try to breathe, try to think of what I need to do.

I need to be free of them. Yes. I need to escape.

They start pulling me toward the lab.

I dig my heels in best I can, but it's a pathetic attempt.

"What the fuck are you doing?" I hear Kincaid roar.

My heart skips a beat.

He's here, he's here.

I try to lift my head to look at him, but I can only stare at the muddy ground where his black combat boots come into view.

Is that…blood splattered on them?

Fear twists into me like a knife.

I remember that Kincaid lied to me about Clayton.

Oh god, what has he done?

"You're a little late, doctor," Michael says coldly. "She's breaking."

"She's fine," Kincaid says, and he steps forward to grab me, but Michael blocks him.

"Stay back, Wes," Michael warns.

"Stay back?" Kincaid sneers. "Are you serious right now? She's my fucking patient."

"And a patient you're fucking," Everly says under her breath, so bitterly that it causes something to dig in the back of my skull.

She's jealous.

"Fuck off, Everly," Kincaid says. "This doesn't concern you."

"She's breaking," Michael says again. "And your sessions have been no help, that much I can see. Preventative, my ass. *We* need to do something. Take a look at her brain, see what her problem is. See if we can fix her."

Excuse me, what? I think. I moan, trying to run, to scream, but I can't.

"Hold on, Syd," Kincaid says to me, trying to sound calm. "You entrusted her into my care. Both of you did," he says to them, his voice brimming with raw anger. "So you're not laying a single fucking finger on her head, or I swear to god I will burn this whole damn place down with you in it. *Especially* with you in it."

"Idle threats," Michael says. "You've said this before, and yet you're still here."

"I don't make idle threats," Kincaid growls. "She's mine."

Everly sighs. "Such a caveman. Fine, fuck, what do I care what you do. I don't."

Michael lets out a derisive snort.

"What?" Everly snaps. "I don't care."

"Right, *dear*," Michael says sarcastically. "Sometimes I can't tell who will be your downfall here, Sydney or Wes? Perhaps both of them, hmmm?"

Everly suddenly lets go of me, and I slump toward the ground, held up only by Michael's cruel grip.

"All of you can go to hell," Everly says, and I hear her walking off.

"You first," Michael says under his breath, but he's still holding me at an angle, as if I'm diseased.

"Michael, you're traumatizing her," Kincaid says in a low voice. "You think she can't hear this right now, can't feel this?"

Michael grunts and starts to release me. Suddenly, Kincaid rushes forward and grabs me by the waist, hauling me up.

"You need to be careful," Michael says as Kincaid cradles my head against his chest. My entire body lets go, slumped against him. "You need to be a lot more careful."

"Sounds like you're the ones who need to get things under control," Kincaid says. "One more mistake will put all of us over the edge. And you have the most to lose."

Michael laughs bitterly. "That's where you're wrong, doctor. That's where you're wrong."

Then he walks off, leaving Kincaid and me alone.

"Jesus," he swears, exhaling heavily before kissing the top of my head. "Syd, are you okay?"

I try to speak, but it all comes out as gibberish.

"That's okay," he says. "I'll take you to the boat. Come on."

He leans down and scoops me up in his arms, carrying me past the totem pole and boardwalk, down the ramp, to the docks.

He carries me on board and down the stairs, and then takes me to his sleeping quarters, laying me down on the berth.

"You're going to want to sleep for a few hours until the

sedative wears off," he says. "I'm not sure exactly which one they injected you with, but you should be okay. I'll be right here keeping an eye on you. You're safe."

Then he kisses my forehead tenderly and pulls the blanket over me, tucking me in.

Am I safe when I don't know you at all? I think. *You lied to me. You have blood on your shoes.*

Does he have blood on his hands?

"Good morning, sunshine."

I groan, stirring until my head erupts in pain, as if someone is beating a drum inside. I blink my eyes open to see the hatch above me. But there is no sun. Only dark clouds that move quickly in the sky. The boat moves up and down, water sloshing against the sides and the dock.

I slowly turn my head to see Kincaid sitting in a seat in the corner of the cabin, a mug of something that smells like mint tea in his hand. He has dark circles etched under his eyes, his stubble turning into a beard. He looks exhausted, which makes me imagine I must look worse.

"Don't try to get up right away or make any sudden movements," he warns me, voice stern yet quiet. "You'll be groggy for a while. I have no idea how much of the sedative Everly gave you, but it was close to a dangerous amount. You were out cold all night long."

I try to swallow, but my mouth feels like cotton. All the events from last night bubble to the surface, and I try to swat them away, not wanting to face them, not wanting my perception of Kincaid to change.

But it already has. My heart feels heavy.

So terribly heavy.

"I'm sorry," he says, reading my face. "I truly am." He helps me to sit upright, slowly, then hands me the mug of tea before sitting back down.

"You lied to me." I breathe in sharply, preparing for the pain. "Did you kill Clayton?"

He shakes his head. "No."

"Why don't I believe you?"

He shrugs with one shoulder, looking down at his hands. "Because whatever trust of yours I had, I've lost it. Simple as that, Syd."

I take a sip of the tea, letting it warm my throat, trying to gather my thoughts before I swallow it down. "Why did you lie to me?"

He exhales through his nose. "NDAs." He gives me a pained look. "Sorry. It's the truth."

"So now it's a matter of *you* not trusting me," I tell him.

"For all I know, you might leave on the first seaplane right after the storm. Tell the world what you saw here. I advise against that, by the way. Not the part about leaving on the seaplane—that I recommend. I mean about breaking the contract. They will sue you, and even if you think you have nothing to give, they will find something. Do you understand me, Syd? They will make it their mission to utterly destroy you." He pauses. "They will kill you, figuratively. One way or another."

I gulp, fear tickling my ribs. "You recommend I leave?"

He leans back and runs his hand over his jaw back and forth, the stubble scratchy. "I'll have to come with you on the plane. But yes. I think you should leave."

I blink at him in disbelief. "Are you serious?"

"When am I not?" he says, staring at me. "Soon as the storm clears, I'll get you on the first flight out of here."

"And you'll come too? Just leave your boat and your job and go?"

"I'll have to come back at some point. Maybe I can only

leave for a few days, but yes. I'll take care of you, Syd. I told you I would. I'll help you get settled wherever it is you want. You won't have to worry about finances, you won't have to worry about anything."

"Except I will have to worry about my friends up here at Madrona Lodge. Are they in trouble too?"

He keeps his eyes locked on mine for a moment, not saying anything. Then he gives his head a shake. "No."

I let out a shaky exhale. My nerves are so frayed that I can feel them snapping one by one, until nothing will hold me together.

"They drugged me because I knew the truth about Clayton," I say. "They wanted to shut me up. But they were also taking me somewhere. Michael said something about looking at my brain…"

He nods. "Yes. They would have hooked you up to an EEG. Measured your brain waves."

"But they know I was telling the truth," I say. "So why do that? Was it a threat?"

"You're not well, Sydney," Kincaid says grimly. "They have access to my files on the computer. They know what I've logged after our sessions. They know about your hallucinations. Your sleepwalking. They know you've seen ghosts."

"No. No, because the things in the woods, those bears, the wolves, you saw them too. They're real."

"I know they're real," he admits. "And so do Everly and Michael. That's not why they're worried." He pauses. "They're worried for the same reasons I am, except I don't need to look at your brain, and I don't need to prescribe you any medication. I know that all you need is time. Time to get well. Depression is a wound like any other. It takes time to heal. There is no quick solution."

"But she drugged me," I tell him. "She injected me."

"You did try to attack her," he points out.

I narrow my eyes at him. "Why does it sound like you're standing up for her?"

"Believe me, I'm not," he says with a small smile. "I'm just letting you know the answers." He gets up and opens a cupboard, pulling out my leggings, a clean pair of underwear, and my green sweater. "I went to your room and got you some clothes. Figured you would want to change. When you're ready, and if you still want to, we'll go to Everly's office, together, and tell her that you'd like to leave."

The idea of leaving gives me hope, and I'm grateful I don't have to go alone. And yet, the thought of seeing Everly again makes me feel sick. Not just that I tried to attack her, which was kind of unhinged and embarrassing and did me no favors, but that she drugged me. She scared the hell out of me.

And she lied right to everyone's faces.

"Can you tell me anything about Clayton?" I plead with Kincaid before he walks away. "Is he still alive?"

He pauses. "I'm not sure."

"Did they...did they take him to run tests? Did they take him because he was bad? Because no one would miss him?"

Is that why I'm here?

Because they want to run tests on me, because no one would miss me if I disappeared? Was that their plan all along?

Were your sessions a way to somehow prove my worth to stay alive?

Did I prove my worth?

But I don't voice those last questions. I'm too afraid of the answer.

And Kincaid doesn't say anything. The look on his face, the steel grey of his eyes, tells me that he's not allowed.

He leaves, closing the cabin door behind him for privacy, and I stare down at my tea for a couple of minutes, lost in thoughts that don't make any sense, choked by a growing sense of fear.

I think I'm right.

I think they picked me because I was broken and alone, and they wanted to see whether I would crumble further or whether I could be saved.

How many times did Kincaid tell me he wanted to save me?

That he was supposed to protect me?

It wasn't to protect me from myself, not entirely. It was also to protect me from them. It must have been a happy accident for them that I lost my scholarship—no one would notice at all if I never came back home.

Something snags in my thoughts, a prickle of unease, but when I try to focus on it, it floats away. It seems if I try too hard to think about anything, everything just dissolves.

I slowly get dressed, breathing deeply to keep the mounting dread at bay. The boat continues to rock, the waves coming in a little harder now, and on deck, the ropes start to bang against the mast.

The storm is almost here.

After I'm dressed, I make my way out of the cabin, pausing at the doorway to see Kincaid sitting at the chart table, staring at something in his hand that he quickly tucks away. He clears his throat and straightens up.

"How are you feeling?" he asks.

"How do you think? Like I've been drugged. Like I am losing my fucking mind because of the shit heap of lies everyone keeps telling me. Like if I stay here one minute longer, it's going to be me in that tree next time, getting shot and dragged away to who knows where." My heart is starting to race with anger, leaving me feeling woozy, and I have to lean against the doorway.

Kincaid crosses the boat in seconds, arms holding me up. "Don't be ridiculous, Syd. You're letting your mind get away from you, and you're still feeling the effects of the drug. Look, there's a storm coming. You have nowhere you need to be today. You can just stay here and take it easy. You're safe. I mean it." He pauses. "I'm the one with a rifle, and I have a lot of bullets left," he jokes.

I nod carefully. "I know. But I want Everly to know my intentions. I want her to tell me it's okay to leave. I need to hear it."

"Alright," he says, leaning down to peer at me. "We can do that right now if it makes you feel better. I'll let her know I'm leaving with you."

"She won't like that," I say quietly.

"Probably not."

"She's jealous, you know. She's jealous of me, I think. Or maybe she's jealous of you."

He smiles faintly. "I know that, too."

"But she's married."

"Let's just say they aren't happily married," he informs me. "There's a reason that Michael is rarely here. But divorces are costly, and they both have a lot to lose. Some days, it's easier for them to turn a blind eye. Other days…Michael likes to make my life a living hell, as much as he can."

Hearing this little drama, that Everly isn't as put together as she seems, makes me feel a bit better, even if it means that Michael is out to get Kincaid.

Still, I have to ask. "Did you ever, uh, sleep with her?"

"God, no," he says, wrinkling his nose. "Everly is beautiful, of course, but she's a snake. Not in a good way."

"But she's tried."

He laughs. "Yes. She has tried. But that's enough about that. All you need to know is that things were an awful mess for a while." I'm watching him as his face falls, the laughter dying on his lips. Darkness falls across his eyes. Then he clears his throat again and nods at me. "Shall we go?"

He leads me to the doors, and as soon as he opens them,

cold, wet wind blows my hair back. He helps me up the steps and out of the boat. The dock is wet and slippery, and I have to lean into him to keep my balance, but at least it's not raining.

We walk up the ramp and toward the north dorm. I never realized Everly had an office here at all, albeit down the opposite way from Kincaid's.

"Do you know if she's here?" I whisper to him.

He nods and raises his hand, about to knock, when the door opens and Dr. Janet Wu steps out. It feels like I haven't seen her in a really long time.

"Hello," I say to her, wondering if she's innocent in all this or if she's the one working on Clayton, testing their drugs on him.

Her eyes go round, and she steps away from me so she's backing up into Everly's office.

"Ah, it's Sydney Denik," Everly says in an overly cheery voice as she gets up. "Janet, have you properly met Sydney yet? I don't believe you have."

Janet smiles stiffly at me and shakes her head. "No. I think you were in the class when I had one of my, uh…"

"Episodes," Everly says. "One of your episodes. It's okay, Janet, you're among friends here. If anything, Sydney is a lot like you. Also has these episodes, some of which include trying to attack me, but that's better than just breaking down in tears in the middle of class, isn't it?"

"Everly," Kincaid snipes at her.

"Save it, Wes," Everly says, rubbing at her temples. "The air pressure from this storm is making my head feel like it's about to implode. Now, what is it that you want? Janet, you're dismissed again. Go." She shoos her off with a dismissive flick of her wrist.

God, was Everly always like this? Did she blind me with her grace and beauty so that I didn't even see it?

"So, what do you want?" Everly says, sitting back down

with a sigh as Janet scurries out of the room. "I had a hell of a night. At least you were drugged." She jerks her chin at me. "Bet you slept all the way through, lucky bitch."

I clench my teeth at that, and Kincaid gives my hand a squeeze.

"Sydney would like to fly home on the first flight out of here," Kincaid says.

Everly fixes a tired eye on me. "Is this true? Or is this his idea?"

"It was my idea," I tell her. "I would like to go home."

Her eyes narrow at me while she smiles sourly. "I see. Of course you would, especially after last night. I suppose I do owe you an apology. I didn't mean to drug you; you just left me no choice. You were becoming violent, Syd. Now I guess the apology is in your court."

Fuck that.

"Just put her on the next plane," Kincaid demands. "And make sure I have a seat next to her."

"Et tu, Brutus?" she asks, picking up a pen and tapping it rapidly against the desk as she looks between the both of us. She sighs and stops tapping. "Well, I'm not surprised. So is this your formal resignation, Wes?"

"He's coming back," I tell her. "He's just going to help me get settled."

She snorts. "Oh, sweet summer child. No he's not. If he gets on that plane with you, he's quitting. He'll only come back for his boat. Still, quite the risk in assuming the boat will still be here. So many storms come through…"

He stiffens. "I'll be back to collect *Mithrandir*. That's it."

I turn to him in awe. "What? No. You can't quit. This is your job, your life."

"Maybe you're his life now, Sydney," Everly says in a mocking voice. "Isn't that precious, a love story happening before our very eyes." She flashes a wry smile at me. "I'm sorry, am I ruining things? Is he coming on too strong for you? It *is* a lot, isn't it? Has he already told you that he loves you, that he would lay his heart on the blade and die for you? Hell, he's already quitting his fucking fantastic job and running away with you somewhere, and you don't even know one fucking thing about him, do you?"

"Everly," Kincaid growls at her. "First plane out of here. And if you don't make the arrangements, I will."

She laughs. "Fuck, you're a serious one this morning. Whatever, Wes. Stay, go, I don't care. It will be your loss in the end. You'll both lose, you know that, don't you?" She looks off and waves her hands at us. "It doesn't matter. You'll be back. You always come back. Anyway, you'll be joining Dr. Wu on that same flight. Must be the season for idle threats of resignation."

"Not an idle threat," Kincaid grumbles. "I don't make idle threats."

He then squeezes my hand and pulls me toward the door.

I look back at Everly to see her laughing again and shaking her head, like she doesn't believe him at all.

"We will get out of here, won't we?" I ask him as he leads me down the hall to his office.

"I'm calling the seaplane companies right now. If I have to charter it personally to get you and Dr. Wu out of here as soon as possible, I will."

He unlocks his door, and we go inside, where he picks up the phone.

"Lines are down already," he rumbles, throwing the phone down on the receiver. "Fuck. Well, satellite internet should still work."

He goes to his computer and types away while shooting furtive glances my way as I sit down across from him.

"What? You think I'm going to knock you out with a paperweight and check my email?" I tease.

He grins and slips on his glasses. "It occurred to me."

I sit back and watch as he types, studying his handsome

face. There's a scar above his eyebrow, but I don't know where he got it from. His hair is so thick and dark but with a reddish sheen to it, and I wonder if he got that color from his mother or his father. And where were they born? Where was he born?

Everly was right. He's giving everything up for me, and I know nothing about him.

But do I have to? I've had boyfriends before where I did know everything, and all it did was result in me being either bored or brokenhearted. Maybe this time, under these circumstances, I can just learn everything along the way.

Far away from here.

"Well, because we're not on any regular seaplane route, you can't just book a charter flight online," he says with a sigh, typing quickly. "But I just sent a request to Harbour Air, and now I'm going to try some of the private fishing charters. Guarantee that as long as I pay their price, they'll come here and get us."

"We could take one of the Zodiacs," I suggest. "Maybe go to Port Alice. You mentioned Winter Harbor has a road that connects to Port Hardy. That's a legit town."

He shakes his head. "The storm might pass, but the swells will be big for a few days. We're exposed the moment we leave the inlet. There's a reason why Captain Cook called the peninsula the cape of storms."

"Then we take the ATVs," I tell him.

He looks amused. "We're not escaping a villain, Sydney. ATVs are slow and would be a last resort. Hell, *Mithrandir* is the last resort if we can't charter a plane in time."

But that's where he's wrong. He's so close to it that he doesn't even see it.

There is a villain here.

And its name is the Madrona Foundation.

CHAPTER 26

THE REST of the day is uneventful as the storm continues to roll in. I'm too embarrassed to face my friends, so I go back to Kincaid's boat with him. My brain keeps on wanting to think about Clayton, to talk about Clayton. I want to talk about the animals in the woods. I want to know if Madrona picked me for a purpose. All of the questions are on the tip of my tongue, threatening to spill, but I decide to deal with it the way I've been dealing with everything else. I put it in a box, put a bow on it, and shove it in the back of my head. Once I'm out of here, once I'm free from this goddamn fog and this fucking lodge, then I'll take all the boxes out and face them. Unwrap the bows and deal with them head-on.

But for now, in order to survive these next few days, I have to focus on the present. If I start opening those boxes now, I will crumble and be of no use to anyone.

Kincaid takes care of me, which makes it easier to concentrate on him. He cooks for me, we have sex, and then I play the role of shrink.

I make him talk.

"Where were you born?" I ask him as we lie beside each

other in bed. Above us, rain pelts the hatches, the sound soothing. The only sunshine of the entire day slanted down on us a couple hours ago, a peculiar, deep yellow light from a break in the storms, but the showers have picked up again.

He picks up my wrist and kisses the underside where the belt cut into me earlier when he had me tied up on the floor.

"Vancouver," he says. "The real one, not the fake one in Washington."

"What year?"

He pauses. "Are you going to judge me for being old?"

I laugh. "No. I like older men."

"Fair enough. I was born in 1985."

"So you're thirty-seven."

"Yes." He hesitates. "Does that count as old?"

"Sure does," I say playfully. "At least you're not forty."

"Heaven forbid," he says, hand at his chest in a dramatic fashion.

"And where were your parents from?"

"Scotland," he says. "Aberdeen. When I was younger, I had a Scottish accent because they taught me how to talk. I went to kindergarten sounding like Mike Meyers in *So I Married An Axe Murderer*. You know, 'Head! Move! Now!'" He says this in a pitch-perfect brogue, even though I have no idea what movie he's talking about.

"Bah," he says, giving my shoulder a tap. "I forgot that you youngins don't know what good movies are."

"Sounds like I'll have to watch it," I say. "As soon as we get out of here, unless you're allowed to break the rules and show me a movie right now. Is the satellite still running? Maybe we can pull it up on Netflix." I look at him with puppy dog eyes, dying for a distraction. "I'll beg."

He growls at me. "You know I can't say no to you begging, sweetheart." Then he gets up. "Alright. Stay here. We'll watch it."

"Are you for real?"

"I am for real, Syd," he says with a grin as he disappears into the boat.

My stomach flutters with excitement, at the fact I'm going to actually watch a movie after I've been deprived of media for so long, but then my heart starts to flutter too. Like there are butterflies unleashed in my chest.

I'm not in love with Kincaid, despite what the butterflies are trying to tell me, but he must be feeling something if he's willing to do all of this for me. And I don't just mean showing me a forbidden Mike Meyers' movie. I mean willing to quit his job to make sure that I get out of here, that I'll have a life to return to. I know Everly was being sarcastic, but perhaps this could be the start of a precious love story.

Or maybe I need to rein it in and take this one day at a time.

He comes back with his iPad. I can't help but relish the view, considering he's buck naked too. "Alright, everything is working, and it's on Netflix, all lined up to go."

He climbs into bed with me, places the iPad against a pillow, and presses Play.

I squeal with delight as the TriStar Pictures logo comes up.

"Thank you," I whisper to him.

He leans over and places a kiss on my cheek. "You deserve it. Something to take your mind off things. You've been through so much, Syd. And I am so proud of you for how you've been handling it."

Wrapping it up in a box and shoving it aside, I think, and turn my attention back to the movie. *And I can keep doing it for a few more days.*

Just a few more days.

Morning rolls around with a bang.

At around 6:00 a.m., the bed started shaking, the bumpers squeaking relentlessly against the dock as the boat was lifted up and down out of the water by the swells. Neither of us could sleep after that, so we got up, and Kincaid went outside to add more lines to secure the boat to the dock.

"It's probably best you go back to the lodge," he says as we drink our coffee, rain lashing the boat. "There will be nothing but squalls all day. It won't be very pleasant to be down here."

I sigh. I'm still feeling embarrassed about the other night, even though I know what I saw, even though it was Everly who drugged me and tried to take me somewhere, Everly who made me look like a crazy liar.

"I talked to your friends yesterday when you were having a nap," he assures me. "They asked about you. They're all worried about you. You matter to them, Syd."

"Fine," I say, finishing the dregs of the coffee. "I just wish I could tell them I saw a movie last night." It turns out, at about the point where Mike Meyers starts doing his slam poetry about Harriet, that I remembered I had seen the movie before. It still was enjoyable though. And to see Kincaid laugh, like hunched over, full-on belly laughs, was completely new to me.

I think that brought me one step closer to falling in love with him.

"You can tell them, but only if you feel the need to make them hate you with jealousy," he jokes.

He's probably right.

After breakfast, Kincaid walks me up to the lodge, and I'm absolutely soaked by the time I get there. He leaves me, tells me to come find him at his office or the boat later, and it takes a lot of courage to step inside the common room.

But the moment I do so, everyone who was sitting there comes running toward me. It's not even Lauren and

Munawar and the usual gang; it's Christina and Toshio and Albert, people I don't normally talk to.

"We were so worried about you."

"We thought you were sent home."

"Gosh, that was so scary."

"I thought I would never see you again."

"Did you ever find out what happened to Clayton?"

I do my best to explain what I can, leaving out the part where Michael and Everly wanted my brain examined. I tell them I'm adamant that I saw Clayton in the trees though, that it wasn't some cougar.

"So the place got locked down because Clayton escaped?" Munawar asks.

Good question. "I have no idea. Maybe there was a cougar. Maybe Clayton took the opportunity to run."

"So where do you think he's being kept?" Lauren asks. "Do we need to, you know, stage an intervention?"

I think about the shadowy figures running around with guns. I think about Kincaid's warnings about how dangerous Madrona is. I think about lawsuits that would ruin every single one of us.

I shake my head. "I don't know. I don't know enough. Kincaid is bound by NDAs. He can't talk about what's happening."

"But did he confirm it was Clayton that you saw?" she asks warily. "That he's still here?"

I mull that over. Did he?

"He said he wasn't sure if Clayton was still alive," I say slowly. "He confirmed he didn't kill him."

"Well, that's helpful."

"But no, he didn't exactly say he was still here. I know what I saw though. I know it was him."

Now, I'm starting to see skepticism in some of their faces, even Lauren's.

Oh fuck, they don't believe me, do they?

"Maybe something did happen to Clayton, but they aren't allowed to talk about it," Christina suggests. "Doesn't mean he's still here."

"You know who really wouldn't believe you about all of this?" Patrick says with a laugh. "Clayton."

A few people laugh along with him, but I don't. Because this was exactly the thing Clayton kept talking about. It was what he was trying to warn me about.

"Well, I'm glad to see that you're okay," Lauren says, nudging me with her shoulder as everyone else goes back to their spots by the fire, already bored with me. "You really had me worried."

"Kincaid told me he came by and talked to you all, told you where I was."

Her smile tightens. "Doesn't mean I didn't worry. I still meant what I said. He's taking advantage of you."

Anger burns through me, swift as a forest fire. "Why are you being so negative? You always joked about us getting together."

"It was always a joke, Sydney. He's in a position of power. He's your damn psychologist." She lowers her voice, looking around. "You're his patient. And you're having mental health issues, we all know that. He knows exactly how your brain works, how to wield it, how to manipulate it. It's a systematic abuse of power, and it's gross."

I don't even know what to say to that because most of what she said is correct. But he's not using me. I know he's not.

I just grumble and push past her, going to my room to get out of my wet clothes.

I close the door and get changed into my red sweater and jeans, then sit down on the bed and try to do a few breathing exercises. Now that I'm away from the boat and Kincaid, away from Everly, away from the classes, which have been canceled because of the storm, I can finally think.

And when I think, I feel the need to take out those boxes I've shoved in the back of my head.

No, I think as I mentally reach for them. *Stay focused on the now.*

But because Kincaid isn't in front of me, forcing my attention on him, I can't.

I start pulling them out and unwrapping them.

The first box is one so recently wrapped, given to me by Lauren just moments ago.

Is Kincaid manipulating me somehow? With his deep knowledge of who I am and my lack of knowing who he is, is he able to make it so that he gets what he wants while having it seem like it's my idea? He's already established he's a liar. Is he a gaslighter, too?

He had blood on his shoes, I think, another box unraveling. He had blood on his shoes. Whose blood was that? Clayton's? Did he shoot him out of the tree? He is someone who knows how to use a rifle. We're in Canada; it's not a common skill here.

What are they doing to Clayton? His chest looked cut open. His face was full of blood. Did they cut his head open too? Michael had said they wanted to take a look at my brain, see what my "problem" is. *See if we can fix her*, he said. But Kincaid insisted that they would just attach electrodes. What if that wasn't it? What if Kincaid knew that?

Another box opened.

Then another one.

What if Madrona brought me here because they knew I had nothing? Then, as a fail-safe, they decided I needed to lose my scholarship. That's what had been bugging me earlier, on the tip of my tongue. What if they're the ones who called the dean, told some lies, took my scholarship away? I shouldn't have lost it because of a viral video that I was clearly set up for.

Oh my god, what if they went as far as to tell Professor Edwards' daughter, putting it all in motion?

I press my hands against the sides of my head, my brain feeling like it's about to explode. It's too much. I try to stay away from conspiracy theories, but everything here feels like a conspiracy.

And the boxes won't stop unraveling. Monsters spill out of them in the form of rotting wolves and bears and squealing baby goats, mycelia holding me down in the forest, the native who thought I was Everly, the unearthed grave, Amani twirling in the snow, a dead girl in the shower, the whispering trees who tell me I'm home.

No. This isn't my home. This will never be my home.

I get up. I can't stay here. I know what Kincaid said, but I can't trust him. Not until he gets me on that plane and breaks all of his NDAs.

And I'm not the type who can just sit around and wait and put all of the control in someone else's hands.

What if Kincaid never emailed the airlines?

Don't even think that, I tell myself, but I can't help it.

The lodge feels like it's looking inward right now, watching as I fight for agency.

And it doesn't like it.

I grab my raincoat and put it on, taking a half-full water bottle and slipping it in my pocket, along with my wallet and passport, then run down the stairs.

"Where are you going?" Munawar asks, but he doesn't follow.

No one follows.

I slip out the door and start walking up the path. The wind is strong, but the rain has stopped for now, and my pace is quick. I go past the lab and the north dorm until I hit the logging road, and then I start walking east. I keep my head down against the wind, trying not to get distracted by the forest. I can feel the pull of it, the trees swaying in the gusts, whispering my name, but I keep focused on keeping one foot in front of the other.

That's how you escape. That's how you get anywhere, one foot in front of the other.

I don't really have much of a plan, but it's better than sitting in my room and waiting for Kincaid to make things happen. I know that eventually, there will be a fork in the road. If I take the road to the right, it will lead to the peninsula and those...bears.

If I take the road to the left though, the one that snakes up the mountainside, it will take me to camp nine. The closest neighbors only sixteen kilometers up the road, however long that is. Is a logging camp really going to be of much help? Maybe. Maybe there's reception there and they have phones. Maybe they have a truck that can handle the roads and take me to Campbell River. I have a credit card that has just enough on it to get me somewhere. Maybe they'll be a better help than anyone at Madrona Lodge, Kincaid included.

God, I want to trust him. I want to with all my heart. But no matter what, he knows things that I don't, and until we are equal and even, no secrets, then I'm going to have to keep him at a distance.

And if you get out of here tonight? If the loggers are of help?

Then I'll email Kincaid and let him know I couldn't wait. If he cares about me like he says he does, he'll understand. Perhaps he'll still help me. If he doesn't though, I'll figure it out. I always do.

Buoyed by this new sense of control and, dare I say, hope, I start walking faster. The wind isn't as strong as it is on the water, but even so, the gusts push me along from time to time, as if the weather wants me to hurry too.

I round the corner, looking up at the magnificent lone maple amidst the cedar and hemlock, its leaves bright green and full, waving in the breeze.

I pause slightly, something about the look of the tree that's troubling me.

That's when I hear it.

At first, I think it's just the wind, making strange noises through the trees.

Then I realize it sounds familiar.

A roar. A rumble.

An engine.

My heart sinks as I turn around to see an ATV racing toward me. I expect to see Kincaid behind the wheel, and if it's him, I hope I can convince him to drive me to the camp.

But as it gets closer, I realize it's not Kincaid.

In fact, it's someone I've never seen before.

An older man with a thin face, thick bushy brows, long grey hair, and strange, piercing eyes.

And that's when I remember I *have* seen him before.

He was on the seaplane with me, sitting at the back with the other new staff member at Madrona.

What the hell?!

"Where do you think *you're* going?" the man says to me, his voice low, his hand resting on the wheel as his eyes bore into me.

"Uh, for a walk," I say.

"You're not allowed to leave," he says, the wind whipping back his straggly hair. "We can't let you leave."

Oh fuck.

"You're going to have to come with me," he says, starting to get out of the vehicle.

Hell no!

I start running.

I sprint down the logging road until I hear the start of the engine, and then I quickly veer to the right and run into the forest, wondering if I can lose him for long enough that I'll find the road again. I crash through the bushes, blackberries ripping at my leggings, reminding me of being a child, pushing myself off the trunks of spruce and pine.

I run through thickets of sword ferns that tangle at my feet, through pockets of aspen groves, until I finally come to a stop, leaning over with my hands on my thighs, spitting on the ground and trying to catch my runaway breath.

"Okay," I wheeze. "Okay."

I glance up, looking around. I'm surrounded by cedar, the undergrowth primarily salal in patches, though most of the ground is bare, covered in needles. Blue stain fungi show up on the trunks of some of the trees; on dead ones, oyster mushrooms abound.

I spit again and stare at the ground, straining my ears for sounds of the ATV or that man running in the forest after me. I don't hear anything but the wind howling.

I try to think about what to do next, where to go, when something on the ground steals my focus.

The blob of spit that just came out of my mouth…

…it's *moving*.

I lean in closer to get a better look, frowning.

Did I spit on an ant or something?

But I don't see any insects.

Except a worm.

Except *worms*.

Tiny, thin white worms are wriggling in my spit.

"Ew," I say, looking around at the soil. But there are no other worms around.

No.

No.

I put my hand to my mouth and hastily wipe at it.

When I take it away, thin worms wriggle against my wet fingers.

"Oh my god," I cry out, stumbling backward until I hit a tree. I open my mouth and start retching, dry heaving violently, until I'm able to vomit up the bacon and eggs from this morning.

And in the pile of vomit is a mass of them.

White, thin, wriggling.

And with increasing terror, I realize they aren't worms at all.

They're mycelia.

"Oh god!" I say again, trying once more to vomit, my face straining. When nothing happens, I dig my fingers into my mouth, finding them pouring out of my throat, writhing on my tongue. Screaming, frantic, choking, I pull the strands out of my throat, over and over again, throwing them on the ground in sloppy heaps. Tears stream down my cheeks at the horror of it all.

Finally, it seems like there's none left, and I don't know what to do. What does this mean? How did this happen?

A branch breaks behind me.

I whirl around to see something brown slinking through the trees.

Oh god, no. How are things getting worse?

The creature comes closer.

Brown fur.

White bones.

A cougar.

Half-dead and coming for me with slow, deliberate movements.

I scream, but it dies in my throat, already so raw from everything. I push back against the tree and stare at it in horror.

Maybe I was wrong about Clayton. Maybe I hallucinated him like I did with Amani. Maybe there really was a cougar on the loose. This very one.

And yet, this cougar doesn't look like it can do anyone harm. The way it's looking at me—two glassy white eyes, a panting black tongue—doesn't seem like it's about to attack.

Like the other animals, I can see mycelia wrapped around muscle and the bones underneath, but it's mainly intact, though its patchy fur sloughs off with each step.

It stops right in front of me, staring at me with a blank look that I feel deep in my marrow.

Friend, it thinks, or something like that word.

It thinks I'm a friend.

I reach out, trying to touch it, my actions not controlled by me at all but something else. The very thing controlling the whole forest.

I press my fingers against the velvety bridge of its nose and watch in horror as mycelia reach out from beneath its eyes, pushing them out until the eyes fall from the cat's sockets and land on the ground with a plunk.

I nearly vomit again, my stomach churning, until I'm distracted by the same filaments that are now coming out from underneath my fingernails—underneath my fingernails! —reaching and snaking forward until it connects with the ones from the big cat.

And becomes one.

For a second, we are joined.

I see myself through the cougar's eyes as it stares up at me right now. I look exhausted, frightened, vomit staining my jacket.

Then, the forest shifts, and I'm in an operating lab.

On a table with bright lights above me.

"The cat should be asleep soon," a woman's voice says, and then Everly and Michael appear in my vision, wearing scrubs, masks, and goggles as they stare down at me.

The whir of a saw vibrates louder and louder.

Terror fills my veins like an IV drip.

And suddenly, I'm pulled out of the bright room. I'm back in the storm, in the trees. I'm on my knees, crying on the forest floor. Tears spill to the ground, and I'm so afraid, so fucking afraid of what's happening that I collapse onto my side, curling into a ball.

The cougar nudges my leg with its snout, a purring sound, then pads off into the woods until it disappears.

Leaving me all alone.

As if it was never here.

But I'm here.

CHAPTER 27

THUNDER RUMBLES IN THE DISTANCE, shaking the common room slightly.

"Sweet," Lauren says, rubbing her hands together. "We almost never get thunderstorms on the island."

I stare blankly at the fire, lost in the flames. I feel like it's cleansing my brain, clearing it from everything I saw today. If I had enough strength to put the incident with the cougar and the mycelia inside me away into a box and wrap it up, never to look at it again, I would.

But I don't have any strength left. I lay on that forest floor for quite a long time until I decided there was only one thing left for me to do. I could try and find the logging road and continue my journey, but I started to worry that there would be no help when I got there. What if the camp was empty because of the storm? What if there are people, but they take one look at me and think I'm crazy, only to bring me right back to Madrona?

What if I can never truly leave?

So I walked toward the direction of the wind, where I knew it would be strongest coming off the water, and once I found the shore, I followed it as it undulated around the inlet, waves crashing against the rocks, and I ended up at the lodge.

I went straight to my room, had a shower, spent an hour trying to throw up, then brushed my teeth twenty times and swished a whole bottle of mouthwash. Then I knocked on Justin's door, because I knew he had vodka, and had a couple of shots of that, much to his concern.

Now, I'm kind of drunk, definitely out of it, and terribly scared. Even though I'm surrounded by friends as they laugh and drink hot chocolate or wine by the box, I feel unmoored and distanced.

And, quite frankly, disgusted. I avoided looking at my vomit when I left the woods, so I have no idea if the mycelia were real or not, and the front of my jacket showed nothing but a stain. And I have no clue if the cougar was really there or if the vision was something real, but I don't think it matters.

I think what I saw is the heart of the matter. The cougar was dying, yes, but it also seemed fine. Same goes for the bears. The wolf was half-dead. The baby goat…I don't even know. But Madrona isn't just doing experiments with fungi on their livestock. They're doing it to the wild animals. At first, I thought perhaps the wildlife was eating the *Amanita excandesco*, but I don't think that's the case. I don't think any of this is a result of eating mushrooms. I think Everly and Michael have been purposely capturing the creatures and using them in their experiments, then turning them out when they don't work out.

Or maybe they are working. Maybe the animals are fitted with cameras; maybe they're monitoring their health when they release them back into the wild.

I doubt it though. I feel like the animals are experiments, drug trials and testing gone wrong, and they are tossed aside, just like they seem to do with everyone else.

"Sydney?" Lauren says, waving a hand in front of my face. "Hello?"

I'm about to answer when suddenly the lights go out.

Someone shrieks.

"Power's out!" Munawar says, getting to his feet and sounding panicked.

"But we're on solar with generators," Rav points out. "Our power can't go out until someone turns it off."

"Someone turned it off," I say blankly. "This has happened before. They're diverting all their power elsewhere."

The lab.

"Alright, well, time to get all our flashlights and candles lit," Lauren says. "Keep the fire going too."

"Yes, boss," Munawar says.

"Come on," Lauren says, pulling me to my feet. "I'm not letting you wander off anymore, and I'm certainly not letting you go to bed in the dark."

I haven't said much tonight. I think Lauren thinks I'm mad at her for what she said about Kincaid, but that's not the case at all. I should thank her for pushing me in the right direction, to remind me to keep my guard up about him, even though all I want is to let it down.

We go up the stairs to my room, and she takes my flashlight out of the drawer, which I've already left on a few times by accident, the batteries too weak now to work properly. Then she takes out a candle and lights it, plus another one on top of my dresser.

"You going to be okay?" she asks me as I sit on the edge of my bed, the smoke from the match wafting across the room.

"Are you tucking me in?"

"No," she says with a wink. "But I'm going to take advantage of having the power out." She wags her brows suggestively, and I know that Rav is on her agenda again.

I also think she wants me to stay put and not go looking for Kincaid. I don't blame her for that. I don't even know what I would say to him. I've said so much to him already, and he always has an answer.

It's in your head, he'll say.

The wild animals I know he's seen.

He probably knows exactly why they are that way.

But me, throwing up mycelia?

Me, seeing the secret lab through the cougar's eyes?

He'll just tell me it's all in my head.

And maybe it is.

Maybe everything is truly in my head.

But I trust myself to figure it all out before he does.

"Take it easy tonight, okay?" Lauren says as she walks to my door. "You've looked better."

"Thanks," I say sarcastically.

She sticks her tongue out at me, but in that last second before the door closes, I see the gravity in her expression, how much she truly worries.

Leaving her behind will be hard.

But it's necessary.

I sit on the side of the bed for a while, watching the candles flicker, my thoughts going nowhere and thinking everything. Then I decide to pick up my diary, flipping through the entries, of which I only remembered to write in every couple of days. Everything I thought and felt is recorded, and reading it reminds me that if anyone were to find this, they would only think I'm crazy. This reads like the rantings of a lunatic, not someone to be taken seriously.

Maybe even I shouldn't take myself seriously.

Still, I pick up my pencil and start writing down everything that happened today, forcing myself to relive it, forcing me to record every detail. I fill pages of it.

Finally, after what feels like hours, I get to my feet and

grab the candle, walking it over to the mirror, wanting a good look at myself.

Woof. Lauren wasn't lying when she said I've looked better. My face is as pale as a ghost, purple bags under my eyes, my lips cracked and dry. I stand there, staring at myself, the flickering candles creating light and shadows to dance on my face.

They dance until my appearance changes.

My nails are long and black.

My hair brown.

Then it goes back to blonde again, and Kincaid appears behind me, hands on my shoulders.

I glance down. My shoulders are bare. He's not here.

And when I lift my head again to look in the mirror, there's no one there.

I'm alone, dressed as I was before, my appearance the same as it ever was.

I reach up and touch the tips of my hair just as a cold breeze blows at my back, snuffing out the candles in the room.

Plunging me into darkness.

I shriek and turn around, checking to see if I left the window open a crack.

But instead, I see a figure in my room.

Standing in the corner.

Wearing white.

Oh my god, no.

Not her, not again.

The girl's face is dark in the shadows of her long black hair that hangs to the side like a sheet.

Her neck is broken, at an angle.

It's Farida.

White eyes glow from the darkness, staring at me.

"What do you want?" I whisper. My body starts to

tremble all over, my mouth tasting like pennies. Dread seizes my bones, paralyzing me with a sense of helplessness so acute that I might just pass out.

The girl doesn't say anything.

She just stares.

The air in the room thickens, feeling oppressive, filling with smoke from the snuffed candles. I feel like I can't breathe, like I'm suffocating.

Then she takes a step toward me.

A gasp chokes in my throat, and I drop the candle, wax spilling onto the floor.

She takes another step.

She's going to kill me, I think. *She's jealous I'm alive, and she's going to kill me.*

"Please," I plead. "Please don't hurt me, I'm not your enemy."

She pauses at that.

Then slowly tilts her head to the other side.

CRACK, CRACK, CRACK, goes the vertebrae in her neck, the awful sound filling the room.

I pinch my eyes shut, hoping that maybe she's not real, maybe it's in my head, maybe I can convince my brain to get rid of her. Make her disappear, poof.

I open my eyes.

Her face is inches away, eyes bugging out, mouth stretched impossibly wide in a silent scream.

Fuck!

My own scream chokes me, rattling in my throat.

I almost collapse to the floor.

Then the girl turns away from me, and I feel her arm as it brushes past mine. I *feel* it. Cold, so fucking cold. And I watch in terror as she walks toward my door. She opens it and looks back at me, her head still at a horrible angle.

She's trying to tell me something. Her eyes go back to

normal, and they don't seem as scary anymore. I'm starting to see the real girl underneath.

She steps out into the hall. It's quiet except for the howling wind, and dark, with only the white emergency light on. The power must still be out.

Farida continues to stare at me, perhaps more expectantly than before.

She wants me to follow her.

My heart seizes up at the thought. The storm is still battering the lodge, rain pattering against the roof.

But I put one foot in front of the other.

She nods and keeps walking, going down the stairs.

And so I follow the dead girl once again.

We creep down the stairs and across the common room, where the fire is still roaring, but there isn't a soul in sight, and then she opens the door and steps outside.

I'm immediately met with lashings of rain, my hair flying around.

Farida's nightgown doesn't even move with the breeze. She turns and walks toward the lab.

Oh no.

I stop immediately, too fearful to go on.

But she turns around and gives me a look, one that brims with intensity, and keeps walking.

I have to follow.

I have to know.

I hurry after her, glancing around wildly, expecting to see someone.

But it's just us and the trees and the storm.

She walks to the door to the lab building and opens it, no key card needed.

I'm at her heels, scared to be inside but eager to be out of the storm. She walks down the middle of the learning lab, heading straight to the door at the end.

Just like before, she doesn't need a key card to open it, and she steps inside the stairwell.

Oh Jesus, I think, stepping in behind her until the door closes with a soft click. I stare down at the flickering light at the bottom of the narrow stairs. I'm no longer afraid of the dead girl. I am afraid of this place. The real lab.

"What if Everly is down there?" I whisper to the girl. "Michael?"

She doesn't say anything, just starts walking down the stairs.

Well, fuck. At first, I thought maybe this girl was trying to help me in some way or was trying to get me to help her.

Now I'm wondering if she's leading me into a trap.

I'm still paused at the top of the stairs, too afraid to keep going, when Farida finally looks up at me from the bottom, her hand on the door to the left, the room I've never been in. She raises her finger to her mouth, a strange sight with her head at such a terrible angle, and tells me to be quiet.

Fuck, fuck, fuck.

I start walking quietly down the stairs, feeling like I want to throw up all over again. Every molecule in my body is frozen in terror, the feeling so palpable that waves of goosebumps constantly wash over my skin.

I'm shaking as I reach the bottom of the stairs, and she turns the handle and opens the door.

The room is dim, with only a light in the corner.

It's an operating lab, just like the one I saw through the cougar's eyes.

There are three tables spread out in the middle, all of them empty. Machines beep softly all around us.

And in the corner of the room, where the single light is, is another table.

This one has a body on it.

Clayton.

He's lying there, strapped to the table. Various machines

are hooked up to him: IVs and electrodes and oxygen snake in through his nose. Beside him is a ventilator that is on, the sound of the pump steady, but it isn't attached to him. There are A-fib paddles beside him too, as if he'd just died of cardiac arrest and someone tried to revive him.

I slowly step forward, fear a knot in my throat, and realize that he's not dead at all. His chest is rising slightly. The heart monitor shows a very slow and shallow pulse.

I come closer still, staring at him in horror as I realize that he was shot in the chest, a bloody bandage covering the area.

Even worse is when I look at his face.

His eyes are open, not blinking, staring at the ceiling.

At first, it doesn't look like anything has been done to his head, but then I see the staples along his hairline.

I turn around to look at the ghost, to ask her what I should do.

But the ghost is gone.

The door is closed.

It's just Clayton and me alone in the room.

Sydney, he says.

I gasp and spin around to see him staring at me.

You came, he says.

But his mouth isn't moving.

I can hear him in my head.

"What the fuck?" I breathe.

He attempts a smile, but it's crooked. His eyes start to water.

Suddenly, his face goes blank.

She's coming, he says. *Hide.*

"What?"

Hide!

I hear someone starting to thump down the stairs, and I look around wildly for a place to hide. Oh fuck, oh fuck.

Holy shit, what do I do?

I go behind the ventilator and crouch down. With the deep

shadows away from the light, there's just enough coverage from it and the cloth-covered operating tray beside it.

I'm barely in position when the door beeps, and I have to freeze. I suck in my breath as I hear it open. Quick footsteps follow.

"And how are we doing, Clayton?" asks Everly as she steps closer to the table. Too close. Oh god, what if she can see me? She's only a foot away!

"Are we feeling more up for discussion?" Everly goes on. "Hmmm? Have you learned how to talk again?"

Clayton makes a rumbling noise, his breath wheezing.

"That's it. You can try. It will make things a lot easier for you if we can converse."

"Everly," Clayton whispers, his voice hoarse and faint.

"That's a good boy," she says cheerfully. "Do you know why you're back here, Clayton?"

"No."

"Do you know why we had to shoot you?"

He doesn't say anything but takes in a ragged breath. My brain is filled with the *woosh woosh* of my heart as I strain to hear him.

"Because you were a bad boy," Everly says. "You knew what would happen if you tried to escape. This is only your fault and no one else's."

Speaking of gaslighting.

"You can make it up to me though," she goes on. "You can speed up the process. I just want to ask you a few questions, and I want you to be truthful with me. Do you understand?"

"Yes," Clayton says after a moment.

"You died a second time," she says. "When you were shot out of that tree. Do you remember?"

"Yes."

"Do you remember dying this time?"

Silence.

So much silence that I fear she can hear my heart. I can

barely breathe, and my muscles are starting to shake from holding the crouched position.

"Yes," he says.

"Tell me about it. Tell me what you saw. Tell me about death."

"She knows," he says.

I stiffen.

"Who knows?" Everly says sharply.

Please don't say me, please don't say me.

"Sydney," Clayton hisses. "She knows."

"What does she know? Do you know where she is? I was just in her room. I couldn't find her."

Oh my fucking god.

"I was in the tree, and she saw me get shot," he goes on. "She knows what you're doing to me."

Everly snorts. "She doesn't know shit. She never did. And we had such high hopes for her. But perhaps you'll be our star pupil, Clayton. You've already died twice, and we've used the mycelia to bring you back. That's never happened before."

"Fuck you."

She laughs. "See? Even your personality is starting to come alive. That means nothing was erased. This is a good thing, Clayton. You're doing a good, noble thing. You're sacrificing your lives for science, for the greater good. It's not enough that we can temporarily cure Alzheimer's. We can temporarily cure death."

My eyes widen at the truth of it all.

They're using their fungi to bring back the dead. Those animals in the woods weren't byproducts of the experiment; they were the whole point. That testing didn't go wrong...

It went right.

I gulp, dread sticking to my throat, then freeze, afraid that she heard me.

But the machines drone on, burying the sound.

"Of course, we had to make some adjustments," Everly goes on. "You weren't good enough before, but you are now. We made you better, Clayton. The mycelia can have a mind of their own sometimes, but it just takes some corralling to get them to behave the way we want them to."

Suddenly, her phone beeps, making me jump.

"I have to go," she says tersely. "Try not to go anywhere, okay?"

Then she hurries out of the room. I don't exhale, don't move, until I hear the door slam shut and the sound of her footsteps on the stairs fade.

I let out a whimper and then stagger to my feet, my muscles cramping. I hurry around to Clayton's bedside, staring at him in a different light.

He died.

He was dead.

Now, he's not.

"I'll get you out of here," I say to Clayton, trying to undo the straps that hold him down.

But he shakes his head slightly.

I'm not alive anymore, Sydney, he says inside my head. *But you are. You need to get out of here, now, tonight, before you become like me.*

"I can't leave you like this," I tell him.

You have to, he says sadly. *Or you will die, I promise you this. Please go. She's going to come back any minute, and then you'll be strapped down beside me.*

Panic starts to claw through my chest. He's right.

"Answer me something," I say quickly. "Does Kincaid know about this? Is he one of them?"

He stares at me and blinks. *Yes.*

My heart sinks.

Now, go. She's coming.

I swallow down my sorrow and fear and turn away from Clayton. I run through the lab to the door, opening it and expecting to see Everly on the other side. But it's empty. I quickly rush up the stairs, then through the learning lab. I run along the windows, knowing that no one can see in, especially at night, watching for the signs of flashlights in the storm, but there's nothing.

I open the door to the outside and start running.

Right to Kincaid's boat.

CHAPTER 28

THE RAIN LASHES at my face as I run down the ramp and the dock, nearly wiping out a few times. The wind batters me from the sides, making me wobble, waves smashing up against the sides of the boats as they're tossed violently in the swells.

I reach *Mithrandir* and pull myself aboard, bursting through the saloon doors and yelling down into the cabin.

"You knew!" I scream.

I scramble down the stairs in time to see Kincaid coming out of his quarters, pulling on his jeans.

"What happened?" he says fearfully.

"You liar!" I yell, storming toward him and slapping him across the face. The CRACK echoes in the cabin, and before he can adjust, I shove him hard against his chest.

He moves back a step, hand at his cheek, staring at me in horror.

"You asshole!" I scream again. "I saw Clayton! I went into the operating lab—I saw him there. He's dead. He's dead, Kincaid. You killed him."

His face pales, and he swallows hard. "I didn't."

"Liar! I saw the blood on your boots! I asked Clayton, and he said you knew! He said you were one of them!"

"You just said he was dead," he says calmly.

"And you know why he was able to speak despite that! You killed him, one way or another, you killed him, and you're making him come alive. You're bringing him back from the dead again and again so you can experiment on him." My heart breaks at the endless cruelty of it all. "All so you can peddle your fucking drugs."

He presses his lips together in a fine line.

"Fuck your NDA! I'm reporting you to the police! I'm reporting you all to the police!" I start looking around for his phone.

"There's no reception here. The storm is causing service dropouts from the satellite," he says. He reaches for me, and I try to pull myself out of his grasp, but he holds tight. "Listen, Sydney, I can explain everything, and I will. But you're not safe now. Neither of us are."

"Why? No one saw me down there. And Clayton wouldn't tell them that."

Would he?

"If they suspect something, they just need to check their monitors. Everything here is recorded, everywhere, all the time. Even in this very boat."

I look around wildly, trying to spot the camera.

"We have to go," he says, grabbing both my shoulders now and peering into my face. "Do you hear me? We *have* to leave. On the boat. Now."

"I'm not going anywhere with you, and especially not in this storm!" I yell, wriggling myself out of his grasp. Off-balance, I land against the chart table, then spot the VHF radio.

I can call the coast guard!

I reach for it, but then Kincaid grabs me from behind and

pulls me away. "Not until I've explained," he grunts, holding me in place.

I squirm, trying to fight him, but he's just too big and too strong.

"Let me go!"

"I can't do that, Syd," his voice rough at my ear. "I'm sorry."

Then he's pulling me backward, and with one hand, quickly reaches under the chart table to pull out a spool of rope.

"No!" I yell. "Help!" I scream. "Someone help me!"

Oh my god, what is he going to do?

"No one will hear you in the storm," he says grimly, wrapping the rope around my shoulders quickly, pinning my arms to my sides. Then he steers me to the couch, plunking me down.

I try to bite him, but he has quick reflexes.

"Stay here!" he commands, his eyes flashing dangerously. "Don't move. I'm doing all of this to help you, Syd. You have to trust me."

"Trust you?" I exclaim as he turns and goes up the steps two at a time until he's on the deck. He turns the engine on, and it comes to life, loud, rumbling and shaking the boat.

Oh my god. He's really going to try and leave with me. He's serious. He's kidnapping me and taking me with him into the storm. We're going to die!

I'm going to die.

I'm going to die and wake up strapped to an operating table.

I get up and run over to the galley kitchen. With the way my arms are pinned down, I struggle to open the drawers. I keep watch through the portholes at the side, watching as Kincaid's legs go past, the sound of ropes being unfurled. I manage to pull a drawer open, leaning just so to try and get my fingers around a knife. I have no idea how I'm going to stab him like this, but it's better than nothing.

By the time I have the handle in my grasp, the boat starts moving backward, waves slamming into the stern.

We're loose, no longer tied to the dock.

"Oh fuck," I whimper. Suddenly, the GPS console at the chart table comes alive, and I can hear beeps from on deck. Kincaid must be plotting a course, using the autopilot on the system in the cockpit, which is showing up on the downstairs chart.

I go over to it, trying not to accidentally stab my thigh with the knife, and watch as the boat's location shows on the chart. He's plotted a course out of the inlet and across the open to Winter Harbor.

Fuck.

I eye the VHF, wondering if I can get up on the table, if I can then manage to grab it. Maybe there's some emergency button to hit. Or if I hold down the depressor on the mouthpiece and shout for Mayday, maybe they'll hear me.

Kincaid will hear you too, I think. *And then what will he do?*

I have to take my chances. It's worth a shot.

I drop the knife, unable to climb with it safely, then get up on my knees on the bench seat. I'm trying to balance, leaning toward the table, when a wave hits the boat from the side. I yelp and go flying against the communication consoles, knocking loose something that had been stuck in there.

Feeling bruised, I stare at the small square piece of white paper that flutters down onto the table.

A Polaroid picture.

The Polaroid picture I've seen Kincaid carry with him, seen him staring at with so much longing that I was always too afraid to ask what it was.

But now, it's staring at me, right in the face.

And it's *my* face.

I'm staring at a picture of myself.

Except, I'm...different.

I have long brown hair, black nail polish, wearing my Miss Piggy shirt with my pajama bottoms. Kincaid is sitting on the floor next to me, his arms around me, clad in ugly reindeer pajamas, and there are some unwrapped presents at our feet.

We're both smiling at the camera, looking happy.

At the bottom of the photo, in my handwriting, it says:

Syd + Wes Xmas at Madrona 2023.

I stare at it, blinking hard, trying to comprehend.

2023?

But it's 2022.

I *know* it's June 2022.

Why does this say 2023? Why am I with Kincaid? Why am I calling him Wes? Why is my hair my natural color? Why don't I remember any of this?

And then, in the back of my head, puzzle pieces start to fall, not enough for me to put them together, but enough to let me know that I'm missing something.

Something terrible.

Suddenly, I hear Kincaid coming down the steps.

"We'll go extra slow, but I've plotted a course for—"

He stops.

I turn to look at him, shaking my head, my whole world starting to disintegrate. Tears spring to my eyes because I don't understand.

But you do understand, you do understand.

"What year is it?" I ask him, my words trembling. "Please. Tell me what year it is."

Kincaid's face crumbles. He walks over to me slowly and picks up the Polaroid, glancing at it before putting it back into the spot where it was stuck in between the instruments.

"It's 2025," he says.

I shake my head, my chin trembling. "No. It can't be. It's 2022."

"It *was* 2022," he says patiently, though his eyes are sad. "It's now 2025. Three years have passed, Syd."

"Passed since what? What was that, what is that? Why are we…why don't I remember?"

He reaches down and unties the rope from around me, the boat shaking as the waves slam into it, the autopilot in control but going slow.

I feel like I'm on autopilot too.

None of this is real.

Nothing is real.

What the hell is happening?

He then disappears into his quarters, leaving me reeling.

Reality seems to slip away, leaving me raw and exposed to the elements.

It's 2025.

I've lost three years of my life.

How?

Why?

When he comes back, he's holding a shoebox. He places it on the chart table and lifts off the top, gesturing for me to look inside.

I hesitate, the fear so acute that I don't think I can move.

But then I do. I peer over into the box.

It's full of Polaroid pictures.

I reach inside and start rummaging through them.

There are pictures of me and Kincaid together. Many pictures of us together. Kissing under mistletoe. Dancing. Having beers in the sunshine on the boat. Playing bocce ball in the field. Feeding a seal.

There are also pictures of me and Dr. Wu laughing about something. As I flip through, there are a lot of pictures of me and Dr. Wu. Going for a hike, roasting marshmallows, working in the lab.

Janet, I think. *You called her Janet.*

There are pictures of Everly too. Some at Christmas where

she's posing with a Santa hat or making a small snowman. One while whale watching, Everly smiling at the camera with the wind in her hair. She and I on the couch in her cabin, drinking pink martinis.

There's even one of me and Amani, lying in a pile of autumn leaves and throwing them up in the air.

Amani.

Tears start to burn behind my eyes as the truth slowly creeps up on me.

I'm starting to remember.

I look up at Wes, at his familiar, beautiful face. His eyes are brimming with emotion, barely restrained.

"Wes?" I whisper to him.

The corner of his mouth lifts. "Hey, sweetheart," he says quietly.

A tear rolls down his cheek.

Oh my god.

I stare down at the pictures again, my old life coming back to me in pieces, all my emotions coming first.

But so much is missing. Too much is missing.

I know…I know I…

"What happened to me?" I ask, but even as I do so, alarm creeps in. I close my eyes, my mind so desperate to remember.

"I don't know if you're ready to hear," he says.

"Please don't lie to me anymore," I tell him, my eyes flashing open. "Please, I can't bear it."

He shakes his head, his mouth grim. "Later."

"Later?" I repeat, getting to my feet. "What the fuck, Wes? What happened to me? How come I can remember every-thing, but…but…I don't know what the last thing I remember is. I look at these pictures, and I remember the moments, but the moments aren't stringing together. There's no form. There's no function. I remember these things, and that's it. My life is a mosaic."

"We need to get out of this storm first," he says, moving for the stairs.

"No!" I yell at him, punching him in the shoulder. "Stop fucking lying to me! Why were you all lying to me?" I grab my head. "Oh my god, I can't even think. I can't think. I don't know who I am." I stare at him and scream, "I don't know who I am!"

"Calm down," he says, panic in his eyes.

"Fuck you!" I yell. "Don't tell me to calm down!" I go to shove him again, and I slip on the rug.

My body lurches to the side, and out of my peripheral, I see the taped, broken corner of the dining table rushing up to meet my head.

Suddenly, Wes' hands wrap around my arm, pulling me back just enough so that I hit the couch instead.

And that's when it all comes back to me.

Everything slams into me in one horrible, existential moment that blows my mind apart at the seams.

All of this has happened before, and it will all happen again.

I had argued with Wes one night, here on the boat.

We were fighting.

We weren't together anymore, but we were fighting.

Things got physical.

I pushed him, and I think he shoved me back.

Yes, he pushed me.

I fell right here.

I hit my head on the corner of the table.

And that was it.

That was where my life ended.

That was when I died.

CHAPTER 29

I LIE on the couch at an awkward angle, staring up at Wes, and all I can think about is that I died.

I *died.*

I was dead.

And he's the one that killed me.

"You killed me," I manage to say, my heart wrapped in barbed wire.

He shakes his head adamantly. "No. I did not. It was an accident."

He tries to pull me to my feet, but I wrestle out of his grasp, stumbling to the chart table, picking up the knife.

"Stay back!" I yell at him, my head pounding. "Stay the fuck where you are."

"Sydney, please!" he barks, his palms splayed in desperation. "I did not kill you. I didn't hurt you. It was an accident!"

But he's wrong. I know he's wrong. He's lying like he's always lied to me.

"You pushed me!"

"I didn't! It was an accident. You slipped and fell. I tried to stop you, and I didn't. I couldn't. I missed." His eyes search mine, quick and feverish. "God. Please, you have to believe me, you have to! I'm the only ally you have, the only one who can save you."

"Save me?" I laugh bitterly. "We weren't even together, were we? We had broken up."

Is that why he killed me? Because he wanted to get back together and I didn't?

Fucking hell, why can't I remember anything?

Because you died. Whatever they did to Clayton, they did the same thing to you.

And that's when the truth sinks into my cells, infiltrating every part of me.

I died and was brought back to life.

Not by CPR. Not by a ventilator.

But by *Amanita excandesco.*

And before that, before they stuck that mycelia in my brain, I was dead.

I was dead for a long fucking time.

"I think I'm going to be sick," I mutter, my hand pressed against my mouth.

Wes takes that moment to lunge for me, but I'm quick, crying out as I instinctively slash at his arm with the knife.

He howls in pain, holding back his arm, blood pouring over his fingers, and I twist around to pick up the VHF. I press it down. "Mayday, Mayday! This is *Mithrandir* at the Madrona Lodge. We're in Klaskish Inlet and—"

Wes yanks the radio out of my hand.

I quickly drop underneath the chart table, squeezing past him on my hands and knees, but then he's on me, tackling me to the ground.

I roll over, kicking at him, getting him in the face, the crunch of bone as I break his nose. He lets out a yelp, and I scramble to my feet.

I look around the boat, trying to remember where he might have a weapon. I know he has a rifle somewhere and also a flare gun. I'm also not thinking clearly because deep down, I know shooting him with either a flare gun or a rifle is the wrong thing to do, but I'm so panicked, I have to get away from him by any means necessary.

He killed me once, and he can do it again.

And then what?

Keep operating on me, keep me on that table like Clayton, keep bringing me back to life?

Finally, I see the fire extinguisher in the corner and yank it off the wall.

Just as Wes is about to get to his feet, I bring it down on top of his head with a sickening *thud*.

He drops to the ground, out cold.

I stand there and stare down at him, terror starting to shake through my body, my heart free falling in my chest.

Oh Jesus, what if I killed him?

What have I done?

"Wes?" I whisper.

I drop to my knees and feel for a pulse.

He still has one. And there's no blood from where I hit him either.

More memories threaten to come forward. I welcome them, wanting to understand, but they dissolve instead, like snowflakes, my mind too rattled and panicked to process anything. But even though I don't want him dead, I have to get away from here. From him. I have to get help.

The only place I can go is Madrona.

Everly brought me back to life, she's not the one who killed me.

She'll help me, right? Now that I know the truth, she'll help me.

I step over Wes and grab the VHF radio again, putting in another Mayday, saying the captain has lost consciousness, giving the coordinates that are listed on the GPS console.

I then run up the stairs to the deck. The wind and rain blast me, and I look behind me at the lodge. We're further down the inlet but still pretty close to shore. I go to the wheel and drop the speed down another knot so that the boat is crawling. The waves are hitting us, but I know outside of the inlet the swells will be much worse. I know a boat like this is made for blue water cruising and can take a beating, and as long as it stays on autopilot, Wes should get to Winter Harbor. Hopefully, he wakes up before it crashes into a dock.

I look back at Madrona, at the lights flickering through the trees. The power to the main buildings might still be out; it's hard to tell from here.

I only have one choice.

I grab the life ring from the back, slipping it over me like a Hula-Hoop, then step to the edge of the boat.

I stare down at the black water and waves, knowing it's going to be so cold when I land that I'll forget to breathe.

But knowing I've already died once makes it a little easier.

I take in a deep breath.

And I jump.

I land in the ocean with a splash, just as a wave crashes over my head. I hold on to the ring as tight as I can, all the air leaving my lungs, my limbs seizing up immediately. It's so cold I think it's stopped my heart, all the dark water whirling around me as I sink.

Then the buoyancy of the life ring snaps into gear, and I pop up through the water until I'm right side up again, staring at the boat as it slowly moves past me, guided by auto. I turn and start kicking toward the shore. It's only a few yards, and as long as my legs are able to keep moving, and as long as the waves don't crush me against the rocks, I should be able to reach it.

I keep kicking, telling myself to keep going, to not stop, that I'm going to make it, that I'll make it to shore and that everything will be alright, that Wes will be alright.

But at the thought of him, my heart bleeds.

I loved him. I truly loved him, didn't I?

And he loved me.

Why did we break up?

Why was I brought back to life with all my previous memories here erased?

And why can't I remember more? It's like I only remember the bits and pieces, I only remember the Sydney Denik from the Polaroid pictures. I don't know what I did when I was here. I don't remember how Wes and I fell in love, only that I know we were in love. I don't remember why Everly was so nice to me back then and why she's so cruel to me now.

I just don't remember any of it.

I know who I was before I stepped off that seaplane.

I know who I am after I stepped off that seaplane, three years later.

Somewhere in the middle, there is this other Sydney, another version of myself. One who fell in love and made a home for herself here. One who found family in the lodge, who never went back to California but stayed at Madrona year-round.

Did I...work here?

Yes. I worked here.

The realization dawns on me as I kick closer, trying to avoid the rocks. It's too dark to see anything, but I aim for a gentle slope under the trees where the shoreline looks more manageable, and it's here where the waves slam me into the shore, pounding me into the pebbles.

I gasp, spitting out seawater, and then crawl up on the beach. My body is starting to shake, and I know the hypothermia will set in soon if I don't get warm.

I manage to stagger to my feet, my sneakers sliding on the pebbles, and toss the life ring to the side. I glance over my shoulder at *Mithrandir*, bobbing up and down in the inlet as it slowly moves away.

What if you made a mistake? I can't help but think. *What if Wes was telling the truth?*

I can't think about that now. I'm here. He's there. And I don't know what to think. Where to begin. Even before all of this, he was acting erratic. Dangerous. He tied me up. He wouldn't let me call for help. He was kidnapping me. None of those things suggest he's someone with my best interests at heart.

But he loved you. He loved you.

I walk up the shore, my feet numb, but I keep going, making my way through the woods. I hear the trees whisper to me, but they don't bother me anymore, not when I know what's happened. Of course I can hear them; we're all connected by the same things. We are one.

But even though the lodge didn't seem very far at first, the more that I walk, the harder it is to keep moving. I can't feel my feet, my heart rate is slowing, and it's getting hard to breathe. My body won't stop shivering, my teeth chattering so violently I'm afraid I'm going to chip a tooth.

You died, I remind myself. *You fucking died, and you're worried about a tooth.*

I keep going.

Eventually, I see lights through the trees.

"Help," I call out, but I'm too weak to make a sound. I'm too weak to even think of a plan.

What was my plan again?

I escaped Wes, and now…I tell Everly?

The very Everly that probably cut my brain open?

She was trying to save you though, I tell myself. *Everly was your friend. Think of the photos. Think of those moments.*

I stumble out of the forest and collapse right outside one of the staff cabins.

"Help," I cry out again, louder this time. "Help me."

But the storm is too loud.

So I crawl, pulling myself forward over the dirt until I

reach the path, and then I crawl to the front door and start pounding on it with all the strength that I have.

Suddenly, I hear footsteps on the other side.

The door opens.

A flashlight points down at me.

"Sydney?" It's David's voice. "Oh my lord."

I stare up at him. "I think I might have killed Wes," I croak.

His eyes widen, and then he's reaching down and pulling me to my feet and bringing me into his cabin. He puts me on the couch and wraps a blanket around me, then picks up his walkie-talkie as he goes around and starts lighting candles and emergency lanterns.

"Everly? We have a situation here. I have Sydney in my cabin. I think something happened between her and Wes."

The radio crackles. "I'll be right there."

He puts it down and looks down at me. "What happened?"

I can't even answer I'm shivering so hard.

"Fuck," he swears. I don't think I've ever heard him swear before, but then I remember what he's like when he loses at poker.

He disappears down the hall, and then when he comes back, he's got an emergency kit with him. He unzips it and rips open a silver space blanket.

"Before I use this, I'm going to have to take off your clothes and put you in dry ones," he says. "Do you consent to that?"

I snort. Just like I consented to being an experiment?

He gives me an odd look and then takes my sweater off, then my jeans. I make it extra awkward for him since I can barely help.

"I re-remember," I manage to say, teeth chattering. "What a sore l-loser you are."

He pauses to give me an incredulous look.

"At poker," I finish.

His eyes widen, brows reaching the ceiling.

He knows that I know.

His hands are shaking now as he slips a crewneck sweater over me just as Everly and Michael come bursting through the door.

"What the hell happened?" Everly asks. "Syd, are you okay?"

David looks at them tersely. "I think she knows."

Everly and Michael exchange a look of surprise. Then Everly looks back at me. Really stares at me.

I stare right back at her. "Hello, Everly."

Her eye twitches, and she slowly nods. "Hello, Sydney." She lets out a shaky breath and slowly walks over to me, dropping to her knees beside me, placing her hand on my thigh. "Where is Wes?"

"He's gone," I tell her. Her mouth drops open. "He's not dead. But I'm worried he's not alright. He's on the boat. He's out at sea. On auto-pilot. I had to knock him unconscious."

"Why?" Michael asks, crossing his arms.

"Because he kidnapped me. He tied me up. He was taking me away from here."

Everly's eyes narrow. "But didn't you want to leave?"

"Not in a storm. And then I remembered...I remember." I pause. "Did you know that he killed me?"

The three of them tense up and exchange a look I can't read.

"I'll put on some tea," David says quickly. "I have some stuff that will warm you right up."

He disappears into the kitchen, and Everly gives my knee a squeeze. "What do you mean that he killed you, Syd?"

"I mean, I remember," I tell her, though my brain feels fuzzier by the second. "We were arguing on the boat, and I nearly hit my head on the table. That's when I remembered everything. I remembered how I died."

Michael clears his throat. "And you think Wes did this on purpose?"

"He pushed me," I tell him.

"Do you remember him pushing you?" Everly asks.

I nod. Though now that I try and think about it, try to pull up the memory, it changes slightly. It becomes blurry.

"This is new information," Everly says. "You know, we always suspected his anger would get the best of him. He was so obsessed with you, Syd, do you remember that?"

I frown and put my head in my hands. "I have no idea what I remember anymore. I saw the pictures he kept, and I remember those scenes, but everything else…I don't remember what I was doing at Madrona. I don't remember when Wes and I got together and why we broke up. You say he was obsessive…"

"Very," Everly says. "We were often fearful he would do something."

"Everly," Michael says in a warning voice.

"What?" she says, flicking her hair over her shoulder. "It's true. He couldn't let you go, could he? He wanted you to be his, and if you couldn't be, no one else would have you."

I swallow hard. No. That doesn't quite make sense. Wes may have killed me, he may have been violent and abusive in that moment, but that doesn't mean he actually murdered me in cold blood.

"No. No, it was an accident," I say, the memories swirling again. I try so hard to pinpoint the moment, but I can't. Earlier, it had been there as clear as day, but now it's just a haze. Perhaps hitting my head and actually dying did that.

Maybe I don't remember any of it all.

Maybe my mind is filling in the blanks, making me think I do, based on the events that happened earlier.

"Tell you what, Syd," Everly says. "When this storm is over, we'll get the police involved and press charges. Say he tried to kill you."

"Everly," Michael warns again. "Let's discuss this before we do anything rash. There's a lot here that will be hard to unpack for anyone, let alone the cops." He looks to me. "You said you left him on his boat. Do you know he's alive for sure?"

I nod as David comes out with a hot mug of tea. "He had a pulse. The autopilot is set for Winter Harbor. But what if he dies on the way there? What if I killed him?'

"Hmm," Michael says, not seeming bothered by that idea in the slightest. He takes out a walkie-talkie and presses the button. "Keith? Is Roderick with you? Send a Zodiac out to intercept *Mithrandir*. It should be out in the inlet. Navigation lights on. And yes, I'm aware there's a storm."

"You're stopping him?" I ask.

"The cops might not be able to do anything, but we can," he says with a grin that sets my teeth on edge.

"Can I just say how wonderful it is to have you back, Syd?" Everly says, squeezing my knee. "You're one of us again. You gave up on trying to change the lodge. See what happens when you let the lodge change you?"

Change me into what? I think as I take a sip of the tea. It's bitter and acidic, but the heat is soothing. *What am I now?*

"But how was I one of you?" I ask. "Why did I stay at Madrona?"

I try to think, but my head starts to pound. I wonder if the mycelia in my brain are working extra hard. The idea of it, of what's actually happening in there, makes my mind spin. I have so many questions, and I don't even know where to start.

"You had nowhere to go without that scholarship," Michael says.

Scholarship? Oh yes. That was real. That happened.

"You stayed because you were ambitious," Everly says proudly. "Because you wanted success above all else. Because you know you are made for great things. Because you proved your worth. That brilliant mind of yours discovered the secret to all of this, after all."

I stare at her woozily, not understanding.

"It was you who eventually found out the receptors needed for the fungi to grow and create new synapses," she tells me. "It was you that took this from a groundbreaking cure for inflammation and brain injuries, from Parkinson's and Alzheimer's, and managed to do something even more profound. *You* found a way to cheat death."

I blink at her, the room spinning slightly.

"What do you mean?" I ask, but my words sound funny.

"You're the one who made the breakthrough, Syd! It took time, but you did it. It was your research and discovery that made it possible for us to kill that mouse, to bring it back to life. And then when we were ready for human testing, well, you're the one who found us our first patient. We couldn't have taken that leap without your lapse in morals."

The world drops out from underneath me. I go still, but the room keeps spinning.

No.

"What?" I whisper, my heart full of lead as memories threaten me.

"A suicide was a happy accident," Everly says. "Poor Farida just couldn't stomach the program. But when you suggested we cut open her head and use the mycelia on her, well, we couldn't refuse. Sure, it didn't go right the first time. Or the second or the third. But you were very persistent, and eventually, you got it right." She pauses. "Too bad you never saw that advancement. Because we had to use it on you."

"No," I gasp, trying to shield myself from the memories that keep flooding in.

No, I would never.

I would never.

But I remember, I remember.

I remember who I was.

The Sydney of back then.

I remember…

I was the bad guy.

The horror is a blade to my throat.

I'm the villain here.

The mug drops out of my hand, tea splashing on me.

"That wasn't me. It wasn't me. I could never…"

"You'd be surprised what humans are capable of when certain parameters are removed, when the rules no longer apply," Michael says. "It's part of what makes this field so fascinating."

I try to move but I slump back into the couch, my limbs growing heavier by the second as I realize what has happened.

The tea.

"You…you drugged me," I say, dread taking hold.

"Well, we had to, Syd," Everly says wryly. "We don't want you fighting back like last time." She looks up at David. "Call Carvalho and get the OR prepped."

"I'll go myself," David says. "You sure you both can handle her?"

Everly looks back at me and smiles. "Of course. Don't worry, Syd. Soon, you won't remember any of this. We'll rewire you and start again. Do you know how many times we've had to stop and start your brain?" She laughs. "No, of course you don't. That's the whole point. How many times your mind has died and been brought back, well, I stopped counting. But don't worry, your body is keeping count."

Michael smiles at me. "You're used to it."

Then David leaves the cabin.

Everything blurs.

And Michael and Everly step closer.

CHAPTER 30

THE COUCH SEEMS to swallow me whole. I open my mouth to speak, to scream, but I can't utter a word.

What the fuck was in that tea?

My mind feels sharp, at least as sharp as it can be, considering I'm not one hundred percent right in the brain, but I can't think of a way out of this. I don't even understand what's going on.

I don't want to understand.

All I wanted was the truth, but now I want the truth to stay buried.

Everly sighs and sits down on the couch next to me. "I know you have questions. You said you saw the photos, and they jogged your memory. I guess I shouldn't be surprised that Wes held on to that box. He's a sentimental one, that boy. Oh, I told him not to. I told him there was a chance that one day you could find it, and then what? How would we explain it?"

"You see, Sydney," Michael says, sitting on the coffee table. "We had no idea what you would be like this time around. How smart would you be? Would you be the same person? Would the mycelia have changed your personality, the core of who you are?"

"We know it got rid of your ADHD," Everly says. "At least most of it. That's why Wes asked you to go off your meds. They would have done you no good, and we had to be sure you were operating unaltered. When the mycelia created new pathways, it started from scratch. We wanted to study you in a live environment; we didn't want you to remember anything from your days here. We wanted to see if you could, in fact, be the same person again. Nature versus nurture."

She pauses and gives her head a shake. "I have to say, the person you are is much more pleasant. Still a firecracker but with a lot more morals. Your ambition has waned. I don't know if it's because you fell for Wes earlier than the first time around and that he's been a good influence on you. But I suppose we'll never know."

"The problem is," Michael adds, "when we got rid of your ADHD, we got rid of a lot of things that made you brilliant. That were also a hindrance, yes. But you didn't have that focus anymore. That drive or ambition. It wasn't the same. The Sydney you were before was able to give everything up for the chance to feel worthy and you, *this* you? You didn't have it in you."

"You're just not smart enough," Everly says simply. "Don't get me wrong. There's nothing wrong with that. You're still really smart, Syd. But you're not a genius. You had a genius in you, waiting to be untapped at the right moment, but now...the well has run dry. Frankly, I do blame Wes. You didn't fall for him so fast the first time around. You took your time to find each other. And before you fell in love with him, you found your role here at the foundation. You and I? We became friends. Really good friends."

She sighs, staring down at her hands and shaking her head. "The first time around, you blew me away with your thoughts. Your ideas. And I thought, yes, this is exactly who we need on our team. You were the answer to our prayers. When Wes staggered into our cabin that night…" She looks away, gnawing on her lower lip. "I thought my world was over. He said you were dead. I looked at you, at the blood coming out of your head, and I knew. I knew you were gone."

A shaking breath escapes her lips, tears spilling down her cheeks that she angrily wipes away. "But there was hope, you know? I thought, why not do to Syd as Syd would do unto others? So we did. And it worked. It fucking worked, Sydney. You're here right now, proof of that."

"It's just a pity you're not the same girl," Michael says gruffly.

Thank god I'm not the same girl, I think.

"Wes got to you before your brain had time to redevelop," Everly says, brow furrowing with disappointment. "You fixated on him. Not your work. Not your dreams. You ignored all that for a man you barely knew. But I suppose you did know him, all this time, on some level."

I did. I did know.

I felt the connection.

I knew we were inevitable.

"It's romantic, isn't it?" Everly adds with a dreamy sigh. "The fact that you found him and fell for him all over again. That you can be separated by time and death, and still nothing can keep you apart."

Nothing could keep us apart.

"You know, you made his dreams come true," she contin-ues. "He didn't want to do it. He didn't want you to come back, not this way, but he was so desperate to see you again that in the end, he decided he would do anything. He never stopped loving you, Syd. No matter what. Even when he mistook obsession for love. Even through death, he didn't give up. Of course he had no idea how hard it would be on him to see you alive again. To watch you walk into Madrona not knowing who he was, while inside, he was dying for you.

He's had to pretend every single day that you weren't the love of his life."

Michael laughs dryly. "He didn't do a very good job of it. But he had to keep an eye on you, eh? He had to make sure there were no problems, that your brain was functioning. Poor fucker. I almost feel sorry for him. But nothing will hurt him as much as what's to come."

He gets up from the coffee table, looming above me.

"And while I'm sure you want time to come to terms with all that we've told you, that time has an expiration date," he says, the words sending ice through my veins. "Originally, we thought the experiment was only successful if we could study you without you knowing what had happened. Without you remembering death. It's why we reset your brain to start over again on the seaplane, setting it back to your first flight over. We hoped that had been seamless."

"But now that we have Clayton, we realize there is the capacity for the brain to reconcile death. That knowing you've died won't break you. That you can continue on with the same memories. But unfortunately for you, Sydney, you know too much. The person you are doesn't coexist with the person you were. It can't. If we let you go, you'll only cause trouble."

She's right. I'll cause a world of trouble.

I'll follow through with what Wes promised and burn this place to the ground.

"So we have to let the mycelium start again," Everly adds. "Fungi is so much smarter than we give them credit for. To think we barely know anything about them, that we've barely tapped the resources of these organisms. The future is exciting, isn't it? Don't worry, you'll be a part of it. You still have your part to play. You just won't know it."

Michael reaches down and pulls me up to my feet with a grunt. I'm limp in his arms. "Come along now, Sydney. We need to reset."

I scream internally.

I don't want to be reset.

I don't want the connections to be severed.

I try to fight back, but the drugs in the tea have me incapacitated, helpless, useless.

I've made a huge mistake. I never should have left Wes.

Wes, my god, Wes.

I remember now.

I remember as Michael takes me under the arms, as Everly holds my legs and they carry me out of the cabin and into the storm.

I remember the first day that I stepped off the seaplane, that real first day.

Amani had been chatting my ear off the whole flight. There were two staff members at the back; I remember them as Roderick and Melly. I got off the plane, and David came to greet us, escorting me and Amani up to the lodge.

And that's where I first laid eyes on Wes.

He was standing by the totem pole, talking with Janet.

David introduced us, and Wes locked eyes with me, and I locked eyes with him, and I remember thinking, *He's going to ruin me, isn't he?*

But I had just had my scholarship fall through because of Professor Edwards. I purposely reined in any attraction I had to Wes. He was another older professor, and I had been so thoroughly burned. And Everly latched on to me instead. I bonded to her first.

As the months went by and I found my footing in Madrona, it was only then that I started to let my guard down around Wes.

He wasn't my psychologist the first time around. There had been no mandatory counseling then. But he was my teacher. I was around him a lot, in the classroom and outside of it.

We grew closer. I found him attractive, of course I did.

How could I not? Wes was a neurosurgeon. The man oozed sex and competence. And even then, I had an inkling that underneath his steely, composed exterior, there was an animal waiting to be let loose. There usually is.

I remember our first kiss. He'd invited me to go whale watching with him, just the two of us. We saw a pod of transient orcas within meters of the boat. We turned off the engine, as per the law, not wanting to get too close or to accidentally strike them. Too many whales die needlessly because of boats getting too close. But even then, with us just drifting on the big swells off the coast, the orcas swam right past us. It was the most thrilling thing I'd ever seen, and I guess adrenaline caused me to do it because I leaned in and kissed Wes on the cheek, so grateful that he took me out to see them.

Then he kissed me on the lips, kissed me for real.

After that, I was smitten with him.

I fell head over heels and fast.

We kept it a secret at first. I would sneak out of my room and go to the boat. Sometimes we would meet in the office. Sometimes in the gazebo after dark, where he scratched our initials underneath the picnic table so no one would see it.

I fell in love with Wes with my arms spread wide in a freefall.

I didn't hold back.

He didn't hold back either.

I even talked to his parents on the phone. Moira and Ross Kincaid. They lived in Vancouver at the time, in a beautiful estate overlooking Howe Sound that Wes had bought for them. They told me to visit whenever I got a chance to leave the lodge.

They sent me Christmas presents.

I sent them Zoom calls.

I never got a chance to leave the lodge.

And then, the more I fell in love with Wes, and the more he fell in love with me, the more that Everly grew cold.

She became jealous. Possessive. It didn't matter that she was married to Michael—she wanted my attention, and she wanted Wes' attention, and neither of us would give her what she needed.

She started to turn me against him.

She manipulated me, and I was so gullible I fell for it.

She told me I'd never make it as a researcher if I was so wrapped up in Wes. I needed all my focus to be on the fungi, on the science. I was reminded that my relationship was against the rules, something she seemed to make up on the spot, and she was adamant about making an example out of me.

She broke us apart because I was too weak, too fixated on the wrong things. I followed the rules while Wes said he would gladly quit his job so long as I was by his side.

I wanted love.

I wanted his love.

But I also wanted fame, significance, admiration.

I lost my way.

I lost Wes.

And in the end, I found just how far I would go to make my mark on the world.

CHAPTER 31

Now, I'm being carried by two people who I once trusted through a raging storm, toward a lab where I'll surely be killed again.

Or at least my brain will be. Perhaps they won't stop my heart. They'll probably keep me alive. I can't imagine how hard it was to keep my vitals going after my brain was thoroughly gone. They'll want to make quick work this time, cutting through the mycelia until every part of me—*this* me—is gone.

"God, she's heavy," Everly complains to Michael as we approach one of the maintenance sheds, grunting as she carries me. "She was so light when we first brought her back. Remember? I thought for sure she would have noticed something was wrong with the way her muscles had atrophied. Guess she was a lazy bitch back home."

"Everly," Michael warns her, breathing hard. "Now you're just being a cunt."

"Can't help it," she says. "Didn't take long for her stomach to stretch back to normal size. She got her appetite back, and now look at her."

"Well, you know Andrew's cooking," Michael comments.

"Last week, when he made that foie gras pie, I thought I was in heaven. Could have eaten a dozen of them."

"Ugh, yes," she says, huffing away. "But the calories in that were absurd. I mean, fine for you men, but if you want a fit wife, Andrew has to be making concoctions out of carrot sticks. Hey, maybe he can do a cauliflower foie gras. Why not?"

"You ask him." Michael groans as we enter the shed. "That sounds ridiculous." While holding on to me, he swipes a key card, and a hidden door swings open.

Oh fuck. This is the entrance to the tunnels, isn't it? The ones that run to the labs? Which means no one will see me go into the lab. I was hoping that maybe Lauren or Munawar or someone would see me being taken.

But it's still the middle of the night.

I'll probably be dead before the sun rises.

Then I'll be awake again.

Someone else.

With no memories except for stepping off that seaplane and wondering where Amani had gone.

And Wes…

Fuck.

If he's brought back here and he has to see me go through that all over again, with no idea of who he is and who he is to me…

My heart breaks open at the thought.

I can't imagine what he's had to go through this last month. Or the months before that. Or the years before that.

The man has been put through the wringer, accidently killing his ex-girlfriend and then seeing her brought back to life in a myriad of failed attempts until the one that finally sticks.

I want to scream.

But the puzzle pieces rearrange and slide back into place again.

Because it had to have been an accident. Wes never would have killed me. I know he loved me so; I knew back then.

But he pushed you, I think. *He shoved you. Laid his hands against you.*

Did he though? Wes had mentioned that there were cameras on the boat. Could I get ahold of that footage to see? Wouldn't Everly and Michael have seen that footage? Why did she try to make it seem like it was believable that Wes would have done that?

She's gaslighting you again, I think to myself. *She's manipulating you even still.*

All of this has happened before, and it will all happen again.

Everly and Michael carry me down a narrow hallway, not unlike the one in the lab building. I do what I can to scream, to move, but while my mind works, my body doesn't. I'm just a brain with no attachment to my body. Which is ironic because in a few hours, I'm going to be a body with no brain.

The thought is worse than death.

It's erasure.

Everything that I am, everything that is right now, will cease to exist. Some other me, severed from the one that I've known here, will continue, and the same thing will happen again.

And again.

And again.

They carry me down a narrow hallway. There are no lights here except for one midway down the tunnel. It flickers. The walls are dirt. I would have expected something more clinical-looking, but maybe this is their next renovation.

Finally, they bring me through the door and into that narrow stairwell.

We go into the operating room.

I try to look around, but I can't see much without moving my head. I'm placed on one of the three tables in the middle. I think I make out Clayton in the corner, but I can't be sure if it's a body or not.

Now, I'm staring up at the blinding overhead lights.

"Don't worry, Syd," Everly says, looming over me with a Colgate smile. "You'll be as good as new when you're done. All this pain you're experiencing now? It won't exist anymore. None of this will exist. Isn't that wonderful?"

But I don't want to erase it. I don't want to erase any of it.

"Should we strap her down?" Michael asks, putting on his surgical mask.

Everly disappears, and I hear a tap running. "If you want. David gave her a lot in that tea, didn't you?"

"She won't be moving," comes David's voice, and I realize he's in the room with them.

I feel myself sinking further into the table.

I don't know what to do.

I don't know how to get out of this.

I don't know how to free myself.

"We should put her under," Michael says, the surprising voice of reason.

"We can't," Everly says. "It's too dangerous with what she's already consumed. We'll have to operate on her as it is."

No. God, someone, help me.

"Just because she's sedated doesn't mean she can't feel pain," Michael says gruffly.

"Well, look at you, dear husband. Finally having a calling of conscience. Has this been a dark night of the soul for you?"

"It's just a little inhumane."

"You could have grown a set of morals a long time ago, but you didn't. It's too late for you now. Pass me the razors. I feel like we don't have the time to do this properly."

"If you shave her hair, she'll know. It's why Sydney never caught on. There were no scars or marks."

"Well, there is that one mark at the back of her head, but I'm sure she thought it was a mole or pimple. That's the wonderful thing about the back of the head. If you have hair, you have no idea what's going on back there."

I think about the faint bump at the back. I always did think it was a mole of sorts, though it was sort of scabby. Is that where they had gone in?

"Razors, please," Everly says testily. "It will be small. She'll barely notice. Then we can start drilling."

Oh my god. Oh my god.

I hear the razors being turned on.

I yell at myself to move.

I yell at the mycelia in my brain to do something, to override the sedation.

But there is nothing.

Just a barely functioning brain.

No genius. No plan.

Then I hear the door to the lab open.

Everly gasps.

"Wes," Michael says stiffly. "Did Roderick bring you?"

My heart leaps inside my chest.

Wes! He's here. He's alive.

Relief flutters through me like butterflies, giving me strength.

"I saw Roderick when he attempted to commandeer my vessel," I hear Wes say from the end of the room. I wish I had enough strength to turn my head, to lay my eyes on him. "He was easy to subdue."

"Stay where you are," David says. I hear the slide of metal, and I imagine he's picking up a gun or a weapon of some sort. I almost laugh at the thought, but then I see Michael move out of view, presumably taking it from him.

"What are you going to do, Michael?" Wes says. "Shoot me? Shoot me like you did to Clayton?"

"As if you care," Everly snaps. "You're the one who wanted to send him home. All so your little sweetheart could feel better. Pathetic."

"Yes, I wanted to send him home," Wes says adamantly. "But I didn't want him dead. I didn't want him to end up as the next experiment. You promised me this would stop after Sydney."

"Then it's a good thing you're not in charge of the program," Michael says. "All analysis, no progress."

"No death. Clear conscience. Can't lose," Wes states.

"That's funny," Everly says, "because Sydney here is under the impression that you tried to kill her."

"You know I didn't," he says quietly. "You saw the footage. I still have the footage."

Thank god. Thank god!

"So easy to doctor these days," she muses as she peers over me, her eyes glinting beneath her goggles. "I'm sorry your last moments had to be like this, Syd. You find out your ex-lover killed you right before you have your memories erased. To make matters worse, your ex-lover gets killed too. Or maybe he doesn't. Maybe he has to stick around and watch you begin again with no memory of who he is."

"I'll find her again, no matter what life she restarts," Wes growls, and my heart skips hard against my chest as if it's trying to return to him.

Everly makes a face over me. "But it would be so sad. To see you keep dying like that? Oh well."

"So you're going to shoot me. Kill me. Is that it?" Wes says loudly. There's a tone in his voice that makes my nerves dance. It's the voice he uses when he's about to make someone feel like an idiot. Only people in academia know what that is.

"We don't have to," Everly says to him. "I'm sure Michael wants to, but part of me just wants to put you through hell all over again. Just for fun."

"And what does that mean?" he asks.

"It means you staying the fuck where you are while we

operate on Sydney." She jerks her chin at Michael, her expression grim.

"Would you at least explain what it is you're doing?" Wes asks. Again, it's the tone. He's acting like he's in front of a class. Like he's teaching. "Are you killing her?"

"We're not killing her," Everly says tersely. "We're just rewiring her brain. The less she knows about what happens at Madrona, the better."

"And Clayton?" Wes asks. "Where is he?"

"He's in the other lab recovering," Everly says through grinding teeth, her impatience coming through.

"Did you kill him?"

Michael snorts. "Define kill."

"I saw you shoot him."

"Because he escaped from the lab."

Everly sighs, despondent. "Wes, seriously. Either help with the surgery or get the fuck out of here. You're distracting me."

"So you're using the mycelia to rewrite Sydney's brain. Then what? The students will know she's not the same. She won't remember them."

"Well, maybe we can put her back to a couple of days ago," Everly muses. "Then she'll still know them, and she won't remember the last few weeks. Anyway, your students are a bunch of idiots. Honestly, they could all use some rewiring."

I don't know if it's my super mycelia hearing, but I swear I hear Munawar in the distance yelling, "Idiots!?"

And from the way Everly and Michael snap to attention, I think they hear it too.

"What was that?" I hear David ask.

"What was that?" Wes repeats. "Oh. That? Sorry, I should have disclosed this. You see, once I woke up on the boat, I took *Mithrandir* back to the dock. Then instead of coming right here, I grabbed my phone, my iPad, and came straight to the main lodge, where I proceeded to wake up every single student and got a hold of Janet and Gabriel."

Hope rises inside me, tries to bloom.

"I gave one of them an iPad just in case we were separated. Enabled Bluetooth. I kept my phone on me. I led them down here. Made sure the phone was recording before I put it in my pocket. So while you've been blabbing away, they've been hearing everything you've been saying. They're all in the stairwell right now. They insisted on being witnesses, just in case you did something else stupid."

I can hear him grin as he adds, "You can't kill them all."

And that's when somehow, I find the strength to turn my head.

I look toward the door and see Wes standing there, his nose bloodied and bruised where I kicked him in the face, but he's smiling at me. His eyes hold mine, telling me I'm going to be okay.

Telling me to trust him.

I manage to nod.

I trust you.

Then everything turns black.

CHAPTER 32

"SOMEONE'S CUT THE POWER!" David yells as the operating room is plunged into darkness. Everly screams. Students in the stairwell scream. I hear people running, and someone crashes into something, enough to make my table spin to the side, and I roll off, right onto the floor in a broken heap that knocks the wind out of me.

"Help, Wes," I try to call out, trying to roll away, my limbs still useless.

Someone steps on my hand as they run, and I scream.

There's a commotion, people clamoring, fighting.

Suddenly, a gun goes off.

One blast, two blasts that briefly light up the room and blow out my ears.

More screaming follows, muffled now.

My heartbeat is so loud in my head it drowns out everything.

I think I hear Wes cry out in pain, or maybe that was David, and then something else crashes, glass shattering, metal clanging against metal.

"Michael! Michael!" Everly is screaming. "Oh my god, Michael, are you okay?"

Something heavy falls on my legs, maybe the ventilator, trapping me.

Another gunshot.

This time, it shoots something glass, shattering it.

Then there's a WHOOSH!

Suddenly, flames sprout up in the corner of the room, lighting the darkness.

From down on the floor, I can see Michael lying lifeless, blood pouring from his head, his empty gaze staring straight at me. His ice-cold stare is worse in death.

I glance up to Wes, with a handgun in his hand, breathing hard, watching the flames. "That's sodium methylate," he says to himself, then starts looking around. "Sydney! Sydney!" he yells.

"Here!" I call out just as I see Everly appearing from behind an operating table, running toward the door.

But Rav is standing there in the doorway, Hernandez beside him with a rifle, Munawar peeking between them.

Hernandez aims the rifle at Everly.

"Don't even think about it," he says.

Meanwhile, Wes runs to me and lifts the ventilator off my legs with a grunt.

I don't see David at all.

"We have to get out of here now," Wes says, pulling me to my feet. "Take short, shallow breaths. Try not to breathe the chemicals in."

He carries me in his arms and runs to the door, where everyone is gathered and Everly is trying to fight her way through.

"Everyone out now. This place is going to blow!" Wes yells.

Everly starts clawing against Rav, trying to escape, but Hernandez brings the butt of the rifle down on the back of her head, causing her to slump. Justin squeezes through to help them drag her up the stairs, the only light in the stairwell coming from the flames rapidly spreading through the operating room.

Everyone clamors up the stairs, yelling, shouting, fueled by the panic of the oncoming flames. Once the door at the top swings open to the learning lab, air blows through and stokes the fire building below us, spreading across to the other room where Clayton is being kept.

"Clayton," I cry out, trying to get out of his arms. "We have to get Clayton."

"I'm sorry," Wes says, holding me tighter as we reach the top of the stairs. "We have to let him go."

We burst out into the room just as the flames roar out of the stairwell and into the learning lab.

"Go, go, go!" Wes yells as everyone runs for their life through the lab, the heat of the flames at our back. There's a *whoosh, whoosh, whoosh* as various chemicals catch fire and start burning, the threat of an explosion imminent.

We scramble out into the storm, the wind blowing inside the lab behind us.

"Keep running, keep running!" Wes shouts. "To the docks, head to the—"

The lab *explodes*.

Wes and I are thrown to the ground by a wall of heat. My ears ring, and Wes covers my body with his as flames reach above us. I feel like I'm on fire.

I whimper, terrified, and Wes keeps me still, his breath ragged and steady, the only thing I can hear above the din.

"Are you alright?" he asks. "We've got to keep moving."

"Yes," I whisper, and he gets off me, lifting me to my feet. I can move a little more now, so I lean on him, and we start limping toward the docks.

"Everyone alright?" Wes yells, some of the students picking themselves off the ground, covered in mud, others already running down the ramp.

"We lost Everly!" Hernandez yells.

"There she is!" someone says. "The north lodge."

We look over to see her running through the door into the building.

"We need to stop her," I say, but Wes shakes his head.

"We will," he says. "But first, we have to get all of us to safety. That fire is going to spread along the tunnels. The wind is going to carry it to the other buildings. It might be too wet to catch, it might not, but the whole compound could go up in flames, and there's no fire department to put it out."

"Good," I mutter.

He glances down at me as we reach the ramp and gives me a shaky smile. "Music to my ears, Syd. Music to my ears."

We run down the rest of the way, the students gathered around *Mithrandir*, which is hastily tied to the end of the dock where the floatplanes usually tie up. The storm is dying down, and though the swells are large, the waves are less choppy, and the wind is lessening.

"I'm sorry I hit you on the head," I tell him. "I'm sorry I didn't believe you. Didn't trust you."

He squeezes me close to him. "You have nothing to apologize for. I'm sorry I've had to lie to you the whole time."

We stop in front of the crowd. I see everyone, their shocked and worried faces lit up by the fire on shore: Lauren, Munawar, Rav. Justin, Natasha, Toshio, Noor. Patrick, Albert, and Christina. Hernandez, who I realize is someone new to Madrona since I had never met him before, and Janet, who was one of my good friends.

I meet her eyes, and she nods at me. Now I know I was the reason she had run out of the lab crying that day. She couldn't stand to see what they had done to me. Couldn't stand to see one of her friends die and be brought back to life as someone who didn't know her.

But I know you now, I think. *And I promise I'm not the same person.*

"I'm sorry I had to lie to all of you," Wes says to the group.

"You're all brilliant minds. You deserved so much better than this."

"I guess we were liars too," Lauren says, looking at me. "They told us that you were a special case, Sydney. They said that you had a traumatic brain injury and you thought it was 2022. None of us were allowed to mention the year or talk about what was happening in the world."

I think that over. "Clayton kept calling me special."

"He played hardball," Wes says. "He had a harder time lying to you than anyone else."

He was constantly trying to tell me the truth. He just had a weird way of doing it.

"Wait a minute," I say, looking back to Lauren. "You said you missed watching the Kardashians. You mean that's still playing in 2025?"

She lets out a small laugh. "Sadly, yes."

"What else have I missed?"

"*The Last of Us*," Munawar says excitedly. "We could have a watch party!'

"*No*," everyone says in unison.

"Good lord, Munawar, what is wrong with you?" Rav asks.

Munawar shrugs. I've played the video game, and the parallels between that and the poor mutated creatures in the forest are too close for comfort.

"So what happens now?" I ask Wes. "What about the animals around here? They were experimented on." I pause, horror seizing my chest. "Oh no, was I the one experimenting on them?"

"No," he says adamantly. "That was Wes and Everly, and that was after you died. And as genius as you were, sweetheart, you are not a doctor or a neurosurgeon. You didn't do any of the operations or testing. It was just your formula that made it possible."

But I'm the one who dragged a dead girl over to them, I think, remembering bits and pieces now of what happened when I discovered Farida had died. I'm the one who...who...

"You didn't kill anyone," Wes whispers, trying to assure me. "In fact, the moment you found out what had happened to the other students, when you realized that they didn't die by suicide but that they had been purposely murdered, you tried to tell the police. But Everly had a noose around your neck."

"The NDAs," Janet says, walking over to me. "They had us all in shackles." She looks off into the forest. "The mycelia didn't take in their brains the way it did in yours. The animals won't live forever. They aren't in any pain. Everything in the rainforest here is still in perfect balance. It won't be long before they become one with the forest floor. All the different fungi here will devour them. Their remains will sink into the soil as fertilizer, giving the trees here their growth. The trees give us the air. It goes on."

The wind blows back her hair, and she wipes a tear away from under her glasses. It's only now that I notice she's wearing her pajamas under her raincoat. In fact, everyone is, having been woken up by Wes.

We're having a hell of a night.

"Look," Hernandez says.

We follow his gaze. The north dorm is on fire.

"Everly," Wes says grimly. "She's probably burning it down. She's destroying all the evidence."

"All that research," Janet says. "All those years of work, all that life-changing research going up in smoke."

But she doesn't sound sad about it. I know when I first started, all I wanted was to find a cure for Alzheimer's. I wanted to avenge my grandmother at all costs, to stop feeling so helpless over her loss.

It was enough that I let that vengeance become an obsession, let that obsession lead me down a path there was no coming back from.

I still want that, too. I want a cure. We had a cure. Madrona Pharmaceuticals was ready for it. We just needed more testing. But then I got sidetracked by something even greater—the cure for death.

Something there should be no cure for.

I lost my way.

I lost myself.

I lost my *life*.

And yet, somehow, I'm still here.

"I'm tired," I say softly, leaning into Wes.

"I know," he says, kissing the top of my head. "We all are." He clears his throat and looks at the group. "Unfortunately, I don't think it's wise for anyone to head back into the main lodge. Not only could it catch on fire, but I don't know where the rest of the staff is, and it's safe to say, I don't think they're on our side."

"When I went to the generator to cut the power, I saw Roderick—guess he didn't stay subdued for long," Janet tells us. "He was with Nick, Michelle, and Handyman Keith. They got on an ATV. It already sounded like another ATV was in the distance, I couldn't be sure. Maybe the rest of the staff escaped."

"Oh my god, the barn!" I cry out suddenly. "We have to go save the animals!"

"Already done," Janet assures me quickly. "I let the goats and the chickens loose. They'll be alright." She looks at Wes. "You said there was a chance that Madrona could go up in flames. I know you always follow through."

"I don't make idle threats," he says with a shrug.

"So we have to leave our stuff behind?" Munawar says. Then he gasps. "Oh no, all my fungi shirts."

"We'll get you new shirts, alright?" Wes says. "Everyone still have their essentials on them, your passports and wallets?"

The students pat down their pockets and nod. I don't

think any of them are okay with leaving their luggage and belongings behind in their rooms, but we don't have much of a choice.

"Still wish I had my phone," Lauren says.

"And that's why we always back up to the cloud," Wes says.

About half the students groan about not backing them up, and everyone starts griping amongst themselves.

Wes turns to me. "Don't worry, I have your phone. I've had it for a long time."

Realization dawns on me. "Oh, so that's why my grandmother's picture changed."

"I didn't get it right?" he asks. "Sorry, I tried. I knew you had your grandmother as your wallpaper when you first got here because I asked you about her, but I wasn't sure the exact picture. There were a lot of things that were challenging to keep up the ruse."

"Like my sneakers," I tell him. "That's why you snuck them into my room."

"You ruined them on a hike," he says. "I had to get you new ones, but they didn't arrive on time. The perils of having to take a boat to get your mail."

I remember now. Wes and I had gone hiking and foraging for the *excandesco*, and we got caught in a downpour. We had to hunker down in a fallen log for hours before we were able to continue through the mud.

"And my Miss Piggy shirt?" I ask.

He gives me a sheepish look. "It, uh, ripped one night."

Oh. I see. In my mind I have the vague memory of us having sex, him ripping it by accident, then tearing the rest of it up to secure my wrists together.

"I have to admit, the hardest part for me was getting your hair color just right," he says, a sobering look in his eyes.

"You dyed my hair?"

He nods, brushing a strand off my face. "I had to. You

decided to go back to your natural color when you were here. Everly bought the dye, tried to match it. I think maybe I left it on for too long, I don't know. I'd never dyed anyone's hair before."

I stare up at him. "You dyed my hair as I was dead?" I picture my corpse, Wes rubbing the dye into my strands. "I can't tell if that's creepy or romantic."

"It can be both," he says. Then he cups my face in his hands. "I know that you don't remember everything. I know it will take a long time for everything to make sense. And maybe it will never make sense. But I will wait however long it takes for you to trust me again."

He kisses me softly, sweetly, and pulls back, resting his forehead against mine. "I love you, Syd. I love you with all my being. And you don't need to love me back. I know that we were broken up before. I know that this new you doesn't know me like the old you did. I know—"

"You don't know half the things you think you do," I interrupt him, my heart expanding in my chest, blossoming and blooming at his words. "Neither do I. But my soul does. My heart does. It always has."

I run my hand over his face, relishing the feel of his beard, the softness of his lips, the drugs finally out of my system.

"I love you, Wes," I tell him, and in every essence of my being, every part old and new, deep within every neuron, I know I never stopped.

Then I kiss him, and he holds me tight, and I realize that some connections in life can't be severed, not even by death.

Someone claps.

Then, another person claps.

Sarcastic golf claps, but still.

And Hernandez says, "This is all well and good, but are we actually going to get out of here, or do we have to stay here and watch you make out?"

We break apart. We didn't pick the best time for this, did we? One moment of intimacy amidst a world of chaos.

"Well," Wes says, clearing his throat. "What do you all say? Should we get on the boat and get the fuck out of here? Or do you want to stand on the dock and watch the lodge burn?"

Munawar puts up his hand. "I vote for the burning of the lodge."

"Me too," says Lauren.

"Me three," says Janet.

So we all stand there on the dock and watch as the lab and the north dorm burn down. Soon, the fire spreads to the main lodge, then the dining hall. Miraculously, all the surrounding trees survive, their waterlogged trunks and full foliage unable to catch fire, while the wood of the buildings goes up like tinder.

Perhaps the lodge had wanted this all along.

I always thought it was like a sentient predator, waiting to pounce.

But maybe the lodge was never trying to harm us.

Maybe all it wanted was to be set free.

CHAPTER 33

"Good morning, sunshine."

I blink, waking up to the sun streaming in through the window of the hatch.

"Sun," I croak, shielding my eyes. "My god."

It's been a week since we sailed away from Madrona Lodge, and there hadn't been a single day of sunshine on the entire journey from the Brooks Peninsula all the way down to Tofino. To say the sun feels like heaven shining down on me right now is an understatement.

The trip down the west coast only took a few days, with Wes steering the boat day and night and taking shifts with Janet, who has some sailing experience, while the rest of us braved the rough seas. It was a crowded couple of days, with fourteen people on a fifty-foot yacht, everyone sleeping on every available surface, but eventually, we pulled into the surfer town of Tofino, the biggest community on the coast, and kissed the ground the moment we all stumbled onto shore.

After that, we had a day or two to get our heads on straight and enjoy being in civilization. The students frequented coffee shops, bars, bookstores, taco trucks conversing with locals and tourists who had nothing to do with Madrona. Wes generously put everyone up at the local hotels. I opted to stay back on the boat with him, taking the time—and the quiet—to not only piece together the missing parts but to get to know each other in a whole new way.

I had to get to know myself better, too.

To reconcile who I was with who I am.

To think about death and dying.

Wes asked me one night, if I had remembered what dying was like.

I wish I did.

I was dead for months and yet I don't remember any of it. It doesn't make me more afraid or less afraid of it. I still believe in an afterlife—that's deeply ingrained by my grandmother—I just don't remember if I went there.

I think some things are meant to be forgotten.

At the very least, I think my death is what connected me to Farida. I was able to see her as a ghost and she was able to see me, because I had already passed to the other side and back. I think at first she tried to scare me, payback for what I had done, but then was trying to show me what I was, the truth of what I had become.

That's what I tell myself, anyway.

After a few days had passed, it was time for all of us to decide together as a group what to do. The burning of the lodge still hadn't made the news, and we hadn't heard from anyone there. We don't know what happened to Everly, only that she's probably alive. Michael is for sure dead, having been shot by Wes. David is most likely dead as well, possibly shot, too. I try to feel an ounce of remorse over that, but I can't seem to conjure it.

Wes, of course, is taking it hard, but in his own stoic way. Some nights, I'll catch him staring out across the water with a look of dread on his face. I know he's thinking about how they died. I know he blames himself. But then I catch him looking at me, and I see the joy and relief return to his face, and I know he tells himself it was worth it.

Some of the group—Janet and Hernandez and a few other students, Natasha, Patrick, and Rav—wanted to bring Madrona to justice. The other students just wanted to forget about the whole thing and go back home. I couldn't blame them. I'd do the same thing if I were in their shoes.

Wes and I, well, I'd definitely like to take Everly and Madrona to court. I'm not sure exactly how since there are some things that shouldn't come to light. For example, none of us can ever tell the truth about what was done to me. The world is not ready for a person to be resurrected over and over again. If anyone learned the truth about me, I would be subjected to tests and scrutiny for the rest of my life.

Of course, we didn't make anyone sign an NDA. If someone wants to blab one day, they can. No one will ever believe them.

But what we can do is bring Everly to trial over illegal and unethical experiments on the local wildlife. Those poor creatures are still out there in the woods. They are our proof. I am sure we could get the natives involved in this, too, since it occurred on their land; same goes for the provincial government.

The only issue is the NDAs. But if we get a good lawyer, we can prove them to be void.

Wes also paid for everyone's flights back when we reached Tofino, making good with his Madrona salary. Everyone agreed to keep in touch, especially with regard to any legal action. It was especially hard to say goodbye to Lauren, Munawar, and Janet, but at least Lauren lives in the city of Victoria, which isn't too far from here, and Munawar lives in Vancouver. I'll be able to see both of them again soon.

As for Janet, though she flew back to Toronto, I think it's for the best we don't see each other much. She was my friend, but she also represents Madrona. Right now, the only tie I want to that place is Wes, and that's because we're tied so deeply to each other that Madrona doesn't even count. When I remember me and Wes together, I remember him, not the lodge.

As for my own memory, some things are still slow to return. The harder it is to come to terms with, the more likely the memory wants to stay away. I don't want to know what a horrible person I was, though I suppose it serves me right to remember. If I don't, how do I know history won't repeat itself?

I do know, however, that my morals did come through at the last minute, even though they led to my eventual death.

Two things happened in succession. First, I realized what was happening to the natives. I had been under the impression that they were getting a percentage of the stock options from Madrona, as well as being paid flat out. I learned they were getting screwed over when I went onto their land to forage for *excandesco*. The man I saw in the forest, Samson, was the one who confronted me with the truth, assuming I knew more than I did.

Then, I discovered the body of a student in the lab, a girl, Kim, whom I had known well. I knew she wasn't suicidal; I knew she wasn't on any drugs. But she was made to look like she'd overdosed. It was then that I realized what was happening, that Everly and Michael had murdered her and caused another suicide prior, a guy called Jack.

After that, I was so irate and damn scared I blew up at Everly. I told her I was going to take her ass to jail. She neither confirmed nor denied anything but once again mentioned the fucking NDAs. After that, I went to see Wes, thinking he had something to do with it, or at the very least, that he knew and didn't tell me. At least Everly had made it seem that way. We started fighting, not only over the murders and the natives being fucked over, but the reason we broke up, Everly's manipulation of me.

It was a huge blowout.

It got physical.

I slapped him.

I shoved Wes, hard.

I went to shove him again, but he moved out of the way.

I started to fall forward. I overcorrected myself so that I slipped on the rug and then started to fall backward.

Wes reached out to catch me.

But he didn't grab me in time.

I hit my head on the corner of the table, at just the right—or wrong—spot.

And died.

Wes has asked, many times, if I wanted to see the footage because he does have the accident recorded. But I always say no. I remember now. I don't want to see my actual death. I have a hard enough time coming to terms with what happened to me; I don't need to see it with my own eyes.

"Here," Wes says, handing me my coffee.

I sit up in the berth and take the coffee from him, having a long sip. Him bringing me coffee on the boat is the best part of the morning, maybe even the day. Well, aside from the sex, of course.

"Thank you," I tell him, peering at him over the mug. He used to have a mushroom one on the boat, one that Munawar appreciated, but I made him toss out everything fungi related. Suffice to say, I'm not sure being a mycologist is the right career choice for me anymore. "You made it extra strong."

"We have a big day ahead of us," he explains. Once slack tide hits later and the current around the marina stops being so vicious, we're heading back out, deciding to continue sailing to the town of Ucluelet, then spend a few weeks bumming around the islands of Barkley Sound while we figure life out.

There's so much to figure out.

So much to think about.

And so many things I don't want to think about too deeply.

"Before we get ready, though, I have a present for you," Wes says. He reaches into the bottom of one of the cupboards that surround the berth and takes out a shoebox.

"More Polaroids?" I ask. I've spent so much time going through the photos and jogging my memory until I'm certain the memories are there to stay. Wes thinks eventually my own neural circuits will override the mycelia, until one day my brain is completely back to normal and the mycelia are rendered moot. At least he's the right person to help me with that.

"No," he says, placing the box in front of me. He gives me a steady look. "Now, you don't have to do anything with these. You can throw them away if you want. Or I can put them back, and you can decide to do something with it a few years from now. We can decide to do it together. But I wanted you to know."

He lifts off the top of the box.

I look inside.

Papers. There are hundreds of scattered papers, some typed and printed, some in my chicken scratch handwriting. "What is this?" I ask, but as I see a few words and formulas, I realize the truth.

This is all the research on *Amanita excandesco*, the research needed for Alzheimer's and other neurological diseases.

"I'm not sure if it's complete," he says. "And of course, we don't have the fungi either anymore. But it's a step in the right direction. You always kept this on the boat; I guess some part of you was worried it would be taken. So when Everly burned everything down, she didn't burn this. If you want, if one day you're ready, we can tackle this together. We can find another way towards a cure."

My lower lip starts to tremble, a rush of emotions flushing through me.

For one, the fact that I was smart enough, good enough to actually help with this research, the very reason I wanted to join Madrona to begin with.

For two…it's hope. Even without the ingredients for this to work, it's the right start. And hope is such a powerful thing.

"Come here," Wes says, taking the coffee from my hand and placing it on the shelf before pulling me toward him. He wraps his arms around me, and I cry. I haven't cried much since everything happened, but it's all coming to a head now.

"One day, your work is going to save the world," Wes says. "But I'll let you choose when that day comes."

I cry into his embrace, and he soothes me.

He holds me until that feeling of being loved, of being worthy, of being enough for this world, sinks deep into my bones. He makes me believe it.

Then I push the box aside and kiss him.

He climbs onto the bed, and we fall back into it, our clothes coming off in seconds, our bodies tangled in the sheets.

He's gentle and soft with me this morning as the sun streams through, lightly restraining me at times, whispering that I'm his pet, that I'm his forever, that he will always take care of me.

That his soul will always find mine.

I surrender to him like I always do.

I surrender to the moment.

I surrender to tomorrow.

I have no idea what the future will bring for us. I just know we have to keep moving forward, one foot in front of the other.

"The past is past," as Wes always says. "We only have now and tomorrow."

EPILOGUE

OCTOBER 7, 2027

VANCOUVER — Jury selection will begin Tuesday in the trial of former Madrona Foundation CEO Everly Johnstone, accused of capturing wild animals for use in illegal experiments regarding drug trials, a judge decided Friday.

However, on Friday, the judge will also consider a renewed request by her father, Brandon Johnstone, CEO of Madrona Pharmaceuticals, who is also named in the case, to dismiss the case completely, without a trial.

The case was brought forth by former employees Dr. Wes Kincaid, Sydney Kincaid, Dr. Janet Wu, and Dr. Gabriel Hernandez, who say they witnessed Everly Johnstone and her late husband, Michael Peterson, doing unethical and unsanctioned experiments on cougars, bears, deer, raccoons, and wolves in the surrounding land of the former Madrona Lodge Research Lab on northwest Vancouver Island, near and on Mquqin/Brooks Peninsula Park. The BC Provincial Government and the Quatsino First Nation are said to also be considering a separate trial for Johnstone should she be proven guilty.

"Ms. Johnstone wants to proceed to trial, wants to have her day in court," Johnstone's current defense attorney, Langdon Alder, told reporters outside court on Friday. "She's been fairly adamant since the get-go that she wants to tell her side of the story and prove that this case is brought on by disgruntled ex-employees who couldn't stand being let go. She is confident she has nothing to hide and finds the accusations disturbing and inaccurate."

The Madrona Lodge was the site of the foundation's research lab that burned down due to an electrical fire during a storm in June of 2025. That same fire resulted in the deaths of two employees, the aforementioned Michael Peterson, and the lodge's manager, David Chen, as well as one of the visiting grad students, twenty-three-year-old Clayton Wade of Montana. Since then, the Madrona Foundation has said to continue with their research in a new location that has yet to be disclosed.

Two of the employees who were instrumental in the lawsuit, Dr. Wes Kincaid and his wife, Sydney Kincaid, who got married shortly after their careers with Madrona ended, are expected to appear as witnesses during the trial. Currently, they are sailing around the world on their boat, *Mithrandir*, stopping in at countries where Dr. Kincaid can work as a neurosurgeon for Doctors Without Borders.

Thank you so much for reading Grave Matter! I hope you enjoyed the ride (once you've had a moment to process). Reviews are so appreciated, and if you liked the book, word of mouth goes a long way for authors.

Please continue reading for a few special notes from me, as well as the Book Club Discussion Questions, and links to books with similar vibes.

AFTERWORD

While I did endless research about fungi for this book, some (okay, a lot of) scientific liberties were taken. That said, I have to give special thanks to Dr. Anna Rosling, a professor of evolutionary biology at Uppsala University in Sweden. It was her findings on "dark fungi" that inspired me to reach out to her with questions with regards to the research and advancements in Grave Matter and I am very appreciative of her help and suggestions to root the science in reality.

Funny story; in the author's note/afterword of *What Moves the Dead*, a fungi horror by one of my favorite authors, T. Kingfisher, Kingfisher talked about how she was early into writing her book when she picked up *Mexican Gothic* by Silvia Moreno-Garcia (another favorite author of mine) and thought, and I quote "Oh my God, what can I possibly do with fungi in a collapsing Gothic house that Moreno-Garcia didn't do ten times better?"

So, I hadn't read *Mexican Gothic* OR *What Moves the Dead* until I was about halfway through Grave Matter and as I read them, I had the same thought "Oh my God, what can I possibly do with fungi that both Moreno-Garcia *and* Kingfisher didn't do 100 times better?"

(This is your sign to read both of those books, btw).

But as Kingfisher notes, "Yes, it's been done, but *you* haven't done it yet."

And so with that in mind, I went back to writing Grave Matter, putting my own spin on fungi horror. I fell in love with Sydney (giving her all my neurodivergent issues) and Kincaid (who was only trying his best for the girl he loves), Munawar (ask me how many fungi pun shirts I have now), all of the students at Madrona, even Everly at times. I wrote the book with my heart in my throat, scaring myself silly, while trying to blend actual scientific progress with regards to fungi with what I needed the book to be.

Originally I thought the book would be about dark fungi —which is so worth Googling—but after talking to Dr. Rosling, I realized that I needed my *Amanita excandesco* (totally fictional, does not exist) to be more physical (whereas dark fungi is very much not physical).

Anyway, I hope reading this has made you more curious about the world of fungi and the incredible things that the organisms can do, and of which we've barely scratched the surface of. I also hope it's encouraged you to visit Vancouver Island. I promise you, it's beautiful here (and if you want to see pictures of the area where the book is set, please check out my Instagram: @authorhalle), and that the nature is more beautiful than terrifying.

That said, our province's motto is Super, Natural (supernatural) British Columbia for a reason...

ACKNOWLEDGMENTS

If you've been reading my books lately, you'll by now know that I often start my acknowledgements by saying "this book was the hardest book I ever had to write."

Well, I'm here to let you know that Grave Matter was one of the easiest books I've ever had the pleasure of writing. Perhaps "easy" isn't the best word since there was a hell of a lot of research that went into this book, and since it was my first psychological thriller, I had to reverse engineer the book and plot it with even more detail than I'm used to. I do love research, and I do love plotting, but it was still a challenge to branch out like this.

BUT…I thoroughly enjoyed writing every second of this book. I never sat down at my computer and went "ugh I have to write." I never had that ADHD brick wall slide in front of me that prevented me from getting the words down. The words just flowed. Even when I had to stop and start due to fact-checking, or making sure I was leaving the right amount of clues, the words just kept coming. This book was an absolute joy and that can't ever be taken from me.

In the end, it felt like I had been stuck in Madrona Lodge for a month but unlike Sydney, I absolutely didn't want to leave.

Alas, the book is done now and so I must thank the people who helped make it happen.

Firstly, my husband Scott. I got the idea for Grave Matter in May, just before we went on our month-long sailing trip around Vancouver Island (in case you missed the map of the island at the beginning, Vancouver Island is HUGE—it's larger than Vermont or Taiwan). I knew I wanted to set it on the west coast, and when we finally rounded Cape Scott (not named after my husband, unfortunately) we ended up holed up in the "town" of Winter Harbor (full-time population: two) for five days waiting for the weather window to clear so we could round Brooks Peninsula. During this time, Grave Matter really began to form in my head and the plotting and research began. Winter Harbor became the inspiration for Madrona Lodge, even though I decided to set Madrona in Klaskish Inlet, which was about an hour away by boat (next time we sail around Vancouver Island again, we are DEFI-NITELY stopping there, specifically the cove where I set the book).

Anyway, Scott deserves all the thanks, not only for listening to me lament about how much I wanted to write Grave Matter but couldn't (I had various deadlines for other books all summer) but when I finally did start, let me bounce a million different ideas and clues off him. He also very patiently listened to me read out loud the first chapter and told me he knew this book was "special." I could not have done this without his support and enthusiasm (because, again, even 85+ books later, this book and genre was new to me, and I am someone who needs a lot of encouragement!).

I also need to thank Lauren Cox for also being so patient and helping me make this release the best it can be. You truly are the best! Laura Helseth for her edits and beta-ing during a hurricane of all things, Sandy at One Love Editing for coming through at the 11th hour. Kara Malinczak for her proofing and supportive texts. Cora McCormack for all her help with my blurbs (and for being the only person, aside from Scott, who knew the ending to the book). Hang Le and Lisa Ericco for their brilliant cover designs. Betul Ericki for being a wonderful beta.

Last but not least, thanks to all the readers who have been

super supportive and excited about this release. You've truly helped push me to try and make this book the best it can be. Special shoutout to all the book clubs who made Grave Matter their October or November spooky season read!

I hope you enjoyed it!

Oh, and if you're in a book club or just want some extra questions to help you think and process what you've read, flip the page!

BOOK CLUB DISCUSSION QUESTIONS

1. When Sydney speaks about how "they shun us and side-eye us and make pithy comments about how "mentally unstable" we are, especially if we happen to present as feminine" with regards to being neurodivergent, do you think there is a double standard with how women are treated as opposed to men?

2. In Sydney's class with Professor Kincaid he suggests that people might be able to take a pill to get rid of ADHD and other neurological impairments for good. This idea bothers Sydney as she feels that though she does take medication for it to deal with the more debilitating aspects, to get rid of it entirely might take away what makes her *her*. If you are neurodivergent or know someone who is, would you agree with this assessment? Why or why not?

3. As a potential scientist, Sydney has mixed feelings toward animal testing. She knows that for advancements in science and healthcare, such as a cure for Alzheimer's, it's a necessary evil, but as an animal lover, she has a hard time reconciling this. Do you think there's a future where animals won't be tested?

4. Discuss how loss is central to both Sydney and Kincaid's stories, but in different ways.

5. Kincaid and Sydney discuss that ravens have many different meanings, including "Connecting the living world with the world of the spirits. A mediator between life and death." Do you believe Kincaid has taken on this role when it comes to Sydney?

6. Many of the characters are lying. Do you think Sydney was also lying to herself?

7. One of the reasons that Madrona Lodge is so isolating is because of the lack of internet and phone access. Would you be able to survive for three months without checking emails, social media, or texting your friends? Do you think this would be a blessing in disguise?

8. One of the themes of Grave Matter is how dangerous ambition and the climb to success can be. Have you ever been in the position where you had to make a choice between success and your morals? Have you seen this happen with others?

9. The world of fungi is utterly fascinating and deeply unexplored. For example biohybrid robots are part computer, part fungi and a relatively new discovery where fungal electrical signals can be converted into digital commands. Lately, "preclinical studies have shown that there can be improvements in ischemic stroke, Parkinson's disease, Alzheimer's disease, and depression if Lion's Mane enriched with erinacines are included in daily meals." Has Grave Matter changed your view about mushrooms? Is it for better or worse?

10. Discuss how the weather influences the sense of isolation and desperation at Madrona Lodge.

11. Sydney and Kincaid have a deep connection that can't be broken. Do you believe some people are soulmates and fated to be with each other, no matter the circumstances?

12. Wes Kincaid is a mystery throughout this book thanks

to his secretive nature and Sydney's limited POV. Can you imagine what Grave Matter would have been like from his POV? Discuss how different and difficult the events prior to the book and during the book would have been for Kincaid. Bonus work: if you want a novella of Kincaid's POV in the events prior, during, and after Grave Matter, please let the author know because she is dying to write this:)

WANT MORE LIKE GRAVE MATTER?

Check out Blood Orange, from The Dracula Duet.

From New York Times bestselling author Karina Halle comes a dark and delicious Dracula retelling filled with secrets and lies, dangerous liaisons and a forbidden, student-teacher, second chance love story with a twist.

"My heart will always find yours."

Dahlia Abernathy has only known revenge. When her parents were killed at an early age by vampires, Dahlia spent the rest of her life under the thumb of the Witch's Guild being trained to kill them. Her latest mission sends her undercover to a prestigious music academy in Venice, Italy. Her goal? To kill Professor Valtu Aminoff, her teacher and the notorious vampire who inspired Bram Stoker's *Dracula*.

But getting close to a dangerous vampire like Professor Aminoff is one thing. Falling for him is another. With Dahlia's appearance disguised under a glamor spell, Valtu has no idea that the woman who has become his new dark obsession is actually the reincarnation of the woman he loved and lost twice before.

And Dahlia doesn't remember that the very man she has been sent to kill is the love of her life.

Will their love come through and transcend time once again? Or are the fated lovers destined to let history repeat itself?

How about a slow-burn horror romance series that's basically *The X-Files* meets *Supernatural* but with lots of banging?

DARKHOUSE is the first book in the Experiment in Terror Series about a pair of amateur ghost-hunters.

Perry Palomino seems like your average twenty-something girl on the surface. She's had bad luck dating, her job sucks, and she's disillusioned by her place in life, not sure exactly what she wants or where she's even going.

She also sees ghosts, which makes things extra complicated, especially when she'd do anything to be normal.

But normal people don't go exploring an abandoned and supposedly haunted lighthouse on the Oregon coast, where she ends up getting the attention of Dex Foray, an enigmatic producer who wants to exploit her talent for seeing the dead on his webseries.

At first, Perry's not sure she wants to work with Dex on his amateur ghost-hunting show. He's cocky, sarcastic, mysterious, and perhaps a little disturbed, not to mention aggravatingly sexy. But the more Perry works alongside Dex, her sanity tested at every turn, the more she realizes that falling for this man might just be the scariest thing of all.

Sometimes the ghosts we really need to fear are the ones that live in our pasts.

AN EXCERPT FROM
UNCHARTED WATERS

The following is an excerpt from the psychological thriller
Uncharted Waters by Scott Mackenzie:

I open the bottle and let it take its first breath of air since the day it was bottled, then I pour two glasses.

"Today is the day we cross the imaginary line in the middle of the ocean. We're halfway across the Atlantic, halfway to Azores. We honor our ship, and the sea. We drink to celebrate the miles we have sailed and ask Neptune to protect us for the miles that lie ahead." I raise my glass and Tenn raises hers. "To Crazy Lady."

"To Crazy Lady," Tenn responds.

We touch glasses and take a drink. It's an excellent rum that doesn't need ice, and we both drink again, emptying all the rum in our glasses. I pour again, then we drink again.

"There is one more thing to do," I say with a devious smile.

Tenn has expressed a fear of swimming in the open ocean, and she hasn't been in the water since we lost sight of land almost two weeks ago. I wouldn't encourage the idea if I didn't think it was safe.

"Come on, we'll jump at the same time," I say as I hold out my hand.

"I don't know," she says, a genuine fear in her tone that makes me want to forget the idea.

"Fine, I'm sure Neptune will understand."

Tenn fills her glass again to the top and drinks it down with a wince. "Ugh, I can't believe I'm doing this," she says as she stands and walks toward to the stern of the boat. I remove the towel from around my waist, open the gate, and take her hand.

Tenn holds my hand tight, and we both stand there naked, looking at the blue water. I feel like it's best to not have too much time to think, so I lean forward, and she does, too.

Tenn lets out a scream.

We jump.

The water is cooler than I would have thought and shocks me at first. I stay below the water and open my eyes, amazed at how clear it is. I can see the bottom of Crazy Lady. She looks so vulnerable and small from this perspective. Tenn's legs are kicking frantically and there are white bubbles surrounding her. I stay below for a moment to take in this world that seems so surreal, but I also want to see that the coast is clear of sharks or anything else before I tread water with Tenn. There is nothing but blue water, the hull of Crazy Lady, and Tenn's kicking feet.

I surface next to Tenn.

"Ahhhh!" Tenn is shouting a carnival-ride scream that is somewhere between fear and joy.

"Are you okay?" I ask.

"Ahhhh!" she shouts again, this time with joy rather than fear. She then takes a deep breath and disappears below the water.

I follow her beneath the surface. Tenn swims like a fish, kicking her feet, and heads below Crazy Lady, flipping around with an acrobatic grace. She surfaces on the starboard side this time, and I surface about twenty feet away. We slowly swim toward each other. It's a strange feeling, having somewhere around 20,000 feet of water below you. Even I have a looming concern that something will grab at my kicking feet.

As we get close, I can see most of her fear is washed away.

"Okay, darlin', I think Neptune should be happy. I'm done," she says while treading water in front of me.

"Ladies first." I motion to the ladder hanging off the boat.

Tenn climbs up, and I'm close behind.

The hot day had us feeling sluggish, and the swim was very welcomed. I feel clean, rejuvenated, and slightly drunk from the rum.

Tenn pours herself a generous glass and pours me another as well. Her hips sway from side to side to a song that is playing in her mind, the drops of water on her skin sparkling in the sun. She has on her hat and a long necklace that drapes between her breasts, but nothing else.

I look at the half-empty bottle on the table and can't help but let Tenn know the value of the rum we are enjoying.

"We've just drunk about one-thousand dollars worth of rum."

Tenn holds a mouthful of rum in her mouth, frozen in shock. She swallows with guilt. Drinking excessively expensive rum is an extravagance that is against a liveaboard's intuition. That's the kind of money that could sustain the Caribbean liveaboard lifestyle for at least month. I didn't want to tell her until we were halfway done so she couldn't protest.

"I didn't even know rum that expensive existed. What's the deal, man?" she asks.

"It was Stan's. He said we would drink it on a special occasion. Trust me, he would be happy we are enjoying it on a sailboat in the middle of the Atlantic."

Tenn takes a moment, looking at the bottle reflecting on the memory of the man she did not know for very long but clearly liked very much.

"To Stan," she says, raising her glass.

"To Stan," I say, and touch the rim of my glass to hers. We both drink while holding eye contact.

Tenn throws on a yellow sundress that hangs off her beautifully.

"Okay, Vince, we are becalmed in the middle of the Atlantic drinking a two-thousand-dollar bottle of rum. I've been waiting for the right time to tell you something, and this is it."

Tenn looks concerned. I have no idea what's happening, and her concern has migrated into me. I'm making rapid speculations of what she might need to confess. All my speculations and concerns circle my biggest fear. My worst nightmare. I fear whatever she has to say will break the spell we have been under, the deep connection to her that I don't want broken.

"Should I be concerned?" I ask.

"No, it's all good, but I don't know exactly how to tell you this," Tenn says nervously. "Come on, I need to get out of the sun." She grabs the bottle and heads down into the cabin. I follow.

Tenn sets the bottle on the table and slumps onto the deep bench, more like she is on a sofa than at a dining table.

"I think I better lead up to this one, darlin'," Tenn says while she swirls the remaining contents of her glass around. She investigates the glass like there are answers in the rum. Maybe there are.

I sit across from her.

"Like I said, Sylvester would take me on little Caribbean vacations, and we would charter sailboats. It was such a contrast to the winter months in Manhattan, the sun felt so good, and it was nice to be out in the open rather than in that windowless bar. I met people who were living on their sail-boats, couples, families, loners — all types of people. It seemed like such a beautiful escape to me. What surprised me the most is how little these people needed. That's where the dream of living on a sailboat in the Caribbean began. Sylvester and I were doomed from the start. It was only after we broke up that I started to work for him. He knew of my plan to save enough money to buy a sailboat and leave New York behind, so he gave me a few jobs that earned a little more than singing at the chophouse."

"What kind of jobs were those?" I ask suspiciously.

"Well, I drove from New York to Miami, and back. I didn't know more than I had to, and that's how I wanted it. The only rule was I couldn't look in the trunk, and I had to stay at a certain motel and park in a specific spot. In the morning when I left, it was with a different car, and I drove back to New York. I didn't mind it. I always loved road trips, and I liked checking out the little towns along the way. I would listen to the Allman Brothers and dream away on the open highway. I dreamed about my future sailboat, and what I would do once I had her."

"A gal's gotta do what a gal's gotta do. I don't judge you, Tenn," I assure her.

"There's more," she adds with some guilt.

"Okay. I think we might have a two-thousand-dollar hangover tomorrow," I say as I fill both of our glasses.

Tenn takes a slow drink and her eyes deepen as she gets lost in a memory. "I decided I wanted more money. To keep on doing these runs for Sylvester—it would have taken too long for me to save enough for a boat with some savings to get me by. The conversation didn't go well, and I didn't do another run after that. We didn't speak for months. I would see him occasionally at the chophouse, but he would pretend I wasn't there. Other than signed divorce papers, there was nothing I wanted from him. I still put money aside when I could, but I would be old and gray before I had enough to buy a boat to sail away on. Then one day his business partner, Jesse, wanted to have a word with me after my shift."

"Ah yes. Jesse. He seemed nice," I say sarcastically.

"He said Sylvester told him about my dreams to leave New York and buy a sailboat, and he told me he could make that dream come true. He said he had a single job that could make that happen for me." Tenn looks from her glass up to me.

We hold eye contact. Although I have not pieced together what she is telling me, I can tell she is asking me to brace myself. Her eyes are wide and intense.

"Since you are living on this sailboat, I assume you did that last job," I rationalize.

"It's more complex than that," she adds.

Our eyes stay on each other.

"Vince, *this* is the job. We are doing a run right now. Only this time Sylvester is dead, and I looked in the trunk."

Tenn slides off the bench and scoots over to the center of the floor. She then peels up one of the teak floorboards, reaching inside and pulling out a black duffle bag. She slides it over to me, where I pick it up and set it on the table. When she joins me again, our eyes meet, and I know this moment will be a turning point for me on this trip. I will never be able to un-see what is in the bag.

Tenn takes a deep breath and opens the bag. She removes a small black brick-shaped bundle and takes a knife from the galley table, cutting into the bag and revealing a white hard-packed substance.

"This is what I found in the trunk," Tenn says. She is now breathing heavy from the stress of the moment.

I look down at the bag and try to process what is happening. I look back at Tenn, who is still holding the knife she used to cut open the bag.

"How much?" I ask.

"How much is in the floor, or how much is it worth?" she questions.

"Both." My voice cracks.

"I have no idea how much it's worth. All I know is the compartment has eight duffle bags."

"That's a lot." I pick up the brick, surprised at how light it is. It's maybe only two pounds. Looking back in the duffle, I guess there are about thirty bricks. If each bag is the same...

"Holy shit. We are sailing with five hundred pounds of cocaine."

"I think we'll be able to buy another bottle of this rum when we're done," Tenn says.

I notice how she is using "we." I guess we *are* in this together. I want to say something, but I can't find the words. I drink what is left in my glass.

Tenn sits down in front of me and speaks quickly. "The

original deal was for me to bring the boat to Azores, get some land-time in, explore the island, then sail it back to Miami, where Sylvester would meet me. He would take the money that would be hidden in the hull and I keep the boat. That was it. But Sylvester is gone."

"Right," I say.

"Right, so, we make the drop and we sail away with the money and the boat."

"Right."

"We are sailing across the Atlantic with five hundred pounds of cocaine," Tenn says.

"How much is that worth?" I ask.

"I don't know," Tenn admits.

I have no idea why, but I start to laugh, and Tenn laughs with me. I pull her close and we kiss, both out of breath. I want to show her that she is not alone, that I will protect her. I want to show her that I will be strong, that I can handle this. We kiss harder, our hearts running wild with the thought of being encased in walls of an illegal drug, our minds hazy from the rum. I pull up her yellow sundress and we make love on the bench next to the open bag of cocaine.

"Everything is going to be okay," I tell her as we lie together for a moment. I kiss her lightly on the forehead before I step away. We share a smile as she pulls down her dress and walks to the galley for a glass of water.

I make my way up the steps and look around 360 degrees. There is nothing to see but water. But, to my delight, the sails waver, making a loud noise as they move around. We have wind. With a gentle thud, the sails are full, and I feel them push us along.

We are sailing.

ABOUT THE AUTHOR

Karina Halle is a screenwriter, a former music & travel journalist, and the New York Times, Wall Street Journal, and USA Today bestselling author of River of Shadows, The Royals Next Door, and Black Sunshine, as well as 80 other wild and romantic reads, ranging from light & sexy rom coms to horror/paranormal romance and dark fantasy. Needless to say, whatever genre you're into, she has probably written a romance for it.

When she's not traveling, she, her husband Scott, and their pup Perry, split their time between a possibly haunted, 120-year-old house in Victoria, BC, their sailboat the Norfinn, and their condo in Los Angeles. For more information, visit www.authorkarinahalle.com

Find her on Facebook, Instagram, Pinterest, BookBub, Amazon, and Tik Tok.

Made in the USA
Las Vegas, NV
30 November 2024

13014310R00236